Glacier of Secrets

Faith in the Parks, Book 4

J. Carol Nemeth

Copyright © **2020**
Written by: J. Carol Nemeth
Published by: Forget Me Not Romances, a division of Winged Publications

Cover Design: Cynthia Hickey

ISBN: 978-1-947523-94-4

Dedication

I would like to dedicate this book to the memory of my father, the Rev. James W. Pruitt and to the memory of my mother, Mary Sue Amick Pruitt. My parents instilled in my siblings and me the love of camping and the outdoors at an early age. I still remember our first camping trip in an old canvas army tent that closed by tying long strings at the door, and it had no floor. We slept on old army cots. I must have been three or four years old. We soon graduated to one with a floor and a zippered door where creepy crawlies were encouraged to stay out. My parents introduced us to the national parks and monuments as well as state parks, and we traveled from the mountains to the coast as often as we could. We climbed lighthouses, descended into caves, swam in the ocean, visited presidents (homes), and saw where man took flight to name only a few places. Thank you, Mama and Daddy, for spreading our wings and giving us the love of travel!

Acknowledgements

Without the grace of God this book wouldn't have been written or published. I began with a general idea of what I wanted my story to be about, who my hero and heroine and some of my other characters would be, sort of where I was going in the story and kind of how it would end. Nothing more. I struggled almost from the beginning of chapter one with getting this story down. I always pray over every book I write, and as a pantser*, I trust the Lord to give me what He wants me to write. No matter how hard I prayed, with *Glacier of Secrets*, He would only give me a little at a time. Near the end He finally gave me the climax and my "aha moment." Yep, it was even a surprise to me. Imagine what a surprise it was to my characters. It was about that time we found out my mother, who had full-blown Alzheimer's, had Multiple Myeloma cancer and had for years, only the doctors had never picked up on it. My father-in-law had fought cancer since the beginning of the year. Mama declined quickly and we were very involved in her last few months as well as in father-in-law's last months. It was difficult to finish *Glacier of Secrets* and complete my edits before sending the manuscript to my editor for her editing process. We were in the midst of edits when Mama passed away, and they eventually came to a halt as we took care of family needs. We picked them back up again, only to have my father-in-law pass away in the middle of my editor's edits and my corrections. Helping my mother-in-law became a priority, but eventually we were able to get back to editing again. My publisher told me "Family comes first," so I took her at her word. My deadline drew ever nearer but with His help we made it. God's mercy and grace saw us through it all. I give Him all the glory and praise because He is worthy. Praise God!

I'd like to thank Libby Powell, our church nurse, for her expertise in answering some medical questions for me for my story. She's one smart and experienced lady. Thanks, Libby. Your help was of immense value to me. You just never know when I'm going to call on you out of the blue.

My son, Matt, is a well of information when it comes to military hardware and tactical information. Serving in the US Army has helped him pick up information he's been able to pass on to me. He's a huge book lover and reader and a paper book purist. He won't touch an eReader with a ten-foot pole. Give him a paper book (hardback or paperback, it doesn't matter) and he's happy. He's a deep reader and has read Moby Dick as well as many other classics. He's my go-to guy and sounding board for discussing scenes in my books and writing them plausibly, especially when it comes to a death scene or disposing of a villain. He's good. Thanks, Matt, for all of your help. Love you, Son.

Natalya Lakhno is one of my faithful readers. She won a contest several months ago in which she won the chance to have her name used for one of my characters in this book. Congratulations again, Natalya! However, I would also like to thank Natalya for her help in making sure I used the proper Russian words in the right places in this story. She was a great help to me. Thank you, my friend, and God bless you!

To Jan Denapoli Cosmutto, I'd like to say thank you for all your help. Your knowledge of sled dogs, dog sledding and Alaska weather was invaluable. Mark and I had a blast on our fishing trip with you and Eric out to the Valdez Arm and Prince William Sound those four days. Fish on!

Thanks to my publisher, Cynthia Hickey, and her amazing talents, I once again have a beautiful book cover. She always comes through with what fits the story, and this cover is no exception. Thank you, Cynthia.

I would like to thank my editor, Debby Drust, for her editing talents and for her willingness to have a flexible schedule. Due to the fact I lost my mother to cancer January 21, 2020 and my father-in-law last Sunday, March 1,2020, it's been difficult to get this book edited and released. With Debby's flexibility and editing talents, we've finally reached our goal. Thank you, Debby and God bless you.

And last, but never least, I thank my sweetheart and husband, Mark. He's my greatest cheerleader and supporter. The Faith in the Parks series requires a lot of travel and research, and, considering *Glacier of Secrets* takes place in Denali National Park, Alaska, I was able to travel there two summers in a row. Mark and I traveled all over the eastern side of Alaska and saw some amazing sights, but I did most of my research in Denali National Park and the surrounding area as well as in Fairbanks. I fell in love with Alaska. I didn't, however, visit in the wintertime, so I had to get my information from the internet and from the locals. My love for Alaska might have changed had I visited in the wintertime, but I doubt it. It's a glorious state, with so much beauty and wonderful people. Thank you, Mark, for indulging me once again and taking me on yet another research trip (actually two). I love you, sweetheart. More than words can say. What a blessing you are in my life. I thank God for you, sweetheart. I love you and look forward to the next research trip with you! On to the next!

*Panster – an author who doesn't follow an outline and who writes by "the seat of their pants"; an author who "wings it" in their writing.

Prologue

June 12, 1987
State Department, Washington, D.C.

There is one sign the Soviets can make that would be unmistakable," President Ronald Reagan spoke into the podium microphone as he stood in front of the Brandenburg Gate in Berlin, Germany near the Berlin Wall, "that would advance dramatically the cause of freedom and peace. General Secretary Gorbachev, if you seek peace, if you seek prosperity for the Soviet Union and Eastern Europe, if you seek liberalization, come here to this gate! Mr. Gorbachev, open this gate! Mr. Gorbachev, tear down this wall."

Edgar Norton reached over and turned down the volume on the TV. "Those are powerful words, sir. Do you think Mr. Gorbachev will take up that challenge?"

State Department Under Secretary Bradford Scott leaned back in his leather desk chair and ran a hand through his dark hair. He eyed his young assistant for a moment then shrugged. "We can only hope, Edgar. Our president has called Mr. Gorbachev out in no uncertain terms, and if he doesn't follow through, the general secretary will look like a fool."

Just then the phone on Secretary Scott's desk rang and his assistant reached for it. "This is State Department Under Secretary Bradford Scott's office. This is his assistant, Edgar Norton, speaking. How can I help you?"

"Hey, Edgar. Is that no-account boss of yours in the office?" a booming voice came across the telephone wire followed by a chuckle. "If he is, I need to speak to him."

"Oh, good morning, Assistant Secretary Holloway, sir." Edgar stood a little straighter as he spoke. "Yes, sir. He's here, sir."

"You know, Edgar, you could drop half the sirs you use, and you'd still be using too many. You need to loosen up some, son."

"Yes, sir," Edgar nodded, his body still straight and stiff. "I'll try, sir."

A heavy sigh heaved across the wire. "You do that, son. In the meantime...."

"Oh, yes, sir. Here's Under Secretary Scott, sir." Edgar passed the handset to his boss and busied himself straightening up the office.

"What's up, Gabe? Did you call to harass my assistant or are you calling to critique the president's speech? I think he did a pretty good job....what's that?" Bradford Scott leaned forward resting his elbows on his desk. "Wait a second, Gabe."

"Edgar, hold up on what you're doing and head back to your desk. I need a few minutes here, please."

Edgar looked up and realized from the undersecretary's expression that something important was going on. He headed for the door even as he answered, "Yes, sir."

Secretary Scott leaned back in his leather desk chair. "Okay, Gabe. Go ahead."

"Brad, you know I can't tell you anything on these unsecured phone lines. Do I have to remind you there's a cold war going on? Meet me outside in five minutes at the park bench."

The phone line clicked in Scott's ear and the phone buzzed, indicating Gabe had hung up.

Secretary Scott grabbed his fedora from the coat rack and stepped out his door, stopping at his assistant's desk. "Edgar, I'm stepping out for a few minutes. I won't be long."

"Yes, sir." The young man nodded, returning to his computer and the work at hand.

Secretary Scott hurried down the marble corridor of the Harry S. Truman building and out the main entrance. He paused for a moment, his gaze on the park bench in the grassy area in front of the building which housed the State Department. A single man sat on the bench, facing the other direction, a plume of cigarette smoke drifting away on the afternoon breeze. Gabe Holloway. He'd know him anywhere. Even from the back.

Secretary Scott left the sidewalk, strolled across the paved driveway in front of the building then crossed the grass to the park bench. He stopped and faced the other man, grinning at him.

"Hi, Gabe. What's so all fired important that you dragged me out of my air-conditioned office to sit out here and talk to you? It may be mid-June, but it's already getting warm."

Gabe Holloway crushed his cigarette on the sole of his shoe and laid the butt on the seat beside him. "Well, at least it's not August, Brad. Besides, there's a nice breeze, and we're sitting under the shade trees. So quit your griping and have a seat. I have something to tell you. Something that we need to act on. Now."

Scott's brow furrowed at his superior's words, and he took a seat on the wooden bench. "What's up, Gabe?"

The older man crossed one leg over his knee, his foot bouncing in…what? Agitation? Frustration? Excitement? Brad couldn't decide, but lifted his gaze to the older man's face as he began to speak.

"A few hours ago, a Russian pilot attempted to defect to the US." Gabe's voice was low, and Scott strained to hear his words. "The difficulty is we can't find him."

"What do you mean, 'we can't find him'?" Scott's voice matched Gabe's in a low whisper. "Where did he enter the US? Or did he?"

Gabe wiped a heavy hand across his forehead, puffed out his cheeks, and blew out a stream of air. He turned his gaze to meet Scott's. "Apparently, our defecting pilot was picked up by a couple of fishermen on a small fishing trawler off the northwest coast of Alaska. It's unclear how he escaped from Russia or how he made it to the point where he was picked up. They found him floating in an emergency raft. He told them he was from one of the crabbing boats and had fallen overboard."

"Did he speak English that well?"

"Would you hang on, Brad." Gabe held up his hand as a policeman would to hold back traffic.

"How do we know he's a pilot?" Scott crossed his arms over his chest and eyed Gabe.

"Don't get ahead of me, Brad. Let me finish." Gabe glared. "Our pilot in question was taken on board the fishing trawler and talked his way to shore. The fishermen let him go when they docked in Nome. They never asked anymore questions. He made his way to the airport and stowed on board a flying ambulance. Only the pilot was onboard at the time but was preparing for a flight and had the engines running. The Soviet pilot caught him unaware. The ambulance pilot threatened to turn our defecting pilot over to the local authorities, but apparently the defecting pilot has some sensitive Soviet information he's more than willing to hand over to the US government. He explained in broken English that he's a pilot and flew out of the Soviet Union during the night with top secret information. His plane was shot down over the Bering Sea. He talked the ambulance pilot into taking him to one of the military bases in northeast Alaska, using the sensitive information as a bargaining tool. That's where they were headed when we lost them. When I say we don't know where they are, we have a general idea but that's all."

Secretary Scott shifted on the park bench. "That's quite a story, Gabe. What I'd like to know is how he survived the plane going down in the frigid waters of the Bering Sea. You know how cold that water is. And where did he get the emergency raft?"

"Brad, if I knew all the answers to this account, I'd tell you." Gabe scratched his head. "At this point we don't know everything. Maybe he had an emergency raft beneath his ejection seat. Who knows what the Soviets do in their planes? Give me a break, man. Besides, there are more important issues at stake here."

"Fine." Scott waved a hand. "I understand. Where do you think the general area is where they may have gone down?"

"Now that's a more sensible question." Gabe glanced around then turned to look over his shoulder before returning his gaze to Scott. "Mt. McKinley National Park. The pilot of the ambulance called the Ft. Wainwright Army Base in northern Alaska telling them he was bringing the defecting pilot in. Because it was an unsecured radio transmission, he attempted to tell them as much as he could without endangering him and his passenger.

"He indicated he needed a security officer to meet the plane ASAP. His passenger had a 'package'," Gabe held up fingers indicating air quotes, "they would be interested in. We translated that to mean sensitive information. He also told them his passenger was from a nearby country and needed to speak with the officer. Well, that could mean several different countries, but the nearest is Russia, so that's the most likely choice."

"You're reading an awful lot into a few words in a vague transmission, Gabe." Scott swept his hand through his hair. "And if you don't find the plane, it isn't really going to matter much."

Gabe harrumphed. "That's the problem, isn't it? The transmission ended near Mt. McKinley. Do you have any idea how big Mt. McKinley National Park is, Brad?"

"Yeah, actually, I have a general idea. I am from Alaska, remember?"

"Yes, I do remember, and the park is nine thousand four hundred and forty-six square miles. We looked it up. And we have to find a tiny plane in all of that. All because we want whatever it is that Russian pilot has in his hands that the Soviet Union doesn't want us to have." Gabe pulled a pack of cigarettes from inside his suit jacket and tapped it against his finger. Nothing came out. He mumbled, "Empty. Wouldn't you know it."

With a heavy sigh, he jammed it back into his jacket pocket. Reaching into an inside pocket on the other side of his jacket, he retrieved a stick of gum, offering one to Scott.

Secretary Scott waved a hand indicating he didn't want any. Gabe unwrapped a stick and popped it into his mouth. "We begin a search of that park, Brad. I'll call the Secretary of the Department of the Interior, and he can do whatever has to be done to get the park service moving on their end. I want that plane found. I'm sending you out there to oversee things and make sure the search is thorough."

Scott sat up straight. "Me? Search and rescue isn't really my area of expertise, Gabe."

"Maybe not, but it is your home state, and it'll look good on your record if you find them."

"And if I don't?" Secretary Scott quirked an eyebrow. He certainly had his doubts. McKinley *is* a huge park.

"Don't defeat yourself before you've even started, Brad. We'll cross that bridge if and when we get there. Find that plane and hopefully you'll find those pilots still alive. Then find whatever sensitive information that Russian pilot has. Understood?" Gabe looked him in the eye.

"Understood." Scott understood all too well that this mission was nearly impossible. The proverbial needle in the haystack had nothing on him. He'd much rather look for the needle than attempt to find that plane in Mt. McKinley National Park.

Chapter One

Present Day

Pavel eyed his phone as it rang. It was that number. Grabbing it, he clicked on the answer call button and held it to his ear.

"*Da?*"

"You must remain vigilant." A deep Russian voice came across cyberspace as if the man were in the next room rather than the next continent. "He will be arriving soon. We will tell you more when our intelligence has that information."

"*Da.* I understand." Pavel answered in Russian. "How soon, do you think?"

"That is not your concern. You worry about finding it and getting it out when the time comes." He heard the Russian's voice harden. "You will use whatever means are at your disposal."

"Understood."

Only the Russian man's breathing filled the pause that spanned a full thirty seconds causing Pavel to grow uncomfortable. What was he doing? Was this a mind tactic reminiscent of the cold war? Weren't those days over? There were rumors....

"Evgene was a fool." The Russian's words were adamant. "He could have had everything. He was to be given a promotion that would have placed him high in the ranks of the KGB. President Gorbachev himself would have...."

He waited for the Russian to continue.

"What's the use of looking to the past?" The Russian's words were more resigned now. "Just be prepared. You will move when we tell you to."

"I understand, and I'll be ready."

"Good."

"How shall I address you?"

"I am General Kozlov. That's all you need to know." The phone clicked and the line went dead.

~

Maggie Lawrence parked her little green rented SUV in front of the small, brown wooden building at the far end of the runway and turned off the engine. The lake behind her was home to numerous seaplanes. They were tied up along the lake shoreline while a long runway lay between the lake and a long row of buildings surrounded by small land planes. Maggie glanced at the sign over the front door of this building. It read Svenson's Bush Plane Service. Yep. This is the place. Before she'd left New York, she'd done thorough research of all the bush plane services that flew out of Fairbanks, Alaska. Svenson's had the best reviews and the best prices to boot.

Maggie couldn't wait to get a bird's-eye view of the park she'd been hired to photograph, and she wanted to get a jump on it. She would drive down to Healy near Denali National Park later today and find her new home away from home. First things first. She needed to find the pilot who would take her on a flight-seeing tour.

Opening the car door, she stepped out into frigid cold air. The car rental attendant had told her the temperature was -20°. Maggie shivered in her tan parka and pulled the hood up. Having been born and raised in North Carolina, she doubted she'd get used to these temps. Ever. Even living in New York City as she did now, didn't compare to Fairbanks, Alaska, the coldest city in the US.

Locking her car, she tucked her gloved hands into her parka pockets and headed for the front door. With reluctance she pulled one hand back out and attempted to turn the door knob. Locked. Shading her eyes, she leaned close and gazed through the window in the door. There was no one in the room. Just a cluttered desk, a filing cabinet, a bookshelf and a couple of chairs.

Maggie knocked hoping whoever ran this place was just in another room. However, no one came hurrying to let her in. She knocked louder.

"Hello. Anyone here?"

Maggie heaved a heavy sigh. Still nothing. Not good. She had a reservation after all. She glanced around, then heard a faint sound. A gravel road led from the parking lot in front of the building around back. Drawing her parka hood closer, she walked around the side of the building, the sounds growing louder.

Maggie found a larger building located further back. It looked like a plane hangar and the sounds emanating from it were mechanical.

Maggie tried the door on the side of the building, and it opened. She stepped inside to find it was a lot warmer than outside. The smell of petroleum filled the air. Gasoline and oil, she guessed. A plane stood ten feet in front of her, its engine cowling removed. A man stood beside it, his arms buried inside the engine. His loud hum was off key as he worked.

Maggie took a couple steps closer. "Excuse me. I'm looking for Jud Svenson. Is he around?"

The humming stopped, and the man tilted his head slightly to the side as he ceased working. He shook his head and started working again, resuming his loud humming.

Maggie shoved her parka hood back and stepped nearer to the man, raising her voice as she spoke. "Excuse me, sir. I'm looking for Jud Svenson."

The man jumped and yanked his arms from the engine. "Ouch!" he yelled.

Blood dripped from a cut on the back of his greasy hand as he spun around to see who had interrupted his work.

"I'm so sorry." Maggie's gloved hands flew up to cover her mouth. "I didn't mean to startle you. I called out a few seconds ago, but you didn't hear me."

The tall blond man's eyebrows lifted in surprise as his blue gaze landed on Maggie. "No, no, please don't apologize. You did startle me, but it's alright. I had no idea someone had come in."

He strolled over to the wall where a first aid kit was attached, and pulled it down, carrying it to the utility sink near the back of the hanger.

Maggie followed him.

"What's your name?" The man turned on the warm water and pumped soap into his hand from a dispenser on the wall.

"I'm Maggie Lawrence. I called a couple of weeks ago to make a reservation. I tried the front door, but no one answered. I heard a noise back here and decided to come see if I could find someone."

The man scrubbed his hands, removing the grease and washing the cut on the back of his hand. "Lawrence, huh? I don't remember the name, but then my secretary usually handles reservations. Sue Ellen had an emergency this morning. Her daughter went into labor. Wasn't due for another two weeks. Anyway, let me get this cleaned up, and I'll help you out."

"And you are?"

"Jud Svenson. I'd normally shake your hand, but that'll have to wait, I'm afraid." He dried his hands with paper towels he retrieved from the holder on the wall.

"Open that for me, will you?" He pointed to the first aid kit.

Maggie opened the kit and took a look at the cut on his hand. "I don't think it's too deep, and you certainly don't need stitches. One of these should do it."

She pulled out a bandage that would be sufficient and, after applying an antibiotic ointment, applied the bandage. "There you go."

"Thanks, Flo." He grinned at her.

Maggie wrinkled her brows at him. "Flo? I told you my name is Maggie."

"Flo. You know. Short for Florence Nightingale."

Maggie chuckled. "Well, it's the least I could do after causing your injury."

Jud waved her words away. "Nah. I've always got my hands inside the engines of my planes, and I'm always getting them cut up. It's no big deal, believe me."

Maggie returned his smile. "Very well. Now how about we check on my reservation. I'd like to get up in the air and get a look at Denali. I have some photos to take. I hope it's a clear day down there."

Jud snapped his fingers. "You're in luck. I check the report every morning and it said clear skies for Denali today."

"You're not just saying that? It's really going to be clear?" Maggie lifted crossed fingers on both hands and squinted at him.

"I'm not just saying that. It really was the report this morning. I can't say that every day, you know. The majority of the time Mt. Denali is shrouded in clouds."

"Then let's go." Maggie started to walk toward the front of the hanger then stopped. "Oh, but what about your plane?"

Jud stopped next to her and placed his hands on his hips, a question in his gaze. "What about it?"

"You're working on it."

Jud smiled and crooked a finger at her, beckoning her to follow him as he walked around the grounded plane and pointed. "Ta da."

Maggie stepped around the first plane to see a second one, it's engine cowling in place. Red and blue stripes decorated the white Cessna 185.

"Patriotic. Nice. She's ready to fly?" Maggie turned to Jud.

"As soon as we do your paperwork, I'll get her out of the hanger. I'll do my pre-flight check and we'll be on our way."

~

Maggie had flown many times before, mostly commercial airlines. She'd flown a few "puddle jumpers" with six to twenty passengers, but this was her first flight in a four-seater. From her seat inside the plane she watched as Jud followed his checklist, ensuring that everything outside the plane worked as it should. Then he climbed inside and continued to follow his checklist.

When Jud finished, he stowed the clipboard with the list and handed her a set of headphones. "It's going to get loud so put these on. We'll also be able to talk to one another through the mics."

Maggie placed the headset over her ears and Jud plugged the cable into the audio panel. Then he did the same with his own headset.

She watched in fascination as he began flipping switches and pushing buttons. A few seconds later, she felt a vibration throughout the plane as the engine roared to life. Its muted sound stayed a mere hum thanks to the headset.

Excitement stirred within Maggie. She'd been looking forward to this trip since *National Scenic Wildlife Magazine* called three weeks earlier. They'd hired her to do their photo shoot for an article they planned to release in six months covering the scenery around Denali National Park. This gig should put her in the big time for sure.

Maggie glanced out the window as she felt the plane begin to roll down the tarmac. Jud spoke to the air traffic control tower putting in his request for takeoff.

The tower at the Fairbanks airport responded with the need for them to wait while they set up a plan for them. Jud moved the plane to the flight area where they would wait until the tower told them to move to the runway.

He turned off the mic to the tower and turned toward Maggie, speaking only to her.

"How you doing? You okay?"

Maggie nodded. "Yeah, I'm fine, thanks."

"Ever flown in a small plane before?"

"Nope. Not this small."

Jud's eyebrows rose. "Okay. Have you ever had air sickness when flying?"

"No, no. Never." Maggie shook her head.

Concern filled Jud's eyes. He reached under his seat and pulled out a paper bag, handing it to Maggie. "Just in case."

Maggie eyed the paper bag. "I won't need it."

"Just in case. I just cleaned the inside of my cabin. I don't want to have to do it again." Jud's face twisted distastefully.

Maggie snatched the paper bag from his hand. "Oh, for goodness sake."

Jud chuckled as the tower came back directing him to take off.

He turned the Cessna 185 and throttled it up as they taxied toward the runway. Once there, Jud moved the plane into position and throttled the engine. As he pushed the throttle forward, the little plane rolled down the runway faster and faster. Jud pulled the yoke back and the plane lifted off the ground.

The slight sensation of weightlessness overcame Maggie for a few seconds as the plane lifted higher and higher. The plane skipped sideways a few times with wind gusts, causing Maggie to grab hold of her seat.

Jud spoke to the tower again then signed off.

Maggie looked out her window and watched as Fairbanks grew smaller and smaller, drifting away behind them. Soon trees and lakes with the occasional small house, smoke wafting from its chimney, became part of the snowy scenery. A winding frozen river and a road twined through the mountainous terrain. A distant railroad track serpentined through the landscape like a snail's trail. Snow covered the landscape and the midday sunshine reflected off frozen ponds and lakes. Maggie grabbed her sunglasses from her purse.

Jud noticed her actions. "You're coming at a good time. Our days are getting longer now, you know. Here in early March, we have about 10 hours of sunshine per day. Earlier in the winter it was far less with only a couple hours of sunshine. As we move further into spring the days will continue to grow longer until summer when the sun is up all but a couple of hours at night."

"So I've heard. The land of the midnight sun, right?"

"You've got it."

"Isn't that hard to get used to?"

"What? Walking around at ten o'clock at night and it looks more like three in the afternoon?" Jud chuckled. "It's all I've ever known, so I'm used to it. To a newcomer, I suppose it would take some getting used to."

Maggie shook her head and gazed out at the scenery below them. "This is gorgeous. My first real view of Alaska. I sat on the aisle on my flight to Fairbanks and the man by the window kept his shade down so I couldn't see our approach."

"This is a far better view anyway. You're closer and we're going slower." Jud pointed to the southwest. "Take a look at that. Denali is clear today. Not even the usual cloud ring around the summit. What do you think?"

Maggie followed his pointing finger to catch her first glimpse of Mt. Denali, once called Mt. McKinley, and gasped. "Oh, my goodness. It's…it's spectacular."

She reached into her camera bag, that she'd stuffed between her feet, for her camera.

"Hey, don't worry. We're going in a lot closer. I'll angle the plane so you can get some great shots, but you can snap away whenever you want."

Maggie did just that. Jud set up the plane for some terrific shots from great angles. Then he took the plane in low and she was able to get some more great shots of the park landscapes and some of the glaciers.

They flew over a dog sled team whisking across the snowy terrain.

"Oh my goodness!" Maggie snapped more pictures. "Did you see that? It was a dog sled team."

"Yep, they use them here in the park." Jud pulled back on the Cessna's yoke and lifted the plane into the sky. He turned the yoke to the right then pushed it forward, diving back toward the ground, leveling off as they approached the dog sled team once again. Jud waggled the plane's wings slightly on approach.

The musher lifted a hand and waved.

"Do you know him?"

Jud pulled back on the stick, lifting the plane back into the sky. "I know several of the rangers in the park, but I don't know which one that was. He's too bundled up."

"Dog sled teams in the park service. Who knew?" Maggie mumbled as she glanced over her shoulder trying to catch a final glimpse of the musher and his team whisking over the snow.

What an interesting story that would make for a magazine article. Would the editor of *National Scenic Wildlife Magazine* be interested in something like that? Maggie only did the photography. Mr. Charles Radford would have to find a reporter to come up and do the article. Could she sell that idea to the great New York editor?

Chapter Two

With the sunlight waning, Maggie pulled into the Three Bears gas station and shopping mart in Healy and parked. It had been over a two-hour drive from Fairbanks and she'd forgotten to pick up groceries before she headed to the cabin she'd rented for her stay. She'd make a run back to Fairbanks another day when she could stock up on supplies, but she'd just get what she needed to last until then.

She zipped up her parka and climbed out of her SUV. The temps had hovered around -9° all day but it felt like they were dropping. Slipping her purse onto her shoulder, she made her way inside the shopping mart. It was a good-sized grocery store. At least she wouldn't have to drive two hours to Fairbanks every time she needed something.

Maggie grabbed a shopping cart and started down the aisles, dropping items in as she went.

She was reaching for a box of cereal when she felt a tug on the hem of her coat.

"Grandma, look at this," an excited voice matched the excited tug on her coat. "Can we get it?"

Maggie turned to find a dark-haired little boy holding a box of cereal in one hand, his gaze latched onto the front, his other hand tugging on her coat hem in earnest.

"Oh, um, I'm sorry, but I think you have the wrong coat." Maggie kept her voice soft so as not to startle him. She bent over slightly. "That looks yummy. Have you ever had it before?"

The little boy lifted a scared gaze to hers. "Oh, you're not my grandma."

Maggie chuckled softly and shook her head. "Nope, but I can help you find her."

"I'm not supposed to talk to strangers."

"I know sweetie, but I have to help you find her. How about if I walk you to the front of the store and we find the manager? They can call over the loudspeaker and have her come to the front and pick you up."

The little boy looked uncertain then turned and looked up and down the aisle as if hoping his grandma would make an appearance.

"I can't just walk away and leave you standing here, sweetheart."

"I'm not moving till she comes back." Red rimmed the boy's eyes as they grew watery. He wiped his eyes and held his chin up with a brave tilt.

"Then I'll wait right here with you until she returns. I'm sure she's already looking for you." Maggie winked at him trying to reassure him.

They didn't have to wait long.

"There you are, Jeremy, dear. I'm right here."

Maggie spotted an older woman in her early sixties pushing her cart toward them. What once was black hair was now mixed lavishly with gray and pulled back in a bun. She wore wire-framed glasses that did nothing to hide impish brown eyes bracketed by laugh lines. A wide smile lit her round face. She wrapped her grandson in her arms.

"I'm so sorry, sweetie-pie. I don't know how I missed you. I suppose I turned the corner and you were still here staring at this…oh, my goodness. What are you looking at? Do you have any idea how much sugar is in that box of cereal?"

"But Grandma, they look like they would taste good."

Maggie noticed he didn't use a whiny voice to ask. She was impressed.

"Oh, honey, I know they do." Grandma gave him another hug. "That's how they sell this unhealthy stuff. So, I tell you what we'll do. You let me pick a box of healthy cereal that I think you should eat and if you want that box, then we'll get both and you can have half of each when you eat your cereal in the morning. What do you think of that?"

The little boy thought for a moment then nodded. "Okay. Then I'm only eating half of the bad stuff and I'm getting half of the good cereal too. You're so smart, Grandma."

Maggie chuckled and Grandma turned to her and winked. In a low voice she said, "I may or may not fudge on the halves of each cereal depending on the good and the bad, if you know what I mean.

"Thank you for staying with my grandson, sweetie, and have a blessed day." The older woman placed the boxes of cereal in the cart, then the little boy hopped on the front and they wheeled away.

Maggie stood for a moment and watched them disappear around the end of the aisle. She only hoped she would one day have the opportunity to be a wise grandmother like that lady. With a smile on her face she finished her shopping and headed to her cabin. She was exhausted and tomorrow was the first day she'd be on the ground in the park taking pictures.

She was supposed to meet up with her guide, Ranger Troy Donovan. In spite of the exhaustion that threatened to overwhelm her, Maggie was excited to get this photo shoot started. She would be here for a few weeks, and if she could get Mr. Radford to approve another shoot involving the dog sled teams, perhaps she could extend her stay even longer.

Maggie parked in front of a small cedar log cabin and stared at her new home. It was small but well kept on the outside. Hopefully it would be the same on the inside. She climbed out of the SUV and gathered her few grocery bags. She climbed the three steps to the small porch that was adorned with a cedar Adirondack chair. That would certainly come in handy in warmer summer months, but she wouldn't be around to enjoy it. Too bad.

Tugging the key from her coat pocket, she unlocked the front door. Pushing the door wide, she stepped inside to find a rustic, but welcoming, home away from home. A small kitchen was situated on the right with a breakfast nook in the corner while a grouping of overstuffed couch and armchairs around a gas fireplace beckoned on the left. Straight ahead a staircase led up and around to a loft bedroom. She'd bring in her bags as soon as she got her groceries put away.

Making short work of that, she soon had her bags upstairs and a quick meal cooking in the microwave. She was far too tired to prepare anything big.

Maggie ate her microwave meal, changed into her pjs, brushed her teeth and climbed into the big fluffy bed in the center of the loft bedroom. She flipped off the light on the bedside table.

Ooooh. Wow. This was like drifting on a cloud. She was going to like sleeping in this bed. Maggie stretched and yawned, settling amongst the pillows and the warm comforter. It might be -30° outside, but she was warm and snuggly here in her bed.

Maggie turned onto her side and tugged the comforter over her shoulder and up to her chin. The cold wasn't her problem. Being from North Carolina, she wasn't especially fond of it, but she could deal with the cold. No, her problem were the memories. Memories that sometimes led to nightmares. A shiver ran through her unbidden. She squeezed her eyes shut tight then opened them again. Very little light seeped around the drapes at the window. She'd wanted to be out in the remote area beyond the edge of the village, hadn't she? The idea of the Alaskan peace and tranquility had appealed to her. All of a sudden, she wasn't so sure anymore.

~

With her favorite thermal coffee mug in her gloved hand and her camera bag slung over her shoulder, Maggie strolled down the snow-cleared sidewalk to the small grouping of log buildings that comprised the headquarters for Denali National Park. Somehow, she'd expected something a little more upscale yet still rustic. These were rustic for sure and that's where it ended.

A simple board and log sign outside one of the log buildings indicated she'd found park headquarters. The one-and-a-half story log building with a silver rippled tin roof was painted dark brown and the window frames white. A porch with four dark brown log posts supporting a silver rippled tin roof welcomed visitors to enter. The cement floor of the porch had been shoveled clear of snow as well as the walkway to the porch.

Maggie hurried up to the wooden door with a single glass windowpane and turned the knob. She stepped inside and blessed warmth greeted her. Shoving her parka hood from her head, she glanced around the tiny entrance. It was sparse and rustic just like the outside. A reception counter stood to the right of the entrance while straight ahead a hallway led to offices. On the left a closed door led to who knew what.

Maggie spotted a young woman in park uniform sitting behind the reception counter working at a computer. She stepped across to the counter, and the wooden floor creaked loudly beneath her feet. Maggie cringed at the sound that shattered the quiet.

The young blond woman glanced up and giggled. "Don't you just hate that sound when you first enter a new place? It announces you before you're ready to be announced."

Maggie chuckled. "Yeah, I guess you're right. I've never thought of it that way before."

Her photographic eye scanned the young woman's appearance. Her blond hair was fashioned in a twist at the back of her head, not a hair out of place. Her makeup was flawless, she was congenial and her smile genuine. Her uniform was impeccable. She'd be amazing in front of a camera.

The young blond laughed. "You're not the first to cringe at this loud floor. I must say, I get a good chuckle at people's expressions when they come in. Anyway, what can I do for you?"

"My name's Maggie Lawrence, and I have an appointment to meet Ranger Troy Donovan here. I'm a photographer for *National Scenic Wildlife Magazine*. He's scheduled to be my guide over the next few weeks as I photograph the park." She patted her camera bag for good measure.

The blond's smile slipped a notch, her gaze moving to the hallway at the rear of the reception area. "Uhhh, Troy's not in at the moment."

She bit her lip in thought and Maggie could almost see the gears moving as the young woman reached for the phone on her desk. She held up a finger with a perfectly manicured nail.

"Just a moment, please. I'll see if I can locate him for you." She turned toward the window behind her desk and waited for the person on the other end of the line to answer.

Maggie set her camera bag on top of the counter and took a sip from her thermal coffee mug. Her gaze wandered around the small space taking in a few schedules, a calendar and a wildlife poster.

A mumbled conversation took place behind the desk but the words "the superintendent," "she's waiting," and "right now," came across loud and clear. Was the elusive Ranger Donovan reluctant to make an appearance? Why, for goodness sake? She had a job to do and arrangements were made weeks ago through the superintendent's office. There shouldn't be a problem.

The young woman hung up the phone and turned back to Maggie, a smile lighting her pretty face. She stood and opened the office door behind the counter. "Miss Lawrence, this office is empty for now. If you'll please just make yourself comfortable in here, Troy will be back in a few minutes."

Before Maggie stepped inside, she stuck out her hand. "Please, call me Maggie. I don't stand on formalities. What's your name?"

The young woman shook Maggie's hand. "I'm Natalya Lakhno. Just call me Natalya. If you need anything while you're here, don't hesitate to ask. I'll be happy to help however I can."

"Thanks, Natalya. I'll remember that."

Maggie stepped inside the office and took a seat in a chair along the wall and waited. It wasn't three minutes before heavy footsteps sounded down the hallway and a dark figure loomed over Natalya's desk.

"Where is she?" The figure's voice may have been low but from where Maggie sat, he didn't sound happy.

Natalya pointed in Maggie's direction and said in a low whisper that Maggie still heard, "Play nice."

The man turned and made his way into the office. When he'd appeared before Natalya, Maggie had the impression his presence filled the small reception space, but now Maggie was sure she would be swallowed by it. His stormy expression left no doubt he was unhappy about being here.

"Let's go." He turned on his heel and headed back out the way he'd come in.

Maggie grabbed her camera bag and hurried after him, turning a quick glance at Natalya.

"Good luck," the receptionist called as Maggie tried to keep up with her new guide. A couple park employees stared at her as she made her way through offices to a back door that slammed in her face. She opened it and raced after the dark figure that stormed in long strides toward a parked SUV near another building. Maggie was glad she'd worn her warm and comfortable hiking boots. Keeping up with this guy was going to be a workout. By the time she reached the SUV, he was sitting in the driver's seat and the engine was running.

Maggie climbed into the passenger seat and shut the door. Troy Donovan put the vehicle in reverse, slammed it into drive, and gunned the engine. Maggie barely had time to put her thermal coffee mug into the console drink holder and buckle her seat belt.

"I guess we're in a hurry?" she asked. He remained silent and she dared to look at his stormy features that were half hidden by a hunter green baseball cap covered by a knit toboggan of the same color with a park service emblem on the front. She leaned forward and settled her camera bag between her feet and mumbled, "I guess so."

In silence, her new guide drove a few miles down the road then pulled into a parking lot she'd passed earlier, parked the SUV and turned off the engine.

"I'll wait here." He stared straight ahead, his expression stoic.

Maggie looked from her driver to the sign in front of the building before them then back to her driver. "The visitor's center? I don't need to go to the visitor's center. I don't need to see exhibits and photographs taken by other photographers. I need you to take me out into the wilderness so that I can take my own photographs of the scenery and the wildlife in the park. That was arranged through the superintendent's office weeks ago, Mr. Donovan."

For the first time he turned the full force of his gaze on Maggie. The color of a stormy blue-gray ocean, it bore into hers beneath furrowed brows. Chiseled deep between them were two vertical lines indicating his anger. She felt the impact as much as she saw it.

"That's not happening, Miss Lawrence. Not today, not tomorrow, not ever." His voice was low but deep and menacing. "Whatever arrangements you've made, you'll have to change them."

He reached for the keys and started the engine, backed the SUV out of the parking spot and drove back to park headquarters. He stopped in the parking lot above the headquarters buildings and without a word waited for Maggie to get out.

Angry at the treatment she'd received, Maggie grabbed her camera bag and got out of the SUV, slamming the door behind her.

No sooner was she out of the SUV than he sped away, leaving black marks from the tires on the pavement.

How dare he treat her this way. These arrangements had been made weeks ago and whatever ego trip this man was on, he'd have to get over it. Maggie pulled her keys from her parka pocket and unlocked her SUV. She climbed in and dropped her camera bag on the passenger seat, then remembered she'd left her favorite thermal mug in the park SUV.

Maggie banged her head against the soft leather headrest a few times then, realizing just how futile that was, shook her head. She sighed heavily. This morning wasn't going well at all.

Now what, Lord? When I left the cabin this morning, I had such high expectations for the day. I know You're still in control even when things don't go the way I think they should. You've got a better plan, haven't You? Well, I need You to work this out.

Maybe a call to Mr. Radford was in order. He's the editor and he's the one who arranged things. *I'll put the ball back in his court. Then we'll see what happens with Mr. Donovan.*

~

Troy parked his SUV in front of the kennel office and looked over at the sled dogs. They never failed to bring a smile to his face. Even in the dead of winter they still preferred to lay on top of their houses instead of inside. He strolled over to his lead dog, Venture, who lay sprawled on top of his house. Venture cast him a lazy glance as he approached.

"What're you doing, boy?" Troy removed his glove and ran his fingers through the thick silver and black fur of the large husky. Venture's ice blue eyes closed in contentment as he stretched and rolled to his back exposing his stomach for Troy to rub. "Oh, you're just a couch potato, you know that? A real bum."

The dog yawned and stretched again.

"What? Am I boring you? I guess I'm going to have to put you to work, you lazy hound." Troy gave him a thump on the chest and walked away. He glanced back to see the dog lift his head and stare at him with a skeptical gaze.

As Troy headed into the office his cell phone rang. He shut the door behind him and pulled his phone from his pocket, giving a nod to the only other occupant of the office, Bryce West. Troy punched the answer call button and put the phone to his ear.

"Hello?"

"Troy, it's Natalya. The superintendent wants to see you in his office right away."

"Why?"

"He didn't say. He just told me to call you and tell you he wants to see you right away. Like now."

"As in right now?"

"Troy." Natalya's voice held a note of censure in it.

"Alright, I'm on my way." He punched the end call button and dropped the phone into his pocket.

"What was that all about?" Troy's coworker and fellow dog musher, Bryce, was busy repairing a leather harness.

Troy turned and placed his hand on the doorknob. "The superintendent wants to see me."

Bryce lifted his gaze and eyed Troy with lifted brows. "Now what did you do?"

"I have a pretty good idea." Troy didn't bother to restrain the wry note in his voice as he slipped back out the door.

~

"I got a call from Mr. Hayes, the Secretary of the Department of the Interior, telling me his close friend Mr. Radford, the owner and head editor of the agency *Photography International*, called him and he wasn't happy. When Mr. Radford complained that his star photographer was not allowed to take the pictures that were arranged for her to take weeks ago, what am I supposed to say, Troy?"

Troy eyed the superintendent over the man's desk as he leaned toward him, fists planted firmly on the smooth mahogany surface. His boss, a short man in his early sixties with a balding head and wire-framed glasses, was not in the least bit happy. His uniform was pressed to perfection and he generally ran a tight ship, but he also listened when his subordinates needed him to. Somehow, Troy didn't think this was one of those times.

Perhaps he'd gone overboard this morning with the beautiful, auburn haired Miss Lawrence, but there was something about her that reminded him of…. nope. He wasn't about to drag up the past. He'd seen red when he'd seen her and maybe he'd overreacted, but he didn't want another instance… No. No more.

"Troy, are you listening to me?" Superintendent Wade straightened and pushed his glasses further up onto his nose. "What's the matter? You've gone pale."

"Nothing's wrong, sir. I heard you. Perhaps I went a little overboard and overreacted, but I just…I…."

Superintendent Wade walked around his desk and placed a hand on Troy's shoulder. "Son, I understand you're still trying to heal from things in your personal life, but you've got to move on. You've got a job to do, and I don't trust anyone else to take this photographer into the wilderness and help her get the photographs she needs like I trust you. Besides, this is important. Mr. Radford is one of the largest financial contributors to the National Park Foundation. You understand how important it is to keep him happy?"

Troy released a heavy breath. "Yes sir, I do."

"Then, please, for the sake of the park service, go take care of Miss Lawrence and give it your best. I know you can clam up like a…a…well, like a…clam. Please try and treat her like a welcome guest to our park. She didn't come here as an enemy. She's here to do her job as well. I'm sure she wants to do it the best she can so help her to accomplish it, Troy. When she has all the photographs she wants, then she can go home, and I'm sure you'll both be happy."

Troy glanced to the side then back to his boss. "Yes, sir."

"Thank you." Superintendent Wade returned to his chair behind his desk and sat down. He reached for the phone on the side of his desk. "Now, I'm going to call Miss Lawrence and have her return to HQ. I expect you to apologize to the poor woman. Then try and play nice, for heaven's sake."

Chapter Three

Maggie started to enter the headquarters building but heard a shrill whistle to her left, halting her in her tracks. She turned her head and spotted Troy Donovan leaning against the rear of his SUV, one leg crossed over the other, his arms crossed over his green parka-covered chest. On his head he wore his green ball cap and park service toboggan. He waved her over.

Maggie hesitated for a brief moment, unsure of this change in the man. When the superintendent had called, he'd said Ranger Donovan would take her out to begin her photo shoot. She changed course and strolled toward the SUV and her guide, unsure how to approach him. She noticed the SUV was already running. Where was he taking her?

She stopped a few feet away, ready to take off in case he started roaring at her again. Ranger Donovan had made his feelings for her known quite plainly that morning. He lifted her thermal coffee mug from the bumper of the SUV and held it out to her.

"You left in a bit of a hurry this morning and forgot this." At first his gaze was everywhere except on her then as she reached for the mug, he pinned it right on her and held her gaze captive.

"Hey, I'm sorry I acted like such an idiot this morning, okay? I wasn't at all fair to you. I know you're only here to do your job, and I made that impossible for you. I apologize."

Maggie had the strange feeling she was being sucked into a whirlpool and dragged under. She could hardly breathe. She dragged in a deep breath and squeezed the thermal mug tight in her gloved fingers. What was wrong with her? Was it possible to drown in someone's gaze? That was ridiculous. Wasn't it?

"Yeah, it's okay. All's forgiven." Was that her voice that sounded so distant? Those dark blue-gray stormy eyes were no longer stormy. Apparently, the storm had passed and the seas had calmed. The blue was now more sapphire and the furrows had smoothed away. Maggie noticed the jet-black hair peeking from beneath his cap and toboggan. How was his skin tanned even in winter? This man was handsome in a rugged way although his nose was slightly crooked.

"Something wrong, Miss Lawrence?" His eyes narrowed as he crossed his arms over his chest and tilted his head in a question. One brow quirked up beneath his ball cap.

Maggie realized she'd been staring. Had she lost her ever-loving mind? She never stared. Ever. She tore her gaze away and readjusted her camera bag strap further up onto her shoulder. "No, not at all. Um, I accept your apology, and I appreciate it. I understand there are…um…miscommunications, or um…perhaps hard feelings due to…circumstances but we'll…just put those behind us and start over."

She stuck out her gloved hand. "I'm Maggie Lawrence. It's nice to meet you."

He eyed her gloved hand then, reaching out with his, he shook it. His large one engulfed hers, but he was gentle in his grasp.

"Ranger Troy Donovan at your service, Miss Lawrence."

Maggie wondered how much of a struggle it was for him to say those words. What had happened after her phone call to Mr. Radford this morning to elicit the change in this man? She hoped he hadn't been threatened with losing his job. She would feel terrible if that were the case.

"So, you want photographs of scenery and wildlife?" Ranger Donovan scratched his chin. "Well, it's a little late in the day to go too far afield. How about we take a short trip and I introduce you to some friends of mine?"

Maggie waved a hand toward him. "You're the guide. I'm trusting you to take me wherever the scenery and the wildlife are."

"Come on. Let's get in the truck. It may be a balmy -4° today, but we're going to be outside a good bit. Let's get you warmed up for a few minutes anyway."

They climbed into the truck and drove around the buildings, down a short snowy dirt road to another building and parked.

Maggie glanced out the window and spotted twenty or so dog houses with dogs roped to each one and several chain link dog kennels with dogs inside.

"What is this?" Maggie glanced around as they climbed out of the SUV.

"This is where I work." Troy walked around the SUV and waited as Maggie set her camera bag on the seat and prepared her camera. She'd pulled the mitten tops of her gloves back to expose only her index and thumb fingertips. She loved these gloves. They kept her hands warm but gave her the ability to work with her camera.

Maggie snapped on a lens then hung the camera strap around her neck inside the parka hood. She pulled the hood over her hair, covered her finger tips and turned to Troy.

"Ready when you are, Mr. Ranger Guide. Lead on." Maggie dazzled him with a smile.

~

Troy eyed Maggie through narrowed eyes, clenched his teeth and groaned. At least on the inside. Best not give her any ammunition to go back to her editor with. This woman was far too dangerous to him. Career wise and, well, she's a beautiful woman, but he had no intentions of becoming interested in her. He had no room in his life for a woman. Not now. Not ever. He was instantly reminded of the famous last words he'd spoken this morning. Look where *that* had gotten him.

"Follow me." Troy turned on his heel and strolled toward the dog houses. "These are the park's sled dogs. I'll introduce you to a few of them. You can get some pictures if you like. I know it's probably not what you're looking for specifically for your photo shoot, but we'll have to leave a lot earlier in the day to get out and take those shots."

"Sled dogs?" Elation spread across Maggie's features. "This is great. I don't mind at all. I can always save the shots for a future article, if I can talk Mr. Radford into it. Are you a musher?"

"Yep, that's right." Troy reached the first doghouse and petted the silver and black dog laying on the flat rooftop. "This is Ranger Venture. He's one of our lead dogs. He's not as lazy as he looks. If I were to pull a sled out here, he'd be up and barking, pulling at his rope, wanting to go for a run. All these dogs, no matter how much they look laid back and lazy now, love to work. They're working dogs and they enjoy pulling."

"You called him Ranger Venture."

"That's because he is a ranger. All of them are. They work for the park service just like I do. His take home pay may be in kibble and biscuits, but make no mistake, he works hard for his pay."

"Is it okay if I pet him?" Maggie's glance at Troy was tentative.

Troy shrugged one shoulder and nodded toward the dog. "Sure thing. They each have their own personalities, but in general they love to be loved on. There's a couple that are a little shier when it comes to strangers. Venture here isn't one of them. He thinks it's everyone's duty to show him attention."

As if to back up Troy's words, Venture reached out a paw in Maggie's direction.

Maggie laughed. "I see what you mean."

She removed a glove and ran her fingers through his fur. "Oh my goodness. His fur is so thick. It swallows my fingers."

Troy removed his glove and ran his fingers through Venture's fur as well. The husky rolled on his back giving them access to his stomach. "You're a mooch, you flea bitten dog."

Troy roughed up the big dog and Venture yawned and made noises at Troy, wrapping his front paws around his arm, clamping it to his chest. "Oh, yeah? It's like that is it?"

Troy laughed and played with the dog a bit then pulled a treat from his parka pocket and gave it to him.

"The reason his fur feels so thick is because he has two coats, whereas most dogs only have one. Huskies have a long outer coat that repels water and holds in the heat but also allows the skin to breathe in warmer weather. The second coat, or undercoat, is soft and downy-like and traps warmth in during the winter. They lose that coat in the warmer months because they don't need it."

Maggie ran her fingers into Venture's fur along his back. He stretched and eyed her with his ice blue gaze. "He has the most beautiful eyes."

"Yeah, he does, but you can look at a lot of the huskies here and they have similar eyes. Huskies can have blue, brown, a variety of both or various shades of both. They can even have one of each. It's pretty common."

"How many dogs do you have here?"

"Thirty."

Maggie backed up a few steps and snapped some pictures from various angles. Troy got Venture to sit up and stand, posing him for several shots. Then they walked around to visit some of the other dogs. Troy gave her a tour of the site then took her into the office.

Bryce was in the sled room working on one of the sleds.

"Hey, Bryce, I want to introduce you to Maggie Lawrence. She's a photographer who's here to do a photo shoot for a wildlife magazine. She'll be here for the next few weeks." He yanked both hats off and stuffed them in the pocket of his parka then ran his hand through his hair.

Bryce, who sat on the floor, one leg sprawled out, the other leg folded beneath it, turned to look at them over his shoulder. "Oh, hey there. Just a sec."

He finished wrapping some strapping around the framework of the sled and fastened it, then he stood up and wiped his hands on a rag.

Bryce stuck out his hand. "It's nice to meet you, Maggie Lawrence. Welcome to the back of nowhere."

"Miss Lawrence, this is Bryce West." Troy slapped the guy on the shoulder. "He's also a musher. As you can see, we do a lot of things around here. We have to keep our equipment in top running order. That's what Bryce is doing, repairing one of the sleds."

Troy watched as Maggie removed her gloves, unzipped her parka partway, removed her parka hood, and shook Bryce's hand.

"It's a pleasure to meet you, Bryce."

Bryce eyed Maggie then turned his gaze to Troy. "So, is this…?"

Troy cast Bryce a dark look and cleared his throat. "I'm giving Miss Lawrence a tour of the kennels and our facility today. Tomorrow I'll drive her out the Park Road to get her first glimpse of the park."

Troy turned his gaze on Maggie. Had she caught what Bryce was getting ready to ask? The idiot. What was he thinking almost bringing up the fact that she was the one that had caused the ruckus between her editor, the Secretary of the Department of the Interior and the park superintendent? He certainly didn't want to bring that up again.

"Oh. Sure. You'll like that, Miss Lawrence. It's a scenic drive and you'll get a lot of photos out there." Bryce held his thumb up.

"You know, guys," Maggie jammed her hands into her parka pockets, "I'd prefer it if you'd call me Maggie. Miss Lawrence sounds so formal. I'm going to be here for a few weeks, and since we're going to be working together, it doesn't make any sense to be formal."

"Well, I'm game, Maggie," Bryce chuckled.

Maggie's gaze sought Troy's and his breath caught in his throat. Now why did she have to go and get all friendly like? He wanted to keep her at arm's length. A long arm's length. But she wanted to be on a friendly first-name basis. Well, he'd see if he couldn't keep it formal for a while longer.

"Bryce, why don't you show her around the sled room. I've got to check on something in the office. I'll be back in a few minutes."

Troy hurried out the door, letting it slam shut behind him. He escaped into his office and shut the door. He stood leaning against it for a few moments. For the first time since Liz had gone, he had the desire to pray but he couldn't. There was no way he could talk to God after everything he'd said to Him. He'd blamed Him for everything.

His little world had settled into a routine and he was getting along fine without Him. That is until Maggie Lawrence came along and tilted it on its axis. All of a sudden, he didn't know which end was which. With her gorgeous mane of dark auburn hair and her fair skin, she didn't look like Liz but there was something about her and he couldn't say what it was. He just knew that Maggie Lawrence had rocked his world.

~

Maggie put on some soft jazz music then settled on the couch and pulled her laptop onto her lap. She picked up her digital camera from where she'd left it on the coffee table and, opening up the SD card compartment, ejected the SD card. It was time to take a look at the pictures she'd taken from her flight-seeing tour with Jud Svenson. She opened the files and blew up the pictures as large as the computer screen. Wow. The landscape pictures were gorgeous. So sharp and clear. She was glad she'd invested in the new digital camera before coming to Alaska. Definitely worth it.

Maggie took her time browsing through the shots until something in one of the photos caught her eye. She zoomed in as close as she could to try and figure out what the object was. It was slightly darker than its surroundings, and because of a few straight and rounded edges it looked man-made. But what would a man-made object be doing out in the wilderness? And it looked like it was lying at the base of a glacier. No. It actually looked like it was partially buried beneath a glacier. The camera lens she'd been using hadn't allowed her to get in close enough to tell what it was and the snow around it made it difficult to discern details.

Maggie looked at the previous and following pictures but didn't see it in those. This was the only picture of it. Curious.

Maggie stared at the zoomed-in photo and squinted her eyes to see if that would release some clue. Nope. She tried flipping the picture and staring at it from different angles, but nothing provided further information about the object. Should she ask someone about it? Troy Donovan? Jud Svenson? They were the only ones she knew to ask. Perhaps she'd better do some research first. The problem was she'd been busy snapping pictures and had no idea where in the park that picture was taken.

~

"Good morning." Maggie called as she hurried toward the running SUV parked near the headquarters building. Exhaust poured from the tailpipe. Troy stood by the driver's door with one hand in his parka pocket, a thermal coffee mug in the other gloved hand. His ball cap was in place, his parka hood pulled over it.

"Morning. You're late, New York."

"Because I'm from New York automatically means I'm going to be late?" Maggie realized she was arguing for argument's sake, but what the heck?

Troy shrugged. "City people are always hustling and bustling. Cramming so much into their day. I'd think they'd be used to running late and wouldn't think twice about it." He sipped his coffee, his sapphire gaze challenging her.

Maggie bristled inside but she had to be careful how she dealt with this man.

"Nope. I can't seem to get my little SUV started these chilly mornings." She furrowed her brow and compressed her lips as she met his gaze.

"Chilly?" He chuckled. "Are you plugging it in at night?"

Maggie gave him a blank stare. "Can we talk in the truck? I don't think it's a balmy -4° this morning like it was yesterday."

She stamped her feet against the paved driveway.

"You're right, it's not. It's an extremely cold -30°. Climb in and I'll explain."

Maggie beat feet around the SUV and climbed into the passenger seat. She'd brought her own coffee mug and, after belting herself in, she took a swig. The warmth went a long way to ease the chill. The inside of the SUV was toasty, and after a few minutes, she stripped off her gloves, and removed her hood. Troy had already done so and drove them out of the headquarters area up Park Road deeper into the park.

"Have you noticed a short pole with a plug and possibly a heavy-duty extension cord near your parking area?" Troy cast Maggie a sideways glance.

She thought for a few seconds then nodded. "Yes, I think so."

"Pretty much every vehicle in Alaska has been fitted with a block heater. Somewhere on that block heater is a plug for you to connect that extension cord to. The block heater element ensures your fluids don't freeze in the sub-zero temperatures, then it makes it easy for the engine to crank. I'm surprised you got it to start at all. Kudos to you."

"Thanks." Maggie felt warmth flow through her at the compliment. "You wouldn't want to show me where this connection on my SUV is so it's easier for me, would you?"

Troy turned a half grin and a raised brow in her direction. The blue of his gaze sent her heart rate into triple time. "Sure, I can do that. Anything to ensure you're on time."

"You think city people are always late to appointments, am I right?" Maggie took a swallow of her hot coffee.

"Well, I didn't say that exactly." Was he really back peddling?

"Yeah, I think you did say something like that. And yes, I do live in New York, but I'm not from there. I was born and raised in North Carolina."

Troy's curious gaze swept over Maggie before returning to the road. "Hmmm. Interesting."

"You think so? I enjoy living in New York because of all it affords. There's all the wonderful restaurants and the theaters. I love the theaters. So many shows playing. Then there are the concerts."

Troy grunted. "And all the people."

Maggie eyed him. "I enjoy New York, but it's not my roots. I love my roots, Troy. Have you ever been to North Carolina?"

He nodded and kept his gaze out the front windshield. "A time or two."

"Then you must know what a wonderful state it is."

"Where are you from in North Carolina, Miss Lawrence?"

"Are we back to formalities, *Mr. Donovan*?"

When he didn't answer, Maggie answered his question. "I was born in Chapel Hill. My father is a professor at the University of North Carolina."

Troy glanced at her again. "Really? What's his name?"

"Owen Lawrence. He's a history professor. His specialty is world history, but sometimes they tap him for US history. Why?"

Troy shrugged his shoulders. "No reason. Just curious."

"Dad just finished a sabbatical in which he traveled to Jamaica to research a lost golden cross called *La Cruz de San Mateo*. It was stolen from Jamaica by a rum runner back during Prohibition. I was on a photo shoot last summer where my cousin works at Cape Hatteras National Seashore when Dad brought his research to the cape. We all got involved and things got…well, dangerous."

"What happened?"

Maggie took a few seconds to answer. "My cousin, Ruth, and I found the cross. As soon as we found it, we were kidnapped and almost sold…we were…um…we were almost sold…into… human trafficking."

Out of the corner of her eye Maggie saw Troy watching her but she couldn't bring herself to return his gaze. She swallowed hard. "We were rescued by park police and the Coast Guard before the transfer could be made."

She shook her head. "I…I'm sorry. I don't know why I told you that. I should've stopped with the information about my father and his sabbatical. I didn't mean to tell you the rest."

Troy pulled the SUV to the side of the road into a pullover and put the vehicle into park. He turned in his seat to face her.

"It's okay. I don't mind. That's a huge and pretty terrible thing to happen in a person's life." Maggie noticed Troy's voice was low and almost tender. "It's something that's going to take a while for you to get over, I'm sure."

"Yeah, believe me, I know. But I didn't mean to tell *you* about it." Maggie turned her gaze on him. "It has nothing to do with you and it just, well, it just sort of slipped out. Look, do me a favor, and pretend you didn't hear any of that, okay? Let's start over. It's not important where you're concerned, and I'd rather it not be out there. This is my issue to deal with alone."

Troy looked as if he were waging a battle within himself. Was he deciding whether to let things go or not? It wasn't his decision to make.

He removed his ball cap, ran a hand through his black hair and turned back to the steering wheel, putting the SUV into drive. "Ok. If that's what you want. Done."

"Thanks." Maggie sipped her coffee.

They remained quiet for a few minutes until Troy pulled the vehicle to the side of the road again. "Here's your first chance to see some wildlife. There's a herd of caribou in the field over there. We can park here, and you can work your camera magic. I'll wait here."

~

Troy sat in the warm truck and watched as Maggie climbed out and set up her tripod and camera. As cold as it was there would be no way she could hold her camera still. She snapped away with a remote-control button, adjusting the shots in between.

He scrubbed his hand down his face. How in the world had he gotten himself in this situation? Here he was playing guide to the most beautiful woman he'd ever seen. Yes, his Liz had been beautiful, too, but there was something about Maggie Lawrence.

Troy shook his head trying to dispel whatever it was that drew him to her. It was a passing fancy, nothing more. He had no room in his life for another woman. No desire to go through what he'd been through before. He couldn't do it again. She was only here for a short time. He'd play nursemaid to the photographer for a few weeks, then she'd leave and his life would return to normal. That would be the end of it.

~

"He's coming. We don't know yet if he will try again. It's been many years. You *will* find it." The deep, rolling Russian words uttered through his phone sent excitement through his body. Pavel had been waiting for this.

"*Da*. When will he be here?" Pavel spoke in soft tones. He glanced around to see if anyone had heard him. He got up and left the room. He didn't want his coworkers to hear him speaking Russian. There would be all kinds of questions if they did.

"In two days. You *know* what you must do."

"I'll take care of things."

"You are there because you are one of the best. Do not let us down. Your country depends on you, Pavel."

"I am not one of the best. I *am* the best." Pride filled his voice as it rose. He glanced around again to make sure there was no one around.

"Then prove yourself." General Kozlov's voice was filled with a sneer before he ended the call.

Pavel dropped the phone into his pocket and folded his arms over his chest, anger erupting inside him. How dare the general question his ability? He was the best, no matter what anyone in Russia thought. He'd do the job and find it. It was out there. Somewhere.

Chapter Four

M aggie's cell phone rang and vibrated in unison on the kitchen counter as she poured coffee into her thermal mug. She grabbed it and saw it was her boss. She swiped to answer, placing it to her ear.

"Good morning, Mr. Radford."

"Good morning, Maggie. How are things in the wild, cold north of Alaska? Haven't frozen yet, have you, dear?" His booming laugh filled her ear. She held the phone away.

"No sir. I'm holding my own."

"Wonderful, dear, wonderful. As long as you're snapping those fabulous photos you're known for."

"Well, I'm doing my best, sir." Maggie forced cheerfulness into her voice. "Is there something in particular I can help you with or are you just checking on me?"

"That's what I like about you, Maggie. You always get right to the point. I have another job for you in the middle of the one you're doing."

"Okay." This was highly out of the ordinary.

"Yes, my dear. There's a senator who will be arriving at Denali National Park in a day or two for a dedication of some memorial or other. You'll get the details from the park superintendent. This senator is from Alaska. Apparently, he's the state's fair-haired boy. Very popular amongst the citizens. All the country's newspapers as well as the state's local papers will be carrying the story. The local papers will have their own reporters and photographers, but I've brokered a deal with the New York papers to get the first photographs by you since you're already up there. It'll save them money by not having to send up a reporter *and* a photographer. So, your mission is to take photographs of the dedication and get them back to me ASAP. I'll in turn get them to the papers. Got it?"

"Yes, sir. I understand. But will *National Scenic Wildlife Magazine*?"

"Don't worry. I've already arranged an extension on that contract." Mr. Radford's voice was reassuring as he hurried on. "The superintendent will be expecting you to come by for the information you need on the senator's activities."

"Very good, Mr. Radford. I'll go see him first thing this morning."

"Great. I'm counting on you." Mr. Radford hung up without waiting to see if Maggie had any questions.

She dropped the phone back onto the counter and grabbed her parka. Time to go see the superintendent and find out what this new mission entailed.

~

Maggie closed the door of the headquarters building behind her and headed toward the parking lot and her SUV. She'd gotten the scoop from Superintendent Wade. Mr. Bradford Scott, Alaskan Senator from Washington, D.C., would arrive in a couple of days to dedicate a monument to Harry Karstens. He was Denali National Park's first superintendent back in 1921 when it was called Mt. McKinley National Park.

Maggie climbed into her SUV and headed to her home away from home. This little mission wouldn't put a crimp in her wildlife photography at all seeing as how she'd barely gotten that off the ground. A few shots of some caribou were all she had so far. The sled dogs didn't count. They weren't wildlife.

Superintendent Wade had indicated Senator Scott would be in Alaska for several days. Although his itinerary hadn't yet been shared with the superintendent, he'd told Maggie he'd let her know more when he had the information.

Interesting. What could that mean? Was he on the campaign trail? This wasn't an election year. Could it be he was extending his stay to include a vacation? Oh well, she'd find out eventually.

Within a short time, Maggie pulled in front of her log cabin and parked, making sure she plugged her block heater into the electric pole. Ever since Troy had told her about it, she'd made sure she plugged in. No more difficult engine starts in the mornings.

Maggie gathered her camera bag, her laptop case, her purse and her thermal coffee mug, locked the SUV and climbed the porch steps. When she reached the door she halted, her breath seizing in her lungs, her heart pounding in her chest.

The front door stood slightly open. No, no, no. Was someone in there now? Fear gripped Maggie as she backed away. Her boot heel caught on the edge of the porch, and she nearly lost her footing but managed to save herself from falling.

Turning, Maggie eased down the steps and hurried to the SUV, unlocked it and climbed back in. Locking the doors, she pulled out her phone and called Troy.

"Hello," his deep voice came across the line.

"Troy, it's...it's Maggie." Oh, why did she have to stammer now?

"Maggie? What's the matter?"

"I think my cabin's been broken into." Was she sure? Had she just not pulled the door closed all the way this morning? But what if she went in and someone was in there?

"Are you sure?"

"Well, not a hundred percent, but when I came home, the door was standing partly open. I'm pretty sure I closed it this morning. I didn't go inside. What if someone did break in and they're still in there?"

"You're right not to go in, Maggie. Where are you now?"

"I'm sitting in the SUV in front of the cabin."

"I'm on my way. I'll call the police in Healy to meet me there. They know me." There was a brief pause then, "Give me your address."

Maggie gave him the information.

"Maggie, be careful. I'll be there in a few minutes. I was heading home for lunch and was nearly there."

"I will. Thanks, Troy."

Maggie hung up and let her gaze roam over the cabin but didn't see any movement. She spotted the electric pole where she had plugged the SUV in with the extension cord. If she had to start the car and leave quickly, she couldn't because she was tethered by the cord.

She quietly opened the car door and slipped around the front to unplug the cord, then hurried back into the car and closed the door behind her. At least this way she could start the car and get away should the need arise. The engine was still warm enough to start.

In less than ten minutes, a police SUV followed by a blue 4x4 pickup truck pulled in beside Maggie. A policeman and Troy climbed out of the vehicles. Maggie started to climb out of her SUV and join them.

"Ma'am, if you'll remain by your vehicle while we take a look," the policeman waved her back, "then you can join us when we've cleared the cabin."

Maggie nodded and pulled her parka closer around her. Troy gave her half a grin and squeezed her arm as he passed. He then followed the policeman up onto the porch. Both men pulled their firearms from their holsters and held them in an offensive posture then slowly pushed the door open. They went through the cabin, clearing each room then returned and motioned for Maggie to come inside.

Maggie stepped onto the porch and entered the cabin, closing the front door. It was quite cold inside from the door being left open. She gazed around and caught her breath. *What in the world...?*

The kitchen cabinets were all open, dishes scattered on the floor, drawers pulled out and dumped. In the small living room, the cushions had been pulled off the couch and armchair, the drawers on the end tables pulled out and dumped on the floor. This was repeated in the upstairs loft bedroom. The bed was torn apart, the chest of drawers emptied and dumped, the closet had been ransacked and Maggie's clothes strewn across the floor.

Maggie sank onto the edge of the bare mattress, her stomach churning. She covered her mouth with her hand, her elbow in the palm of her other hand. She shook her head in disbelief.

"Maggie, this is Healy's Chief of Police, Garrick Patuk. He wants to ask you some questions." Troy's voice was gentle as he dropped to one knee beside her, his troubled sapphire gaze on her face.

Maggie met his gaze then eyed the dark skinned, dark eyed native Alaskan who stood slightly behind Troy in a navy police uniform. His uniform parka hood was fur lined. His stoic features gentled a fraction.

"How about we move down into the kitchen area, Miss Lawrence. We'll sit at the kitchen table. It's the only area that wasn't completely ransacked."

Troy stood and held out a hand to Maggie. Without a word, she grasped it like a lifeline, following him downstairs to the kitchen.

When they were seated at the table, Chief Patuk removed a notepad and pen from an inner parka pocket and eyed Maggie. "Miss Lawrence, do you have any idea why your cabin was ransacked?"

"I don't have a clue, sir. I've only been here a couple of days. I don't have anything of value except my camera and my laptop, and I keep those with me pretty much all the time." Maggie waved her hand toward the mess in the cabin. "In all of…this, they didn't find anything, because there wasn't anything. Literally my camera and laptop are all that I have of any value."

"Could there be anything on them that someone would want?" Troy asked.

Maggie closed her eyes and thought for a moment. She ran her hand through her hair then shook her head. "No, I wouldn't think so. All my previous shoots were removed onto thumb drives or out on the cloud so I don't have them on my laptop anymore. I only have the shots of Denali that I took from the air on the day I arrived and the caribou I took today. That's it."

A thought popped into Maggie's head. Could it be? It sure seems pretty far fetched. Should she say something?

"What is it, Maggie?" Troy asked. "You look like you just thought of something."

Maggie twisted her fingers together. What would they think of the picture?

"Miss Lawrence, if there's something you have or know that may help, you need to tell us." Chief Patuk tapped his pen on the table.

Maggie pushed her chair back from the table and crossed to the counter where she'd laid her laptop bag when she'd first entered the cabin. Slipping the laptop from its case, she brought it to the table and opened it, booting it up. She pulled up the pictures from her airplane ride with Jud Svenson.

"I took these the day I arrived in Fairbanks and hired Jud Svenson to fly me over the park. There's one picture that I took that has something in it I can't explain. Perhaps one or both of you can. I'm not saying this is what someone was after, because how would they have known I had it?"

Maggie pulled up the picture and allowed the men time to look at it. "Here let me zoom in closer for you."

She zoomed in so they could get a closer look.

"Well, can either of you make it out? I can't tell what it is."

Chief Patuk shook his head. "I can't tell what it is, but I can tell it's man-made. There are too many straight and curved edges for it to be natural."

After a few more seconds Troy sat back. "I agree. Definitely man-made, but I can't tell what it is either."

"You don't think they could've been after this, do you?" Maggie shoved her hair behind her ear and waved a hand toward the picture.

Chief Patuk scrunched up his features and did a slow shake of his head. "It's highly unlikely, Miss Lawrence. This is remote and difficult to ascertain. The only person who knew you'd taken pictures out there was Jud Svenson, and he knows the area better than most. How would he know you had a picture of it? Why would he care?"

Maggie caught an odd expression on Troy's face that was there one second then vanished. Had she imagined it?

"Then why do you think I was broken into, Chief?" Maggie turned to look him in the eye. "Do you have many break-ins around here?"

"No, not really, but I'd say this was a planned break-in by someone who's been watching you. Probably heard you were from New York City. Thought they'd make a good haul and get away with it. They were disappointed. I'll call the rental company for you and have them come change the locks and put a deadbolt in. If you're not happy with that, and they have openings in other cabins, perhaps they'll move you."

"Yes, moving would be nice and making sure there's a deadbolt on the new cabin would be great." Maggie closed down her computer. "I'll gather my things and be ready to move as soon as they have that deadbolt in place."

~

When Chief Patuk attempted to find some fingerprints, he found a few partials that were questionable and lifted them for evidence. There was no guarantee they didn't belong to someone from the rental company or the cleaning crew who cleaned the cabin before Maggie moved in. Whoever had tossed the cabin hadn't left anything to go on, so the Chief left allowing Maggie to pack her things. The rental office had another cabin in Healy that was a little closer to the village but still remote by Maggie's standards. She was happy with that however. It was slightly larger with the bedroom on the main level and for the same price. Troy offered to help her move her things over before heading home.

Someone met them at the new cabin with a key. A deadbolt had been installed previously, so Maggie was happy.

Troy held out his hand. "May I?"

Maggie eyed him before laying the key in his hand. Without a word, she watched as he unlocked both locks and opened the door, turning on the entry light. He carried in Maggie's suitcases and set them down before turning on more lights. He found the thermostat and turned up the heat. He carried the suitcases into the bedroom then returned to the living room. He lit the gas fire to make sure it worked, leaving it on to help warm the room up quicker. It gave a warm and welcoming glow to the room that instantly made Maggie feel better.

"This is nice." Troy glanced around the cabin's interior. "I like this one better than the other one."

"Why? Because there's no drawers and cushions scattered all over the floor? Not to mention silverware and dishes." Maggie strolled to the kitchen and leaned on the counter. "Once we bring in the groceries, I'd be happy to make you a cup of coffee."

"Thanks, but no. After I help bring in those groceries, I need to get home."

Maggie nodded. "Sure. Tomorrow's another day."

"Yeah. Bring that camera of yours and maybe we'll spot some moose. Who knows?"

Maggie chuckled then grew serious. "I appreciate all your help, Troy. I know this isn't the gig you wanted. To babysit a photographer all day every day? It can't be fun for a ranger like you. It won't last forever. I'll be out of your hair in a few weeks."

Troy pointed toward her with his chin. "Don't worry about it, New York. That's the thing about working for the park service. It's all in a day's work."

One lid dropped in a wink before he lifted his parka hood and headed out the door. Maggie's heart beat triple time before settling back to normal. She felt the corners of her lips lift in a grin as she covered her head with her parka hood and headed out the door. Was Mr. Ranger Guide mellowing or what? Well, she didn't have the time or the inclination to worry about it. As he said, it was all in a day's work. She had a job to do in the few weeks before she had to head back to New York. No telling where her next job would be. Most likely it would be far from Alaska.

Chapter Five

You've got to be kidding me." Maggie's camera bag bounced on her hip as she ran beside Troy to his park SUV. Her foot slipped on a piece of ice and she started to fall. "Whoa."

Troy's hand reached out and grabbed her arm, steadying her. "Hey, careful now. We can't have our star photographer ending up in the hospital. Where would all those New York newspapers be today without you?"

"Yeah, well, the better question is, where would I get my next job?" Maggie climbed into the passenger side of the SUV. "Mr. Radford would fire me in a flash if I fail to get great shots of Senator Scott and the dedication."

"As you were saying, 'you've got to be kidding me'." Troy tore out of the motor pool area.

"Why did Senator Scott get here a day early?"

"Why do politicians do what politicians do? Who knows? The dedication is still on for tomorrow, so don't worry about that. He's landing at the park airport in about fifteen minutes. Thought you'd want to get shots of that. There's going to be a dinner for him tonight at the Denali Wilderness Lodge. The local mayors from Fairbanks, North Pole, Nenana, Healy and Cantwell will attend as well as the governor of Alaska and some other dignitaries. Our own Superintendent Wade and some of the other Alaskan National Park superintendents will also attend."

"Sounds schmoozy. I suppose I have to be there to take pictures of all those dignitaries."

"You got it."

Troy parked the SUV near an unmanned dirt runway. People were already gathering to meet the senator. Maggie prepared her camera then they climbed out of the SUV and walked over to stand beside Superintendent Wade.

"There you two are. I was beginning to wonder if you'd make it in time." Wade shoved his parka sleeve up to glance at his wristwatch then shoved his wire-framed glasses further up onto his nose, peering at them through the lenses.

"Sir, we came as soon as we got your message. We were just getting ready to head into the backcountry to look for wildlife when Natalya called."

"Well, I know it was short notice, Troy. Thank goodness she caught you." The superintendent turned his gaze on Maggie. "This is imperative for you, Miss Lawrence."

"Don't I know it, sir." Maggie huffed softly, her breath freezing in the air before her. "Where would you like for me to stand?"

"Just stand here beside me, then when the helicopter lands, I'll go over to greet the senator and his wife. You can move wherever you need to take whatever shots you think are best. Troy, you and Bryce will help watch the senator's back. Park police will keep folks back. The senator and his wife will ride with me in my SUV to the Denali Wilderness Lodge where they'll be staying."

"Yes, sir." Troy gazed around on the small crowd of reporters and park personnel gathered at the airport. "Is your magazine's reporter here, Maggie?"

"Yes. I got a call from him yesterday touching base with me. He'll pretty much be working on his own. He's over there in the press area somewhere."

Maggie felt a tap on her shoulder and turned to find Jud Svenson standing behind her, a smile on his handsome face.

"Jud? What are you doing here?" Maggie turned to give him her full attention. "This is a surprise."

"It's good to see you, Maggie. I spotted you from over there by my plane and thought I'd say hi."

Troy and the superintendent turned at the masculine voice speaking to Maggie. She noticed the less than pleased expression that settled on Troy's features.

"What are you doing here, Svenson?" Troy's body stiffened as he stepped to Maggie's side.

Jud's smile slipped a bit as his gaze moved from Maggie to Troy. "Not that it's any of your business, Donovan, but I have reason to be here."

"Perhaps you'll tell me then, Mr. Svenson. What *are* you doing here?" Wade stepped to Maggie's other side.

Jud's smile was forced as he eyed the two men. "I'm here to fly supplies out to Kantishna Airport, if you must know."

"That's not your contract." Troy folded his arms over his chest. "That's Hal Myers' contract."

"Yep," Jud nodded, his Hollywood smile showing his bright whites. "Normally. Hal's got some troubles with his plane right now. He called and asked me to do him a favor. I told him I'd be happy to, and here I am."

"Show me." Troy held out an arm in the direction of Jud's plane that sat at the end of the runway.

Jud glared for a few seconds. "You don't trust me?"

"Now why would I do that, Svenson? Show me the supplies."

"You don't have the right, Dono…"

"Then show me, please." Superintendent Wade smiled then pushed up his glasses. "Since I'm the park superintendent, and that airport is within my jurisdiction, I have the authority to request an inspection of your plane. Now show me."

"Sure, no problem." Jud shrugged his shoulders as if it really were no big deal.

"And let's hurry. I have other things to attend to."

The two men moved toward the end of the runway where Jud Svenson's red, white and blue Cessna 185 sat, engine running.

"What was all that about, Troy?" Maggie watched the two men walking away. "Why don't you and the superintendent like Jud? I found him to be a great pilot and guide the day I hired him."

Silence met her question until Maggie turned and gazed directly at the man beside her. "Troy? What's going on?"

Troy kept his eyes on the two men who grew smaller the further away they walked. "Let's just say Jud Svenson hasn't always been on the up and up as far as the park is concerned."

Within a few minutes they watched as the superintendent returned by himself.

"Well, sir?" Troy kept his eyes on the distant plane as the superintendent rejoined them.

"He indeed has a plane full of supplies and the paperwork to go with it. I'll give Kantishna a call after the senator arrives and see what they say. I'll also call Hal Myers."

"Good idea, sir."

Maggie wasn't sure what to make of all this. Of course, she knew nothing of Jud Svenson except he was handsome enough to be in the movies, and he'd been nice to her when she'd hired him for her flight-seeing tour. But of course, he would be. She was paying him.

The faint sound of helicopter rotors could be heard and a murmur swept through the crowd as they gazed heavenward, all eyes sweeping the skies for the first glimpse of the metal bird.

"Oh, and by the way, Troy," Wade turned back to Troy and grinned. "I expect you to be at the dinner tonight. Black tie."

Maggie saw the look of distaste that crossed Troy's face as Wade turned his gaze back toward the sky.

"Yes, sir."

Being from New York, she was used to black tie events. It was nothing to put on fancy clothes and head to a dressy business party or event but she doubted Troy attended them often. From his expression he must abhor them. She hoped he owned a tux and black tie. Out here in the wilderness was an unlikely place to need one.

The sound of the helicopter rotors grew louder, and Maggie lifted her gaze to see a brown and green camouflaged CH-47 Chinook with double rotors approaching from the north. It had skis on the wheel assemblies. Well, it is Alaska. Maggie pulled her hood tighter as the helicopter drew closer and the rotors stirred up a wind around them, blowing snowy ice crystals into the air. The giant grasshopper-looking beast lowered onto its skis on the runway then the pilot cut the engines and the rotors began their slow halt.

The bay door on the side of the helicopter opened and one of the crewmen jumped down then reached in and brought out a set of steps. Since the rotors hadn't completely ceased their spinning, Superintendent Wade held his "Smokey-Bear" hat firmly against his head and hurried over to greet Senator Scott and his wife as they descended from the helicopter.

Maggie started snapping pictures as the helicopter landed and didn't stop until the good senator and his wife were in the superintendent's car driving away from the runway.

It had begun to flurry in the middle of everything, but no one seemed to notice.

"Well, what do you think?" Troy asked.

"I think my fingertips are freezing, and I need something hot to drink to help thaw me out." Maggie turned, her head tilted as she observed him. "I suppose you're used to this, aren't you? You don't think twice about -15°."

Troy laughed. "-15° is nothing when our winter norm gets down to -40° or lower."

He turned and walked back to the SUV. Maggie wasn't sure she could ever get used to either one. She hurried after him, wanting to get into the SUV and warm up.

~

"Here, take it." The young Russian man handed the young woman a small package. "This will do what is necessary."

They stood in the poorly lit back hallway of the Denali Wilderness Lodge behind the kitchen near an exit. Most of the kitchen traffic was much further down the hallway so no one paid any attention to them.

"Are you sure it will work?" She accepted the package then opened it, glancing over her shoulder toward the kitchen. Her Russian accent was little more than a whisper.

"I promise, it will work." He kept his voice low.

She nodded, pulling a small vial of liquid from the package. She dropped it into her uniform vest pocket then handed him the wrapping. He crumpled it then placed it in his left jacket pocket. He reached into his right jacket pocket and fingered the smooth cold steel of the Ruger 9mm handgun that rested there.

"Go. You must go. Hurry now." She waved him away and picked up her serving tray, heading toward the kitchen as he slipped out the exit. He placed a small block of wood in the doorway to hold the door partially open, then melted into the darkness.

~

Maggie stood near the entrance to the great room of the Denali Wilderness Lodge. She'd already dropped her parka at the cloak room and been to the ladies' room to make repairs to her hairstyle. Parkas weren't conducive to evening affairs, but when it was -38° there wasn't much choice. Her legs had nearly frozen seeing as how pants weren't really an option for this evening. Thank goodness she had a good heater in her little SUV.

A few people stopped to say hi as she waited for…well, she wasn't really sure what she was waiting for. The senator and his wife to arrive, she supposed. Her camera hung around her neck and she fiddled with the settings to make sure it was set for the lighting in the room.

The oldies band music that played in the background worked its way into Maggie's toes and up her calves into her body. She couldn't help but sway a little to its upbeat rhythm. She may not have been around in the 1940's when Tommy Dorsey and Glen Miller directed their bands, but her mom and dad had loved the music of that era and they'd passed that love on to Maggie.

Her gaze wandered around the room and stalled on Troy Donovan as he stood beside the superintendent. Goodness gracious, he was handsome. No, he was more than that. He was devastating in his tux with his black hair trimmed and combed back so neatly. She'd only seen him with his ball cap and toboggan, his hair rough and longish. This was a new and different look. His sleek and debonair appearance stole her breath away.

~

Troy released a heavy sigh and ran his finger beneath the collar of his snow-white shirt. The black satin tie he wore felt more like a noose than evening attire. He stretched his neck and shifted his shoulders. It promised to be a miserable evening. His gaze swept the room and met Superintendent Wade's. The man lifted a hand and waved him over. Shoot. Not good. His intention had been to stay in the shadows and possibly leave early. What could his diminutive boss want?

He strolled in the man's direction, glancing around the room as he went. He'd been early and so far, only a few people were here. The senator and his wife wouldn't come down from their suite until the majority of the guests had arrived.

Troy stopped beside Wade. "Good evening, sir."

"Good evening, Donovan. Glad you're here. I wasn't sure if you'd actually show up." The man chuckled.

"Sir?" Troy cast him a questioning gaze as he crossed his arms over his chest. "Why would you think that?"

"I wasn't sure if you had a black tie and tux." Wade smirked then chuckled. "I know you'd rather be in the woods or behind your team of dogs, Troy. Nothing wrong with that, but occasionally it'll do you good to come out of the woods and dress up. Builds character."

"I'm not sure that putting on a tux and feeling like a...a...a penguin builds character, sir."

Wade let out a loud laugh and clapped him on the shoulder. "Ah, Troy. You'll survive this evening, don't worry."

Troy heaved another deep sigh. "If you say so. sir."

"Would it help if I gave you an order to relax?" Wade peered at him over the top of his glasses. "Besides, park police have this place covered so security shouldn't be on your mind. The senator told me he's hired a few bodyguards to protect him as well. Unless you're the president or vice-president, you don't get taxpayer-funded security."

"Hmm, who knew?" Troy didn't tell him that security hadn't been at the top of what was on his mind at present.

The crowd began to thicken as guests arrived. Troy's gaze swept the room. He was searching for the one who was on his mind most lately. Maggie Lawrence. Ridiculous. He had no business searching for that woman. Nevertheless, he couldn't prevent his gaze from sweeping the room for her lovely face.

On one sweep past the entrance to the great room he spotted her where several groups gathered but she stood alone. Her gaze wandered around the room, a slight smile curling those lovely lips while she swayed gently to the music playing in the background. What was it? Big band music? She liked big band, huh? His heart hammered in his chest and he drew in a ragged breath. Wow. She was a vision in a black shin-length sheath dress with a black lace overlay. Long lace sleeves covered her arms to her wrists. As she turned to speak to someone in passing, he noticed how her long auburn hair was pulled into a twist held up with a black flower comb. Soft tendrils had escaped and lay against her neck and cheeks. Black strappy sandals adorned her slim feet.

Troy could hardly catch his breath. She'd stolen it from him. Warmth rolled up from his neck and he didn't think it had anything to do with his tight collar. He swallowed hard. Taking a deep breath, he attempted to jumpstart his lung function.

"By the way, Troy, I checked out Jud Svenson's story." Superintendent Wade cast his own gaze around the room.

"Sir?" Troy attempted to figure out what the superintendent was referring to. Right now, his full attention was on the gorgeous woman across the room and anything else was an intrusion on his thoughts.

"You know. From this afternoon at the airport." Wade spoke with patience. "Jud's story panned out. Hal Myers and the Kantishna airport confirmed it. Those supplies were indeed bound for Kantishna."

Ah, that was what he was referring to. The afternoon's event returned to Troy, only sidelining Maggie by a fraction. "That's good, sir. I'm glad that for once Svenson was on the up and up."

"Let's be fair, Troy. Jud Svenson generally is on the up and up. There's only been a couple of times he's had issues with the park."

"That we know of," Troy pointed out, his gaze never leaving Maggie.

"I'll concede that."

Silence fell between them for a few seconds as they watched the crowd in the room grow.

"Well, well. There's Miss Lawrence." Wade shoved his glasses further up his nose. "My, doesn't she look lovely."

He planted a hand on Troy's back and gave him a slight push. "Go greet her, Troy. I'm sure she's feeling a bit overwhelmed with all this, and my wife is signaling me. I need to mingle."

She's feeling overwhelmed? Troy's feet were lead weights as he trudged in her direction. A sixth-grade schoolboy had nothing on him. And why? She was the same young woman he'd taken out to photograph caribou yesterday. Nothing had changed. Right? Except tonight she was stunning in that dress. Why in the world should that matter? *It doesn't. She's the same person inside and out. A dress doesn't matter.* Then why were his palms sweaty and his heart racing?

Maggie turned from perusing the room and her gaze met his, a smile shaping those amazing lips. Troy wiped his palms on his dress slacks and stopped beside her.

"Good evening." Somehow, he'd managed to sound normal.

"Hi, Troy." Maggie's gaze once more swept the room. She kept her voice low. "I thought this was just going to be a few dignitaries. There's a lot of people here."

"Yeah, it's amazing how fast they can get a group of people together considering the senator wasn't supposed to arrive until tomorrow." Troy moved to her side and turned to scan the room. "Speaking of the senator. There he is. Come on. Let's get you over there so you can start snapping pictures."

Troy grasped Maggie's hand and started clearing a path through the crowd. They headed for the superintendent, his wife, the senator and his wife and another gentleman who stood beside the senator.

"Ah there you are, Troy. Maggie." Wade waved them forward. "Let me introduce you. Senator Scott, Mrs. Scott, allow me to introduce you to Miss Maggie Lawrence, our New York photographer who will be taking photos while you're here. She represents all the newspapers in New York City. This is Ranger Troy Donovan, our lead musher for our dog sled teams."

"It's a pleasure to meet you both." Senator Scott reached out, shaking their hands. He put his arm around the woman at his side. "Let me introduce my wife, Miriam. She's my right-hand man, you might say. Goes with me everywhere I go. She's my rock and my support. Couldn't do it without her, you know."

Miriam Scott had once been a brunette but didn't seem to mind that gray was taking over. Her makeup was tastefully done and her satin emerald green evening dress was gorgeous, fitting her slim figure well. It was topped by a matching emerald and rhinestone trimmed evening jacket. Diamonds graced her ears and neckline, glittering in the chandelier light of the dining room.

She held out a gracious hand first to Maggie. "It's a pleasure to meet you, Miss Lawrence. I'm not a huge fan of the media, but I do know how important they are. And you are such a lovely photographer. Far more than most. Don't you think so, young man?"

Troy wasn't expecting her question or the immediate attention she cast on him as she put her hand out. He grasped it and met her twinkling ice blue gaze.

"Yes, of course she is." Had he just blurted that out as bluntly as it sounded to him? Warmth rolled over him in waves as he saw a pleased smile cross the lady's face.

"Are you two a couple then?" Mrs. Scott's eyebrows lifted as her gaze ping-ponged between them, a delighted smile forming on her lips.

"Oh no, ma'am." Maggie waved a wary hand. "He's married. See his wedding band."

"No, ma'am." Troy spoke at the exact same time. He cringed as he glanced at the gold band on his left hand. *Oh Liz…*

"Hmmm." Mrs. Scott tilted her head with an amused expression on her features. "That's too bad. You'd make such a lovely couple."

Of its own volition, Troy's gaze met Maggie's before hers dropped away. He sucked in a deep breath. A drowning man in the ocean couldn't feel any more helpless than he did at this moment. How in the world had he gotten sucked into this situation? Willing the evening to end at this moment or the floor to open up allowing him to escape didn't happen, so he was forced to concentrate on slowing his breathing.

"Miriam, my dear," Senator Scott smiled, "I know you've had great success at playing cupid in the past, but let's not get carried away. Leave these young people alone and let's get on with our evening. I want to introduce them to Jacobs here."

"Oh, Brad," Mrs. Scott placed a gentle hand on her husband's tux sleeve. "I know a match made in heaven when I see one, and this is it."

The senator kissed his wife's cheek and gave her an indulgent smile. "Not if the young man's already married, darling, but let me finish introductions, alright?"

The slim lady waved her bejeweled hand and gave a smug smile. "Of course, sweetheart. Business first as usual."

She winked at Troy then at Maggie. She held the back of her hand up to her lips and whispered, "We'll talk later."

Troy's heart sank even as the senator spoke. "Let me introduce my assistant, Mr. Calvin Jacobs. I don't know what I would do without Calvin. He's my other right-hand man."

"It's a pleasure to meet you, Mr. Jacobs." Troy shook his hand.

The thin to almost skinny middle aged and balding man with wire-framed glasses nodded as he returned Troy's handshake. "A pleasure, I'm sure."

"I'm glad to meet you all." Maggie lifted her camera. "Can I get a picture of you all with the Superintendent and Mrs. Wade? Stand together now. That's right. Smile at the camera."

Maggie snapped a few pictures. "Those should be great shots. Thank you."

"Thank you, Miss Lawrence," the senator nodded in Maggie's direction. "I hope you got my good side."

"Oh dear. Both of your sides are good." Mrs. Scott grabbed her husband's arm. Senator Scott smiled down at his wife with a pleased expression.

A pretty, blond waitress in black slacks, a black vest, white blouse and a black tie carrying a tray of beverages stopped beside their group and smiled.

"Drinks?" She held out the tray to the group and picked up a glass of champagne from the tray, handing it to Senator Scott. "For you, sir."

The senator took the flute of champagne and held it in his hand as she handed a second glass to Mrs. Scott.

"Why thank you, young lady." Mrs. Scott accepted the glass.

Calvin Jacobs refused a drink as did Troy, Maggie and the Wades, each waving away the tray. The young woman faded away between guests.

"Sir," Calvin spoke in a low voice close to the senator's ear. "I don't think I would drink that if I were you."

"What, Calvin? What's that you say? Don't drink it? Why not?" The senator eyed the bubbly liquid in the crystal stemmed flute in his hand. "Why shouldn't I?"

"Sir, think about it. Why would a waitress hand you and Mrs. Scott a specific glass of champagne rather than let you pick from the tray?"

Senator Scott's gaze pinned his assistant with a furrowed brow then eyed the liquid again. He watched as his wife began to lift her glass to her lips. His hand halted hers in its travel upwards. "Hold on, darling. Calvin may be on to something."

"Whatever do you mean, Brad? It's just champagne."

"Perhaps not."

"Has something happened that would make you question it, sir?" Troy stepped closer, his voice low.

Senator Scott pretended to smile, his gaze wandering around the room. "You could say that. Just before we left on this trip, I received a letter postmarked from Alaska warning me not to come. It said if I did my life was in danger."

"What?" The word was barely more than a breath as it slipped from Mrs. Scott's lips. "Brad, why didn't you tell me?"

"Why do you think, my love? I didn't want to worry you, and I wasn't sure that it wasn't just a prank. But now that you know, you need to be careful and follow my lead. Mr. Donovan, is there some way we can have this champagne tested?"

"Sure, there is. We have access to a lab in Fairbanks where we send all our evidence for processing."

His attention turned to his boss. "Superintendent?"

Wade gave a single nod. "Of course, Donovan. You know what has to be done. Take care of it."

"Yes, sir."

"I'm impressed, Mr. Donovan. This park may be at the back of nowhere, but you all get the job done."

Troy gave a slight bow. "Thank you, sir. I'll take that as a compliment."

"You should. That's how I meant it."

"If you'll excuse me, I'll take these and be back shortly." Troy took a handkerchief from his pocket and took the two champagne flutes by the bottom of the stems. "We may get lucky with fingerprints other than yours and Mrs. Scott's. Who knows?"

Troy found one of the park police officers who took the stemware out to his vehicle to package the liquid in containers and wrap the glasses in evidence bags. He then drove them to headquarters where he could process the evidence. Someone would then take the evidence to Fairbanks to the lab the following morning.

"Mr. Donovan," Senator Scott turned to him as Troy rejoined the group, "I would so love to go on a dog sled tour if you can arrange that."

Troy thought that was a terrible idea considering the security logistics, and glanced at the superintendent who nodded emphatically. "Well, Senator Scott, I'm sure that can be arranged."

"Wonderful, wonderful." Senator Scott clapped his hands together. "I look forward to it. Darling, would you like to go?"

He turned to his wife and placed an arm around her slim waist.

"Dear heart, you know I can't abide the cold or the snow." She shuddered and rubbed her jacketed arms. "I'll take a pass on that. I'll remain here at the lodge and stay warm by the fire."

The senator chuckled and squeezed her waist. "Whatever you want, my love. I'll regale you when I return."

"You do that, darling." She reached up and pinched his cheek.

Troy caught Maggie's gaze and winked at her. Her face suffused with a peach blush, and she lifted her camera, snapping more pictures. Hmmm. He'd made the intrepid photographer blush. That was cool.

A dinner bell sounded and everyone moved toward the dining room. Just then a shot rang out, the sound reverberating on the cedar-logged ceiling and walls before a second shot was fired.

~

Amidst the sound of screams, Troy forced the senator to the floor even as Superintendent Wade pushed his wife down. Mr. Jacobs dove to the floor and covered his head with his hands. Maggie dropped to the floor but apparently had the presence of mind to snap pictures of what was happening.

Within minutes park police streamed into the room and took charge of the chaos that had ensued at the sound of the shots. People began to stand up at the encouragement of law enforcement.

"What in the world was that all about?" Mrs. Scott asked what everyone was thinking. "Are you alright, my darling?"

She ran her hands over her husband's face and chest once he was on his feet. The senator did the same to her. "Yes, dearest. I'm fine. If they were shooting at me, they missed. Calvin?"

"Yes, sir?" The thin man's voice squeaked as he stood from his prone position on the floor and straightened his tux and black tie. He glanced around with wide-eyed terror through his glasses.

"Are you alright, Calvin? You weren't shot, were you?"

Jacobs ran his hands over his torso and shook his head. "N-n-o, sir. I'm fine."

Troy suspected from the man's expression that stress was permanently stamped on his features.

"Troy," the superintendent put his hand on Troy's shoulder, "go see what the commotion is all about. We need to get on with the dinner as soon as possible."

"Yes, sir." Troy headed toward the park policemen who were working the scene and pulled one of them aside.

"Hey, Jake. What happened? I have Sen. Bradford Scott over here. Was someone aiming at him?"

The officer tucked his notepad into his parka pocket. "Hey, Troy. From what we're gathering, a lone shooter came into the room as everyone was headed into dinner. He tried to push his way through the crowd toward the front and fired twice. Two people were shot but not fatally. We suspect he was aiming at the senator. Both victims were within the line of fire. We have a helicopter flying down from Fairbanks to take them to the hospital. As for the gunman, the witnesses we've talked to saw him head toward the senator until park police entered the room, then he slipped out the back way."

"Not good. That means he may try again." Troy ran his hand through his hair with frustration.

"Yep, I'd say so."

"Did anyone get a good look at him?"

"We got some vague descriptions. They'll be in the reports." Jake gave Troy a light slap on the shoulder and turned back to his task.

Troy allowed his gaze to roam around the room. Considering there was a US senator in attendance, security was pretty high for this event, and yet someone had gotten through their net. Had the shooter acted alone? Or had there been help on the inside? Could the young blond waitress have been an accomplice? Why was the shooter targeting the senator? They needed answers. They needed to find the shooter before he struck again and possibly succeeded.

As Troy turned to head back to the senator's group, he spotted the blond waitress who had served the champagne to the senator. She peered from behind a drape in the back corner of the room, her gaze on the senator. A sneer marred her pretty features just before she released the drape and disappeared. Troy hurried between tables and chairs, many that had been turned over in the chaos of the shooting and slipped behind the heavy drape where she'd been. He found a short hallway that turned into another hallway that led to an exit. He followed it then stepped outside the exit. A dirt road paralleled the back of the building, and on the other side of the road was the rushing glacier-fed Nenana river. The young woman was nowhere to be seen. Just like the shooter, she'd vanished.

Chapter Six

U nsure what to expect from the weather forecast for an Alaskan snow storm of three to six inches, Maggie headed to Three Bears to pick up some groceries. She was used to a New York snowstorm, not an Alaskan snowstorm. She'd found a snow shovel on the back stoop of the cabin so no need to purchase one of those. She'd been unable to make it to Fairbanks for major grocery shopping so she decided to purchase more than a few groceries.

Maggie turned the corner of one aisle and ran into someone's cart as they came from the opposite direction.

"Oh, I am so sorry. Please forgi…" She peeked around the corner and met a familiar sapphire blue gaze. "Troy?"

A small voice met her ears. "Grandma. It's her."

"Oh, look who it is." A happy chuckle sounded as the little boy's grandmother came into view. "Oh, my, Jeremy. It's a good thing you got off the front when you did. You'd have gotten squashed between the carts."

The older woman came around and stopped in front of Maggie. "How are you, sweetie? It's nice to see you again."

"I'm fine, thanks." Maggie's gaze swept from the woman to Troy to the little boy, who, now that she noticed, looked a lot like Troy. Her gaze lifted back to the taller version. "I'm terribly sorry for running into you."

"Oh, not to worry." The older woman waved a hand, dismissing Maggie's apology. "I think it's rather nice that we ran into you."

"Troy, this is that nice young woman Jeremy and I were telling you about the other day." She turned back to Maggie. "I told him how you kept Jeremy calm when we got separated. Again, I can't thank you enough for that, my dear."

"It wasn't a problem." Maggie's gaze slid back to Troy.

"We've met, Mom. This is Maggie Lawrence. She's a photographer for a wildlife magazine. I'm guiding her through the park to get some photos. Maggie, my mom, Clarissa Donovan."

"It's a pleasure to meet you, Mrs. Donovan. Officially." Maggie reached out a hand only to have it encased between both of Mrs. Donovan's small ones.

"Oh, Maggie, it's my pleasure as well. Welcome to Alaska." She turned to Troy. "We must have Maggie over for dinner."

She turned back to Maggie. "I want to hear all about your photography. I think it's wonderful that you're here to photograph the park, and you couldn't have a better guide. My son knows it like the back of his hand."

Maggie chuckled at the woman's enthusiasm. She cast Troy a teasing glance. "Well, that should certainly come in handy."

"Are you doing anything Saturday night?" Mrs. Donovan took out a notepad and pencil. "We'd love to have you join us for dinner. How about five o'clock? Sound good?"

Maggie noticed Troy had said very little since she'd rammed her cart into his. He seemed less than happy about the invitation. And what about his wife? That gold wedding band flashed like a warning beacon. He'd pretty much worn gloves at all their outings until the night of the senator's dinner when she'd seen that wedding band for the first time. She hadn't been expecting it. What would his wife say about her mother-in-law inviting a single woman to come to dinner? Perhaps she was used to visiting personnel coming. Surely, she wouldn't have invited her if it wasn't something they were used to.

Maggie shrugged. "Yes, sure. I'm free. Five sounds good. Thank you."

Mrs. Donovan wrote something on the notepad. "Here's the address, sweetie. Do you have one of those GPS gadgets or do you need directions?"

"Oh no, I can get there with this. Thank you." Maggie tucked the paper in her shoulder bag. "I'd best be getting on."

Troy tapped Jeremy on the shoulder. "Here, champ. Think you can push the cart for Grandma? I'll be with you in a minute."

"Sure thing, Dad. I'm a big helper." There was pride in the boy's stance.

Troy ruffled his hair. "Of course you are. That's what I can depend on you for. To always be a big helper."

"Bye, Maggie. We'll see you on Saturday." Clarissa Donovan waved as she and Jeremy moved down the next aisle.

"See you, Mrs. Donovan. Bye Jeremy."

"It's Clarissa." A sing-songy voice floated back around the corner.

Troy jammed his hands into his parka pockets and shook his head. "You'll have to pardon my mom. She gets excited about, well, about pretty much everything."

Maggie tilted her head. "And what's wrong with that? We should all have a cheery outlook on life. Our days would be so much easier to go through."

His gaze swept over her face as if he were considering her words, but he changed the subject.

"Call if you have any problems during the storm. My truck is four-wheel drive so I don't have any problems getting around."

Maggie nodded. "Thanks. I appreciate that. Anything I should expect different from a New York snowstorm?"

He shook his head. "Not really. The snow here is light and fluffy. It doesn't generally pack easily until the temps rise and there's more humidity in the air."

"What? You mean no snowball fights?" Maggie's shoulders slumped.

For the first time since she'd met him, the closest thing to a genuine smile appeared on Troy's face, and it nearly stole Maggie's breath away. It was hard to drag in the next one.

"Not at these sub-zero temps. Not enough moisture in the air. When it snows at normal temps, then you can have your snowball fight."

He winked. "See you."

Troy disappeared down the aisle after his mom and his son. Maggie drew in a deep breath and spotted an elderly woman staring at her with a less than pleased expression on her face. Maggie was blocking her path into the aisle.

"Oh, I'm terribly sorry, ma'am." She scooted her cart out of the way and over to the main aisle to a spot where she could think for a moment.

What had just happened? Troy Donovan had actually smiled at her then winked. Maggie closed her eyes. No, no, no. Don't read too much into that. Next time she saw him, he'd be right back to the bear of a man she's come to know and...well, like. Although the other day when she'd slipped up and spilled about her and Ruthie's near human trafficking experience, Troy had been almost...what? She couldn't quite put her finger on it. There had been a quiet, almost tender note in his voice.

Maggie slammed her hand down on the handle of the cart. The man was an enigma to be sure. Besides, there was the issue of a wife in the offing. She turned her cart and propelled it down the aisle. It was time to finish her shopping and head home. It was far more important to get there before the storm set in. She glanced out the front windows of the store. Heavy snowflakes were already drifting past the glass panes. Great. Time to concentrate on the job at hand.

~

The young Russian man slid back the bolt of the Remington model 700 chambered 30.06 rifle, eyed the chamber, then slid it forward. He checked to make sure he had plenty of ammunition in his ammo pouch.

"You must be careful." His younger sister placed a hand on his arm. "It will be subzero temperatures out there. Do you have the proper clothing to stay warm?"

The man cupped a hand to her cheek then patted it and grinned. "You worry like an old grandmother, *melkaya*."

The young woman slapped his hand away and glared at him in anger. "I am not a baby girl. I am a grown woman who wants this man dead just as you do. Go then. Freeze for all I care."

She stomped across the room, her back to him.

The man's laugh was soft as he dropped onto a chair. He tried to appease her. "Do not worry. I won't freeze. I have plenty of warm clothing and all the gear I need. I will be there waiting for them when they arrive. Who cares that snowmobiles aren't allowed in the park? I think I may break more than one law today."

There was silence for a moment then Ivan spoke again. "You did good, *melkaya*. I would not have this opportunity if you had not heard the man say he would be out on this expedition. I still don't know how you found out they planned to go today."

"I have my ways." She poured tea into a mug and doctored it with honey. "I cozy up to park employees. Especially the men. They like me and talk freely."

She spun around, her long, blond hair whipping over her cheeks as she turned. "Kill him, Ivan. Make him pay. Father was foolish, but they could have saved him, and they did not."

Rushing toward him, she leaned against the kitchen table which stood beside the chair where he sat. "He must suffer the same fate and die. Father did not survive, and neither can he."

~

After a bowl of microwave potato soup and crackers, Maggie lay on the overstuffed couch in front of the gas fire and snuggled beneath a fleece throw she'd found draped along the couch back. She spent a while reading until the words in her book began to swim before her eyes and her eyelids began to droop. Maggie dropped the book onto the end table and stood, stretching. The warmth of the fire and the coziness of the fleece had worked their magic.

Maggie padded in her socks over to the front door and flipped on the porch light to see if she could tell how much snow had fallen. A couple of inches. Good. It shouldn't be a problem getting to the park in the morning.

She hurried through her preparations for bed then slipped beneath the covers. *Abba Father, each day has been different since I arrived, and my guide is a…*Maggie stopped and considered what Troy Donovan was. *He's a challenge, Father. I'm sure You put him in my life for a reason. If You're trying to teach me something, help me to learn it quickly. I don't think he likes me although he seems to be making an attempt to be nice. You told us to pray for our enemies, and although he's not an enemy per se, he's not exactly a friend either. However, there's something in his eyes when he looks at me that twists my insides into a knot, and that's not good if he's got a wife. Please make that feeling go away."*

Maggie pulled the comforter beneath her chin and within minutes was fast asleep. She didn't even slip into her nightmare.

~

"Where are you going, Ivan?" Ludmila stopped in the doorway of her dimly lit kitchen and stared at him, the sight of the rifle sending her heart into her throat. "What are you doing?"

"Go back to bed, *Mamochka*." He pitched his voice to be reassuring. "I'll be back before you know it."

"Please tell me you're only going hunting." The older woman crossed her arms and placed a hand at her throat. "Even then, you know it's not hunting season. You have no need to go out with a rifle."

"Yes, I'm going hunting." Ivan turned to his mother, grinned and placed a kiss on her cheek. "You have nothing to worry about, Mama. No one will know if I bring back a caribou for us to eat."

"We have worked too long and hard to become citizens of this country, my son. Do nothing that will bring hurt or shame to this family." Ludmila held her head high. "If you could only remember what it was like…What your father…"

The grin disappeared from Ivan's face, a sneer replacing it. "Yes, what father went through? For his family? You've told us before. Many times. But what you fail to talk about, Mama, is the fact that he left us. Left us to fend for ourselves."

Ivan picked up his rifle and heavy backpack and slung them over his shoulders then headed toward the door. Ludmila grabbed his arm, halting him.

"I knew what your father was going to do, Ivan, and it was his intention to bring us out at a later date. He did not intend to leave us in the Soviet Union for good."

"Ah, yes, but he got himself killed, didn't he?" Ivan yanked his arm away and stormed out the door.

Ludmila clasped her hands together over her heart. She'd attempted to prevent what was about to happen, and she could do nothing more. She only hoped and prayed her son would come home to her.

~

A loud banging noise penetrated the sleep-filled recesses of Maggie's mind, tugging at her until she was awake. She lay for several moments in the warm cocoon of her bed attempting to understand where the noise was coming from. What in the world…?

She reached for her cell phone on the bedside table and squinted at the alarm. She still had ten minutes. Who would dare deprive her of the last ten minutes of her sleep?

The banging continued. Maggie threw back the covers and instantly regretted it. She longed to slip back beneath their warmth. Instead she reached for her burgundy velour bathrobe and belted it around her slim waist then slid her feet into matching slippers. Maggie headed into the living room, flipping on a lamp as she went.

It was nearly six a.m. Who could be pounding on her door at this time in the morning? Maggie flipped on the outside porch light, illuminating the porch and the front parking area. She peeked behind the door curtain. Troy? What was he doing here?

Maggie unlocked the deadbolt and the door lock and opened the door.

"Troy? What are you doing here?" She waved him in. "Come on in."

"Thanks." He stepped inside bringing the cold with him. He removed his parka hood and toboggan, waiting for her to close the door behind them. "I came to get you to the park."

"What do you mean?" Maggie ran her hand through her long, disheveled hair. It must look a mess. She hadn't even thought to run a brush through it before she came to the door.

"Remember that three to six inches they were calling for?" Troy stuffed his hands in his parka pockets as his gaze followed the movement of her hand. Wow, she'd even drawn his attention to it. How embarrassing.

Maggie swallowed her embarrassment and tugged her robe tighter over her flannel pjs then folded her arms over her chest. "Yes."

Troy grinned and shook his head.

"We didn't get three to six?"

"Nope. We got eighteen inches."

Maggie stood for a moment unsure she'd heard him right. "Did you say eighteen inches?"

Troy's grin grew. "Yep, I sure did. That's what we reported to the National Weather Service this morning. The national park records weather information on a daily basis, and we're required to report it to the National Weather Service. When we have snowfall, we report it, and we reported a whopping eighteen inches this morning at park headquarters."

"Wow, I'd say someone miscalculated on their forecast." Maggie's voice was soft and awestruck.

Troy chuckled. "Yeah, I'd say so."

"What's the plan?"

"Like I said, I'm here to get you to the park. I wasn't sure you could get in, so here I am. My personal pickup truck has a plow on it."

Maggie walked to the window and peeked through the curtains. She turned back to him. "Great. Have you had breakfast?"

"You don't think my mom's going to let me walk out the door of my house without feeding me first, do you?" A dry expression settled on his features.

"Probably not." Maggie moved to the small kitchen. "I'll put some coffee on before I get dressed."

While the coffee brewed, Maggie hurried back to the bedroom to change into warm clothes. She put on a touch of makeup and pulled her hair into a ponytail then hurried back out to the kitchen. She found Troy pouring coffee into thermal travel mugs.

"I wasn't sure how you like to doctor yours so I left you room for that." He pushed her favorite travel mug toward her. He'd brought his in and had refilled it.

"Thanks." Maggie removed a bottle of creamer from the fridge and fixed her coffee the way she liked it. "What's on the agenda for the day?"

"The snow's all but stopped. Just a few flurries blowing around now." Without adding anything to his thermal mug, Troy tightened the lid back on. "We have quite the expedition going out this morning. Senator Scott set things up with Superintendent Wade. His assistant, Calvin Jacobs, is going with us. I didn't think it was such a great idea considering the security logistics of a plan like that, but what the senator wants the senator gets. Keep him happy, the superintendent says. Not only do we have to take them out, we have to take the senator's security detail too. That's three extra men who require three extra dog sled teams. Now we're looking at a total of six teams. We only have thirty dogs who comprise five teams. We had to bring in a team from outside the park. We've asked a local guy we know to come and give us a hand. He's a retired park musher who knows the park well."

"Seriously?" Maggie tightened the lid of her mug. She leaned a hip against the counter. "That's going to be quite the flotilla of dog sleds."

Troy ran a hand over his chin. "Tell me about it. It promises to be a headache for sure."

Maggie grabbed her boots from beside the front door, sat on a kitchen chair and slipped them on. "And you thought babysitting a lone photographer was a pain."

"Now I never said that." Troy tugged his toboggan over his head.

"You never had to. Your expressive face said it for you."

Troy leaned against the counter. "Well, since you've been here, I've come to realize you're not so bad to have around. We'll see how you do with dog sledding."

"Thanks. I think." Maggie stood and reached for her parka. "Well, if nothing else, I can add dog sledding to my list of Denali transportation."

"What do you mean?" Troy's brow furrowed.

"My first day in Alaska with my tour. It was obviously from a few hundred feet up so I only saw the scenery from the air, but it was quite breathtaking. The air was so clear that day. It was gorgeous."

"Yeah, I've been up many times. I know what you mean." Troy took a drink of his coffee and wrapped his hands around the mug. "You mentioned before having flown with Svenson's Bush Plane Service. How was your flight?"

"Like I told you before, Jud Svenson was my pilot. It was a great flight. I enjoyed it a lot." Maggie zipped her parka and pulled her gloves from the pockets then reached for her camera bag and coffee mug.

A dark look flashed across Troy's features for an instant then it was gone.

"I got the feeling from the day the senator arrived that you don't care much for Jud. Why?" Maggie wondered at his fleeting expression. Had she imagined it or had a look of distaste flitted across Troy's face.

"Nothing much." Troy gave an offhanded shrug. "We just don't see eye to eye on some things."

He strolled toward the door and reached for the doorknob. "Ready to go?"

"Ready." Maggie grabbed her keys off the kitchen counter and locked up after they stepped onto the porch. "With the airport and a train station in the park, it makes it easy for folks to get there, especially from far away. Interesting. People arrive to Denali by plane, train and automobile."

A few fine snowflakes drifted down as they made their way to Troy's pickup truck. A huge snow plow was attached to the front. He'd used the snow shovel that she'd left on the front porch to clear a path from his truck to the front door. Maggie glanced at her SUV. It was well and truly covered. She'd have to work on that this evening when she returned.

~

Maggie glanced at her watch. Eight o'clock in the morning and the sun was just beginning to shed faint light behind the mountains. The mercury light on the front of the building by the dog sled kennels lit the yard. She stomped her booted feet and watched as her breath froze in the morning air. She tugged her parka hood closer and tightened the strings. Brrrr. It was -20° this morning but it didn't seem to faze the sled dogs.

Troy and Bryce, along with another ranger, whom Troy introduced as Jason O'Rourke, and three others whom she hadn't met were busy harnessing the teams to the sleds. All the dogs were barking in anticipation for the day's run. The whole kennel yard was a cacophony of barking. Excitement stirred in Maggie's midsection as she watched the preparations. She would be riding in Troy's sled and once the sun came up, she would snap photographs as much as she could.

Troy's favorite lead dog, Venture, was harnessed at the front of his team. Venture's harness was clipped to a grommet buried in the ground. Troy had cleared the snow away to expose it and all the grommets holding the leads for each of the dogs in the team. Troy petted each dog, speaking in soothing tones to them as he made his way back to the sled. It was piled with heavy blankets.

He called to Maggie and tossed a gloved hand in the direction of the other sleds. "Everyone's about ready. We've got some miles to make. Ready to get this expedition under way?"

"Ready when you are, boss." With her camera bag slung over her shoulder, Maggie made her way through a path in the snow to the sled. "Where do you want me?"

Just then a man in a navy-blue parka made his way toward them, a smaller man in a forest green parka right on his heels. Both men wore goggles that protruded from their hoods. "Morning, Miss Maggie. Ranger Donovan. It's a gorgeous morning for a ride, don't you think?"

"Good morning, Senator Scott." Troy held out a gloved hand and shook the hands of both men. "Good morning, Mr. Jacobs. I hope you're both ready for this. Have you ever been dog sledding before, sir?"

"I may be from Alaska, Ranger Donovan, but I've never had the opportunity. That's why I asked to come. And my assistant here," he threw a heavy arm over the smaller man's shoulders, "he's not from Alaska. Have you ever been sledding before, Calvin?"

"Oh, no sir." Calvin Jacobs shook an emphatic head and wrung his gloved hands. Maggie had the feeling if he had his way, he wouldn't be going today either. Poor man probably didn't have a say in the matter.

She reached over and patted his arm. "It'll be alright, Mr. Jacobs. These mushers are well trained. Isn't that right, Ranger Donovan?"

Troy's gaze met hers then moved to the little man. Assessing the situation, he smiled. "You bet we are, and not just us, but all of these dogs are well trained too. Believe it or not, there's an understanding and communication that passes between the musher and the sled dogs. You have nothing to worry about, Mr. Jacobs. This isn't a race like the Iditarod. That's not what we're here for today. We're here to give you and Senator Scott a leisurely view of the park. So, when you're seated on the sled, just relax, look for wildlife and enjoy the view."

The senator, who still had his arm across Jacobs's shoulder, patted it then removed his arm. "Come on, Calvin. Let's go have a great ride."

Jacobs adjusted his goggles and gave a slow nod. "Yes, sir."

They made their way through the snow back to their sleds, and their ranger mushers helped them settle onboard.

Troy lifted the blankets from his sled and motioned for Maggie to take a seat.

"Make yourself comfortable, and I'll pile these blankets on top of you. Believe me, you'll want them. We'll be traveling about five miles an hour, and although that doesn't seem like much, it's still going to be quite cold. So bundle up." He lifted the blankets and waited for her to take a seat, stretching her legs out in front of her. She slipped her camera bag and tripod beside her, then Troy settled the blankets over and around her, tucking her in.

"There. How's that?" A grin lifted one corner of his handsome lips as his sapphire gaze met her gaze in the illumination from the mercury light. Then he chuckled. "You look like a mummy."

Maggie huffed then giggled as she lowered her goggles. "Thanks. That's so complimentary. It doesn't help that I sort of feel like one."

"Well, snuggle down." Troy walked to the head of the team and called over his shoulder as he went. "We're about to get underway."

He grabbed Venture's collar and petted the dog, talking to him in soothing tones. Maggie couldn't hear his words. Each dog in the team was barking with eagerness to get on the trail. Troy had told her how sled dogs live to work. He'd told her they thrive on pulling a sled. From their eagerness this morning, she believed it. The cacophony of barking around the yard was ear splitting but at the same time, Maggie enjoyed it. These dogs were special. Nowhere else in the United States were there national park service sled dogs. These were the chosen groups. How cool was that?

Troy unclipped Venture's lead and tucked it into his parka pocket. "Hold, boy. Hold."

All the other teams prepared to leave as well, each musher releasing his lead dog then the rest of the team.

Venture watched Troy with his amazing ice blue eyes. He was all business as he barked then stood at attention and the team went silent. Troy jogged back to the rear of the sled and jumped on the runners.

"Mush," he called in a loud, clear voice. "Mush."

Venture sprang forward at the same time the team dogs did. These were the dogs positioned just in front of the sled. They gave the momentum to the rest of the team and to the sled as the rest of the team took off. Their barks of excitement echoed around the yard and were joined by the second team, then the third and so on until all six teams were on their way. Each team put on speed as they charged down the snowy dirt road and headed away from the kennels.

Chapter Seven

T he sun finally made its appearance at 9:03 a.m. Maggie wasn't sure she'd ever get used to the sun's Alaskan schedule. Every day it rose three to four minutes earlier and set three to four minutes later making the day seem longer. Before long, those minutes would stretch to ten minutes at each end of the day. Eventually, in summer, the sun would stay up pretty much all day. That's when Alaska would be called by its summer name, the Land of the Midnight Sun. Too bad she wouldn't be around to see it.

Since they'd left the kennel yard and before the sun had risen, the senator's sled had been at the center of all the teams while the rest had circled around him keeping as close to him as possible considering each had a string of dogs leading them.

Occasionally the mushers would switch their positions around, moving the senator to the front or to the left or to the right, or to the back. After a while Maggie wasn't able to keep up with where he was. His security team required this shuffle even though it didn't make a lot of sense to her. Who in the world would brave these wintery temperatures and this wilderness to come find the senator out here?

The only sounds were the soft padding of the dogs' booted feet in the snow and the whisking sound of the sled runners as they slid across the powdery surface. Occasionally the dogs barked. Not long after the sun rose, a small herd of caribou stood pawing at the ground some distance away.

"What are they doing?" Maggie turned to ask Troy over her shoulder.

"Looking for mushrooms and lichen near the river." Troy slowed the team and signaled the others to do the same. "Want to take a few pictures? That's what you're here for, right?"

"Right." Maggie tugged her camera from beneath the blanket. "But how in the world can you tell there's a river over there? It looks just like the rest of the ground around it."

"Because I work here and know the area."

Maggie took aim, adjusted the focus and snapped off a few pictures. "That makes sense."

"Besides, I've fallen in a time or two when the spring thaw's begun and it's not fun. You learn fast not to do that again. The snow on top can be deceiving."

Maggie lowered her camera and glanced at him. "So, your mom was right. You do know this country like the back of your hand."

"Yep. You about finished?"

Maggie nodded. "Yeah, I got some great photos. Thanks for stopping."

She turned to cover back up with the blanket when a loud crack sounded and echoed across the valley. Maggie gasped and glanced around. "What was…?"

At the same moment she started to ask, Mr. Jacobs howled in pain. The hired bodyguard detail sprang into action, each one moving to surround the senator and Calvin Jacobs.

The sound startled the caribou causing them all to raise their heads and jerk their bodies in surprise. Then they stood stock still.

"We can't stop here," Troy shouted. "We're sitting ducks. Get back to your sleds. Let's get to that bluff over there and hide beneath that outcropping of rocks. Hurry. Let's go."

Just as the men plopped back onto the sleds, the mushers called for their teams to go and the dogs sprang into action, moving much faster than they'd done previously. Another loud crack rang out across the valley, and the caribou herd startled again, this time running away.

The teams all moved beneath the outcropping of rocks even as a third crack rang out. They squeezed in as best they could. Troy jumped off the runners on the back of his sled and he, along with the other mushers, tethered their teams to the ground with stakes and their harnesses. Maggie climbed from her seat on the sled and followed Troy as he made his way to Calvin Jacobs' sled. His musher, ranger Jason O'Rourke, was already at Calvin's side.

"How is he, Jason?" Troy dropped to Jason's side as he peeled back Jacobs' parka and inner clothing to get a glimpse of his injury.

"We'll know in a moment. He's wearing a lot of layers. There's a first aid kit just below his feet there. Grab it, will you?"

Troy reached under the blankets and pulled out a large red nylon case with a white circle and red cross on top. He unzipped the case and rummaged through the bag looking for a large compression bandage.

Calvin Jacobs moaned, his pale face twisted with pain.

"Troy, look." Jason's gaze met Troy's then directed his gaze to a portion of exposed skin between Calvin's left shoulder and his chest where a bullet hole was bleeding. No sooner did the blood hit the surface than it began to freeze. Jason covered it up again then checked Calvin's back. No blood. No exit wound.

Troy handed him the compression bandage. "Here, get this on him as quick as you can."

Troy looked up at Maggie. Her face was pale, her gloved hand covered her lower face as she averted her gaze.

Jason slipped rubber gloves on and worked quickly but his hands shook from the cold.

When he was finished, he made Calvin Jacobs as comfortable as possible considering their circumstances. He stood and pulled Troy to the side.

"Troy, he needs to get to a hospital. Soon."

Troy lowered the zipper on his parka and reached inside one of the interior pockets removing the satellite phone he always took into the wilderness with him. He may rough it in most other areas when it came to the wilderness and sled dog travel, but he refused to leave his one link to civilization behind.

"I have the satellite phone, Jason. I'll call Fairbanks for a rescue helicopter with EMTs to pick up Mr. Jacobs and the senator. Considering we have an active shooter situation I'll inform them we're pinned down. It's going to be tricky getting them out."

"Mind if I make that call, Ranger Donovan?"

Troy turned to find the senator standing behind him, hands in his parka pockets, his goggles shoved up above his parka hood.

"Sir?"

"I think I can get us more than just a helicopter with some EMT's, Ranger Donovan. That is if you'll loan me your phone for a couple of minutes. You're welcome to listen in, if you like."

The senator grinned as he waited for Troy's response.

Moans reached them from the sled where Calvin Jacobs sat propped up. Troy glanced in his direction then handed his satphone to the senator.

"Make your call, sir. We need to get Mr. Jacobs to the hospital. And you to safety."

~

Maggie averted her gaze from the first aid that Jason O'Rourke performed on Calvin Jacobs. Poor man. He hadn't wanted to come on this trip into the wilderness to begin with and then to be shot by someone way out in the middle of nowhere just didn't seem fair. Maggie closed her eyes.

Oh Lord. Please don't let this man die. Please don't let him bleed out here. Send help and stop the shooter from harming anyone else. Why, oh, why is he shooting at the senator? I'm pretty sure that's who he was aiming at. Please put your shield of protection around us and keep us safe.

"Are you alright?"

Maggie's eyes popped open at the sound of Troy's gentle voice so near. Her gaze met his just inches away. Concern filled his sapphire blues as they roamed her face.

Maggie gave a slight nod. "Yeah. Just praying for Mr. Jacobs and for all of us really. Until that shooter is gone, none of us are safe. How are we going to get out of here, Troy?"

He drew in a heavy breath and released it all at once. "That's a good question. I'm hoping when the helicopter comes and takes the senator away that it'll also take away the shooter's incentive to kill."

"And what will stop him from shooting out of frustration because you robbed him of his target?"

"I was afraid you were going to ask that." He crossed his arms over his chest. "All I know is we're going to get as many people on that helicopter as we can, then three or four of us will take the dogs out of here. We'll come back another day and pick up the rest of the sleds. We can't risk taking everybody back by sled."

Maggie eyed him with skepticism. "What if everyone won't fit on the helicopter?"

Troy's lips tilted in a grin that sent Maggie's heart into overdrive. Why in the world did he have to be so handsome when he smiled? What the heck? He was handsome when he didn't smile.

"Remember the chopper that brought the senator and his wife to the park? The CH-47 Chinook?"

Maggie gave a slow nod, lifting an eyebrow over a wary eye. "Yes."

"That's what they're sending out. If they could've sent two, we could've all gone for a ride, including the dogs. As it is, they could only send one. And you're on it, understand?"

"But...."

Troy's gloved finger immediately rested against Maggie's lips. "No buts. You're on that chopper and you're out of here with the senator and Calvin Jacobs. Take pictures. Do your job. You're out of here."

His hand dropped away, and his gaze roamed her face landing on her lips. Warmth spread through Maggie halting her breath. What was happening? After what seemed like forever, he tore his gaze away and moved toward his dog team.

Maggie stood for a moment unsure what had just happened. Closing her eyes, she attempted to jumpstart her lungs by breathing in a deep breath of freezing air then putting her gloved hands over her face and breathing deeply again trying to warm her frozen windpipe.

A thought struck her. He had a wife. He had a *wife*. That's right. What in the world was she thinking? He had a wife. Then why was *he* looking at *her* like *that*?

~

After what seemed like hours, the whomp-whomp of the Chinook's rotors could be heard before they spotted the big bird in the sky. It was a welcome sound. What they didn't expect was a second set of rotor sounds as a smaller helicopter came into view just ahead of the Chinook.

Troy stepped over to Senator Scott's side and grinned at him. "An Apache, Senator? They must think you're important, sir."

The senator returned Troy's grin with a raised eyebrow. "I am on the Committee for Defense. If I couldn't get two Chinooks to get us out of here then I could at least get an Apache to find the shooter and hold him down while we slip away. I suggest while we get onboard that chopper, you get your dog teams ready to go. That Apache has the ability to find that shooter by his body heat and pin him down. Put your extra sleds on the chopper so you don't have to come back for them, then you can head on back the way you came."

Troy shook the senator's gloved hand. "I'll take whatever senatorial power you've got behind you, sir. Thank you."

He turned to the waiting men standing around. "Mushers, let's get these teams harnessed together and ready to go. I want only four teams running back across country. The other two sleds go back on the chopper."

He called Bryce West, Jason O'Rourke and one other ranger to join him in the cross-country return trip. "Everybody else goes back on that chopper."

There was a beehive of activity as dog teams were joined together and harnessed to four sleds. Two sleds were moved and readied to be loaded on the chopper. One held Mr. Jacobs who waited for Army EMTs to take him onboard for emergency treatment.

The Chinook's rotors kicked up a whirlwind of snow as it set down on its skis in a clearing between the outcropping and the snow-covered river. Its two sets of rotors slowed but did not stop as Troy and Bryce two-man carried a sled to the open bay door. It was decided to try that before taking Calvin Jacobs in case the shooter attempted a shot and got one past before the Apache could stop him.

Indeed, a shot rang out and pinged on the side of the Chinook bay door, just inches from a crewman. Troy and Bryce hit the ground. A mini-burst of machine gun fire sprayed from the Apache as it hovered a hundred feet north-east of them. From their prone positions on the ground they watched as it aimed a hundred feet up the side of the mountain.

Troy and Bryce jumped up and the Chinook crew helped them load the sled into the belly of the huge machine. Calvin Jacobs was next as the EMTs helped him into the chopper and began working over him. Within minutes, the rest of the sleds and the passengers were loaded without any further shots being fired.

Troy stood at the bay door of the Chinook and glanced around the jump seats to where Maggie sat, her camera bag in her lap, her shoulder straps secure. She'd tugged her parka hood off and only her brown toboggan covered her head. She looked exhausted. Turning toward the door, her gaze met his. He grinned then winked before stepping back so they could close the bay door. He caught her smile just before it shut. Keeping that picture before his mind's eye would help him through the next few hours as he made his way back to the kennel. Normally being out here with his team was a joy for him, but knowing there was someone out here trying to kill the senator or any one of them took the joy out of the experience.

Troy tugged his hood up over his toboggan and trotted over to the sleds. They needed to get out of here. The Apache sat in position above the snow-covered road holding the shooter at bay until they were out of sight.

Jumping on the sled's runners, he grabbed the handles and called, "Mush. Mush."

His much larger team took off, eager to go. They'd been laying or sitting under the outcropping for far too long and were ready to move. All four teams moved quickly across the snow heading back toward civilization. It would be late when they returned, and certainly well after dark.

As they moved away from the safety of the outcropping, Troy half expected to get a bullet between the shoulders and urged his team to move faster. The sound of the Apache's rotors reassured him, but what if the shooter took a pot shot? Like he hadn't done that a few times today already. However, they weren't even sure he was still there. Could the Apache have taken him out earlier with its rounds? Hopefully the pilots will give a report when they return.

The sound of the Apache's rotors faded the further they whisked away through the valley along the river and through the patchy wooded areas. None of the rangers said anything. The lighthearted expedition of the morning had turned into a near tragedy and everyone was eager for it to be over. Only the dog teams seemed to be oblivious to what was going on, and they took advantage of the larger teams to move quicker through the snow.

Maggie's smile filled Troy's mind as he settled into a rhythm with the sled and the dog team. She hadn't argued with him when he'd told her she'd be returning on the Chinook. That was a good thing. There was no way he'd wanted to risk anything happening to her should the shooter somehow get another round or more off. Something had happened out there with her and he wasn't sure what it was, but he didn't think he should analyze it too much or he might regret it. If he did, his heart might not survive. He couldn't afford to let that happen.

Their conversation from a few days ago returned to his thoughts. She'd told him she lived in New York, but she was born in North Carolina and that her father was a professor at the University of North Carolina. She'd asked if he'd ever been there. If she only knew. Liz loved it there. She loved it more there than she did Alaska. But when you're from North Carolina what can you expect? Liz had a hard time acclimating to Alaska. She tried. She really did.

One of the sled runners hit a rock and nearly threw Troy off the sled. He grabbed the handles and hung on as he regained his footing.

"You okay?" Bryce called from his left.

Troy tossed his head in the affirmative when he was back in control. Whew, that was close. He needed to pay closer attention. Women. They were too much of a distraction and right now he couldn't afford to be distracted. Liz was gone and Maggie was…Maggie was definitely a distraction. A desire to pray filled his heart but he fought it. How could he go running to God when he'd blamed Him for what had happened to Liz? He'd blamed Him for things that he was ashamed of saying. He'd been so angry when she'd died so needlessly.

Deep down he knew it wasn't God's fault but he'd railed against Him anyway. How could he go back and say he was sorry? What was keeping him from it?

Pride.

The word was spoken as if someone rode along with him right there on the sled. But that was impossible. He glanced over at Bryce and the other rangers. They didn't act like they'd heard anything.

Had God spoken to Him? No, he didn't think so. It was more like an impression rather than a spoken word. He shook his head. How could he ever think about a relationship with another woman when he couldn't even talk to God about what had happened concerning the death of his wife? He had some serious thinking to do.

What he hadn't told Maggie was that he'd attended the University of North Carolina at Chapel Hill to study wildlife conservation and biology. In his sophomore year he'd been a student of Maggie's father, Owen Lawrence, for world history. He was a great teacher.

Maggie's additional information about her experience last summer when she and her cousin had nearly been trafficked had hit him hard. No one should have to go through something like that.

And now here she was, another beautiful woman from North Carolina, stirring up feelings within him that he hadn't felt in... well, since before Liz died. He'd tried to bury those feelings deep. He'd hidden them beneath anger and resentment, but somehow Maggie Lawrence had managed to scratch away the surface to expose his buried emotions. And the real kicker? She didn't even know it.

Chapter Eight

Maggie stood at the door of a beautiful, if rustic, log home in the middle of a clearing in the woods on the northwest edge of Healy. The porch where she waited for someone to answer her knock was long and wide on both sides of the front door. A few rocking chairs with a couple of inches of snow on them sat waiting for a summer that would come fast, stick around for a couple of months then vanish just as quickly as it arrived. Too bad she wouldn't be around to see what an Alaskan summer was like. She doubted Mr. Radford would let her stay and do a story on that but, oh, it would be fun and interesting to experience it.

She spun around at the sound of the front door opening. A gorgeous dark-haired young woman with a slim build held the door wide.

"Please, come in. You must be Maggie Lawrence." She closed the door after Maggie stepped inside. A beautiful smile lit her face. "It's a pleasure to meet you. I'm Skye Donovan. Here, let me take your parka. I'll hang it up for you. Make yourself at home. We don't stand on formalities here."

Like an automaton, Maggie moved without rational thought as she removed her parka and handed it to her hostess. This was Troy's wife. She was beautiful and gracious. Maggie wanted to grab her parka back, turn around and head back out the door. What was she doing here? Oh yeah. She'd been invited by Troy's mom. Ok, so she'd enjoy her visit and the meal, then leave as quickly as she could without being rude.

"Maggie? Are you okay?" Skye's question penetrated Maggie's thoughts and she glanced at the other woman.

Maggie shoved a lock of hair behind her ear and nodded. "Oh, yes I'm sorry. I was wool gathering for a second. I'm fine."

Movement around her ankles drew her attention to an orange tabby cat winding around her knee-length leather boots.

Mmeeeoooowww. The cat wound around one ankle then twisted around the other, rubbing its head against the leather.

"Oh, you have a friendly cat." Maggie glanced back at Skye.

"Yes, Michael's friendly when he chooses to be and with whom he chooses. I guess he likes you. Took to you pretty quickly, didn't he? Come on back to the kitchen."

Skye led the way down a short hallway to a large country kitchen where Clarissa Donovan was busy at the stove and Troy was setting the table. Jeremy followed him with napkins, placing them by large bowls.

"Look who's here." Skye headed for a cabinet and opened it, removing glasses.

Maggie stopped in the kitchen doorway, fighting the awkward feeling that threatened to overcome her. She'd been in far more difficult situations than this so why in the world was she feeling this way? Then a sapphire blue gaze met hers from across the room and she was reminded exactly why. Her breath stuck somewhere between her throat and her chest even as her heartbeat took off like a jackhammer. The comforting pressure of Michael rubbing against her ankles was again welcome.

A grin lifted a corner of Troy's lips as Jeremy whooped, "Hey Miss Maggie. Lookie who's here, Grandma. It's Miss Maggie."

Clarissa turned from stirring a pot of something that emitted a delicious aroma and set her spoon down. She made her way over to Maggie and wrapped her in her arms.

"Oh, my goodness, I'm so glad you could make it. I've been looking forward to your visit for days. Come on in. Don't stand here in the doorway like you're going to run away. I won't let you do that."

Maggie returned the diminutive woman's hug and began to feel better. It touched her heart to know this woman truly wanted her here. "Thanks for inviting me, Mrs. Donovan. It's a pleasure to be here."

Clarissa held her at arm's length. "Now that won't do. You must call me Clarissa. Everyone does. I don't answer to Mrs. Donovan. Isn't that right, Troy?"

"Yep. I haven't heard anyone call her Mrs. Donovan since I was a kid."

Maggie watched as Troy walked over and placed an arm around Skye and tugged her close. She averted her gaze. She'd just have to get over whatever little attraction she'd started to feel for him. It was ridiculous anyway. She'd known all along he was wearing a wedding band. How could she have let it grow? *Lord, I was weak, wasn't I? Help me get over it.*

"Maggie, let me introduce you to Skye. This is my kid sister. She's up for the weekend from Anchorage. She's a teacher down there in a Christian school."

It took a couple seconds for Troy's words to sink in. Sister? He said sister. Not his wife?

"You're his sister?" Maggie's words came out almost incredulous sounding. At least to her ears. "I...I mean, now that you mention it, I suppose I do see a resemblance."

"Troy actually looks more like his dad used to, and Skye looks more like me, or so we've been told." Clarissa moved back to the stove and stirred the pot again. "Dinner's almost ready. Come on and finish setting that table, fellows."

"Is there anything I can help with?" Maggie stood to the side as the others moved around the kitchen accomplishing their tasks.

"Thank you, dear, but everything is just about done. I hope you brought an appetite." Clarissa turned and smiled at her.

Unless Troy's wife was still going to come walking into the room, which was quite possible, her appetite was growing. "Yes, I can eat."

If Troy's wife wasn't here, which when Maggie counted the place settings at the table indicated she wasn't, then what did that mean? Was Troy divorced? Was he a widower? She glanced at Jeremy. Poor little man. He must only be four or five years old. Either way couldn't be easy for such a little guy. Maggie's mom had died when she was in college and that had been hard.

The orange tabby cat had been wandering between everyone's feet and Jeremy picked him up now, hugging him, his back legs dangling. The cat sniffed Jeremy's face.

"Hold Michael's back legs, Jeremy. Don't let them dangle like that, remember?" Clarissa came over and helped him hold the cat the right way. "There. That's better."

"Michael?" Maggie asked. "That's a cute name for a cat."

"It's Michael Jordan," Jeremy smiled, "You know after the basketball player."

"Of course, I know who Michael Jordan is. I was born in Chapel Hill, North Carolina. Everybody there knows who Michael Jordan is."

"Oh really?" Clarissa's face lit up. "Well, did you know...?"

"Mom, isn't it time to eat?" Troy opened the oven and pulled out the pan of bread. "Jeremy, put Michael down and go wash up. It's time to get to the table."

"Alright, Troy. I'm ready for you to take the pot to the table." Clarissa shrugged and stepped back from the stove, making room for her son. "Be careful, that cast iron is hot."

Troy carried the cast iron Dutch oven to the table and placed it on a heavy trivet. Skye placed a large basket of warm sliced bread on the table.

Troy held out a chair next to the head of the table and seated Clarissa there then seated Maggie across from her. Then he held out the chair for his sister next to Maggie. Jeremy sat next to his grandmother. Troy took his place at the head of the table.

Clarissa said grace then they began to serve the food. Maggie noted that it was Clarissa that prayed and not Troy. Interesting.

"Maggie, this is caribou stew. I hope you'll like it." Clarissa handed a ladle to Troy.

"If it tastes as good as it smells, then I'll love it." Maggie watched as Troy filled his mother's bowl then reached for Maggie's. "Did you take the caribou, Troy?"

"Not this one. I usually hunt and get a caribou each winter, but Skye brought this one to us."

Maggie turned to the young woman beside her. "You hunt, Skye?"

Skye nodded and grinned, digging her spoon into her stew. "Oh yes. I love to hunt. Dad used to take both Troy and me out when we were young. Taught us all his hunting skills."

"These kids are self-sufficient, Maggie." Clarissa smiled. She turned and patted Jeremy's head. "One day Jeremy will be too.

Troy's already started teaching him. When you live in Alaska, you have to learn to survive because it can be harsh living up here. Just because you may have power or water today, doesn't mean you'll have it tomorrow or next week. Many Alaskans live without those things all the time. It's called subsistence living. It's a way of life. My grandmother and my great-grandparents were Athabaskan native-Alaskans. My grandmother taught me many of the ways of her people."

Maggie had an "aha" moment. Troy's mom resembled the beautiful native-Alaskans. It wasn't something she'd thought about, but now that she knew, she realized her black hair, tanned skin and almond shaped eyes were features of the Athabaskans. Troy and Skye had more muted elements of those features.

Her gaze was drawn to her right like a magnet and met Troy's sapphire gaze. Now those weren't Athabaskan. He must've inherited those gorgeous blues from his father. A tingle ran down her spine as she lowered her own gaze to her delicious bowl of stew and spooned a bite into her mouth. He may have inherited the color but there was something there that drew her and that was all his own. Was it intentional? There was no doubt she was attracted to him and she was fighting it even though she now knew he had no wife. Could he be attracted to her? She would be leaving this great far-north state in a few weeks and that would be that. Besides, she had no idea where he stood with the Lord. That was important to her. *Is he yours, Lord? Does he know you as his Lord and Savior?*

~

"Senator Scott has postponed the dedication ceremony for a couple of days." Troy wiped his mouth with his cloth napkin and reached for the ladle to refill his bowl. "He's refused to move forward with his schedule until Calvin Jacobs can attend."

He eyed Maggie then glanced at her empty bowl. "Have some more stew?"

She held up her hand. "No thanks. That was a huge bowl, and I'm quite full. It was delicious."

Troy filled his bowl and offered to fill everyone else's.

"Then when will the ceremony take place?" Maggie linked her fingers and rested her elbows on the edge of the table.

"Friday morning. That gives Mr. Jacobs two more days to recuperate. He was shot through the meaty part of his shoulder and fortunately, no bones were involved. They were able to get the bullet out without any problems. He was lucky he wasn't injured worse."

"I'd say so." Skye reached for a piece of bread and the butter. "Did they capture the shooter?"

"Well, they actually put him out of commission." Troy returned the ladle to the pot. "The Apache helicopter fired on him when he fired on us and the US Army took him out. The helicopter landed and they retrieved his body."

"When did this happen?" Clarissa cast a wary eye around the table. "Did something happen that you didn't tell me about, Troy Donovan? Were you in danger?"

Troy chuckled. "No more than usual, Mom. Just a disgruntled person trying to take the senator out while we were on an excursion yesterday. He had us pinned down and the senator used my satphone to call in the US Army. They sent a Chinook helicopter to take most of the group out along with an Apache helicopter for cover."

"Did you come out on the helicopter, son?" Clarissa dropped her spoon into her bowl as she looked directly at him, all ears. "Or is that why you were so late getting home?"

"No, mom. Four of us rangers had to take all the dog teams back to the kennels. That's why the Apache was there. To give us cover so we could get out."

Clarissa's gaze moved to Maggie. "Were you there, Maggie?"

Maggie nodded. "Yes, ma'am."

"Oh, my goodness." Clarissa's hands moved to cover her cheeks. "Had I known I could've been praying for you all. It's a good thing I pray for you daily, Troy James Donovan."

Troy's gaze was on his bowl of stew as he swirled his spoon through its contents but kept his thoughts to himself. It wouldn't do any good to say anything. She'd only tell him he needed to pray and they'd had this conversation time and again. He certainly didn't want to have it with Maggie here.

Skye smiled at her mom across the table and spoke in a gentle voice. "Mom, keep it up. Your kids will always need your prayers."

Clarissa brushed away moisture from beneath her eyes. Then she shoved her chair back and headed to the refrigerator. "Hey, I almost forgot. I made dessert. It's Jeremy's favorite. Chocolate pie with whipped topping. I hope you all saved room."

Skye pushed her chair back and followed her mother. "I'll help you, Mom."

"Sweet." Jeremy squealed and squirmed in his chair. "Grandma makes the best chocolate pie."

With a grin on his lips, Troy reached over and mused his son's hair. "You bet she does."

He glanced at Maggie and found a sweet smile on her lips as she watched them. Her eyes lit as she watched Jeremy. Did this big-city, New York photographer have a tender spot for his son? Would she ever settle down to a family of her own? Although she hadn't mention it, as beautiful as she was, she was bound to have a boyfriend back home. Somehow that thought didn't sit well. It shouldn't matter to him. Maggie would be leaving in a few weeks then that would be that. Besides, he'd already made up his mind. He was done with women. Loving them only brought pain.

~

Troy stepped into headquarters Monday morning and stomped the snow off his boots. He pulled the hood of his parka back and glanced in Natalya's direction as he tugged off his toboggan and ballcap.

"Good morning, sunshine."

"Good morning, Troy." Natalya's chipper voice never ceased to make him grin. Nothing ever seemed to get her down or irritate her. Not even him, and he'd tried.

He started to head to the rear of the building but her words halted him in his tracks.

"Hold up, Troy. Superintendent Wade wants to see you in his office right away."

"Like, right now? Can I get some coffee first?"

Natalya smiled and held up a thermal cup with a lid. "I'm way ahead of you."

Troy heaved a heavy sigh and strolled to the counter above her reception desk. "Sometimes I don't know whether to dislike you or hug you."

She gave him a pert smile, closed her eyes and shrugged a shoulder. "Any or all will do."

Troy grabbed the cup of coffee and took a sip. "Thanks. It's just how I like it and hot to boot. But then you knew that, right?"

"Of course." Natalya turned to her computer, dismissing him, and returned to her work.

Troy shook his head and headed down the hallway to the superintendent's office, knocking on his door.

"Come in." The words were loud enough for Troy to hear.

He opened the door and stuck his head in. "You wanted to see me, sir."

"Troy, come in and close the door. Have a seat."

Wade was pecking two-fingered, one index finger from each hand, on his computer. He finished what he was doing and turned to Troy.

Without a "good morning" or "how are you today," Superintendent Wade jumped right to his subject.

"I received the coroner's report this morning from the US Army. It's obviously a courtesy. Since our park police are investigating the shooting from the evening of the dinner, the Army thought it might be helpful in our investigation to have the information concerning the shooter who was taking pot shots at your dog sled excursion. It begs the question: Could this shooter be the same one that shot at the senator at the dinner the other evening?"

"Yes, sir, it does."

Wade picked up a form from the desktop and handed it to Troy. "Here's the report."

Troy reached for the paper and began to scan the information. The cause of death had been by shooting from an Apache AH-64. The detailed explanation indicated the shooter had been killed when the repercussive rounds had been fired into the mountain behind him sending a shock wave and shrapnel away from the mountain. The impact of the shock wave and flying shrapnel of rocks had killed him, not the repercussive rounds. Had the Army personnel in the Apache fired directly at him, he'd have been disintegrated. The man had been identified as Ivan Evgenevich Orlov. Born in Russia, he immigrated to the US in 2014. There were no identifying marks on his body other than a birthmark on his torso. Nothing out of the ordinary physically. The only other marks were made by flying rock shrapnel that impacted Orlov when the repercussive rounds hit the mountain.

"Sir, there are a lot of Russians in Alaska who immigrated here over the years. What we have to find out is why he wanted to kill the senator. And since he's dead, he can't tell us that."

Wade released a heavy sigh and dropped back against his leather desk chair. He shoved his glasses up onto his nose. "Exactly. We'll have to find other clues to answer that question."

"Anything on the champagne and possible prints on the glasses?"

The superintendent snapped his fingers and pulled a paper from a file on his desk. "Oh, yes, that reminds me. Of course, the senator and Mrs. Scott's prints were found but there were also another set of latent fingerprints. We got lucky."

He handed the sheet of paper to Troy.

Troy glanced at the fingerprint report. "The champagne was laced with cyanide. Cyanide? Who knew you could still get that stuff anymore?"

"Are you kidding, Troy? You can get anything on the internet these days."

Troy tilted his head. "I suppose you're right, sir. Now on to the perpetrator. Laurel Oliver. Her record's clean except for one DUI a year ago in Fairbanks. The only record we've found so far indicates she was born in New York City in 1985. She's sure a long way from home, don't you think?"

"I do, but it wouldn't be the first time we've found out there's more to the story than meets the eye. She lives in McKinley Village outside the park now. Apparently, she's working three different jobs in the area. I looked her up. Perhaps it's time to pay her a visit. Take Bryce with you, Troy. I don't know what to expect from this young woman or who may be with her."

Wade handed him a slip of paper from the file folder. "Here's the address. You may have trouble locating her since she's working three jobs, but I've listed her work places on there as well. Good luck."

"Thanks. I'll let you know what happens." Troy stood and walked to the door, his hand on the knob.

"Troy," the superintendent's words halted him.

He turned around. "Yes, sir?"

"Be careful. So far we have a dead Russian shooter and a young woman who may have tried to poison the senator and his wife, plus someone who slipped in to take shots at the dinner the other night who may or may not have been the same shooter as the one out in the park. All this and no idea what the motive is."

"Yes, sir. We'll be careful."

Chapter Nine

W ho is this woman?" Bryce gazed out his side window as Troy turned the SUV left out of the park and onto Parks Highway heading into McKinley Village. It was a touristy place made up of hotels, restaurants, gift shops and tour guides of all kinds. This time of year, most of the shops were closed and wouldn't open again until later in spring.

"Laurel Oliver. She lives and works in the village. I'm not sure how she got hired to work at the dinner for the senator the other night, but I imagine she snuck in somehow just to deliver the tainted drink to him and his wife."

"Wouldn't she have had to get an approved badge to get in?" Bryce glanced at Troy. "With security as high as it was, that couldn't have been easy to do."

"For the right price, you can get a fake ID for anything, Bryce." Troy slowed the SUV as he crossed the glacier-fed Nenana River and turned right onto a dirt road that twisted and turned up behind the businesses and shops. It led to some housing for the people who worked in the village. Troy glanced at his GPS then back at the road.

Since most of these businesses were closed during the winter months, the extra help was temporary until the season reopened. A few stayed open year-round other than the lodges, and since Laurel was here, she was most likely a year-round worker. Troy pulled the SUV to a stop in front of a small house that looked like it had seen better days. He and Bryce climbed out of the SUV and approached the tiny house. Only two steps led to the front door. Troy reached up and knocked on it. Would they get lucky and find Laurel home? Or would they have to hunt her down?

Within two minutes the door opened three inches and part of a feminine face appeared. A chain across the door prevented her from opening it further. It was the young woman from the dinner the other evening. The one who gave the Scotts their tainted champagne flutes. "Yes?"

Troy noticed her face was damp. Had she been crying? What was that all about? Troy flashed his credentials.

"Miss Oliver? I'm Ranger Troy Donovan and this is Ranger Bryce West. We're with the National Park Service. We'd like to talk with you for a few minutes, if we may."

Her gaze ping-ponged between them in the sliver of door space. "What is this about?"

Troy caught her accent. Russian. Interesting but not unusual. These shops hired Russian exchange students all the time to work from early spring until late fall. Some stayed and worked year-round.

"You were working at the dinner the other evening when Sen. Bradford Scott was there. I just have some questions for you. Perhaps you may be able to help us." *Get in the door before she slams it in your face.*

"*Da*, I was there. I was called in to waitress."

"May we come in, Miss Oliver?" Bryce spoke for the first time. Her gaze flew to his face and narrowed as she searched it.

"Very well." She closed the door and they heard her remove the chain just before the door opened and she stepped back, allowing them to enter.

"Thank you." Troy led the way inside what could hardly be called a living room. More like a sitting room kitchen combination. A small love seat with a bistro table and two chairs backed up to a tiny kitchenette. A door led to what he assumed was a bedroom. That's about all this tiny house would hold. At least it was warm inside.

"Please. Sit." Laurel removed a jacket from the loveseat and indicated they should sit there while she pulled out one of the bistro chairs. She dropped the jacket on the other bistro chair and sat in the one nearest to them. She wiped her eyes with her fingers and sniffed. "I will sit here."

"Thank you." Troy and Bryce dropped to the loveseat which was a little close for their liking but what choice did they have?

Bryce attempted to move to the right but didn't actually move anywhere. He eyed Troy then looked away.

"Are you alright, Miss Oliver?" Troy leaned his elbows on his knees then leaned forward.

Laurel nodded and kept her eyes lowered. "*Da*. I just received some bad news about a…a friend. He…he died."

"I'm sorry to hear that." Troy pulled out his notepad and pen then tried to look as sympathetic as he could.

"Do you live alone, Miss Oliver, or do you share your home?" Troy watched her expression for signs of unease.

"I live alone." She met his gaze then looked away.

"Miss Oliver, when were you asked to work the dinner the other evening?"

The young blond dropped her gaze immediately. "I was called in that afternoon."

"Do you normally work prestigious dinners at the Denali Wilderness Lodge?"

"Sometimes." Laurel still avoided his gaze.

"Where do you normally work?"

"I work at the Gateway Snack Bar, Alaskan Gifts and Merchandise and Svenson's Bush Plane Service."

The last business caught Troy's attention. "Do you drive all the way into Fairbanks to work for Svenson's?"

The pretty blond shook her head and a slight smile lifted her lips. "No, no. I help run a shop here for Svenson's. We don't have much business yet. Too early in the year, but business will pick up in May."

"Yeah." Troy watched her with a close eye. "So how did you come to work the dinner at the Denali Wilderness Lodge the other evening?"

Laurel's gaze flew to his face then moved away. "One of the regular waitresses was sick and I was called in."

"I see. As you know, I observed you serve Senator and Mrs. Scott each a glass of champagne. Once you served them, you hurried away. What you may not know is they didn't drink the champagne."

Troy continued to scrutinize Laurel's reaction closely. Her gaze flicked to his for a couple of seconds then moved away.

"Answer me this. How did cyanide get into the senator and his wife's champagne?"

Her eyes were instantly back on his. "What? Cyanide? I have no idea. Why are you asking me these questions?"

"Because your fingerprints are the only other fingerprints on the glasses, Miss Oliver."

Troy noticed that Laurel's breathing had picked up and she was breathing out of her mouth. She probably wasn't even aware that she was breathing heavily. A dead giveaway that she was stressing out.

"Laurel, you obviously speak with a strong Russian accent. Where are you from? Originally?" Troy jotted something on his notepad then lifted his gaze to her face.

The young woman hesitated for a brief moment, uncertainty warring on her features. "Siberia, but I am now a US citizen. You may check. I immigrated."

"We'll do that, but you need to tell me your real name."

"My...my real...name?" Laurel's eyes darted around the room. From what Troy could tell, the front door was the only way out of the little house, unless there was an exit from the bedroom. He sure hoped there wasn't.

"Please." He smiled at her, trying to put her at ease.

Laurel twisted her fingers together, her breathing still heavy. "My name is Laurel Oliver."

"Laurel, you just said you were born in Siberia. You and I both know Laurel Oliver isn't a Siberian name, don't we? And according to the records we found, Laurel Oliver was born in New York City. Now, you can't be from Siberia *and* New York City. Would you please clarify for us?"

She released a heavy breath and nodded. "Yes. My name is Dafna Orlov, and I was born in Siberia, not New York City. I had those records faked. I did not want to be Dafna Orlov from Russia anymore. I wanted to put that life behind me and start over."

Laurel paused and a faint smile lifted the corners of her full lips. "In Russian, Dafna means Laurel. My mother loves the delicate leaves of the laurel bush. You may know them better as bay leaves. They're used in cooking. My mother is a wonderful cook."

"It's a beautiful name in both languages." Bryce's voice was soft.

Troy glanced at his partner with a raised eyebrow. With that kind of comment, he wasn't helping.

"Where did you immigrate to when you came from Siberia?" Troy prepared to jot the information in his notepad.

"We immigrated here, to Fairbanks. Then when I became a US citizen, I moved to New York City and changed my name."

"Then why did you come back to Alaska?" Troy eyed her closely.

She gazed at Troy with her chin held a tad higher. "My family needed me."

"I see. Laurel, getting back to the champagne glasses, yours were the only other fingerprints on them. You put the cyanide in the champagne, didn't you?"

Laurel merely looked away and said nothing.

"Why do you want the senator dead? Did someone hire you to kill him, or did you do it on your own? For what purpose?"

Laurel refused to answer any more questions. She clamped her lips together and sat with her arms crossed over her chest.

"Very well." Troy reached beneath his parka and pulled a pair of handcuffs from his utility belt and stood. "Laurel Oliver, a.k.a. Dafna Orlov, you're under arrest for the attempted murder of Sen. Bradford Scott and his wife, Miriam Scott."

A wounded expression settled on her face as she looked first at Troy then at Bryce. She dropped her gaze to the floor then stood, turning to allow Troy to place the cuffs on her wrists.

"You have the right to remain silent. Anything you say can be used against you...." Troy administered the Miranda warning to Laurel, but he didn't put the cuffs on immediately. "Do you understand what I just told you, Laurel? Do you understand that you have the right to have a lawyer present when you're questioned?"

"*Da*." She nodded, gazing at the floor.

"Get your coat on then I'll cuff you." Troy waited as she put on her parka, then he cuffed her hands behind her back.

"Do you have a key to the front door so we can lock up?" Bryce was the last one out the door.

"It's on the table by the little sofa." Laurel spoke over her shoulder as she trudged toward the park SUV.

Bryce looked to Troy for direction.

Troy nodded. "Grab it."

Bryce grabbed the key and locked the door behind him. They settled Laurel in the backseat of the SUV, seat belted her in, pulled up the cage barrier between the front and back seats and hit the road back to headquarters. The superintendent wanted to be in on any further questioning of Miss Laurel Oliver, a.k.a. Dafna Orlov.

~

"Hello?" Maggie dropped her computer and camera bags on the kitchen counter and placed her cell phone to her ear.

"Maggie? How's it going?"

It took Maggie a few seconds to recognize the voice. "Jud?"

His warm chuckle sounded across cyberspace. "So, you do remember me?"

"Well, of course I do. You gave me a memorable plane ride."

"Hmmm. Thanks. I think. Was that all that was memorable? A guy kind of hopes a girl might remember him as well." He cajoled with a chuckle.

Maggie released a soft laugh. "Yes, I must admit, you left a pretty good impression as well, Jud. You were a great guide that day, and your knowledge of the park was amazing."

"Well, that's not exactly what I was talking about, but I guess it's a good starting point. I'll take it." He chuckled again.

"What can I do for you, Jud? Surely you didn't call to work up a fan club." Maggie pulled off her parka, switching hands with the phone as she worked one arm out of a sleeve then the other. She hung it on the coat tree by the front door then untied her boots and kicked them off, plopping onto the couch.

"Hey that's not a bad idea, but no, that's not why I called. I thought perhaps dinner in Fairbanks would be a fun getaway for you. You know, get you out of the woods for a change."

Maggie thought for a second. A date? In Fairbanks? "That's a long way to drive, Jud?"

"Yeah, it is, but it just so happens, I have this little plane that cuts the time down by a lot. I could pick you up in Healy, fly you to Fairbanks for dinner and have you home by ten-thirty. What do you say?"

"I say it sounds intriguing. Where are you taking me?"

"There's a restaurant downtown called the Majestic. It's to die for."

"I hope you don't mean that literally," Maggie laughed. "I want to make it back home, and I still have a job to do."

"Funny lady, aren't you? How about Friday night?"

"Mmmm, I don't think so. I might be rushed. Something going on Friday." Maggie wasn't sure what time the dedication was or when it would be over. "How about Saturday night?"

"Saturday it is. I'll make the reservations for the Majestic and pick you up at the Healy airport at, say two-thirty. Then if there's anywhere you'd like to go shopping, I can run you around, and you can shop while you're in town before we go to dinner. Sound good?"

"Sure. I could use a little shopping time while I'm in Fairbanks. See you then."

Maggie hung up the cell phone and dropped it on the couch beside her. She wasn't sure why but she felt a niggle of apprehension bumping at her anticipation of this date. Was date even the right word? She shook her head. Then why was she feeling apprehensive? Could it be because of what Troy and Superintendent Wade had said the other day when they'd seen Jud and how they'd responded to his presence in the park? They'd been less than pleased. That's probably how Troy would react when he found out she was going out to dinner with Jud. Did he have to find out? Was it any of his business? No, it wasn't.

~

"Laurel, or Dafna," Superintendent Wade paced in front of the chair where Laurel sat, her hands no longer in handcuffs. He turned and motioned toward a man who sat at a table across the room. "You have been provided with a court appointed lawyer. Are you ready to answer questions?"

"*Da.*"

"Please answer in English, if you will."

"Yes." Her tone was snide, and the superintendent chose to ignore it for the moment.

"Thank you, Laurel." Wade shoved his glasses up onto his nose and clasped his hands together behind his back. "Are you related by blood to Ivan Evgenevich Orlov?"

Troy, who leaned against the wall across the room, watched Laurel for any signs of distress when the question was asked. He was rewarded with an immediate response.

Laurel's nose flared and her eyes turned red even as tears threatened. She swallowed hard and failed to answer immediately.

"Laurel, please answer the question." Wade's voice was gentle.

She dropped her gaze to her lap then closed her eyes as if attempting to compose herself.

"He was my brother." Her voice was barely audible. She lifted her head as tears streamed down her face. She made no attempt to wipe them away. It was as if she was unaware of their presence.

"Laurel, do you know how your brother was killed?"

She gave a slow nod.

"Do you know why he was trying to kill Senator Scott?"

"Laurel, you don't have to answer that question." Her lawyer spoke from the table across the room.

"Yes, I know why he wanted to kill him." Laurel wiped her tears with a bare hand and looked directly at the superintendent. The lawyer watched her with uncertainty, a tense expression lining his forehead.

"Will you tell me why, Laurel?" Superintendent Wade's question was soft in an attempt to encourage confidence.

The young blond wrapped her arms around her body in a defensive posture and looked at the superintendent with loathing. "You killed my brother, Ivan. Perhaps *you* didn't pull the trigger, but your people did it. I won't help you. Your senator must die. You can all die for all I care. What has been set in motion will continue. Your senator will die."

Wade propped his hands on his hips and turned to face Troy. His expression was haggard and bleak. Troy scrubbed a hand down his face as his heart sank. He felt like they'd just been shoved back to square one.

~

"What's your take on things, Troy?" Superintendent Wade dropped into his desk chair in his office as Troy shut the door and took a seat in front of the desk.

"Let me do some research on Ivan and Dafna, sir. Let me check out their immigration records and possible Russian connections. I've got a buddy at Ft. Wainwright. He owes me a favor or two. I'll see if he can help me out."

"You do that. Don't forget about the dedication tomorrow. Two o'clock sharp."

"Right. You know, with the senator here, there's been no time to take Maggie out for her wildlife photography." Troy stood and made his way toward the door.

"Has she said anything?"

"No, sir. She's had orders to photograph the senator's activities first. She's been a good sport about it."

A wide smile lit the superintendent's face. "You like her, don't you, Troy."

Troy shrugged. "What's not to like, sir? But that's as far as it goes. Like is a far cry from deeper emotions, and I've got no time for those."

Wade's smile gentled. "You may find as you grow older, Troy, that you'd enjoy having a companion by your side. Someone to sit with, to stroll with, to talk with, heck just to be with. Don't think that you don't have time for those deeper emotions. Just because you've been hurt doesn't mean you won't heal in time. Growing old alone can't be fun. I'm not saying Maggie Lawrence is the one for you, but I'm not saying she's not either. Just something to think about."

Troy wasn't sure what to say to that. The man was old enough to be his father and was a lot wiser than he was.

"Yes, sir. I'll give it some thought. Goodnight."

"Goodnight, Troy."

Chapter Ten

I t is my great honor to dedicate this monument to Harry Karstens, the first superintendent of Mt. McKinley National Park, as it was called in 1921."

Senator Bradford Scott reached over and tugged off the thin white fabric covering to reveal a bronze head and shoulder bust of Harry Karstens supported on a marble base. The invited guests clapped as they took in for the first time the sight of the monument. Senator Scott rolled up the fabric and handed it to a young uniformed park ranger standing close by waiting to take it away. He returned to the slim podium and gripped the sides lightly as the clapping subsided and the crowd awaited his next words.

"Harry Karstens was chosen for the job of superintendent because he was a man of Alaskan wilderness experience, honesty, indomitable courage and character. He would need all those things in the early years as the park was established. It wasn't welcomed among the locals who were used to hunting, mining and trapping whenever and wherever they chose."

Maggie snapped pictures as the senator spoke. She'd taken photos of the unveiling and several of the monument itself. She'd be sure to get some close-ups of the senator along with the current superintendent in front of the monument. She snapped another photo then released a sigh. Would these pictures of the senator's activities never end? She was eager to get on with her wildlife shots. So far, she had pictures of caribou. Nice. Caribou. True, she had some awesome shots of them, but she wanted something other than just caribou.

She was happy to see Calvin Jacobs in attendance. The senator's assistant sported his ever-present expression of stress along with a sling that supported his injured shoulder. Poor man.

He was in the wrong line of work if he was always so stressed. He would do better in a job with less stress. Something like a cotton candy vendor at carnivals or a ticket salesman at a movie theater. Assistant to a US senator was far too stressful for him. He was sure to have a heart attack one of these days.

Maggie sensed the presence of someone on her right and glanced over to find Troy standing beside her. He glanced down and grinned.

"Hi." His whispered word sent a thrill down her spine.

"Hi back. You're late, and you're not even from New York," she whispered back.

He released a huff of air indicating a quiet chuckle as he covered his mouth with his hand.

"I'll turn the program back over to Superintendent Wade. Thank you for coming." Senator Scott moved to a chair behind the podium as the superintendent made his way forward.

"Thank you, Senator. We appreciate your willingness to be here and to dedicate this monument to the first superintendent of Denali National Park."

The collected crowd clapped just before they began to disperse.

"I'd say I got here just in time." Troy whispered behind his hand.

"Yeah, you missed pretty much the whole program." Maggie leaned close to his shoulder. His woodsy aftershave drifted her way. Mmmm, nice. She straightened. "Gotta go take pictures."

She *had* to escape his heady presence, was more like it. Okay, so she was using her responsibility as photographer to do that. So what? She couldn't afford to let him into her heart. *Help me be strong, Lord. I only have a few weeks then I'm gone. No need to allow myself to think something could grow between Troy and me. Right? Besides, he's never given me any indication he's interested in me. Then why am I struggling with my emotions where he's concerned? Are you listening, Lord?*

While she directed the senator and the superintendent to stand beside the new monument and pose shaking hands, Maggie's heart was heavy. She knew He was listening and had heard her prayer, but she got the impression the Lord was silent. She would just have to concentrate on her photographs. If the Lord wasn't answering, best to err on the side of caution.

~

Maggie hit the send button and shut down her laptop, laying it on the coffee table. It always felt good when she did that. When a job was completed, and Mr. Radford had all of her project photos then she could breathe a sigh of relief. The dedication photos would be in all the major newspapers in the lower forty-eight just as the banquet photos had been. She had only briefly met the reporter who had come up to write the stories. It didn't matter. The reporters didn't generally interact with her much. They had their job to do and she had hers.

It was time to relax a little. Maggie reached for the TV remote and pulled the afghan down over her. Between the gas fire and the afghan, it was cozy in the little cabin living room. Flipping through the channels, she found an old comedy movie she could lose herself in for a while, and she settled back against the sofa pillows.

She was engrossed in the movie when a sound at the front door made her jump. The hair stood up on the back of her neck. What in the world could that have been? She tossed off the afghan and stood slowly, looking around for something to take to the door with her as a weapon. On one side of the fireplace were a poker and a shovel on a stand. It was purely for looks considering it was a gas fire, but they would make great defensive weapons. Maggie reached for the poker and hurried to the front door. She flipped on the outside porch light and pulled the curtain back enough to see out. There was no one in sight. Were they out there in the darkness somewhere watching?

Maggie glanced around to see what could've made the noise, and as her gaze roamed over the lit porch, she spotted a piece of paper held down by a rock. She gasped as the feeling of ice flowed through her veins. There on the paper in bold block letters were the words "Go Home."

~

"They found what?" Troy spoke into his cell phone. He sat at his desk in the kennel office.

"The other gun, Troy." The superintendent's voice crossed through cyberspace. "Park police found a Ruger 9 mm handgun suspected to be used the night of the dinner at the Denali

Wilderness Lodge and fired at the senator. It's been dusted for fingerprints, and it and the prints have been sent to Fairbanks for analysis."

"Where did they find it?"

"In a dumpster behind the snack bar near the visitor center inside the park. One of the kitchen workers was getting ready to drop a bag of trash in. He opened the lid and spotted the handle sticking up between two other bags. Apparently when the perpetrator threw it in after the dinner, he thought he'd dropped it in far enough. Unlucky for him or her. Lucky for us."

"I'm surprised it hasn't been covered over already by other bags." Troy leaned back in his chair and ran a hand down his face.

"As am I. A couple other bags were thrown in, but they missed it somehow."

"I think Maggie and my mother would call it a God thing." Troy chuckled.

"Well, don't discount it, my boy. Who knows?"

Troy shook his head. Why did he have to bring up that topic?

Superintendent Wade continued. "Now we'll wait to hear back about that evidence. We'll see if either Ivan or Laurel, a.k.a. Dafna, were behind the trigger."

Troy sat forward, leaning his arm and elbow on the desk. "Sir, the night of the dinner after the shooting, I spotted Laurel peeking out from behind the drapes at the back corner of the room, then she disappeared behind them. I took off after her but couldn't find her. The area back there had a hallway that ended in another hallway that led to an exit. There were no park police covering that exit. If she was the shooter, it was easy for her to get away."

The superintendent released a heavy sigh. "I understand what you're saying, Troy, but we only have so many park police officers and they were spread pretty thin for that event. It's hard to cover everything. I'm not making excuses, just stating facts."

"I understand, sir."

"I'll look into the situation and see if anyone was supposed to be guarding that exit."

"Thank you, sir. It's quite possible her reason for being there was to kill the senator and no other reason."

"That very well could be, Troy, but we need more evidence than the fingerprints on the champagne glasses. Someone with rubber gloves could have poisoned the champagne while hers were there only because she was serving it to them."

"Yes, sir. I know." Troy released a heavy breath. "Let's hope this gun delivers the evidence we need."

~

Maggie parked her car in the small gravel area near the runway at the Healy airport. She was used to airports having at least a small control tower or pilot-controlled runway lights when there was no tower. Here there were neither. The runway was paved and that was it. A pay-at-the-pump airplane fuel pump sat in a small tin-roofed shelter near the taxiway. A couple small planes were tied down with wheel covers. Other than that, there was nothing except snow covering the vegetation around the edges of the runway.

Maggie sat in her little SUV until she spotted Jud's plane coming in for a landing. Once he'd touched down, he came around to the plane parking area but left the plane running and waved at Maggie. She'd stepped out of her car and locked it as she'd watched him approach. Stepping carefully around icy spots on the pavement, she made her way to the patriotic Cessna and moved beneath the wing, climbing into the passenger seat and shutting the door behind her.

Jud handed her a set of headphones and motioned for her to put them on. She adjusted the earpieces then the microphone and turned a smile on him.

"Hi, Jud."

"Hi back. Ready for an adventure?" He flashed his Hollywood smile in her direction and gave her a wink.

Maggie chuckled as she snapped her seatbelt in place and settled into her seat. "Sure am. Let's go."

As Jud taxied the little plane back out to the runway, Maggie wondered why his wink did nothing to her insides like Troy's did. His flashy smile failed to send tingles down her spine or make her weak kneed like Troy's. Why? What was the difference? Jud was a handsome guy, and he had a plane that was fun to explore with. Big deal. Troy was handsome and far more reserved. One might say he was standoffish. Then there was his dog sled team. A girl could get up close and personal to nature to snap photos of them, and it was a lot of fun. You got the magnificent, big picture from the airplane but you missed all the closeup neat things you could see from the seat of a sled. Maggie supposed both had their advantages.

"Where do you want to go shopping first when we get to Fairbanks?" Jud's voice in her ears brought her attention back to him as the little plane lifted off the ground.

"I need to go to a department store to pick up a few things." Maggie looked out her window, thrilling at the sight of the earth falling away as they climbed higher. She reached into her camera bag. Never miss an opportunity to catch a great shot was her motto. You just never knew when "the award winning" shot would be around the corner or out the window.

"You're always prepared, aren't you?" Jud laughed.

"Of course. What great photographer isn't?" Maggie snapped a few shots out the side window.

"How did your photos of the park turn out from our tour on the day you arrived?" Jud tilted the plane a bit, adjusting their direction northeast toward Fairbanks then straightened it out. "Get any great shots that day?"

"I sure did. You may remember Mt. McKinley, or Mt. Denali, as some people prefer to call it, was visible and beautiful that day. I got some gorgeous, clear shots. The colors were vivid and bright." The picture of the strange man-made object at the base of the glacier came to mind. Should she ask Jud about it? She'd planned to do some research on her own before involving anyone else. She'd already asked Troy and Police Chief Patuk about it and they didn't know anything. She decided to keep it to herself for now.

Maggie turned the conversation around to Jud's flight-seeing business and how he delivered supplies to the remote areas of Alaska during the winter months. There wasn't much call for flight-seeing tours in the dead of winter. Only occasionally. Within a short time, Jud was calling to the control tower at Fairbanks International Airport requesting permission to land at the small regional airport. He received permission and soon was on the path to land on the small paved runway. Minutes later their wheels touched down and they rolled nearly to the end where they turned and continued on to park at Svenson's Bush Plane Service. Rather than park in the hanger, Jud parked on the paved area in front of the building.

He cut the engines and removed his headphones. Maggie followed his lead. "Stay in the plane for a couple minutes, will you?"

"Okay, if you say so." She shrugged her shoulders.

"I have to chock the wheels and put a heater on the engine. It's -25° out there, but it'll be -35° by the time we get back this evening. We want it to start later, don't we?" He grinned and reached for the door handle.

"Uh, yeah, we do. I'll sit tight."

A few minutes later, Jud returned and opened Maggie's door. He took her hand and helped her step down from the plane. She tugged her parka hood up against the bitter wind that was blowing, then gathered her shoulder bag and camera bag from the plane. Jud led her to a 4x4 SUV parked in front of the building. He opened Maggie's door and helped her inside, then walked to the front of his vehicle and unplugged the extension cord keeping his SUV block heater warm. Jud walked around and climbed in, starting the SUV. It started right up.

"I guess no one would go anywhere in Alaska without those block heaters." Maggie pushed her hood back and ran a hand through her long hair. She had no idea how fancy the Majestic was going to be, but she'd decided to simply curl her hair and leave it down. Parka hoods were a necessity in Alaska this time of year and it made it hard to wear an updo. She'd nearly frozen the other night at the senator's dinner when she'd sported one. She wasn't going all out tonight. A trip to the restroom at the restaurant would suffice to make repairs.

"Oh yeah. A simple fix for a huge problem." Jud turned the SUV out of the airport and headed into town. "Now to get you to a department store. I know just what you need. We have one where you can buy pretty much anything except a car."

"Sounds good. Let's go shopping."

~

"Paul, how are you doing, buddy? I hope I'm not interrupting your weekend too much." Troy leaned back in the office chair at his desk in his small home office, his cell phone to his ear.

"Troy? Hey. What are you up to?" Paul Mitchell's deep voice came through cyberspace. "It's been a while since I've heard from you. If I know you, you're staying out in the backcountry with those dog sled teams of yours."

"Well, we do keep them working. They love pulling, you know."

"Yeah, I do, but I think you love it as much as they do."

"What can I say?"

"Well, you can start by telling me why you called. I know it's not because you wanted to talk about your dog teams." Paul chuckled. "What's up, Troy? What's going on?"

Paul always could see right through to the meat of a problem before Troy could even explain it. "I need your help."

"Well, I already knew that. What do you need?"

Troy heaved a sigh and explained the situation concerning the senator, the shooting and the attempted poisoning the night of the dinner, the dog sledding expedition and the second attempted shooting of the senator. He went on to tell Paul about the death of the shooter, Ivan Orlov and then about the arrest of his sister Dafna Orlov, alias Laurel Oliver.

"Wow, things been a little boring for you, Troy? Not enough excitement in your neck of the woods?" Incredulity crept into Paul's voice.

"Well, you know how it gets during the winter. We needed to liven things up a bit." Troy answered with a dry note to his response. "Anyway, what I'd like from you is if you could do some checking on these two for me. We know Ivan immigrated to the US in 2014. The only information we have on Dafna is that she was born in New York City in 1985 under the name Laurel Oliver. Then she told us she immigrated to the US from Russia in 2014 under the name Dafna Orlov. She claims she's the sister of Ivan Orlov. I'm sure you can retrieve that information quicker than we can. The Army shared Ivan's death certificate with us because he died in the park and because we're doing an investigation of our own. We're also running an investigation of Dafna, but so far, we've not been able to find as much on her. Can you help me, Paul?"

Silence met his question for a few seconds. Just as he was beginning to think he'd lost the connection, Paul spoke.

"Yeah, I can do that. If I run into anything marked classified in any way, you know I can't share that without special permission and that's a real hassle. You know the drill."

Troy ran a hand through his hair. "Yeah, I know the drill. Thanks, Paul. Anything you can help with is much appreciated."

"I know. I'll do my best, Troy. Give me those names again."

Troy repeated them for Paul then they hung up. Troy leaned forward and shut down his computer. He'd already attempted to do his own research on the brother and sister from Russia but had come up empty handed.

He started to push his chair back then glanced at his wristwatch. It was still early. He, Jeremy and his mom were planning to watch a movie and eat snacks shortly. Why not invite Maggie to join them? He could even say Jeremy would love for her to come. Which would, of course, be the case because his son thought the world of Maggie. Before he lost his nerve, Troy clicked on her number in his phone. It rang three times before she answered.

"Hello?" Her sweet voice came through loud and clear causing his heartbeat to pick up.

"Maggie?" He had to clear his throat and repeat himself. "Maggie?"

"Troy? Is that you?"

"Uh, yeah, it's me." He heard noises in the background. Was she with other people? "Um, where are you? I hear other people?"

"Yes, there are other people here. I'm actually shopping in a department store in Fairbanks so you're hearing the other shoppers."

Fairbanks? She drove to Fairbanks? "You drove up to Fairbanks to shop?"

"Um, well, no not exactly. Jud flew down and brought me up here. I needed to get some things and he offered."

Jud Svenson flew her to Fairbanks? The movie and snack's invitation were long forgotten as unpleasant emotions filled Troy.

"I see. Well, have fun."

He lowered the phone to click the end call button and heard Maggie say, "But, Troy, why did you call?"

Clicking the button, Troy sat for a few moments, varied emotions swirling through him. Why had he called? All along he'd known he wasn't going to get involved with someone who wouldn't be staying in Alaska. He didn't have time for a woman in his life. He didn't want the heartache that brought with it. The superintendent's words returned to him. Would he end up at the end of his days old and alone? Maggie was a beautiful woman with a beautiful character and a beautiful love for God.

But Jud Svenson? Oh, Maggie, no. Not him. He would only bring heartache and disappointment.

"Dad?" Jeremy stood leaning against the office door frame. "Are you coming to watch the movie? Grandma's done in the kitchen and says she's ready when you are. She's got the snacks ready."

The expression on his eager face tugged at Troy's lips until he felt a grin form. Standing from his chair, he hurried over to the doorway, grabbed his son up into his arms and tickled him.

"Is she now? Well, we'll just have to see about that, won't we?" He tossed him over his shoulder, sending Jeremy into a peel of giggles. Troy reached up and tickled him again. "What was that you said? I didn't hear that?"

They laughed and giggled their way to the living room as Clarissa brought in a tray of soft drinks and snacks. Saturday movie night at the Donovan house was about to begin.

Chapter Eleven

Your expression says that wasn't a pleasant call." Jud pushed the cart for Maggie as she dropped her phone back into her purse.

She cast him a slight smile that faded as she shook her head. "It was Troy. He called then when he found out I was here in Fairbanks, he just hung up and never said why he called."

Jud gave a snort and turned the cart down another aisle. "It's more likely he wasn't happy when he found out who you were with."

"Why is that, Jud? What's the dislike between you two? It doesn't seem all one way?"

Jud leaned his arms on the cart handle and shrugged. "Perhaps not. Several years ago, I got in trouble with the park and he hasn't liked me since. Holds it against me. He tarred me with the brush of distrust and thinks I'm still that same person. He won't even give me the benefit of the doubt that I may have changed and turned my life around."

"Have you?" Maggie stopped the cart with a hand on the side and gazed at him. "Turned your life around, I mean?"

"Of course, I have." Jud stood straight again, returning her gaze. "What I did was a long time ago, long before I started my business. I keep my nose clean and mind my own. I haven't done anything against the park or anyone else since then. He's got nothing on me."

"You may have to prove that to him, you know."

"I don't have to prove myself to anyone, honey. I don't care what Troy Donovan thinks of me. I'm making my way in northern Alaska and there's plenty of folks who know and trust my business. Troy Donovan can go pound salt for all I care." A snarky smile crossed his handsome features. "My advice to you, sweetheart, is to stay as far from him as you can. He's a real loser. If you need help with your photos, I can find you a dog sled guide to take you into the park."

"I didn't think other dog sled teams were allowed into the park other than the ranger teams." Maggie tilted her head and narrowed her gaze at Jud.

He narrowed his own back at her. "Not technically. It can be worked around. I guarantee it."

Maggie wasn't about to risk such a thing. "Thanks. I'll keep it in mind."

She glanced into the cart. "I think that's all I need, but shopping has given me an appetite. When's our reservation?"

Jud glanced at his watch. "Let's get checked out and head downtown. By the time we get there it'll be about time."

~

Maggie watched as Jud's plane lifted off the ground and flew away into the darkness of the Alaskcan night. As she stood watching the lights of the plane disappear, a flicker of green moved across the sky. What? She strained to see if she could spot it again. Yes, there it was. Another flicker, then a longer one. Why, it was the aurora borealis. She grabbed her camera out of her bag and set it up on her tripod that was strapped to her bag. She set the settings to record and aimed it at the night sky.

Oh my...Lord, this is beautiful.

A ribbon of green shot across the night sky, the stars twinkling through the transparent color. It was soon joined by a lavender ribbon that turned to magenta and a silent dance of the duel colors began. Green and magenta ribbons intermingled and danced across the heavens delighting Maggie and filling her with awe.

Abba, Father, You paint such beauty in the heavens. I can't wait to see the heavens where You are. They must be something to behold. One day....

Maggie watched for a while then turned off the camera, packing it all up and walking to her car. God had allowed her to view something special this evening. She drove home filled with a sense of awe, peace and contentment.

As she approached her cabin, every bit of it fled, however, as she spotted the front door standing wide open, all the lights on in every room. Her heart froze in her chest. Was someone still in there? She didn't see any movement. Maggie backed her SUV down the driveway and pulled to the side where she could watch the cabin from a distance. Pulling out her phone, she called the first person who came to mind.

"Hello?"

"Troy? It's happened again."

"Maggie? What happened again?" He almost barked into the phone.

"Someone broke into my cabin. The front door is standing wide open and all the lights are on this time."

"Whatever you do, do not go inside. I'll be right there."

"I've backed away from the cabin, pulled over to the side of the road and turned off my lights. Although I haven't seen any movement, I can't tell if anyone's in there."

"Stay put. I'll call Garrick Patuk." The line went dead.

Maggie turned up the car's heater and hung onto the phone like a lifeline, her eyes on the cabin. She saw no movement against the lighted windows. There was no vehicle there, so perhaps whoever had broken in had already gone. Nausea swirled in Maggie's middle region. They would have to go in and most likely will find the place torn apart again. They'd find her things scattered and touched by an unknown assailant. She was sick and tired of this. Then a thought struck her, and the nausea grew.

She'd left her laptop in the cabin when she'd flown off to Fairbanks.

~

Troy pulled up next to Maggie's SUV and rolled down his window. She did the same. Her face was pal,e and she looked ill.

"Are you alright?" He leaned out and spoke in a low voice. Another vehicle pulled up behind him with only parking lights on.

"I left my laptop in the cabin when I went to Fairbanks this afternoon." Maggie was shaking. "I have a horrible feeling about this, Troy."

"Stay here while Garrick and I check things out. You'll have the opportunity to find out more when we know it's safe."

Maggie gave a slight nod and rolled her window up.

She wasn't the only one with a bad feeling. With his headlights off, Troy parked away from the cabin, followed by

Garrick Patuk. With sidearms drawn, they made their way silently toward the cabin. Troy climbed up onto the front porch while Garrick went around to the back entrance. They cleared the small building, finding no one inside. Troy hurried out to signal for Maggie to come. He waited as she drove her SUV up to the parking area and plugged her car in then followed her inside to find the same horrid destruction as the first break-in.

Troy closed the front door behind her as she sat down on a kitchen chair and stared at the freezing cold, dismantled room.

"Would you like to look around and tell me if anything is missing, Miss Lawrence?" Garrick Patuk stood nearby, hands on his hips, concern stamped on his features.

"I don't have to look far to tell you that." Defeat covered Maggie like a blanket and it tore at Troy. He wanted more than anything to tug her into a hug and comfort her.

"What's missing?" Chief Patuk pulled out his notepad and pen.

"My laptop." Maggie's words were little more than a whisper. "When I saw the door open and the lights on, I knew it would be. I felt sick."

Troy knelt beside her chair and took her gloved hands in his. "Are all of your pictures gone?"

"No, I still have them all on my camera, but just knowing that someone else has them, too, makes me ill. They're personal. It makes me feel…well, violated."

Maggie turned and met Troy's troubled gaze. "This is the second time they've broken into my home. Two separate ones. They've been following me to know where I live. Do you think my laptop is what they were after when they broke in?"

Troy glanced up at Chief Patuk who shrugged. "It stands to reason they've been looking for something and the fact they took it, it could be."

"Miss Lawrence, take a look around and see if anything else is missing." Chief Patuk dropped his notepad into his pocket.

Maggie nodded and began walking through the mess in each room.

"Where was the laptop when you left?" Troy followed her as she searched.

"It was in a laptop bag by the couch. That's how I knew so quickly that it was gone."

"Then why all this destruction?" Troy waved an all-inclusive arm as he looked around the room.

"Unless they were looking for something else." Chief Patuk planted his hands on his hips. "Can you think of anything else of importance they could've been looking for, Miss Lawrence?"

"Nothing other than my camera, and I had that with me when I was in Fairbanks this evening."

"Thank goodness you did." Troy wasn't happy Maggie had gone to Fairbanks with Jud, but what if she'd been home when the thieves had come calling? Then a thought niggled in his brain. What if Maggie was taken to Fairbanks to get her out of her cabin so the thieves could do their dirty work without her stumbling on them? Could Jud Svenson be in on it? For what purpose? What did she have on her computer that would be of interest to the thieves? Or to Jud, for that matter? Was he assuming too much?

"Well, you can't stay here tonight, and I'm not sure the rental agency is going to have another rental they can get you into this quickly." Chief Patuk glanced around the room and released a heavy breath.

"It's alright, Garrick. She can come home with me. Mom will be tickled pink to have her, and she'll get her settled in a room at our house until something can be figured out."

Maggie turned to stare at Troy, her cheeks taking on a pink tinge. "That's thoughtful of you, but I wouldn't want to be any trouble."

"Have you met my mom?" Troy lifted an eyebrow in question then winked. "You won't be any trouble."

Garrick chuckled. "Clarissa Donovan doesn't know the word trouble. Look, I'll call the rental company in the morning. I'll have to let them know about the break-in. I'll see what they have, if anything. Then we'll go from there."

Maggie nodded. "I guess I'll grab a few things."

She eyed her clothes scattered across the floor and hesitated.

Troy's heart lurched. He felt for this woman. No longer did these break-ins seem random. She was being targeted, but why? And by whom?

"Maggie," Troy's voice was soft, "just gather enough for a few days then maybe we can come back and take care of the rest. Maybe mom can help you wash everything before you wear them. That would probably make you feel better."

Maggie's gaze met his. "That would be nice. Thanks."

She grabbed a couple reusable shopping bags from the kitchen and tossed some clothes in, enough to get her through a few days. Then she gathered her toiletries from the bathroom floor and sink and put them in her toiletries bag.

"I think I'm ready." Chief Patuk turned out all the lights and closed the front door. He placed crime scene tape across the doorframe and across the front porch.

"Hopefully that'll keep everyone out." He waved at Maggie and Troy as they headed to their vehicles. "I'll be in touch."

Maggie followed Troy to his house and parked next to his pickup truck. She climbed out of her SUV and gathered her bags, purse and camera bag.

Troy came around and held out a hand. "Here, let me help with that."

"Thanks." Maggie gave him the bags of clothes and the toiletries bag. "Are you sure your mom won't mind me camping out here tonight?"

"Are you kidding?" Troy led the way up the back steps to the kitchen door. "She adores company. The more the merrier."

Troy turned and stopped suddenly before opening the door. Not expecting it, Maggie ran right into him bumping into his broad chest. Troy dropped the bags to the porch and caught her arms to steady her.

"Umph. Oh, I…uh…I…I'm sorry." Maggie stepped back a pace, her gaze anywhere but on Troy.

"Oh no, it's…it's my fault." Troy's hands still held onto Maggie's arms. "I just remembered you'd done some shopping in Fairbanks. Do you have anything that needs to go into the fridge or freezer? Something that'll go bad if you don't store it properly?"

"Oh." Maggie looked as if she couldn't think straight. With her this close, Troy was having the same problem. His gaze wandered over her gorgeous features and settled on her lips. She was so close. His heart was beating triple-time. If he only leaned closer…

"Milk. I have milk, cheese and ham."

"What?" Troy couldn't comprehend what she was talking about. Milk, cheese and ham? Oh, wait. Fridge food. He'd asked her what she had to go in the fridge. Idiot. He swallowed hard, took a deep breath and stepped back, releasing her arms. "Right. Milk, cheese and ham."

The kitchen door flew open and Clarissa Donovan turned on the backporch light. "Maggie, sweetie. Please come on in. Troy called and told me what happened. You are more than welcome to stay as long as you need to."

Troy opened the screen door and handed his mother the bags of clothes. "Here are some of Maggie's things, Mom. She can explain more about what happened. Maggie, hand me your keys and I'll bring in all of your groceries. We don't want any of them freezing in the car overnight."

The women went inside, and Troy escaped to Maggie's car. He breathed in a lungful of cold air. He'd almost kissed Maggie. What in the world was he thinking? He'd almost succumbed to a moment of weakness. Weakness or madness? Did it matter? He couldn't afford to succumb to either. Maggie was beautiful, and Maggie was sweet, but Maggie was not for him.

~

The man handed Pavel the laptop and he in turn handed the man the roll of cash. Without a word, the man scurried away, disappearing into the darkness of the alley. Pavel glanced around as he hurried to his car. It wouldn't do to get mugged and have the laptop stolen after just acquiring it. He'd paid a lot of money to have it stolen and brought to him. There was no guarantee there was anything on it, but he was almost certain there had to be.

Pavel slid into the driver's seat of his car and laid the laptop on the passenger seat, locking the car doors. This wasn't the best part of town. Truth be told, it was the worst.

The engine turned over and he slipped it into gear. He wouldn't speed though. It wouldn't do to get pulled over. His cell phone rang in the drink holder of the center console. Grabbing it, Pavel pushed the answer call button and held it to his ear.

"*Da?*"

"Well?"

"I have the woman's laptop, and I'm on my way home. Hopefully there will be something there to see."

"I hope so too. Call me when you find something." The phone clicked and General Kozlov was gone.

Pavel was tired of his demands. He was doing this job the best he could because he was the best.

~

Maggie pulled back the curtains in her borrowed bedroom early Sunday morning. The sun wasn't up yet. Of course not. This was still winter in Alaska, she chuckled to herself. She'd noticed a change, though, in how each day grew a little longer. It was more noticeable here than back home.

Dressed in a pair of jeans and an over-sized, long-sleeve Henley, she slipped on a pair of moccasins and made her way to the kitchen. She smelled coffee brewing. Mmmm. Someone else had the same priority she did.

Meeooowww. Michael met her at the kitchen doorway and wound his furry body around her legs, rubbing his head against her in an affectionate way.

"Well, good morning, Mr. Jordan." Maggie bent down to rub his head and the cat purred with pleasure, leaning into her hand. "And how are you this cold morning?"

"I do believe you've made a friend." Clarissa stood over the large stove. "Michael Jordan chooses his friends with discretion. I'd say you've made the cut, though. You should feel honored. Not everyone does."

Clarissa chuckled and Maggie joined her. "I suppose I do. Think he'll allow me to pick him up?"

"You can try, then you'll find out."

Maggie reached down and picked up the orange tabby. He settled into her arms as his purr grew louder.

"Well, there's your answer." Clarissa reached for the coffee pot. "Coffee?"

"Oh, yes please."

"I'll pour it then you can fix it the way you want it."

As Maggie used one hand to prepare her coffee, she asked, "So how did Michael Jordan get his name? He's a long way from the University of North Carolina. A lot of people may not know that the real Michael Jordan went to UNC and played college basketball before he ever made it to the Chicago Bulls. He's a North Carolina legend."

"Don't I know it." Clarissa palpitated her hand over her heart. "I'm one of his biggest fans. But I'm surprised Troy didn't tell you. He went to UNC. That's where he received his degree in wildlife conservation and biology."

Maggie dropped the spoon she'd been stirring her coffee with onto the counter, the sound a loud clatter. She placed her hand over it to still the noise.

She stared at Clarissa who was preparing pancakes. She hadn't even looked up at the racket Maggie had made.

"Um no, he never mentioned that." Maggie attempted to keep the tone of her voice light rather than shocked. He'd failed to mention that on purpose was more like it. She'd told him her father was a professor there. Had he been one of his students? There were other history professors, so there was a chance he hadn't been, but he could've mentioned he'd attended the university. Why hadn't he? Emotions swirled within Maggie and she had trouble pinning down a single one. Disappointment? Anger? No maybe not quite anger. Certainly disappointment. Hurt? Yeah. Hurt gnawed at her as it sank in that he hadn't opened up to her like she had to him. Of course, after she'd opened up to him about her human trafficking experience, she'd been humiliated that she had. She'd even wanted him to forget all about it.

"Hmm. That is strange." Clarissa started stacking pancakes on a plate. "Must've slipped his mind. Or it could have something to do with the fact his wife was from North Carolina. Oh well. I've probably said too much, sweetie. Pancakes are ready. Make yourself at home at the table while I call Troy and Jeremy. Jeremy and I attend church on Sunday mornings. You're welcome to go with us if you like."

She placed the plate of pancakes on the table and Maggie set Michael on the floor.

Maggie strove for a light tone as she shoved the shock of Clarissa's information about Troy to the back of her mind. She'd have to deal with it later. The subject of it would appear in a minute. "I'd love to. I attend church at home, but I don't really know where to attend here."

"Then come with us. We have a wonderful church." Clarissa stepped out into the hallway by the stairs and called, "Troy! Jeremy! Breakfast is ready!"

~

Troy ducked as he came through the kitchen door with a giggling Jeremy sitting on his shoulders. He spotted Maggie sitting at the kitchen table, a cup of coffee between her hands, a thoughtful expression on her gorgeous features. He walked over to his mother and he and Jeremy both planted kisses on her cheek.

"Morning, Mom."

"Morning, Grandma."

"Good morning, my favorite guys. Get to the table before the pancakes get cold." Clarissa set the coffee pot on the table along with the creamer and sugar bowl.

"Good morning, Maggie." Troy set Jeremy in his seat and took his own. "I hope you slept well."

She nodded but didn't meet his gaze. "Yes, I did, thank you."

Clarissa prayed over the food then passed the pancakes around.

Maggie took a swig of her still steaming coffee and returned it to the table, accepting the plate of pancakes as it was passed to her.

Troy observed Maggie from the corner of his eye. Something wasn't right with her this morning. What in the world had happened?

"Have you heard from Garrick this morning, Maggie?" He stuffed a bite of pancake in his mouth.

She shook her head. "No."

He waited for something to follow but she said nothing more. He sucked in a deep breath. Yep, something was wrong. She hadn't even looked at him when she'd answered with that one-word reply.

"Maggie will be attending church with us this morning, son." Clarissa reached for the coffee pot to top off her cup. "She said she hasn't been able to find a good church to attend since she's been here. I think she'll like ours. I've put an elk pot roast in the crockpot for dinner. You won't have to worry about fixing anything while we're gone."

Troy glanced between his mother and Maggie, who still kept her gaze on her plate. She shoved a piece of pancake around and through the syrup on her plate, only occasionally taking a bite.

"That sounds good, Mom. Maybe I'll go with you this morning." Troy couldn't believe those words had slipped from his lips. What made him say them? Was it the woman sitting next to him? Was it the superintendent's little talk the other day? Was it time to re-evaluate his life and take a closer look at things? Did that mean the spiritual aspect of his life as well? He wasn't so sure about that part, but he didn't think that a visit to church once would hurt too much.

Jeremy jumped up and down in his seat. "Yay, Dad! You're going to church with us. Yay!"

Troy felt a grin lift the corners of his lips.

"That makes your old mom happy, son. I think I'll have another pancake. How about you, Jeremy?"

Troy's gaze shifted to Maggie and found hers on him. She gave a slight nod then dropped it back to her plate. She stabbed a bite of pancake and ate it.

He had the funny feeling he'd done something wrong but had no idea what. However, he had every intention of finding out.

Chapter Twelve

Ludmila waited as the uniformed corrections officer unlocked and opened the door to the visitation room. He led her to a seat in front of a half wall of glass with stools in front of it.

"You'll only have a few minutes to talk, ma'am. I'll let you know when your time is up." He spoke in kind tones to her.

Ludmila nodded. "Thank you, sir."

"She'll be out in a few minutes. Just have a seat and wait here."

The officer left the room and closed the door behind him. There were no other visitors waiting, so Ludmila glanced around the room spotting cameras in every corner. They made her uncomfortable, but she reminded herself she had nothing to be uncomfortable about. In the mother country there had been eyes everywhere. At a moment's notice you could be hauled off to a *gulag* for nothing more than looking cross. Here in America, she'd done nothing except try hard to be a model citizen. Too bad she couldn't say the same for her children. She'd tried to teach them the importance of being good American citizens. It's what their father had wanted for them and that's why he'd done what he'd done.

The door in the next room clicked open and she turned to see Dafna walk in. Her beautiful daughter Dafna, who had changed her name to Laurel, was wearing a bright orange coverall, her hands shackled as well as her feet. They were attached to chains that led to a chain around her waist. Her beautiful long blond hair was pulled back into a ponytail, her face washed clean from all makeup. She was more beautiful without the makeup she'd always worn.

Another uniformed corrections officer led Dafna to the seat at the window across from Ludmila. Dafna gave a faint smile to her mother before allowing it to slip from her features. She reached for the phone handset and placed it to her ear, then pointed at the one on her mother's side.

Ludmila picked up the handset and copied what Dafna did.

"*Mamochka*, it's good to see you." Dafna spoke in soft Russian.

Tears filled Ludmila's eyes and spilled down her cheeks. She shook her head, her own Russian spilling out from a broken heart. "It's always good to see you, my darling Dafna, but not like this. Never like this. And my Ivan is gone. He is dead. Why did you both have to seek revenge? Why couldn't you just let it go?"

"He let Father die, Mama. That man, that senator let him die. He didn't rescue him. He could have continued the search and rescued him, but he did not."

"No, my Dafna. Your father chose his path and died trying to walk it. Senator Scott had nothing to do with the death of your father. He tried to rescue him. He tried. Don't you see?"

"No, Mama. You're wrong. That's not what the KGB records state." Tears ran down Dafna's cheeks now. "They were going to make him a state leader and the American's let him die."

"Dafna, you cannot trust what the KGB records said, no matter that they were public records. Believe what I tell you because it's what your father told me. He had a plan to bring his family to America to give them freedom."

Dafna sneered. "Well, Mama, we all made it, didn't we? But whatever Father's plans were, they didn't work out the way he wanted. Now he and Ivan are both dead, and I'm going to prison. You will be all alone. Then what?"

Ludmila shook her head as tears streamed down her cheeks. "If your and Ivan's hate and bitterness had not consumed you, I would not be all alone."

~

Troy drove the family SUV back home from church, Jeremy and Clarissa's chatter a constant back and forth conversation. They attempted to include Maggie and Troy but Maggie sat in the back seat looking out her side window and replied in monosyllabic answers. Troy risked glances in the rearview mirror but never caught her gaze.

It had been a long time since Troy had been to church. Three years to be exact. Not since Liz had gone had he darkened the threshold of that building. The preacher was happy to see him but hadn't been over the top about it. For that Troy was grateful. The rest of the congregation had been glad to see him as well. The church had grown. There were a lot of new faces since he'd attended last.

Troy had tried not to listen too closely to the message. He wasn't eager to have his heart worked on. Troy was conscious of Maggie sitting beside him. She allowed him to hold the hymn book for her and she'd shared her Bible with him. Then there were several times when her arm had bumped into his and vice versa. She'd tried to scoot to her right, but his mom had been there so she couldn't move far. For some reason that had sent pleasure coursing through him. Perverse? Nope. Not at all. Genuine, happy-that-she-couldn't-move-away-from-his-side pleasure. If he could've gotten away with it, he'd loved to have put his arm around her. Now where in the world had *that* come from?

Maggie still wasn't looking at him if she could help it. When they'd walked out to the SUV after church, she'd made sure she had hold of Jeremy's hand and she'd walked beside Clarissa.

Troy was determined to get to the bottom of this. Today.

~

Maggie helped clear away the dishes from the table. "That was delicious, Clarissa. I can't say I've ever had elk before. Now I can."

"Well, I'm glad you enjoyed it." Clarissa picked up the plate of pot roast to carry it to the counter and glanced out the sliding glass doors past the deck. "Oh, my goodness, Maggie. You should grab your camera. Look!"

Maggie turned and stared out the glass doors to see a cow moose and her calf standing in the snow in the backyard. "Wow! I'll be right back."

She fled up the stairs and grabbed her camera case, hurrying back to the kitchen as fast as she could. Setting the case on the kitchen table, she opened it and pulled out her camera, attaching the correct lens for the distance and making the right adjustments.

They were far enough away she could step out onto the deck and not send them scurrying.

"Here, put this on, Maggie." Troy held her parka out for her to put her arms in.

Her gaze met his and she cast him a faint smile. "Thanks."

Maggie slipped into the parka and zipped it up then he slid the glass door open for her. She pulled up her hood as she stepped out and over to the railing. She aimed her camera at the moose pair and started snapping pictures. They moved a few steps, altering their positions, but didn't leave.

After she'd taken enough shots of the animals, she stood watching them for a few minutes. Amazing creatures, these Alaskan animals. *Thanks for allowing me to come on this assignment, Lord. It's not been easy, what with the break-ins, and the concerns someone's targeting me, but I'm so glad I'm here.*

The sliding glass door opened, and Troy stuck his head out. "Maggie, your phone's ringing."

She hurried inside and picked her phone up from the table where she'd left it while clearing away the dishes. "Thanks. I missed the call and I don't recognize this number. Isn't this a local number?"

Troy glanced at her phone. "Yeah. That's Garrick."

"Oh, good. Maybe he has news for me." Maggie set her camera on the table and took off her parka, hanging it back on the coat rack by the door. She hit dial and called Garrick back.

"Hello?" His voice came across the line.

"Hi Chief Patuk. It's Maggie Lawrence. Sorry I missed your call."

"Oh no problem. I just wanted to let you know I got hold of the rental company. They don't have any more rental cabins at this time, and nothing's opening up any time soon."

"Wow. That long, huh?"

"Yeah, I'm afraid so. I'm sure sorry about that."

"Hey, however long you need to stay here is fine." Clarissa waved a hand. "You're welcome here no matter what. Right, Troy?"

Clarissa slapped Troy's arm. "Of course, she's welcome, Mom. You don't have to hit me to get me to agree."

Maggie shrugged her shoulders and covered the receiver on her phone. "I'm so sorry. I had hoped to be gone in a day or two."

Clarissa waved her words away. "No worries. You're welcome to stay as long as you need to."

Maggie uncovered her phone. "Thank you so much for checking on it for me, Chief. Is it okay if I go over to the cabin today and get the rest of my things?"

"Yeah. I had my guys go through this morning. We didn't find anything helpful to the case. I'm sorry about your laptop, but I highly doubt there's any way to get it back. We have nothing to go on. We found no fingerprints except yours. Whoever was there, knew what they were doing. I suspect they used gloves and got what they came for."

"Yeah, I think you're right. Thank you for everything. I'll clear out my things later today."

"No problem."

Maggie hung up the phone and dropped into a chair. She leaned an elbow on the table then her chin on her hand. Yes, she had her photos, but there were a lot of her personal articles and information on that laptop that were gone. For good.

Troy sat in a chair across from her. "Well, what did Garrick say other than there's no more cabins available?"

"They couldn't find anything that would help lead them to the thief or thieves. My laptop is gone, most likely for good. He thinks they got what they came for, and there were no fingerprints leading them to who may have taken it."

"I'm really sorry, Maggie."

"Thanks. At least I have all of my photos. I had articles and stories on there that I can't replace, but the photos are far more important."

"I'd be happy to go over to the cabin and help you gather your stuff." Troy leaned forward, his arms folded on the table in front of him.

Maggie allowed her gaze to meet his. "I would appreciate that. I'm not crazy about going over by myself. I doubt the thieves will return, but it's just the idea…you know?"

He nodded. "I think I do. Why don't we go now and get that chore behind you?"

"Let's go."

~

It wasn't hard to get into her computer. Silly woman didn't use extensive precautions or difficult passwords. She thought she had the proper protections just as the average American did. It was easy to stay ahead of the cyber protection companies these days.

Once past her firewall, Pavel had gone through file after file of photos. Apparently, she never deleted anything. He growled as he opened what he thought must have been the hundredth file. There were photos from all over the world. She was a busy, well-traveled woman. Lucky her. She wasn't so good at naming her files, however. She must have a secret code that only she understood. Not so lucky for him. Why couldn't she name them simple names like Alaska?

After opening dozens of files, Pavel was eventually rewarded with a file of pictures of Alaskan mountains and terrain. Ahh. Could this be in the Denali National Park? He clicked on the photos making them as big as the laptop screen. Scrolling through the photos, Pavel grew tired of the incessant views of white mountains until he clicked past a photo and had to go back. He'd almost missed it.

Pavel stared at the photo. He had no idea where this was in the park. Denali was huge and there were so many mountains and glaciers. That's what this was. A mountain and a glacier. Something lay buried at the base of the glacier. He turned the photo every direction trying to figure out what it was. He knew what he wanted it to be, but he wasn't sure if it was that.

Could this be the plane that had crashed in 1987? It certainly didn't look like an airplane. Nor did it look like a part of an airplane. Even if it did, he had no idea where in the park this was. Without the plane's location, Pavel wouldn't find the packet.

~

Maggie and Troy soon had everything picked up and packed in garbage bags. She wanted to wash all of her clothes before wearing them again. The thought that some stranger had touched her personal belongings made her shudder.

She carried two garbage bags from the bedroom and set them by the front door. Troy was replacing the couch cushions and straightening them. He'd already returned the lamps to their places on the end tables and returned all the kitchenware to their rightful places in the kitchen cabinets. The rental company would come through and clean before renting the cabin again.

Maggie picked up the afghan from the floor and returned it to its place along the back of the couch. She ran her hands over it to smooth the wrinkles out.

"You okay?" Troy's voice sounded soft and gentle from beside her.

Maggie glanced up and met his gaze. She attempted to tug hers away, but for the first time that day, she found it impossible to do.

"Yeah, I'm fine." She nodded, her voice not sounding like hers.

"Maggie, what did I do to get you riled at me today? You've barely said more than a few words to me, and you've hardly looked at me all day."

Maggie managed to rip her gaze away only to have him tip her chin back up with a finger.

"No, we're not moving from this spot until you tell me."

Maggie's chin came up and she met his gaze then, crossing her arms over her chest. "Fine. You want to know? Let me ask you this: Why didn't you tell me you went to the University of North Carolina for college? The day I told you I was from there and that my dad was a history professor, why didn't you say something? Your cat is named after Michael Jordan, for goodness sake. Why not say something when that came up? Why, Troy? Why didn't you trust me enough to tell me?"

Troy exhaled a sigh and met her gaze. "It has nothing to do with trust, Maggie. It has everything to do with being a chapter of my life I prefer not to talk about."

All of a sudden Maggie felt cold all over. Her words were little more than a whisper. "Your wife?"

His brows lowered as his gaze penetrated hers. "How did you know…"

"I don't know anything except your mother said she was from North Carolina."

"Sometimes my mother talks too much," he grumbled.

"Perhaps she's unaware it's dear to your heart and something you don't want shared." Maggie placed a tentative hand on his arm. "Maybe you should have a talk with her so she'll understand."

Troy's gaze dropped to Maggie's hand. He reached up and took it lightly within his, his gaze returning to hers. "Maybe you're right, but just so you know, my mother named the cat."

It took a second before Maggie caught the humor in his words, then she spotted the corners of his lips lifting and the spark of laughter in his eyes.

"Is she a big UNC basketball fan?" Warmth flooded up from her collar as he twined his fingers with hers.

"Yeah, she is. She doesn't miss a game." His voice grew husky and she saw his Adam's apple bob as he swallowed.

"So, who was your history teacher?" Maggie attempted to keep her voice light and void of emotion. Not an easy thing with her heartbeat racing, and breathing was difficult with Troy standing so near, the warmth of his fingers seeping into hers.

"Who do you think? Owen Lawrence, professor of world history." Troy tugged Maggie closer and released her hand, sliding his arm around her waist, holding her close. As he slid his other hand behind her head and into her hair, his gaze searched her features then landed on her lips. Maggie's heart beat like a jackhammer in anticipation of his kiss. No, there was no wife to keep him from this, but there was the memory of a wife that he might not be over. Was that a bad thing? She had no idea, but she found she wanted him to kiss her.

He wasn't where he should be with the Lord, and this couldn't go anywhere until he was. He lowered his head as she started to protest.

Troy's phone rang, it's discordant sound breaking into the emotional silence of the cabin. Troy jerked back just as Maggie did. They pulled apart. Troy yanked the phone from his pocket and took a deep steadying breath as he clicked the call answer button.

"Hello?"

As Maggie walked over to the front window, she noticed his voice was husky and not quite steady yet.

"What? When did this happen?"

Maggie turned to stare at Troy as he listened to the caller relay their message. His face drained of color, a look of horror etching his features.

"Yeah, got it. I'm on my way." He hung up, his gaze flying to Maggie's.

"What, Troy? What's happened?" Maggie hurried to his side.

"Senator Scott, his wife, Calvin Jacobs, Superintendent Wade and his wife were in a car crash this afternoon. It just happened about an hour and a half ago."

"What? No! Are they alright?" Maggie took his arm and tried to lead him to the couch.

Troy pulled his arm away. "No. There's no time to sit. I'm driving up to Fairbanks. They're in the hospital. I don't know all the details, but that was Bryce. He got the report from the State Highway Patrol. Mrs. Scott is in the ICU and may not make it."

Maggie gasped. "Oh, no. What about the others?"

"I'm not sure about them. He didn't have all that information." Troy reached for his parka and slipped it on. "Come on. I'll drop you by the house. I may be at the hospital a while."

"Oh, no you don't." Maggie put her parka on and zipped it up. "I'm coming with you."

"You can't take pictures of this part of the senator's life, Maggie." Troy grabbed the garbage bags and reached for the front doorknob.

"Really? Is that what you think? That I would be so heartless as to take photos of this terrible time of their lives?" Maggie grabbed her purse off the kitchen counter and grabbed what was left to take to his pickup truck. "Then you don't know me at all."

She pushed past him and stormed out the door and down the porch steps to his truck. Maggie tossed the bags in the truck bed and climbed into the passenger seat, slamming the door behind her.

Who did he think he was? How could he think she would be so cavalier as to snap pictures of the senator and his wife when they'd been hurt and their lives may be hanging in the balance. She thought they were making progress. He'd...well, he'd almost kissed her, and she'd almost let him. Were they moving in that direction in their relationship? She'd been angry with him that morning for not opening up to her about his university time in North Carolina, but when he'd explained that it was a time he didn't want to talk about, she'd tried to understand. It was personal. She got that. Her experience last summer was like that.

Troy tossed his burden of bags into the truck bed and climbed into the driver's seat and started the engine. She felt more than saw his glance in her direction but he said nothing. Backing the truck around, he put it into drive and headed down the dirt road where he turned onto the main highway to Fairbanks. It was a long, quiet hour and a half ride to the hospital.

~

"Well, have you found anything?" General Kozlov's deep voice was beginning to grate on Pavel's nerves. If he didn't have to report to him, he would....

"Answer me, Pavel."

"*Da*, I found a picture. There seems to be a man-made object. It could be a plane, but it's far away and impossible to make out for sure. Also, there is no way to know where the object is located. It could be anywhere in the park."

"Send me the picture. We will have it analyzed. Perhaps then we'll know more and can better direct your next move."

The phone clicked. Pavel dropped the phone on the desk and rolled his eyes. The man had no manners. He never said goodbye. Pavel was tired of being talked down to. One day....

~

When Troy and Maggie arrived at the hospital, they were told Superintendent Wade, his wife, Margaret, and Calvin Jacobs were still in the emergency room. The nurse sent them down to the superintendent's cubicle.

"Sir," Troy and Maggie stepped into the entrance where the curtain was half opened. "I've seen you looking better."

"Believe me, I've felt better too." The superintendent grumbled as he dropped his head back to his pillow after seeing who had entered his temporary residence. "I'd much rather be at home right about now. They won't even let me go down to Margaret's cubicle. They're getting ready to take her down for a CT-scan. They believe she has head trauma. I'm worried sick over her."

Maggie stepped to his bedside and grasped the superintendent's hand, squeezing it. "I'm sure you are, sir. Would you like for me to pray for her?"

Troy watched as his boss opened his eyes and smiled at Maggie. "Thank you, Maggie. I've been praying for her since they told me what they're doing, but I'd love it if you'd add your prayers to mine."

Maggie bowed her head while still holding the superintendent's hand and prayed. "Father, I ask that you would be with Mrs. Wade as she goes for a CT-scan. Help the doctors and technicians to know how to identify any injury she may have. Help her to rest in Your hands and help Superintendent Wade not to worry, but to let You take care of her. You are the great physician. We love You, Father. In Your Son's precious name we pray, Amen."

Troy never closed his eyes, but watched Maggie's face as she prayed. An earnestness descended onto her features as the words spilled from her. How could she put her trust in a God who took loved ones from you? Had she ever lost someone she loved? He sure had. His dad. Liz. Both far sooner than they should've gone. But Liz…. Not now. No, this wasn't the time or the place.

"Thank you, Maggie. When you've been married to someone for forty-one years, perhaps you'll understand." A wry smile flitted across the superintendent's face then faded away.

"I may not understand that part, sir, but I do understand loss and near loss. You want to hang onto your loved ones and hold them close." Maggie patted his hand holding hers with her other hand.

"Yes, you're right."

Troy wondered at her loss, but he suspected her near loss had been her cousin when they'd both nearly been trafficked. He wanted to know more about that. Could he get her to open up to him? Not unless he could get her to forgive him for the stupid comment he'd made earlier. How stupid could he have been to accuse her of being heartless and mercenary? Open mouth and insert foot. He needed to apologize in a big way.

"So, what are your injuries, sir?" Troy tilted his chin in his boss's direction. "I see you have a brace on your left arm."

"It's broken. Eight weeks in this thing. That's the worst, fortunately." He pointed at his face. "Just a bunch of lacerations over my face, arms and upper body. They'll heal okay. They're from flying glass."

"What about Senator Scott?" Troy crossed his arms and leaned his elbows on the high tray table next to the hospital bed. "When

Bryce called, he told me Mrs. Scott is in ICU but he didn't know anything about the senator. And what about Calvin Jacobs?"

"The senator wasn't hurt much, thank goodness. He had some lacerations on his face and upper body. His left arm was sprained. They patched him up and he's sitting with his wife in ICU. They tried to make him leave. That didn't go over very well, as you can imagine. Since he's there, so are his bodyguards. They're standing outside in the hallway at the entrance to ICU, so I've been told."

Just then Bryce stepped into the cubicle. "Oh hey, Troy. Maggie. Glad you made it."

"How's Calvin, Bryce?" Wade asked. "You can give us the latest."

Bryce shook his head. "Poor man. They're still patching him up. I think he's regretting coming on this trip. Actually, I think he's regretting being the senator's assistant right about now."

"That bad, huh?" Troy straightened from the tray table.

Bryce started ticking off on his fingers. "He's still healing from his gunshot wound in the shoulder, now add to that a compound fracture of the right forearm, a broken right shoulder bone, and a couple of fractured ribs."

"Oh, my goodness. The poor man," Maggie gasped, placing her fingers over her mouth. She shook her head.

"Sir, what happened?" Troy leaned in on the tray table again. "What caused the accident?"

The superintendent remained thoughtful for a few moments as his gaze met Troy's. "Want my honest opinion?"

"Well, of course, sir." Troy shrugged.

The superintendent motioned for Bryce to close the curtain of the cubicle. "Close that curtain, Bryce. Everyone gather close."

Wade eyed Maggie with candor. "Maggie, this can go no further than this room. No newspapers. If you can't promise that, then I'll have to ask you to leave the room."

She held up a hand. "It'll go no further, sir. I promise."

He nodded. "Good. Our SUV was T-boned, and I believe we were targeted. It was a hit and run. In the midst of everything that happened, I may not have gotten a license plate, but I did notice it was a huge truck with a heavy-duty grill guard. One of those contraptions so that when you hit a moose, it'll destroy the moose, but not the front end of your vehicle. I daresay there was little to no damage to the truck. It was black with tinted windows, by the way."

"That's all good information, sir." Troy pulled out his notepad from his jacket pocket and jotted down notes. "What you're saying is...."

"What I'm saying is... someone tried to kill us. We were fortunate. At least most of us were. Mrs. Scott wasn't."

Silence descended on the cubicle as his words sank in.

The curtain slid back, and a doctor stepped into the cubicle, splintering the silence. "Well, well, Mr. Wade. Visitors already. You must be a popular man."

"These are some of the personnel who work in the park, Dr. Sayers." Wade kept his eyes on the man. "What news do you have? And you can talk in front of these folks. It's not a problem."

"Very well." The doctor's gaze swung around to each face then returned to the superintendent. "It's a lot better than we feared. Your wife has a concussion and a pretty bad headache, but she's going to be fine. Just like you, she's suffered from an array of lacerations that will heal over time. Other than that, she's fine. We've given her something for the headache, and she's going to want to sleep when she gets home, but it's best if she doesn't. Not for a while. The nurse will come in and give you some directions for you and for her. She'll go over them with her as well, but it's probably a good idea if you hear them too."

"I understand."

"Hang tight. The nurse will be in shortly and we'll get you both discharged. Then we need to get Mr. Jacobs discharged. I guess you all came in as a package deal, huh?" The doctor grinned and exited the cubicle.

"Sir, what can we do to help?" Troy turned to his boss. "I have my pickup with the extended cab. "If Maggie doesn't mind sitting on the rear bench seat, you and Mrs. Wade can ride with us. Bryce, can you take care of Mr. Jacobs."

"Me? Well, I suppose, but what do I do with him? I mean he's going to be pretty bandaged up with two bad shoulders and fractured ribs."

"He'll need a wheelchair, sir." The nurse breezed into the cubicle, paperwork in her hand. "There's no way he can do crutches with those shoulders. Don't worry, sir. We'll take care of it."

~

It was after midnight by the time Troy parked his pickup behind the house. They'd taken Superintendent and Mrs. Wade to their home in Denali National Park and helped get them settled before leaving them. They'd driven home in silence. As Troy turned off the truck, Maggie started to climb out, not waiting for him. She was exhausted after the emotional day they'd had and she just wanted to go to bed.

Troy reached across, stalling her progress with a hand on her arm. "Maggie, please wait."

Maggie's gaze went first to his hand then raised to his face. She could make out his features by the faint glow from the backporch light that Clarissa must have left on for them. His normally blue irises were black in the faint light.

Releasing the door handle, Maggie leaned back. She waited to see what Troy would say. With everything that had happened throughout the evening, she wasn't really still mad at him, but she hadn't been sure if he was ready to talk to her or not.

Troy pulled his hand back and draped it over the steering wheel with his other one. "Maggie, I owe you an apology. What I said this afternoon was uncalled for. I may not have known you long, but I think I've known you long enough to know you wouldn't behave in an unethical manner. After what I saw tonight, it just reaffirms that."

Maggie tilted her head sideways and narrowed her gaze at him. "Out of curiosity, what did you see tonight that reaffirms that?"

Troy released a chuckle then grew serious again. "When you prayed with the superintendent. That was... well, that was really nice. It seemed to mean a lot to him."

"How does that reaffirm your opinion of me?" Maggie lifted an eyebrow.

Troy huffed a heavy sigh and scooched around in his seat to face her. "You're not making this easy for me, are you?"

Maggie tilted her head back and rolled her eyes up to the roof of the truck then back to him, drawing in a deep breath then releasing it slowly. "Should I?"

Troy shook his head then swallowed hard, his Adam's apple bobbing in the V at the opening of his parka. His voice was a tad husky when he spoke. "No, not really. Not after what I said."

Maggie smiled, her own voice soft in the close space of the truck cab. "I forgive you, Troy. You'd just gotten the call about the accident, and you were worried about everybody. Sometimes we say things in a moment of stress that we wouldn't normally say. Everything's fine."

Troy reached across and picked up her gloved hand. He tugged the glove off and twined his fingers with hers.

"Thanks. I don't know if I deserve that explanation, but if you're happy with it then okay."

A soft laugh bubbled up from Maggie until she realized Troy was leaning closer. His hand came up and touched her cheek. A thrill raced through Maggie at his touch. He was going to kiss her. Anticipation matched the warmth that flooded over her as Troy's hand slid beneath her hair to the back of her neck, tugging her toward him. Was she going to let him kiss her? Was this wise, knowing he wasn't where he needed to be spiritually? Not to mention she would be leaving before long?

"Maggie," his voice was like sandpaper over wood. His breath stroked her cheek as his lips descended. Her heart threatened to pound right out of her chest. Maggie swallowed hard as she tried to decide what to do.

Bang. Bang. Bang.

Troy yanked back just as Maggie did, her heart pounding like a sledgehammer. What in the world was that? Had someone shot at the truck?

"What are you two doing out here? You're going to freeze to death."

A short person was attempting to look through Maggie's window, but the windows had fogged over and it was impossible for them to see in.

Bang. Bang. Bang.

Maggie clasped her hand to her heart while Troy shook his head, yanked off his toboggan and ran a hand through his hair. He eyed Maggie's window.

"It's Mom."

Maggie patted the area over her heart. "I think I just had a heart attack."

"I know the feeling. She won't stop until we go inside. We better go." He cast a grin at Maggie. "By the way, I don't apologize for what almost happened."

Troy opened his door, climbed out and slammed it behind him.

Maggie sat for a few seconds longer trying to compose herself. Wow. For not having been kissed, she sure felt like she had been.

Chapter Thirteen

W hat are you doing here, sir?" Troy stood next to Natalya's reception counter Monday morning, his cup of coffee in hand. "You should be home recovering from your weekend."

"There's nothing I can't do from here, Troy." The superintendent continued down the hallway. "But thanks for your concern."

His last words floated back to them as he headed to his office.

"Did you know he was coming in?" Troy turned to Natalya.

"I assumed he would be here. What happened over the weekend?"

Troy filled her in, leaving out the part about possibly being a hit and run and a target to kill the senator.

"Oh, my goodness. Poor Mrs. Scott. I hope she'll be alright." Natalya shook her head. "I'll take up a collection here in the office and send her some flowers."

Troy pulled some folded bills from his pocket. "That's thoughtful, Natalya. Here. I'll be your first donor. I'm sure they'll be greatly appreciated."

"Thanks, Troy."

The phone on her desk rang and she picked up the handset. "Yes, sir? Of course. I'll send him right in."

She returned the handset to its cradle.

"Troy, Super...."

"Wants to see me. How did I know?" He winked and picked up his coffee cup, downed the last of it and tossed the paper cup in the garbage. "See you later."

She waved. "Bye."

Troy knocked on the superintendent's door and opened it, sticking his head in. "You wanted to see me, sir?"

"Come on in, Troy." He waved him in. "Have a seat."

Troy lowered himself into one of the chairs in front of his boss's desk. "How's Mrs. Wade this morning, sir?"

The superintendent shoved his glasses back up onto his nose and grinned. "Just as stubborn as ever. She's still got a bit of a headache, but that won't keep her down. My daughter and grandchildren are at the house with her. I didn't want to leave her alone, so they came down from Fairbanks to stay with us for a few days. My son-in-law, of course, has a job in Fairbanks, but they'll be company for her."

"How's your arm?"

The superintendent lifted the braced, wounded appendage and waved it around. "Oh, it's still there. A bit painful but it's to be expected. One of the aides came by and picked me up this morning."

"Good. It won't hurt you to be waited on for a change." Troy crossed his foot over his knee. "What did you want to see me about, sir?"

"Just wondering if you've heard from your Army buddy. Since this accident, it appears things are escalating. I don't need to tell you, Troy, we need to get ahead of this. Someone's going to get killed, and from my viewpoint, they're trying to kill the senator."

The office door opened near the end of the superintendent's comment and Senator Scott walked in. "That's my viewpoint as well, Glen, and I'm not happy with what I'm seeing. Especially since they nearly succeeded with my Miriam."

The senator's booming voice filled the room as he stepped in and shut the door behind him.

Troy and the superintendent both got to their feet as the big man approached the desk and shook hands with both of them.

"Sit. Please, both of you sit down." Senator Scott took the chair next to Troy.

"Senator. How did you get here?" Wade sat in his leather desk chair.

"The US Army flew me here in a UH-60 Black Hawk. I love those birds." He slapped his knee and chuckled. "Warhorses, they are. Anyway, I'm here, and we need to talk."

"Very well." Wade nodded and leaned back in his chair. "Troy and I were just discussing the next step in this investigation. The end of last week, Troy asked an Army buddy at Ft. Wainwright if he would research our dead shooter as well as the young woman who tried to poison you and your wife. Troy was just getting ready to tell me if he'd heard back."

Both men turned their expectant gazes on Troy. Great.

"No sir, I haven't heard back yet. I only spoke with him on the weekend when you asked me to. He's probably still in the process of researching. These things do take time."

Disappointment crossed the features of both men as they nodded.

"Of course it does, but we don't have a lot of time." The senator shifted in his seat as he crossed his knees. "There's no telling how long we'll have until the next strike. I've hired extra bodyguards to protect my wife at the hospital while at the same time I have bodyguards shadowing me. When word gets out that I'm still alive, you can bet there will be another strike."

He heaved a heavy sigh as he swiped his brow. "I had no idea this trip would be a dangerous one. I truly thought that letter was a prank."

"It's unfortunate that it wasn't, sir." Wade leaned forward, resting his arm brace on the desk. "This is what we know so far. The young man that shot at you on the dog sled expedition was a Russian immigrant named Ivan Orlov. We're still trying to gather further information on him. We don't know yet if he's the first shooter from the banquet, although we have the weapon. The fingerprint analysis hasn't come back yet. The young woman who tried to poison you and your wife is Dafna Orlov, his sister, also an immigrant. The information is slow in coming in."

Senator Scott nodded as he rested an elbow on the arm of the chair, his fingers on his chin. "Unfortunately, when we deal with immigrants from certain countries it is difficult to find information."

"Sir, I have a question that you may or may not be able to answer." Troy turned to face the senator better. "Other than your wife now being in the hospital, why are you still here? I mean, you did what you came to do. You dedicated the memorial in the park. What other purpose could you have for lingering in Alaska?"

Senator Scott glanced down at his pant leg and picked off a piece of lint, dropping it to the floor. He leaned his elbows on the arms of the chair and twined his fingers together, resting them in his lap. Clearing his throat, he looked from one expectant face to the other.

"Gentlemen, I think perhaps it's time I let you in on a secret. But before I do that, you're going to come for a little ride with me."

~

Maggie stepped into park headquarters and smiled at Natalya as she stopped by the reception counter.

"Good morning, Natalya. Did you have a good weekend?"

"I had a great weekend." The excitement on her face made Maggie chuckle.

"Oh really? Do tell?"

"I had a date with the sweetest biologist you'll ever meet." A dreamy expression settled on Natalya's features as she heaved a soft sigh. "He was amazing."

"Wow. That's great. I'm happy for you."

"Thanks. How about you? How was your weekend?"

"Well, my cabin was broken into and my laptop was stolen, but other than that...."

"What?" Natalya's shriek was accompanied by her surge to her feet as she hurried around the counter in front of her desk to wrap Maggie in her arms. "Oh, Maggie. That's terrible. I'm so sorry. Here I'm going on and on about my terrific weekend when yours was, well... pooh. That's awful."

Maggie hugged Natalya in return then pulled back and smiled. "It's ok. I'm filing a renter's insurance claim for the laptop. I'll get a new one. At least I had my camera with me. I have all my pictures and that's the important thing."

"Well, thank the Lord for that." Natalya returned to her seat. "Where are you staying? Did they find you another cabin?"

Maggie shook her head. "Not yet. I'm staying at Troy's with his mom and son until they can find something."

Natalya's eyebrows shot up. "Are you serious? At Troy's? You mean "Grumpy ol' Troy?""

The memory of the near kiss in Troy's truck and how Troy was anything but "Grumpy ol' Troy" came to Maggie's mind and warmth flooded up from her parka collar.

"Yeah, well it…it's…uh, working out okay. Look is he around yet? He said he'd take me out for some animal photos. It's been nearly impossible with everything that's been going on with the senator."

Natalya shook her head and scrunched her nose. "Sorry. You just missed them. The senator came in and whisked Troy and the superintendent away. I have no idea how long they'll be gone. They didn't say anything. Just left."

"That's not like Troy." Maggie cocked her head and furrowed her brows.

"It's not like the superintendent either." Natalya crossed her arms over her chest.

Maggie walked over to the window and gazed out. "This leaves me at a loose end. I have no idea what to do."

She turned back to Natalya. "Any ideas?"

"How soon were you planning to buy a laptop?"

Maggie snapped her fingers and smiled. "Great idea. Then I can get back to work with the pictures on my camera. I'll see you later, Natalya. I'm heading into Fairbanks. Do you need anything?"

"Nope. I'm good, but watch out for moose. They like to meander along the roadside and occasionally cross it too."

"I'll do that. See you later."

~

Troy sat by the window in the UH-60 Black Hawk helicopter and watched as it flew into Ft. Wainwright Army base. All the buildings looked more utilitarian than decorative and were built in an orderly fashion as though there was a purpose in mind for each one. The senator had been deliberately vague in telling him and the superintendent where they were going, but it was pretty clear now. The helicopter came to a halt in its forward motion and hovered for a few seconds before beginning a slow descent. Troy saw the pavement below and recognized a helipad. It was a gentle touch down, a demonstration of the pilot's abilities, and immediately the sound of the rotors shutting down followed.

The crewman who had shared the bay with them but had remained silent throughout the flight, got up and slid the bay door open. Troy, Superintendent Wade, Senator Scott and his security guards unbuckled their seat belts and removed their headsets. They climbed out and found an Army colonel approaching from a building near the helipad.

He held out his hand toward the senator. "Welcome back, Senator."

"Colonel Williams. It's good to see you again." The senator shook the colonel's hand then turned to the men standing just behind him. "Let me introduce Superintendent Wade and Ranger Troy Donovan from Denali National Park."

"Welcome gentlemen." Colonel Williams shook their hands then indicated they should all follow him. "I have a vehicle right over here. The general is waiting in his office."

The colonel led them to a large military SUV then drove across base to a building where he parked. He led Senator Scott, Superintendent Wade, Troy and the three security guards inside. Here he signed them in with a military policeman who issued them visitor's passes and made them go through a metal detector.

Troy's pocket knife set off the alarm, but he was cleared and allowed to enter with the approval of the colonel. This certainly wasn't what Troy had expected to happen when he'd gotten up this morning.

Colonel Williams led the men to an office on the third floor, his shiny chloroform oxfords clicking on the polished tile as he walked. Troy glanced at the occasional military person who passed them in the hallway, nodding as they made eye contact. They scrutinized his uniform just as he did theirs. If he'd ever felt like a fish out of water, this was it.

Colonel Williams opened an office door and led them into an outer office where a young uniformed woman sat behind a wooden desk at a computer. She turned as they entered. Standing, she saluted the colonel.

"Good morning, sir."

Colonel Williams returned her salute. "Good morning, Sergeant. Phillips. These gentlemen and I have an appointment with General Harding."

The sergeant took her seat and nodded. "Yes sir. He's expecting you. Please go on in."

Colonel Williams knocked on the door near the sergeant's desk and waited a moment.

They heard "come in" and he opened the door, ushering Senator Scott, Superintendent Wade and Troy inside then closing the door behind him. The security guards remained in the outer office and took seats.

Colonel Williams approached a desk where a large, balding man sat, an array of colorful medals and ribbons on his uniform. A few long strands of hair were combed over his bald pate and his jowls reminded Troy of a bulldog. He supposed the general didn't get where he was by being namby-pamby. There were three stars on each shoulder of his uniform. Troy bet he earned every one the hard way. He could see it in his eyes.

Colonel Williams halted in front of the desk, went to attention and saluted. "General Harding, Colonel Williams reporting for our meeting with Senator Scott, Superintendent Wade and Ranger Donovan."

The general returned the colonel's salute. "Thank you, Colonel. Please, won't you all be seated."

The general waved to the four chairs arranged in front of his desk and turned his gaze on the senator.

"It's good to see you again, Brad. It's been awhile."

Before the senator took his seat, he leaned across the desk and shook the general's hand. "I'll say it has, General. You know how it is. When you get to Washington, you get mired down and it's hard to get out. When I do come home to Alaska, it's usually back to the capital in Juneau. I don't remember the last time I've been to Fairbanks."

"I understand, Brad." General Harding leaned forward and clasped his hands together on the glass-like surface of his mahogany desktop. He allowed his gaze to roam from one newcomer to the other. "Welcome gentlemen. It's a pleasure to meet you Superintendent Wade. Mr. Donovan. I just wish it were under far less, shall we say, unpleasant circumstances.

"Brad has asked me to bring you up to snuff on a situation that began a few decades ago. I wouldn't have to do this except Brad's life is now in danger and you folks are investigating the attempts on his life in the park. By default, you've been dragged into this whole sordid mess."

The general glanced at the senator who nodded. Troy's senses were on high alert and didn't miss a thing. What in the world was he and the superintendent getting themselves into? He glanced at the superintendent who wore the same cautious and concerned expression Troy was sure must be stamped on his own features.

"Gentlemen, before I begin, I have some papers you must sign. These papers indicate that you agree to never divulge any of this information. It's called a Non-Disclosure Agreement. You may or may not have heard of it before."

He pulled a file folder from a corner of his desk and opening it, handing each of them a sheet of paper.

"Please read it carefully before signing." The general opened a desk drawer and provided them with pens.

When they'd done as he requested, he returned the papers to the folder and the pens to the drawer.

"Good. Let's begin."

General Harding informed the superintendent and Troy about the Soviet pilot who had escaped from the Soviet Union in 1987 and brought with him top secret information the Soviet Union wanted back. He told them how the man, Evgene Antonovich Orlov, had defected with the plan to hand over the information to the US Army back in 1987 but the plane he had confiscated had gone down within Denali National Park.

"Brad, would you like to say something?" The general waved a hand in his direction.

The senator turned his gaze on the two park rangers. "I was directed by the Assistant Secretary of State, Gabe Holloway, to come to Denali and find the plane, and if he was still alive, the defected pilot. Ultimately, I was to find the top-secret documents and bring them back to Washington. With the help of the US Army and the Denali rangers, we searched for a month. We found nothing. Nothing that even resembled a plane. We had nothing to go by and, due to terrible weather, eventually had to call off the search."

"Well, gentlemen, extrapolate from that, and tell me what you think." The general sat back in his chair, causing it to squeak and groan under his shifting weight.

Troy didn't have to think for long. "You said the man's name was Evgene something Orlov? He must have been related to the man that shot at the senator, Ivan Orlov. Then there's Dafna Orlov, the woman who tried to poison the senator and his wife. Who are they to the defector? Considering their ages, are they his children?"

The general folded his arms over his chest and smiled. "Very good, Mr. Donovan. Yes, they are. Ivan and Dafna immigrated to the US in 2014 along with their mother, Ludmila Orlov. According to our records they settled in Fairbanks then Dafna moved to New York and changed her name to Laurel Oliver. She faded into the millions that live in New York City and no one really paid any attention. Ivan secured work and lived with his mother in Fairbanks but stayed off the radar. At least until he fired those shots at Brad week before last. It was the last thing he would ever do."

The superintendent nodded. "Yes, and we have a smoking gun from the night of the banquet for Senator Scott. We're still waiting on the fingerprint results to find out if both shooters were Ivan Orlov or if we have a third person involved. The young woman is being held without bond until her court hearing. It's a serious thing to attempt the poisoning of a US senator."

"Indeed." The general nodded in agreement.

"What about the mother, sir? Where is she? What's her role in all this?" Troy leaned forward, his elbows on his knees, hands clasped.

"That's unclear. She's given us no reason to think she's involved in anything subversive." General Harding lifted his hands for a brief moment as he shrugged then clasped them on his desk. "She works in a restaurant in Fairbanks and goes home at night. Minds her own business. Goes to church on Sundays. That's about it."

"You've had her under surveillance?" Senator Scott raised an eyebrow.

"Of course, we have. Especially since you arrived in town. She's now added visiting her daughter in jail to her list of places to go." The general shook his head. "It must break her heart."

"It's doubtful this is what her husband had in mind when he defected." Senator Scott shifted in his seat.

"Sir," Troy's gaze moved to the general, "What are your plans for us? You know we have an open investigation, but we're hampered by, well, the facts of your case. We can't exactly solve ours with yours still pending. What are we supposed to do?"

The general leaned forward resting his forearms on his desk, a wide grin lifting his jowls and softening the bulldog expression. "I'm glad you asked, Mr. Donovan. We want to search for the plane again, avoiding all the areas that were searched thirty-two years ago. The senator tells me you're more familiar with the park than most anyone employed there."

His gaze flashed to the superintendent who didn't hesitate to answer. "There's not a doubt about that, General. Troy Donovan knows that park like the back of his hand."

Troy shook his head. "But I've never come across that plane. I have no idea where it's at."

No sooner were the words out of his mouth than a thought struck him. Maggie's photo.

"What is it, Mr. Donovan? You look like you've just had a lightbulb moment." General Harding chuckled, the senator joining him.

Troy got up and paced behind the chairs as he tried to remember what the photo looked like. He came back and stood behind his chair, hands on the back of it. He closed his eyes trying to form the picture in his mind's eye but it just wouldn't come.

"Troy?" Superintendent Wade's voice was soft on his left. "Are you alright?"

Troy nodded as he straightened. "General Harding, the photographer who has been taking the pictures of Senator Scott's visit has a picture on her camera that may be of interest to this case. Then again it may be nothing, but...."

He explained the photo and how Maggie came to take it. General Harding leaned further forward, Troy having grabbed his attention.

When he was finished explaining things, the general's jowls were set like a bulldog's once again. "Mr. Donovan, I want to meet this young woman. Bring Maggie Lawrence and her camera as soon as you can."

"I'll do that, sir. You might also find it interesting that Maggie's cabin was broken into. Nothing was taken, the first time.

Her rental company moved her to another cabin. It was also broken into and her laptop stolen because she left it behind that time. Maggie said the only things of any value or importance she has are her camera and her laptop."

"Why didn't I hear about this?" Senator Scott asked.

"It didn't seem to be related to your case, sir." Troy turned to the senator.

"Perhaps not," General Harding folded an arm over his chest and rested his elbow on it, stroking his chin in thought, "but once we see this photograph on Miss Lawrence's camera we'll know more. Bring her to see me tomorrow. I'll send a helicopter for you."

Troy realized his words were more an order than a request.

"Yes sir."

~

Troy stepped inside the kitchen and closed the back door behind him just as his cell phone rang. Digging it from his parka pocket, he saw it was Paul Mitchell. Good. Maybe he had some information for him. He hit the answer button and held the phone to his ear.

"Hey, Paul. Tell me you've got some intelligence that'll help me out."

"Well, I think you might like this." Paul's voice lilted with the promised information. "Not only did Ivan Orlov immigrate to the US in 2014, his sister Dafna Orlov and his mother Ludmila Orlov did as well."

"Yeah, Senator Scott took Superintendent Wade and me to see General Harding today. He told us that much. What else do you have?" Troy halted on his way to the pegs to hang up his parka. "What's the mother's name again? Do you have an address for her? Is she local?"

"Hey, buddy, hold on. One question at a time. Ludmila Orlov, yes and yes. Ludmila lives in Fairbanks. She's been to visit her daughter, Dafna Orlov, in jail a couple of times. Seems that when Dafna took off for New York City and changed her name to Laurel Oliver, Ivan stayed in Fairbanks and lived with dear ol' mom. He kept his nose clean, pretty much staying out of trouble until Senator Scott's current trip. Even though the good senator is from Alaska, they never tried to make contact until this visit."

Troy dropped onto a kitchen chair. "I wonder why."

"Well, the best I can figure, he never really came to this area except when he was campaigning. Most of his official business has kept him in the capital of Juneau."

Troy remained silent for a few minutes thinking.

"You still there, buddy?" Paul asked.

"Yeah, I'm here. Just thinking. There were two attempted shootings and the attempted poisoning. Our photographer had her cabin broken into twice and her laptop stolen but that was *after* all three and after Ivan was killed and Dafna was put in jail."

"Are you sure the break-ins are connected with the senator?"

"I can't explain why, Paul, but it's connected somehow." Troy heaved a heavy sigh. "I'm under orders from General Harding and I can't say anything. Sorry, buddy."

"Hey, if General Harding said keep your trap shut, you'd better do it." Paul's tone was dry. "So then…"

Silence filled a few moments as the men mulled over all the information they had.

Paul was the first to break it. "Troy, have you considered you may have another player in your game?"

"Unfortunately, that thought just crossed my mind."

Chapter Fourteen

I have a little something for you, Jeremy." Maggie held her hands behind her back as she walked into the family room. The little boy was playing in the corner with his cars while Clarissa sat on the couch watching a TV show. "It's not much, but I thought you might have fun with it."

Clarissa picked up the remote and turned off the TV. Jeremy dropped his cars and hurried over to Maggie, excitement and wonder lighting his eyes and stamping a smile across his face. "What is it?"

"Well, why don't you sit beside your grandma, and I'll give it to you," Maggie instructed, her hands still behind her back.

Jeremy hurried over and climbed onto the couch, his excitement growing. It made him wiggle until Clarissa told him to sit still.

"When I was in town this weekend, I thought about you and decided to pick you up some things that would be fun for you to do." Maggie pulled a colorful backpack from behind her back and handed it to Jeremy.

"A backpack?" His excitement faded a bit, a pucker appearing between his brows.

"Well, it's not just any old backpack. This backpack holds all kinds of fun inside." Maggie pointed at the zipper. 'You have to open it to find the fun."

Jeremy pulled the zipper on the bag and spread the opening wide. His face lit up as he started pulling out the items.

"What's in there, Jeremy?" Clarissa tried to see inside. "Oh, my goodness. There's lots of fun in there."

"There's a coloring book and some new crayons. I love to color, Maggie." Jeremy held them up for Maggie to see as she knelt beside the couch. "Wow. There's a puzzle, too, Grandma. You can help me with that."

He dropped them on the couch beside him and kept digging in the bag. "Here's a game. I bet Dad'll play with me. Maggie, you can play too. Oh, look, Grandma, there's a cool cereal bowl with a straw on it. There's a bunch of stuff in here."

Jeremy kept pulling out items and showing them to his Grandma who exclaimed over every item.

"Why did you get this stuff for me, Maggie? It's not my birthday." Jeremy stuffed all his gifts back into the bag at Clarissa's suggestion.

"Just because I wanted to." Maggie tweaked his nose eliciting a giggle.

Jeremy jumped off the couch and wrapped his arms around Maggie's neck, giving her a squeeze. "Thanks, Maggie. I love you."

A lump formed in Maggie's throat and it took two tries before she managed to get out her response. "I love you, too, Jeremy."

~

The excitement coming from the family room made Troy pause in the hallway and sneak to the doorway, peering around the doorframe covertly. He saw Maggie hand Jeremy a backpack and watched as the excitement rippled through his son. Jeremy could hardly keep his seat. Troy grinned at the scene yet was touched that she would do that for Jeremy. Maggie was a multi-faceted woman, and she never ceased to amaze him.

When Jeremy wrapped his arms around Maggie and told her he loved her, it squeezed Troy's heart. It hadn't occurred to him until now that his son might miss his mom. Troy had always thought Jeremy had been too young to remember Liz and wouldn't realize what he was missing. He had his grandma, but she wasn't the same as his mother, was she? His heart ached at the thought. He'd assumed he and his mom were enough for Jeremy, but maybe that wasn't the case. The little boy needed a mother.

"I'd better go start supper."

His mother's words sent him scurrying to the kitchen where she found him by the back door.

"Oh, hi Troy. You're home early."

Troy dropped a kiss on his mom's cheek. "Yep."

Maggie and Jeremy walked in just then. "Hi Dad. Look what Maggie gave me. It's a backpack full of fun stuff."

Troy picked up his son and swung him around, hugging him and kissing him. Then he let Jeremy show him all his "fun stuff."

"Okay, pal. Why don't you run along and play with your fun stuff for a bit? I need to talk with Maggie, then I'll come in and play with you before dinner. How's that?"

"Okay, Dad, but hurry." Jeremy picked up Michael Jordan who had wandered into the kitchen and carried him out.

"Hey, Maggie." Troy hung his parka on a peg by the backdoor and put his boots on the boot pan beneath the parkas. He pulled out a chair at the table and sat down. "That was an awesome thing you did. Jeremy's pretty happy with that backpack of goodies."

Maggie reached for some potatoes that needed to be peeled and sat in another chair at the table and began to peel them. "It wasn't much. When I was in Fairbanks this weekend, I wanted to do something special for him, so I did. That's all."

"Well, thank you."

"Oh, you should've seen his face when Maggie handed him that backpack, Troy. He was so excited." Clarissa stood at the stove, her back to them.

"I'm sure he was, mom."

After a few seconds of silence, Maggie cast a glance from the potatoes to Troy. "I came in to headquarters this morning to find you and the superintendent had been whisked away by the senator. That's what Natalya told me."

"She was right. I can't really say more yet, but we need to head north tomorrow." Troy tried to catch her gaze and she finally glanced up again. He tilted his head toward his mom then put his finger over his lips. Maggie's eyebrows lowered in confusion but she nodded.

"I was up in Fairbanks today, but if we need to head back up there tomorrow, that's fine."

"What did you do in Fairbanks, sweetie?" Clarissa stirred a pot on the stove.

"I replaced my laptop that was stolen. The guy in the store helped me set it up, and he installed a better photo program than the one I had. I'm looking forward to trying it out. He said it's user friendly yet has better capabilities."

Clarissa turned around and walked over to the table. "Oh good. I'm sure you'll be happy with that. Is it one of those programs you can have fun playing around with photos?"

She picked up the potatoes and placed them in a bowl, carrying them to the pot and dropping them in.

"Oh yes, and I'm going to have fun." Maggie chuckled.

"Mom, can you do without Maggie for a few minutes? I'd like to see this new laptop she has." Troy stood and walked over to his mom, wrapping an arm around her shoulders.

"Please, I was cooking before Maggie came to stay. Of course, I can do without her for a few minutes. Take your time." Then she called as they headed out the kitchen door. "And don't forget to go play with your son."

~

Maggie brought her laptop to Troy's home office where he waited.

"You know we could've done this after dinner." She plugged the laptop into the wall. It wasn't completely charged yet.

"This wasn't the only reason I wanted to get you out of the kitchen."

Maggie cast a wary glance in his direction before returning it to the laptop. "Okay. What's up?"

"Tomorrow morning a helicopter will pick us up at the park and take us north to Ft. Wainwright. I can't say more now, but take your camera and your laptop. Remember the picture with the strange indiscernible object beneath the glacier? See what you can do with this new photoshop program this evening to bring out that object. Maybe you can. Maybe you can't. Just see what you can do."

Maggie straightened and turned a troubled gaze on Troy. "What's going on?"

"I can't say anything more now, Maggie. But trust me. You'll find out more tomorrow, I'm sure. I don't know how much, but your photo may be important."

Maggie laid a hand on Troy's arm. "Is that why my laptop was stolen?"

"I don't know, but I hope we can get some answers soon."

~

Troy left to play with Jeremy while Maggie sat down at his desk and inserted the SD card from her camera into her new laptop. Pulling up the new photoshop program, Maggie played around with it for a bit trying to get used to its capabilities. She was impressed and happier with it than what had been on the old laptop. Searching for the photo of the unknown object beneath the edge of the glacier, she zoomed in and tried some of the new adjustments she'd figured out. Maggie's hand flew to her mouth, her heart pounding in excitement as she gasped at the object on her screen. She'd done it. The photo was still a bit pixelated but it was so much clearer, and she was able to tell exactly what it was.

Maggie saved a copy of the picture then attempted to zoom in further. The picture distorted too much and lost its clarity. Zooming back out to where she'd been, she stared at it, looking for any details she could make out. The front of an airplane fuselage stuck out from under the retreating glacier. A small section of what looked like a wingtip protruded from the ice on the right. It was barely discernible but it was there. She hadn't seen that from the original photo, only the indiscernible fuselage.

Why didn't Troy want his mother to know about this? What on earth was going on?

~

Jeremy had been put to bed earlier and Troy, Clarissa and Maggie watched TV for a while until Maggie excused herself and said goodnight.

"Hold up, Maggie." Troy followed her into the hallway.

She turned toward him, allowing curiosity to etch her features. It had been a long day and tomorrow promised to be longer. She was ready to turn in.

"What's up?"

Troy eyed her with a raised eyebrow as he pulled a piece of paper from his hip pocket.

"Mom found this in the wastebasket in your room and was concerned. She brought it to me. Why didn't you?" His tone was almost accusing as he opened it up. Maggie read the note that had appeared on her cabin porch. The words "Go Home" in bold print nearly screamed at her again.

She drew in a deep breath and released it slowly before answering. Her steady gaze met his. "I found it on the cabin porch one night. I thought I heard someone put it there but when I looked, I didn't see anyone. All I saw was the note held down with a rock. After the cabin was ransacked, I didn't think about it again until yesterday when I found it in my things. I threw it away, and I guess your mom found it."

"Maggie Lawrence, sometimes…" Troy shook his head and closed his eyes, jamming the note into his pocket. He heaved a heavy sigh then opened his eyes and pulled her into his arms. Before Maggie knew what was what, Troy's lips descended on hers, a light, gentle kiss that stirred her insides and stole her breath away. After a few seconds, he pulled back mere inches, his gaze roaming her features. Then he kissed her again, longer and fuller, making Maggie forget what they'd been talking about. All she could think about was Troy. Her heart beat in rhythm with his. Her arms wrapped around his neck and her fingers slid into the hair at the nap of his neck.

Troy groaned then pulled back, a slight grin lifting the corners of his lips as his hands dropped to her waist. He shook his head and whispered. "You're potent, Maggie, but don't think this lets you off the hook. This note means you're in danger. If someone's warning you to go home, then that's probably what you need to do."

Ahh. The note. That's what they'd been talking about. Maggie drew in a deep breath and slid from his arms, allowing quite ire in her voice. "I'm not going anywhere, Troy Donovan. The Scotts are my case, and I'm going to see this through."

~

Troy watched Maggie from his jump seat across from her in the UH-60 Black Hawk helicopter. They'd taken off about a half hour earlier and she'd had her eyes glued out the window ever since. If she'd been allowed to have her camera, he was sure she would've been snapping away. Colonel Williams was accompanying them on this little excursion and had confiscated her camera and laptop bags, promising to return them once they were at their destination. Although Maggie knew where they were going, she didn't know why they'd been whisked away in an Army helicopter in the company of an Army officer. She had no idea what this meeting was all about.

Troy took the opportunity to allow his gaze to wander over her beautiful features. A mistake? Probably. Yet he couldn't help himself. The memory of their kiss last night came to mind. Maggie Lawrence was beautiful both in her character and in her features. Her gorgeous green eyes, delicately shaped nose, and those luscious lips set in her heart-shaped face certainly did things to his heart rate. The little dimple beside her lips made him itch to…."

"Mr. Donovan." Colonel Williams's voice in his headset yanked Troy's attention to the man sitting two seats to his left.

"Yes, Colonel?" Troy attempted to reign in his heart rate. And his thoughts.

Colonel Williams chuckled. "We're almost there. Did you hear the pilot? ETA five minutes."

"Yeah, sure." Troy lied. Okay so he didn't exactly hear the pilot. His mind had been, well, a bit preoccupied. He needed to get it in gear and on matters at hand. Maggie Lawrence was a distraction. A beautiful distraction, but a distraction nonetheless.

He heaved a heavy sigh and dropped his head against the square cushion headrest of the jump seat. This was going to be a long day.

~

Maggie clipped the visitor's badge to her sweater and carried her parka over her arm as she followed Colonel Williams to the third floor. She wasn't happy he'd confiscated her camera and laptop bags, but Troy had reassured her that everything would be alright. She glanced up at him now as he walked beside her. He was the only familiar thing in this whole day, and she was thankful he was here.

Troy must have noticed her glance. Turning his gaze on her, he smiled then lifted his hand and gave her arm a gentle squeeze.

At the end of the hallway, Colonel Williams ushered them into an outer office. The desk inside was unmanned, so he approached the inner office door and knocked. A gruff voice told them to enter.

Maggie was taken aback by the bulldog-featured general who sat behind the shiny mahogany desk. She watched as Colonel Williams approached and saluted the man. He received a salute in return and they were all told to sit in the chairs in front of the desk. She had no idea what she'd been expecting at their journey's end, but it certainly hadn't been a US Army general's office, that's for sure.

The general's dark brown eyes were immediately on Maggie. Was that a smirk on his lips or his usual smile? It was hard to tell. Maggie decided to tread lightly until she could figure this man out.

"Well, Miss Lawrence. It's a pleasure to meet you. I'm General Harding. I'm glad you were able to join us. I've been told you're quite the photographer and that you've captured a photo that may be of significance to us. I would very much like to see this photograph."

Colonel Williams handed Maggie her camera and laptop bags, then retook his seat.

Before opening either of them, Maggie pinned the general with a direct gaze. "Thank you, General Harding. I'm aware of my abilities as a photographer, but what I'm not aware of is why I'm here. Other than the fact that you want to see one photo. You've basically disrupted my day and flown me to a US Army base north of nowhere and no one has given me an explanation. They've just said come and bring your camera and laptop. May I ask why?"

General Harding leaned back in his desk chair causing it to groan and squeak beneath his shifting weight. He chuckled then his slight smile dropped from his face, the bulldog returning.

"No, Miss Lawrence, I'm afraid you may not. You don't have a need to know at this moment. If that need changes, I'll be the one to decide that and I'll let you know."

Maggie held the neoprene envelope laptop case in her arms and against her chest in a protective posture. For a moment she held out the hope that she could defy this man and withhold the picture, but she had a feeling that was going to be impossible. He must have sensed what she was thinking.

"Come now, Miss Lawrence. Your cooperation is necessary for us to accomplish an act on behalf of national security. You wouldn't withhold the photograph and prevent our success, now would you? We can be very persuasive, but we would rather you would cooperate of your own free will."

Maggie glanced at Troy. He nodded slightly, his gaze imploring her to co-operate. She hadn't come all this way not to, but she thought she'd find out why they needed her photograph. It was hers after all.

Just then the phone rang on the general's desk and he reached to answer it. "Yes? Yes, of course. Send him in."

The door opened and Senator Scott strolled in.

"Good morning, General. Good morning, everyone. Well, good morning, Maggie. They dragged you in, I see."

"Good morning, Senator." Maggie smiled a thin smile, her laptop still clasped against her chest. "Yes, I'd say dragged is a fair assessment."

The senator chuckled as he grabbed a chair from beside the wall and brought it closer.

"Well, where are we? Bring me up to snuff."

"Miss Lawrence is hesitant to hand over her photograph because I won't read her in on the mission." General Harding's tone was snide as he leaned forward, his arms resting on the shiny surface of the desk. "I was just telling her that…"

"Hold on, General," the senator interrupted him. He turned to Maggie. "Did he also tell you that by not telling you anything, it's for your protection, Maggie? What you don't know will keep you safe?"

"No, he failed to mention that." Maggie turned a lifted brow in the general's direction and continued in a dry tone. "He pretty much threatened to get the photo from me one way or the other."

Senator Scott turned to the general. "Really, General? High handed tactics? Vinegar instead of sugar? Didn't your mama teach you anything?"

General Harding turned his bulldog face on the senator. "I'm a general in the US Army, Brad. Not a politician. Now I want that photograph, and she's not being read-in on this mission at this time. She has no need to know, and we are wasting time."

Bradford Scott turned to Maggie and shook his head. "Sorry, Maggie, but it is important that we have that photograph. With whoever stole your old laptop having it, it's only a matter of time before they figure it out. We need to get a jump on it before they do. It's a matter of national security."

Maggie heaved a heavy sigh and lowered the laptop, pulling it from the case. Without a word, she opened the lid and booted it up. No one spoke as she opened the file where she'd saved the photos. She opened the original first and set the laptop on General

Harding's desk, turning it so everyone could see the screen-sized photo.

"This is the original photograph that I took the day I arrived in Alaska and took my flight-seeing tour. As you can see it's not very clear, but you can see there's something man-made beneath the edge of the glacier."

She closed out that photo and opened the new, zoomed in photo. Before she could say anything, there were exclamations of "Oh my," "Well look at that," "I believe that's it."

Maggie couldn't help but grow angry at the situation. Most everyone in the room knew what was going on except for her, and they weren't about to tell her. It was her photo, for goodness sake. How unfair was that?

"Miss Lawrence," General Harding reached into his desk and pulled out a thumb drive then turned to Maggie, his bulldog demeanor at the forefront. "I'll need you to place both of those photos on this thumb drive for me, then delete them from your computer and your camera. You have no need of them and should either piece of your equipment get stolen again, they won't fall into the wrong hands again. Especially the new zoomed in photo."

Maggie started to argue but knew it would be futile. How could she argue with the US Army? Besides, she had all her pictures backed up on a thumb drive in her purse. What he didn't know…

"Certainly." She reached for the thumb drive and inserted it into the USB port on the laptop, dumping the two photos onto it. Then she deleted the two photos, making a show of hesitation and irritability. She glared at the general. "This is unfair, general. You get what you want. I get nothing."

"My dear, you get the satisfaction of knowing you've helped your country's national security." He held out his hand and accepted the thumb drive when she handed it to him.

"Right." Maggie turned off her computer, then made a show of deleting the original picture from her camera, showing it to him as she did so.

"Very good." General Harding turned to Troy. "Mr. Donovan, do you have any idea where that plane might be located? Does the photo help in any way?"

"I've stared at it several times, sir, and I can't be certain, but I may have a general idea or two where it could be. Sir, there are forty named glaciers in the park and hundreds of unnamed glaciers. Glaciers grow and recede all the time. This particular one could have covered over the plane and is just now receding for the first time in years. The best thing I can suggest is to take a plane up and check the glaciers out. You know, see what we can find."

General Harding turned his cold gaze on Maggie. "Miss Lawrence, you don't have access to the mission, but I'll grant you one thing. When Mr. Donovan takes his reconnaissance flight, you may accompany him and Colonel Williams. Colonel Williams will give you an SD card for your camera and you'll take all the photographs. They won't be landing on this trip, so you'll only be taking photos from the air. When the flight is over, you'll hand the SD card to Colonel Williams and he'll bring it back to me. Deal?"

Maggie's heart soared. She could live with that. For now. "Deal."

Chapter Fifteen

W ell, what have you found?" The arrogance in General Kozlov's voice grated more and more on Pavel's nerves. He grew more demanding with each call.

"I've searched through all of her photographs and only found one that looks the least bit promising. It's hard to tell what it is, but it has possibilities. The photoshop program on her computer is useless." Pavel heard the frustration in his own voice. Surely the Russian general would hear it as well. He hated weakness. "If I had a better program, I'm sure I could find what clues the picture holds."

"Send the photo file to me." The general's voice was dismissive. "I will put our experts on it. They can do what her program cannot."

Irritated the situation had been removed from his hands, Pavel had no choice but to agree. "*Da*. I'll send it via our secure method. What do you want me to do next?"

"I'll let you know as soon as we look at the picture." The line clicked and the phone went dead.

Pavel dropped his cell phone onto the desk in front of him and scrubbed his hand down his face. He'd be glad when this was over and he could get back to... to.... He wasn't sure what he was going to do when this was completed. He'd waited a long time for this mission and he needed to keep his focus on the goal. Getting those papers at any cost. That was all that was important now. The future was still in the future. He must finish this mission. No matter what. No matter who got in the way.

~

Maggie parked her SUV in the tiny parking lot next to the McKinley National Park Airport flight line, slipped on her heavy mittens and grabbed her camera bag. She pulled her parka hood over her head and stepped out of the SUV. Oops. She almost forgot her travel coffee mug. She leaned in and snatched it from the cup holder then locked her car.

An olive-green plane sat at the end of the runway, it's prop spinning. Standing a few feet from it were Troy and Colonel Williams. She hurried in their direction.

"Good morning." Maggie raised her voice to be heard over the plane's engine noise.

"Morning." Both men spoke in unison.

"Sorry we had to drive separately." Troy wrapped an arm around her shoulder. "Did mom tell you I had to come in early?"

Maggie nodded. "Yes. She said one of the dogs was sick. How is he?"

"Yep, it's Party. He's not feeling up to partying right now, but he'll be alright. He's got an intestinal infection that's put him in isolation. Nothing some time and some medication won't help."

Colonel Williams pulled his phone from his pocket and put it to his ear, covering his other ear with his gloved hand. "Yes?" he spoke in a loud voice. "Good. We're all here. Okay, then. Sounds good."

He hung up and dropped the phone back into his pocket. "Let's get aboard the plane. It's time."

Maggie followed the colonel as he led the way. He opened the small door and helped her into the front row of the four-seater. She was surprised she would be sitting up front, but supposed it made sense. She had the camera.

Troy and Colonel Williams climbed into the back seats, and when everyone was seated, Colonel Williams introduced everyone to the pilot, Capt. Joe Barnes.

Maggie decided his Hollywood good looks had nothing on Troy. He flashed an interested smile at her and nodded when she was introduced, but although Maggie acknowledged him as she would anyone, she wasn't interested in anything more. She was already fighting one heart battle. She wasn't about to get involved in another one.

Within minutes they were in the air, and she heard Troy's voice in her headset telling the pilot the coordinates for the first glacier.

"We'll start with the closest and work our way out. We can always hope it's closer rather than further away." Troy's words came through loud and clear.

"What's the name of it?" Maggie surveilled the scenery out her window as she grabbed her camera bag from the floor between her feet.

"Sunset Glacier."

"Hmm. Beautiful name." Maggie prepped her camera as Colonel Williams handed her the SD card as promised.

Within minutes the pilot pointed out the glacier in question. "There it is. I'm taking us closer."

He did a flyby and Maggie snapped a series of pictures just in case.

"That's not it." Troy's voice held a hint of disappointment. "There's nothing there."

"On to the next." Colonel Williams encouraged from beside him. "You said there were forty named glaciers and hundreds of unnamed ones? Well, we've got our work cut out for us."

Maggie peered out the window at the snowy scenery below them. This could take a while.

~

Troy methodically called out the coordinates of each glacier and Captain Barnes flew them there, taking them in as close as possible. Maggie snapped pictures as they zoomed in for a closer look. They tried to keep their spirits up as each glacier had nothing to share. Troy ticked it off the list and they moved on to the next. The hours passed on and it was necessary to fly northwest to Kantishna airport to refuel.

Once they were refueled, they headed back toward the glaciers and, as they moved at a particular angle, Maggie spotted a glint of sun reflecting off something.

"Did you see that, Captain Barnes?" She couldn't help the breathless note in her voice.

"See what?"

"Are you kidding me? The sun was reflecting off of something just over there at the end of that glacier. It was the way we were lined up with it. What would the sun reflect off of out here, Troy?"

"Nothing in nature that would cause that kind of reflection. Sure, there's ice, but it probably wouldn't cause that kind of glint."

"Does that glacier have a name?" Colonel Williams asked.

Troy searched his glacier map. "That's Peter's Glacier. It's at the foot of the western buttress of Mt. Denali."

"Take us down there, Joe. Let's see what's there causing the reflection," Colonel Williams ordered.

"You got it, sir."

The plane circled around and came in at a lower elevation, approaching the glacier on Maggie and Troy's side, giving her ample opportunity for photos.

As they approached, the sun indeed reflected off something, giving them a target to spot.

"That's a plane, lady and gentlemen." Elation filled Troy's voice. "I don't know if that's the one we're looking for, but it's a plane. Great eye, Maggie."

"Thanks." Maggie was busy snapping picture after picture as they flew past. "Can you get any closer, Captain Barnes?"

"Does a bear live in the woods?" he chuckled. "Give me a minute to circle around."

Maggie's insides tightened with excitement. They'd found it. And all because of a reflection. No telling how much longer they would've searched with the map had they not spotted the sun reflecting on the windshield of the fuselage.

"Peter's Glacier, huh?" Maggie looked up from her view finder. "Anything significant about it being at the foot of Mt. Denali?"

Troy folded his map. "I don't know unless the weather that often hangs around Mt. Denali was bad that day and messed with their instruments, causing them to crash. It's one of those things that most likely will never be answered."

"Unless you find an answer inside the plane. You never know," Colonel Williams leaned forward to get a better look.

"Here we go. We're coming in closer." Captain Barnes steered the plane low as Maggie snapped away.

~

"Wow. Look at that." Maggie's voice was hushed amazement in Troy's ears. It matched to a T the emotions thrumming through his veins. Wow, indeed. The sight of the plane and knowing the remains of two men waiting inside to be found, made Troy catch his breath. They'd found them thirty-two years too late.

"Do you think you have enough photos, Miss Lawrence?" Colonel Williams asked.

"I don't think there's much else I can take from here. I'd love to get down there and take pictures, but I know General Harding isn't about to let *that* happen." Maggie capped the lens as Captain Barnes gunned the engine and sped away into the late afternoon sky.

"No, I'm afraid you're right. He won't." Colonel Williams held his hand out over her shoulder.

Troy spotted the wry expression she cast in the colonel's direction before popping the SD card from her camera and dropping it into his hand.

"Thank you for your service to your country, Miss Lawrence. You are to be commended."

"No problem." Maggie tucked her camera in its bag and sat back gazing out her window.

Troy watched as Captain Barnes kept eyeing her. He'd have to put a stop to that. No more interlopers if he had his way about things.

When the plane landed back at the park, Troy hopped out and hurried around to help Maggie out. "Don't forget your coffee mug."

She reached back inside and grabbed it. "Thanks."

"Nice meeting you, Captain Barnes. Colonel Williams. Give my best to the general."

Troy turned Maggie toward their vehicles hoping to get her out of there before Barnes decided to ask her out. They were halfway there when they heard him call her name.

"Miss Lawrence?"

Both Maggie and Troy turned to see Captain Barnes approaching, a big Hollywood smile exposing his pearly whites.

"Yes?"

"May I call you Maggie?" Barnes stopped in front of her.

She considered for a couple of seconds. "That depends."

"Well," he glanced at Troy then back at Maggie. "I was wondering if I could take you out to dinner sometime soon."

Maggie smiled gently and shook her head. "Thank you, Captain Barnes, but no. I'll be heading back to New York soon, and I don't think I want to start a long distant relationship. I'm just not up to that right now. You might say it's just dinner, but that's not where it usually ends. But thanks anyway. It was nice meeting you."

Maggie tossed him a little wave and turned around, walking toward her SUV.

She unlocked it and climbed in. Just before she closed the door, she spotted Troy behind her and left her door open, gazing up at him.

He grinned at her. "If I glanced back, I think I would've seen scorch marks on the ground where he was standing. Ouch. I almost feel sorry for the poor fellow. Almost."

Pucker lines appeared between Maggie's brows. "I tried to be nice and not brutal. I spoke gently, and I didn't lead him on. Was I harsh?"

Troy removed his glove and leaned forward, tracing a finger over the lines between her eyebrows. His heart beat faster at the feel of her skin against his finger. It was cold but soft.

"No. You weren't harsh at all. You let him know you weren't interested and to move on. Nothing wrong with that. You were being honest with him."

His finger moved from between her brows across her brow down her cheek to her chin. He tilted her face up a smidge. "Who can blame him for being interested. You would catch any man's eye, Maggie."

Her gaze met his with a question. Her voice was little more than a whisper. "Any man's?"

Troy gave a slight nod, his gaze never wavering. He swallowed hard, his Adam's apple bobbing, shifting his parka. "Yeah. Any man's."

~

Ludmila sat on the molded plastic stool waiting for a guard to bring Dafna out. She glanced around her. There were other visitors today visiting inmates. She was thankful she was able to visit her daughter. Once she had her hearing, it was possible she would be sent far away where it would be hard to visit her.

The door behind the tiny cubicle opened and she watched as Dafna approached and took the seat behind the glass. She was dressed in her usual orange jumpsuit and shackles. Ludmila was surprised to see she had cut off nearly all her beautiful blond hair. It was cut short and she had a hard look about her.

Once she was seated, Dafna lifted the handset just as Ludmila did.

"Hello, *Mamochka*. How are you?"

Ludmila noticed her daughter didn't smile and her gaze didn't quite meet her mother's. There were bruises on her face.

"I am fine, daughter, but what of you? You have bruises. What has happened? Who has done this?"

Dafna shrugged. "There's nothing to worry about, Mama. I'm fine. It's jail after all."

"Are the guards mistreating you?" Ludmila dropped her voice.

"No, Mama. It's not the guards. There are prisoners in a jail, and they have to prove they're big and tough. Don't worry, I'll be fine. Ivan taught me to take care of myself."

Ludmila nodded and tried to smile. "Yes, he did, didn't he? He tried to make you as tough as he was. You used to follow him everywhere like a puppy, so he taught you to fight and defend yourself. I suppose that was a good thing."

Dafna glanced at the inmates on either side of her then down to the shelf in front of her. "Yes, it was."

Ludmila sighed and shook her head. "Oh, my Dafna. I wish you would cooperate with the…"

"Shhh. Hush, Mama." Dafna's gaze flew to her mother's, severe and cautious, as she warned her then let her gaze trail back to the inmates. She lowered her voice to a whisper. "Do you want me to be killed in here? If anyone should hear you say those words, I'm dead. Do you hear me?"

Ludmila dropped her chin and glanced around from the corners of her eyes. She whispered, "I'm sorry, Dafna. I just think it would help your case to help them."

"How can I help them?" Dafna whispered. "And why should I? They killed Ivan."

"No, daughter. Ivan was on a suicide mission. He killed himself."

"I won't help them, Mama. I won't."

"Not even for me?" Ludmila pled with every emotion from her heart. Dafna's eyes met hers momentarily, and Ludmila saw her waver.

"I must go, Mama. I will see you next week." Dafna started to hang up.

"I'm praying for you, my daughter. I love you."

The area around Dafna's eyes turned pink and watery, but no tears fell as she blinked them away. "I love you, too, *Mamochka*."

Dafna hung up the phone and stood, turning her back and walking toward the door leading back into the prison. The waiting officer opened the door and led her inside. She never looked back.

Hot tears streamed down Ludmila's cheeks as she closed her eyes and dropped her chin to her chest. *Oh Lord. Help my Dafna to understand she needs You. She's lost her way in a world of bitterness and hate.*

"Ma'am, you must leave now." A tap on her shoulder brought Ludmila's head up. She wiped her tears away, not caring what the officer thought. Surely, he'd seen his share of loved ones crying in the prison visitation room. If not, it was too bad. This mother's heart cared and would weep for her daughter.

"Yes, of course." Ludmila stood and held her head high as she made her way toward the door and out to her car.

The pastor who had shared the gospel with her after Evgene had escaped the Soviet Union had perished when he was discovered by the secret police. Fortunately, he never gave up the members of his underground church. As a young mother, Ludmila had cherished the few pages of the book of John that she'd hidden away and read daily. Now, she had her own complete Bible and it meant the world to her. She had tried to teach the children about Jesus Christ, and they had kept the secret of the church. At first, they longed to be with their father. Their family was highly scrutinized by the government after Evgene's defection. Eventually the children were taken in and told lies to confuse them and stir ill-will toward their father, suggesting he was a traitor to his country and had abandoned his family.

When the Soviet Union fell and democracy was introduced, the children had already been indoctrinated. It was 2014 before Ludmila and her children successfully immigrated to the US.

She climbed into her car and closed the door behind her as memories of the past continued to flood her mind. Evgene had the best of intentions for his family, but he'd gone about it all the wrong way. He'd stolen military secrets in order to ingratiate himself with the US government, thinking as a soviet pilot they would accept him more readily.

Ludmila sighed and closed her eyes. In the end, he'd gotten himself killed and his children were bitter and angry at him and at the US senator who they think failed to rescue him. She had no doubt Evgene was dead when his plane hit the ground.

Lord, one of my children is dead and beyond saving. Only You can save the other one. Please work a miracle and save her. Ludmila's mother's heart was heavy as she started her car and headed for home.

Chapter Sixteen

I sent you the file with the photograph of the plane." General Kozlov said without preamble. "Our experts zoomed in and got a closeup. You already have the original. I have the location and will forward the coordinates to you. Make your plans to go there and retrieve the packet of papers."

Pavel ran a hand through his hair as excitement coursed through his body. While the general spoke, Pavel opened the file and stared at the elusive plane. A smile lifted the corners of his mouth. Ahh. There it was.

"Pavel. Are you there?" The general's voice raised in frustration.

"Yes, General. I was bringing up the photo as you were speaking. I see it. They did an excellent job of zooming in. Are they certain of the coordinates? Let's hope they did as equally good a job on locating that particular glacier as they did with the photograph."

"You needn't worry about that." General Kozlov's words were clipped. "You just do your job."

"Yes, well, they've never encountered the Alaskan outback of the Denali National Park, have they? There are hundreds of glaciers. They must get it right the first time."

The phone clicked indicating the general had hung up. Apparently, he was none too happy with Pavel's lack of assurance in his expert's abilities to find the right glacier.

Leaning forward Pavel stared at the photo of the plane. He felt a smile lift the corners of his mouth as excitement filled him. "Ah yes. You and I will meet. Soon."

~

"Miss Lawrence, I haven't heard from you in a while, and I'd really like to know what's going on up there in our 49th state." Mr. Radford's voice was patient but stern. "We have a contract with *National Scenic Wildlife Magazine* for wildlife photos and so far, you've sent nothing in. Are you still working on Senator Scott's visit or what the heck's going on?"

Maggie admired the man for keeping his temper in check. He'd been in the magazine and newspaper business for a long time and knew what he was doing. He was also right in his disapproval of her lack of contact lately and the fact that she'd failed to send the contracted for photos.

"Sir, are you sitting down? There's a lot going on up here in the 49th state, and it may take a few minutes for me to tell you about it." Maggie paced across her bedroom and back several times as she gave him a brief rundown of the occurrences over the last few weeks. From the attempted shootings, to her break-ins to the accident putting dear Mrs. Scott into intensive care.

"Sir, she was moved into a regular room a few days ago and she's expected to go home today. I've given them privacy when it comes to the hospital, however I did get a statement from the senator this morning making a public announcement about his wife's condition. I sent it to you right after, and it should be in your inbox."

Maggie heard the creak of Mr. Radford's chair across the line. "Maggie, why didn't you call and tell me all this was going on?"

"Sir, things have been moving rather quickly, and unfortunately, lives have been in danger." She paused for a moment. "You know you can't put any of this in print, right?"

"Of course, I do. You'd be surprised at what my previous life involved. But if I told you...."

"I know, I know." Maggie chuckled. "You'd have to kill me, right?"

"Something like that." He gave a short laugh then grew serious again. "Don't worry. It'll go no further. When the Scott situation came up, I stalled the wildlife magazine. I'll stall them some more."

"Thank you, sir. I'll get back on it as soon as I can."

"You do that." He paused. "And Maggie, stay in touch. I don't like having to call to find out what's going on. For all I knew, a polar bear had gotten you."

Maggie laughed. "Not before I would've snapped a picture of him."

~

"How's the arm, sir?" Troy knocked on the superintendent's open office door.

Wade glanced up from his task over the rim of his glasses and waved Troy inside. "Oh, it's mending, I suppose. I'm just thankful I didn't end up in ICU like poor Mrs. Scott."

"Yes, sir. Aren't we all?" Troy tossed a thumb over his shoulder toward the front of the building. "Natalya said you wanted to see me."

"Yes, please have a seat."

Troy dropped into one of the chairs in front of his boss's desk just as Wade handed him a paper. "What's this, sir?"

"The results of the fingerprint analysis on the Ruger 9 mm handgun found in the dumpster behind the snack bar. They match the fingerprints on the rifle used the day Calvin Jacobs was shot and in the attempted shooting of the senator."

Troy glanced up from the paper. "You're saying Ivan Orlov was the shooter the night of dinner at the Denali Wilderness Lodge."

"I'm saying that's what the results indicate." Wade pointed at the paper.

"So that solves that mystery." Troy leaned forward and laid the paper back on Wade's desk, then he leaned back in his chair and propped one knee across the other. "My question is, since Ivan Orlov was killed the day Jacobs was shot, and Dafna was arrested and jailed a few days after her brother was killed, then who broke into Maggie's cabin and stole her laptop? That happened *after* both of those incidents."

Troy had Wade's full attention now. His boss leaned back in his swivel chair, causing it to squeak as he moved.

"That's an interesting point, Troy. Go on."

"Sir, I'm thinking perhaps there's a third person in this game. At a minimum. In other words, the senator may not be safe with Ivan dead and Dafna behind bars."

Superintendent Wade leaned forward. "It would sure make sense. Maggie's laptop was the only thing stolen, and General Harding and Senator Scott ascribe a sinister national security reason behind it."

"Yes sir. Remember my Army buddy who was looking into things for me?"

"Yes." His boss nodded, a pucker between his brows.

"Well, not only did he dig up information concerning Ivan and Dafna's immigrations, but he also discovered that their mother, Ludmila Orlov, immigrated to Alaska at the same time. That corroborates what General Harding told us."

The superintendent leaned forward resting his arms against his desk. "It sure does. Troy, I want you to find this woman and interview her. See which side she's on. You'll know before long if she supports her children or not."

"Yes, sir."

"See if she knows anything about a third party or a radical group that the kids belonged to."

"Want me to take Bryce along?"

Superintendent Wade rubbed his chin as he thought for a moment. "No, I don't think so this time."

He let his gaze trail sideways, not landing on anything in particular. Troy could tell he was still considering his question so kept quiet and waited.

The superintendent's fingers drummed on the desktop as his facial features screwed up in thought.

Moments later his gaze swung back to Troy's. "I have a better idea. I want you to take Natalya along with you."

"Natalya, sir?" Troy had no idea where this was leading. Their receptionist was *not* an investigative officer.

His boss chuckled. "No, I haven't slipped off my rocker. I understand she has no experience in investigation, but she does have an empathetic heart. She might be able to help draw this mother out."

Troy scratched the back of his neck and shook his head. "If you say so, sir."

"I'll have a talk with her before you go."

"Whatever you say, sir."

~

Natalya called Ludmila and made an appointment for her and Troy to stop by for a visit. With Natalya's disarming personality, she made it seem like they were calling to make their condolences with just some small park business to attend to on the side.

When they arrived later that afternoon, Ludmila opened the door with no hesitation and allowed them entry. Natalya immediately gave the woman a warm hug. Troy, ready to get down to business, felt like things had been taken right out of his hands. He wasn't about to hug the woman who he knew nothing about except she was the mother of two killers. Instead he settled with shaking her hand.

Troy sized her up as best he could which wasn't much. She was about five foot three or four and slightly plump as some of the best Slavic cooks he'd met were. Her blond and gray hair was styled short around a broad face. She seemed to wear a mantle of sadness that matched features that bore the same emotion. He supposed when your children lived in hate and bitterness with the goal to kill it would be heartbreaking to a mother.

"We're so sorry for your loss, Mrs. Orlov." Natalya held Ludmila's hands in hers. She introduced herself and then Troy.

"Please, call me Ludmila. Come. Come. Please have a seat." They had no trouble understanding her in spite of her Russian accent. She led them into a sitting room and waved them to sit down. "May I get you something to drink?"

"No, nothing for me, thanks." Troy waved a hand as he took a chair.

"No thanks." Natalya sat down.

Ludmila also sat. "Your name is Russian, Natalya, but you have no accent."

"My grandmother is Russian." Natalya smiled and clasped her hands in her lap.

"Here or in Russia?"

"Oh, she's here now." Natalya turned to Troy and smiled.

Troy leaned his elbows on his knees, leaning forward. "Ludmila, we're sorry about what happened to Ivan and to Dafna, however…"

"Please, you must not apologize for anything my children have done, Mr. Donovan. Ivan and Dafna chose their paths themselves. No one forced them to attempt to kill Senator Scott." Her voice wavered as tears gathered in the corners of her eyes.

"Are you certain of that, Ludmila? Was there ever any indication that they may have been working with someone?"

Ludmila stared at Troy for a few moments before dropping her gaze to her clasped hands. "As you may or may not know, Dafna did not live here, but she was often here when she was not working. I'm not one hundred percent sure, but sometimes there was someone who would come to the door and ask for Ivan and Dafna. Mostly they would go out and meet someone. I would hear them whispering sometimes. I would hear them mention the name Pavel."

"Pavel?" Troy asked. "Any other names besides Pavel?"

"No, no other names. Just Pavel."

"Did Pavel have a last name?"

Ludmila thought for a moment. "Dub, Dub, Dubro."

She shook her head then closed her eyes. Her brows furrowed, and she remained silent for several moments. Then her eyes popped open. "Dubrovsky. Pavel Dubrovsky."

"You're amazing, Ludmila." Her cheeks pinked slightly at his words. "Now can you tell me what this Pavel Dubrovsky looks like?"

Ludmila closed her eyes again and scrunched her brow in thought. "Most of the time he had a hat pulled low over his face, but I remember once he removed it for a few moments when he thought I wasn't looking. He had blue eyes, and blond hair. He might have been in his late twenties or early thirties. Other than that, I don't know."

She opened her eyes and shook her head. "I'm sorry I can't be of more help."

"Perhaps you can, Ludmila." Natalya reached across and placed a hand on the older woman's work-worn one. "Do you think you could get Dafna to talk to us? To tell us who this man is"

Ludmila turned her hand over and patted Natalya's. She shook her head, a resigned expression on her face. "I've tried to do this thing already. I've asked her about talking to the authorities so she could possibly get a lighter sentence at her hearing. She refuses because she thinks the inmates will kill her. Dafna had bruises all over her face the last time I saw her at the jail. It broke my heart."

"Oh no." Natalya cooed and took Ludmila's hands in hers again.

Troy heaved a heavy sigh. "Jails and prisons have a hierarchy or a pecking order, if you will. They're letting her know where she fits in. If she'll co-operate and help find this guy, then her sentence would be lighter. Most likely by a lot."

Ludmila turned pleading eyes on Troy. "Somehow, someone must tell her this."

"Who is her lawyer?" Troy asked, a thought attempting to form in his mind.

"She has a court appointed lawyer." Ludmila shook her head. "I don't like him. He's...he's...how do you say? Slimmy?"

"You mean slimy?" Natalya chuckled. "Some lawyers are known to be like that, yes, but not all."

Ludmila stood from her chair and walked to a table across the room, picking up a business card and handing it to Troy. He took the card and read it.

"I've heard of this guy. Not the best reputation in Fairbanks. I'll see what I can do, but don't say anything to Dafna yet."

"No, no I won't." Ludmila shook her head with vehemence and dropped back onto her chair.

Troy leaned forward, his hands clasped loosely between his knees. "Ludmila, before Senator Scott came to Alaska, he received a warning not to come. He was told he would be in danger if he did. Do you know who might've sent him that warning?"

Ludmilla's gaze dropped to the floor and her cheeks pinked. Her fingers had been loosely clasped in her lap but now they began to tighten and fidget. She couldn't meet Troy's gaze.

"Ludmila?" Troy's voice was soft. "I'm not asking to get that person in trouble. It actually saved the senator and his wife's life. It warned them enough that they didn't drink the champagne when Dafna tried to poison them. Was it you, Ludmila?"

Her gaze lifted to his. "I didn't know for sure what my children had planned, but I suspected they were going to try to do something, Mr. Donovan. I tried to talk them out of whatever they had planned, but they wouldn't talk to me and they wouldn't listen. All I could do was send an anonymous warning."

Natalya smiled and placed a hand over Ludmila's clenched fingers. "Well, even though the Scotts came to Alaska, your warning still worked, Ludmila."

"Exactly." Troy stood and smiled at Ludmila. "You've been helpful to us today, ma'am. We need to find this Pavel Dubrovsky before he finishes what your children started. I hope you're not offended by that."

Ludmila placed a calloused hand on Troy's cheek. "I am not, Mr. Donovan. I cannot save my son, but I would like to save my daughter. I pray and pray for her. Only God can do the miracle that will save her soul. Do you believe, Mr. Donovan?"

Under the scrutiny of this woman's clear eyes, Troy had the sudden urge to race out the door. He knew she wanted an honest answer. "Sometimes I'm not sure what to believe, Ludmila."

A sweet smile brightened her face for the first time since he'd walked in the door. "I believe God will make a way, Mr. Donovan, but if He chooses not to, He'll give me the grace I need to go on. You had better decide what you're going to believe and stop walking the fence. There's God's joy on one side and the devil on the other. Which are you going to give in to?"

~

When Troy and Natalya climbed into the park SUV, Troy pulled his cell phone from his pocket and called Superintendent Wade.

"Sir, Ludmila Orlov was quite cooperative and would like to see her daughter be the same with the authorities. However, Dafna has a court appointed lawyer that Ludmila finds is less than squeaky clean. She needs someone who can help her get better advice and a plea bargain for information on a guy named Pavel Dubrovsky. He's possibly our third party. We don't know yet if he has others involved or not."

"Good work, Troy. How did Natalya do?"

Troy glanced over at the receptionist. "She was amazing, sir. Swooped in and disarmed Mrs. Orlov, but there was no doubt she meant every word of it. She earned her investigative pay, that's for sure."

Natalya's face pinked as she gave him a cheeky grin. Troy shook his head and grinned back.

"Great. I had a feeling she would be the one for the job." Wade paused a moment then added, "I know a good lawyer who takes pro bono cases, Troy. Let me give him a call and see if he would be willing to take Dafna's case. Considering she attempted to murder a US senator, he may not want to be anywhere near it, but if he doesn't, maybe he knows a guy who knows a guy. I'll see what I can do."

"Sounds good, sir. We're heading back."

~

As Troy drove the park SUV south out of Fairbanks toward Denali, he realized it had grown quiet in the cab. Glancing over, Troy noticed Natalya had dropped her head back against the headrest, her eyes closed and mouth wide open as she emitted soft deep breaths. A grin tugged at his lips. With two-and-a-quarter hours to drive back to the park, she'd get a good nap in. The receptionist had always treated him like a big brother, and he'd always treated her like a little sister. They got along fine that way.

Maggie's beautiful face took shape before his mind's eye. Now she, on the other hand, was nothing like a sister. Maggie made his heart race, his breathing seize in his chest, his palms turn sweaty, his mind…well, she was always on his mind. Troy was in love with Maggie. There was no reason not to admit it, but she would never settle into a relationship with him until he made things right with God. He had no doubts about that.

Ludmila's words returned to his mind. *"You had better decide what you're going to believe and stop walking the fence. There's God's joy on one side and the devil on the other. Which are you going to choose?"*

Troy had never thought about his spiritual wellbeing in those terms before, but it was a simplistic view that made sense. He *was* walking a fence, and he'd put off making a decision. He'd placed his trust in Christ a long time ago but when Liz had died, he'd just stopped talking to God. He hadn't really blamed Him, but he'd pretty much walked away from Him. Was it the same thing? In his own way, had he actually blamed Him by walking away from Him?

Troy gripped the steering wheel tighter than necessary then realized what he was doing. As his fingers began to ache, he made himself relax his grip. He glanced at Natalya. Still sound asleep. Her deep breathing had turned to soft snores.

What do You want me to do, God? I'm kind of floundering here. You know my feelings for Maggie. I admit I love her, but it's not going to go anywhere until I get things straightened out with You. I'm not sure how to do that. Another thought struck him. *Even if I do get things right with You, she's still going back to New York, isn't she?*

That thought dropped like a lead weight into the pit of his stomach and weighed heavy on his heart. It shouldn't. He'd known all along she wouldn't stay here forever. She'd come to do a job with the intention of leaving when she was done.

Releasing the steering wheel with one hand, he scrubbed it down his face and breathed in a heavy breath, releasing it all at once.

So, what now, God? I'm done walking the fence, as Ludmila called it. I'm ready to let Liz and what happened to her go and move forward, but I'm going to need Your help. Whether Maggie leaves or not I need You back in my life. I can't keep going down the fence line of spiritual instability. I've got Jeremy to think about. I need to be a godly example before my son. Will you forgive me for walking away from You? Please forgive me for all of it: my attitude, my bitterness, my grudge. Everything.

Right there in the driver's seat of the park SUV with a sleeping Natalya in the passenger seat, Troy made things right with his Creator. Who said you had to go to church and kneel at an altar to talk to God? Peace settled over Troy as he shared his heart and allowed the heavenly Father to cleanse and forgive him. He remembered from scripture the thief that hung on the cross beside Jesus and asked him to forgive him of his sins. Jesus answered with "Today thou shalt be with me in paradise." That thief didn't have to get down from the cross and find a church to be baptized in. He was promised a place in heaven that day. As his own heart filled with forgiveness and peace, Troy was thrilled that he could talk with the Father anywhere, anytime. And the especially amazing thing? Without a shadow of a doubt God was listening.

Chapter Seventeen

Since we have the location of the plane, I want to know your plans for retrieving the papers." General Kozlov's voice grated on Pavel's ears. He would be so glad when this mission was over. Disappearing into the Alaskan outback was looking pretty good about now, in spite of the general's orders to return to Russia. "If it doesn't meet with my approval then I will tell you what I want you to do. I'm giving you the opportunity to see if you can come up with a workable plan first."

"Well, I'm sure what I have planned will certainly be workable, General." Pavel's tone was dry. He was sick and tired of being talked down to by this egotistical man.

"We shall see...."

"Yes, we will, General. I'm not one of your fresh-out-of-the-academy soldiers. I'm sure you will be pleased." Pavel had no intention of returning to Russia and his insubordination was growing. He didn't care.

Silence met his comment for several seconds before the general spoke.

"Pavel, I understand you have been on your own for a while now, and you have been in a holding pattern for some time as you await instructions. However, your attitude of insubordination will *not* be tolerated. Do I make myself clear?" The general's words grew louder and more clipped as he spoke.

It was a good thing there was no video along with the phone call. Pavel rolled his eyes and slunk down in his chair. "Yes, sir."

His words were appropriate even if his tone was a bit insincere.

"Make your plans and have them ready for me to approve at my next call." The general hung up with a click.

Pavel was used to being dismissed without courtesy. Whatever. When this mission was over and those infernal papers were in the hands of the general, he would fade into the Alaskan wilderness. No one would ever find him to boss him around again. No one.

~

"Hey, Paul. How's it going?" Troy held his cell phone to his ear as he crossed one ankle over the other on top of his desk in his office at the sled dog kennels.

"It's going alright. What do you need?" Paul's voice held a note of resignation.

"Aww, come on Paul. You make it sound like I only call when I need something."

"Well, yeah. I guess that's about right."

Troy chuckled. "Can I help it if you're good at what you do? You can find anything about anybody, my friend. The problem is, we don't live anywhere near each other so it's not like we can hang out or anything."

"Well, there is that." Paul chuckled. "What's up? What are you looking for now?"

"I need information on Pavel Dubrovsky. He's possibly our third guy in the assassination attempt of Senator Scott, but we won't know for sure until we have more information on him. Can you see what you can dig up for me?"

"Anything else you can tell me about him?"

"Blue eyes and maybe blond hair. Late twenties or early thirties. Nothing else to go on for now."

"Right. I'll see what I can find out and I'll let you know." Paul paused. "You know the drill."

"I know. If it's secret or blah blah blah. It's okay. I'll take whatever you can give me. Thanks, buddy. I appreciate it."

"Sure thing."

Troy ended the call and dropped his cell phone on his desk then meshed his fingers in his lap, his elbows on the arms of his desk chair. He sat staring at his hands for a few moments. The overhead lights glinted off his wedding ring drawing his attention. Why was he still wearing it? That question hadn't really occurred to him until now.

He'd always been faithful to his wife the whole time they'd been married. Not once had he ever considered…. Troy swiped his hand over his face as if to dismiss that thought, then spun the wedding band on his left hand between the thumb and index fingers of his right hand. Suddenly he slipped it off and held it up to eye level, looking through the gold circlet. *Why did you do what you did, Liz? Why did you leave? You might still be alive today if you hadn't.*

She'd made her choice and she was gone. He was a widower now. He didn't have to wear this gold band anymore. Troy closed his eyes and Maggie's beautiful face was right there. He saw it more now than he did Liz's.

Troy opened his eyes slowly and again looked at the gold circlet. With determination, he stood and dropped it in his pants pocket. No more. When he got home, he'd put it away. If he was no longer married to Liz, then why wear it? It was time to move on.

~

"Hello?" Maggie propped her cell phone on her shoulder as she rushed around her bedroom gathering her things together for the day.

"Hi Maggie. How's it going?"

She halted in the middle of the room and took the phone in her hand. "Jud? Is that you?"

"Well, of course it is. I'm just calling to see how you're doing and see if you're ready for another dinner flight." Jud chuckled. "I don't know about you, but I had a great time. It's been over a week since we went out. Want to try another restaurant? I'll be happy to fly down and pick you up again? The days are getting longer by about ten minutes. It's been about nine days. We've added an hour and half to our day already. What do you say?"

Maggie laughed. "I say you'd make a great salesman, but I have to turn you down right now. Sorry, Jud. I have a job to do."

Silence met her answer for a few moments.

"Jud? You still there?"

"Yeah. Yeah, I'm still here." Jud's reply was a little more clipped than Maggie expected. "Then we'll try another time. See you soon."

He hung up with a click.

Maggie stared at her reflection in the dresser mirror, uncertainty drawing her brows together in a pucker. What was that all about?

She dropped her phone in her purse, grabbed it and her camera bag and headed toward the kitchen.

Clarissa was pouring coffee into a mug. "Good morning, Maggie. Want some coffee?"

"Yes, please. That would be awesome." Maggie reached for her parka. "I'll take it to go."

"Where are you going in such an all-fired hurry?" Clarissa poured coffee in Maggie's travel mug and set out the creamer so she could doctor it how she liked.

"I'm meeting up with Troy shortly. He's actually going to take me out for a wildlife photography shoot. Imagine that. After all this time, I'm actually going to go out looking for wildlife." She pulled the zipper up on her parka and pulled her gloves from the parka pockets. "I'm excited about it."

Clarissa patted her cheek. "My Troy will see that you find what you need for your photographs. He knows that park like the back of his hand."

Maggie gathered Clarissa's hand in hers. "I know he will."

"You need to eat breakfast before you go. It'll be a long day if you don't." Her words of wisdom fell on deaf ears as Maggie prepared her coffee.

"I'll just grab a couple trail mix bars." Maggie reached into a cupboard and took down a box, pulling them out and dropping them into her camera bag. She returned the box to the cupboard.

"Have a great day, Clarissa."

A sudden movement around her ankles made Maggie look down to find Michael Jordan rubbing himself against her boots. "Well, good morning, Mr. Jordan."

She reached down and rubbed between his furry orange ears. "You have a wonderful day, too, sir."

A light snow was falling when Maggie drove into the employee parking lot and parked her small SUV then walked to the sled dog kennels. She opened the door to the kennel offices and stepped inside the warm building. The main room was rustic with exposed beams on the ceiling. Former sled dog name plates were hung all around the beams, at least a hundred and fifty or more. A rustic wood counter stood at the back of the room, but the room was empty at the moment. She heard a voice in Troy's office and strode over to the open door. Leaning on the doorframe, she saw him talking into his cell phone and waited for him to finish.

Troy glanced up and noticed her in the doorway, his gaze lighting up as he lifted a finger indicating he'd only be a minute.

"Yes, sir. I understand. Of course. I'll be right there." Lowering the phone, he pressed the end call button and dropped the phone into his jacket pocket. Troy turned his attention to Maggie as he crossed the room and stopped right in front of her.

"Good morning." A half grin lifted one corner of his mouth while the other remained drawn downward.

"You don't look like that was a good call." Maggie reached up and touched the side of his face that was drawn down. "This side isn't smiling. What's wrong?"

Troy took her finger in his hand and kissed the tip, then gathered her hand in his. "It wasn't. At least it's not for today."

Maggie's heart dropped. Now what? "What do you mean? Who was it?"

"It was Superintendent Wade. He just got a call from General Harding's office. He's asked, and I think the word 'asked' is a loose term, that the superintendent and I come for a meeting with the general, Colonel Williams and Senator Scott. Today they're making plans for the trip to Peter's Glacier."

Maggie felt her shoulders slump. There went her wildlife photo shoot. She shook her head, a heavy sigh escaping as she leaned against the doorframe.

"Even though I don't know why, I know this whole deal with the senator is important, but at the moment, I have nothing to work on, Troy. Not even Senator Scott."

Frustration threatened to overwhelm Maggie as she turned and left Troy's office. She strode across the larger outer room toward the front door. Just as she reached for the long, carved wooden door handle, Troy placed a hand on the door, preventing her from opening it.

His voice over her shoulder was soft and tender. "Maggie, please don't go away angry."

Maggie paused for a few seconds then turned to find him close. Far too close. His arm was still over her shoulder, hand against the door, his face way too near hers.

She dropped her gaze and stepped away from the door where she would be able to think. Away from his close proximity.

Maggie stepped to the middle of the room and turned to face Troy, waiting for him to turn around.

Troy turned and crossed his arms over his chest. "I'm sorry I can't take you out as we planned today, Maggie. Once they have the plan down, I'm sure we'll implement it and get this done. We found out some more information yesterday that should help in our investigation into who's trying to kill the senator. Hopefully that, too, will draw to a close."

Maggie nodded. "Good. I hope so. I got a call from Mr. Radford. He wanted to know what's going on and why I haven't sent any wildlife photos. I explained things in a nutshell to him, and he's going to stall the magazine for a while longer, but they won't accept that forever."

Troy nodded, his expression grim. "I know."

Maggie took a few steps in his direction. "Troy, if you can't help me, then I may have to ask Bryce or one of the other rangers for help. You know this park so much better, but I have to get some photographs soon."

Maggie watched as a look of distaste replaced Troy's grim expression. "Hold off for now and give me some time, Maggie. Please."

She nodded. "Alright. Mr. Radford understood and is working on it. So will I. But only as long as he can."

~

"Mr. Donovan, I want you and Colonel Williams heading into the park tomorrow night." General Harding's bulldog face glowered across his desk at Troy. "The US Army will take you in by UH-60 Black Hawk helicopter where you'll retrieve the packet of Soviet Cold War papers. Understood?"

"No, sir." Troy shook his head. "We won't go in by helicopter. That's not how we do things in Denali National Park."

General Harding harrumphed and glared at Troy then turned his glare on Superintendent Wade. "I do believe your young ranger is being insubordinate, Superintendent."

Troy's boss grinned at the general and eyed him over the rims of his glasses. "I don't think that's possible, General. Number one, he answers to me, not you. Number two, we do things differently in Denali, and we have certain policies that we operate by. We don't allow helicopters in the park except in extreme emergencies and, in my opinion, this isn't one. I'm in charge of the park and that decision is mine to make."

The superintendent turned to Troy and grinned. "Carry on."

Troy turned to the general. "Sir, no disrespect intended, but as Superintendent Wade said, we have certain policies that we follow and have for decades. Planes are flown over the park but don't land in the park except at designated landing strips. There's no knowing the landing conditions anywhere else in the park, so it would be too unsafe to try and land a plane anywhere else. The only other option is our sled dogs. They're trained to go anywhere in the park, and they don't leave an ecologically hazardous footprint that mechanical transports like the helicopter do. In the case where we called in the helicopters to retrieve the senator, Calvin Jacobs and the senator's security team, that was indeed an emergency."

Troy turned to Colonel Williams. "Have you ever mushed before, Colonel?"

Colonel Williams shook his head. "No, I haven't."

"No problem. You can ride on the sled." Troy turned back to the general. "This will be a piece of cake, sir."

General Harding leaned back in his chair, his bulldog expression firmly imprinted on his features. It was clear he was less than happy the park service had taken charge of what had started out as a US Army mission. Troy had no doubt he would have a long talk with Colonel Williams before they headed into the wilderness. It wouldn't matter. Troy would still be in charge of his team of sled dogs.

After a few moments of thought, the general leaned forward.

"Our ultimate goal, gentlemen, is to retrieve that packet of Soviet papers. No matter what."

He turned his gaze on Senator Scott. "Senator? Do you have anything to say?"

"Be careful, Troy. Colonel Williams." Senator Scott looked first one man then the other in the eye. "We suspect there's possibly someone out there looking for that same packet. They didn't steal Miss Lawrence's computer just to look at her pictures. There was purpose behind that theft. If we could figure it out, so can they. If they haven't already gotten there, they may be on their way."

~

Maggie had no idea what to do with herself. The public road into the park was closed for the winter and wouldn't open until sometime at the end of April. That would do her no good for pursuing photographs of wildlife herself. She drove back toward the entrance to the park with no goal in mind, thinking she should just head back home. Perhaps she could help Clarissa with something. As she turned left toward McKinley Village and passed Denali Wilderness Lodge, an idea popped into her head.

Mrs. Scott was back at the lodge now recuperating from the car accident. Perhaps she would be up to a short visit. Maggie wouldn't stay long. Just long enough to see how she's doing and let her know Maggie was praying for her.

Maggie turned around in one of the gift shop parking lots and headed back to the Denali Wilderness Lodge. She parked near the entrance and hurried inside. Just inside the entrance, she dusted the snow from her parka and glanced around. It looked completely different from the night of the senator's dinner. In daylight it looked more like what it was, a rustic Alaskan lodge. She spotted the gift shop beyond the reception desk and thought flowers for Mrs. Scott might be a welcome gift.

Ten minutes later she climbed the main staircase to the second floor with a bouquet of colorful flowers in a vase. When she reached the senator's suite, she found the security guards just as she'd expected.

"Good morning, gentlemen." Maggie flashed her disarming smile. "Would it be possible to visit with Mrs. Scott for a few minutes? I brought these for her hoping to raise her spirits. I know she's recovering, so I won't stay long. I promise."

Both guards eyed her with narrowed gazes, as one of them said, "Good morning, Miss Lawrence. I'll see if Mrs. Scott is accepting visitors. Wait here."

His stern voice and cool gaze sent a chill down Maggie's spine. Hmmm. At least he was doing his job to keep the senator' wife safe. She'd just have to be careful not to get on their bad side.

He knocked on the door and waited until an older woman opened it. The guard mumbled something then the woman smiled and nodded before closing the door. The guard turned to face Maggie but said nothing as he waited.

Maggie had the urge to tap her toe on the carpeted floor, but it wouldn't be loud enough and would lose the effect she wanted. Too bad it wasn't ceramic tile.

A few minutes later the door opened wide and the woman waved Maggie forward. "Please, won't you come in? Mrs. Scott is eager to see you."

"Thank you." Maggie stepped inside a small entryway as the woman closed the door behind her.

She followed the woman as she led her down a short hallway into a sitting room where Miriam Scott half reclined on a suede sofa amidst pillows and afghans.

Maggie approached and took the hand that Miriam held out. "Pardon me if I don't get up, my dear. I'm still a bit weak, and I reserve what energy I have for when I do have to get up."

"Oh, no. Don't worry." Maggie released her hand and set the vase of flowers on the coffee table in front of the sofa. "You stay where you're the most comfortable."

"Oh, dear Maggie. Those flowers are simply gorgeous. Thank you so much. They do so brighten this room, don't you think?" Miriam leaned over to touch the petals of several of the flowers. "My, my, they are lovely. And such a variety you've brought. How wonderful."

The housekeeper waited to take Maggie's coat then slipped out of the room as Maggie made herself comfortable in the chair near the couch. "I'm sorry I couldn't visit sooner. There's been a lot going on."

Miriam nodded. "Don't I know it. Brad has kept me abreast of things for the most part. At least once I got out of ICU. He told me your cabin was broken into. Not once but twice. And they stole your laptop. How terrible. I'm so sorry, Maggie. It seems there's been a lot of bad things happening lately."

Just how much did Miriam Scott know, for goodness sake? "Yes, there has been. It seems I may have taken a picture of something, and someone wanted it badly enough to steal my laptop."

"Oh yes. The picture of the plane. Well, the fellows will get out to that glacier and they'll retrieve whatever it is they need to retrieve then Brad and I can go home to Washington."

Did all senator's wives know this much about their husband's business as this wife did? Maggie certainly hoped not or the fate of the country was most likely doomed. It was terrifying to think the senator was sharing this much information with his wife and she in turn was sharing it with a freelance photographer, neither of which had security clearances. Yikes. At least it sounded like she didn't know what they were going to retrieve. Thank goodness. Of course, neither did Maggie.

"How are you feeling, Mrs. Scott?" Maggie decided a change of subject was in order.

"First off, you must call me Miriam." The lady shoved a tendril of hair away from her forehead and attempted a faint smile. "I'm still quite sore and grow fatigued easily. You might not have heard. I had quite a bit of internal bleeding, and I lost my spleen due to the accident. That, of course, is *not* good. I'll have to be extra cautious for the rest of my life as I'll be susceptible to infections, you know."

"Gracious, no I hadn't heard that. I'm so sorry." Maggie shook her head. "Anything they can do to prevent them?"

Miriam nodded. "Mostly antibiotics for the rest of my life as well as vaccinations."

"Well, I'm glad they have a plan for you." Maggie shoved a lock of hair behind her ear that had fallen forward against her cheek.

"Oh yes, my dear." Miriam waved a hand. "But please, I want to know how that handsome Ranger Donovan is doing. Please do tell me. And how is his wife, dear?"

Maggie's heart leapt into her throat. Uh oh. Where was *this* going? "I assume Ranger Donovan is doing well. He sure stays busy with this case he's working on, that's for sure."

Maggie released a light chuckle. "He's in and out of the office all the time, and he hasn't had a chance to take me out for the photo shoots the magazine sent me to take. It's just been crazy."

Would Miriam forget about the second part of her question?

"Oh, my goodness. Brad told me how they've had so much going on, like I mentioned when you came in, Maggie." Miriam tilted her head a tad and narrowed her eyes at Maggie before continuing. "How is his wife taking him being so busy with all this?"

Maggie drew in a deep breath and released it slowly. Nope. She hadn't forgotten the second part of her question.

"Um, well, it seems Ranger Donovan is a widower." Maggie's lips felt dry all of a sudden and she reached into her purse for her Chapstick. Anything to avoid Miriam's searching gaze. What did she want from her anyway?

"Really? How sad." Miriam raised one brow as a grin lifted the corners of her thin lips. She looked anything but sad. Instead she looked as if she might be devising a plan in her head.

Maggie stood and gathered her purse. "I won't keep you, Miriam. You need your rest. I just wanted to drop by and let you know I'm praying for you."

Miriam tilted her head as a curious expression settled on her features. "I'm not sure I've ever had anyone tell me that, dear Maggie. Thank you. I appreciate it."

"My pleasure."

Hortense appeared with Maggie's coat and helped her into it. Maggie thanked her then started walking toward the exit. Miriam halted her.

"Maggie."

She stopped and turned around. "Yes?"

"Would you like to come tomorrow evening for dinner and perhaps visit with Brad and I afterwards? We haven't had a nice quiet evening in a while, and we'd love to have you come share it with us."

"Do you think the senator will agree with this?" Maggie laughed.

"He will." Miriam winked then smiled.

Chapter Eighteen

M*aggie grabbed the gun from the deck and held it between her trembling hands. She wasn't going to let him get away with this. He was evil and had done evil things to too many people. He had to be stopped. Here and now.*

The sneer on his face as he laughed and tugged her cousin, Ruth, closer to the edge of the boat deck made her sick. Maggie had to act quickly or he'd get away and her cousin would be lost to her. He raised his gun and aimed it at her friend, Gage. Maggie screamed "Nooooo" and fired the gun in her hand. Bang. Bang. Bang. She spotted three bright red marks blossoming on his chest as he fell to the deck.

"Maggie, sweetheart, wake up."

Maggie opened her eyes and found Troy sitting on the side of her bed, her hand in one of his. His other hand brushed her hair back from her forehead as he spoke to her in gentle tones.

"What? What's going on?" Disoriented, Maggie sat up. "Wh...what happened?"

"You were screaming 'Nooooo' just as I knocked on your door. I called to you, but you didn't answer. I came in thinking something had happened. It must have been a nightmare." Troy still held her hand in his.

Maggie ran her other hand through her tousled hair, her gaze meeting his. "It was. It's the nightmare from the day my cousin and me were nearly kidnapped."

Troy reached up and cupped her cheek in a tender hand. "Want to tell me about it?"

She drew in a ragged breath then nodded. "I...I was on a photography job at Cape Hatteras. My contracted employer was Antonio Amato who turned out to be a mafia boss from a long line of mafia bosses. To make a long story short, he kidnapped my cousin and me and attempted to sell us to human traffickers. A national park policeman and a Coast Guardsman came to rescue us. Antonio was using my cousin, Ruth, as a human shield in an attempt to get away onboard the trafficker's boat. A huge wave hit Antonio's yacht, knocking everyone off their feet. Ruth fell away from Antonio just as the Coast Guardsman lost his grip on the gun. It fell in front of me. I picked it up and aimed it at Antonio as he turned his gun on Gage, the park policeman. I shot and killed Antonio."

With gentle fingers Troy pushed a tendril of hair behind Maggie's ear, then ran a finger down her cheek. "Wow. I had no idea what a heroine you are."

Maggie dropped her gaze to her lap and shook her head. "Sometimes I think just how differently it all could have gone. Why did that gun land at my feet instead of one of the professionals? My hands were shaking so badly, I have no idea how I hit him."

"Who knows why God chooses to do things the way He does, but He must've known you could handle the situation, because you did." With a gentle tug, he pulled her into his arms and just held her. "You're a strong woman, Maggie Lawrence, and you should let the past go. It was a bad experience for you and your cousin, but the Lord used you to end it. Seems I recall a verse in the Bible somewhere that says 'All things work together for good to them that love God, to them who are the called according to his purpose'. I've been thinking along those lines a lot myself lately and working through some things. I may have a way to go, but at least the Lord and I are on speaking terms now."

Maggie lifted her head and pulled away from him. A look of astonishment on her face was soon replaced with a happy smile. "Troy? Really? That's awesome. That's answered prayer."

Troy's eyes narrowed. "You've been praying for me?"

She shrugged and scrunched up her face. "Maybe a time or two."

"Thanks. I'm glad you did." Troy stood and walked toward the door. "The reason I was knocking on your door to begin with was to ask if you'd be interested in seeing us off on our expedition this morning. You can drive over to the kennels with me if you like. Colonel Williams will be meeting me there in an hour, so hurry up if you'd like to go."

Maggie grabbed her cell phone from the bedside table and looked at the time. 5:00 am. She threw back the covers and dropped her flannel clad legs over the side of the bed.

"Okay. I'll be ready in a few minutes. Since you're dressed, can you get the coffee going?"

Troy chuckled as he walked out the door. "Already done, slacker."

~

"Are you sure this is the right glacier?" Pavel compared his park map with the information General Kozlov had sent him. "It makes no sense they would have flown in this direction from where they started in Nome."

"It would if they were blown off course by a storm as our experts suspect." General Kozlov cleared his throat. "You had the chance to make a workable plan, but it was not workable like you thought it would be. Peter's Glacier is where you will go. That's where they have determined the plane to be."

"And if it's not there?"

"It *is* there. Take the senator with you. I want him there when you find the packet of papers. He failed to find them in 1987." General Kozlov rendered a malicious laugh. "I want him to know what he missed."

"How are you so certain it's Peter's Glacier?" Pavel didn't think the general's experts were all that dependable.

"My source is reliable, I assure you." The general's laugh dried up and his voice hardened. "Are you getting cold feet, Pavel? Do we need to look elsewhere for a man with more strength and determination to complete this mission, or will you finish what you've begun without question?"

Even though the general couldn't see him, Pavel lifted his chin with pride and forced confidence into his voice. "*Nyet*, General. You do not have to replace me. I *will* complete this mission as planned and take the good senator with me as you desire."

"Good. And as a reward for your cooperation, my good Pavel, I will meet you at the plane crash site. Aren't you a lucky man?"

Pavel was irritated when the man hung up laughing in his ear. He was a smug man, and it made Pavel sick to his stomach. This mission couldn't end too soon for his liking.

~

Darkness faded away as the early April Alaskan sky began to show signs of sunrise. Maggie was beginning to adjust to the strange daylight or lack thereof in Alaska, but the days were growing longer by ten minutes or so each day. As winter would soon give way to spring, then spring to summer, it would become just the opposite. The days would be all daylight with barely any night. Too bad she wouldn't be around to witness it.

When Troy parked his truck, they climbed out and went inside the kennel office. It was too early for the rest of the kennel personnel to be around yet, but a few minutes later, the door opened, and the superintendent walked in.

"Good morning, sir." Troy stepped over and shook his hand. "To what do we owe this pleasure? You don't usually come up to the kennels, especially this early."

The superintendent removed his parka hood and lowered the upper part of the parka zipper. "I thought I'd see you and Colonel Williams off, Troy. I see Maggie had the same idea."

Warmth flowed through Maggie right up to her cheeks. She unzipped her own parka and shrugged her shoulders. "Well, I thought perhaps I could help with something before they take off. Doubtful, since Troy's the sled dog musher, but I wanted to see them off anyway."

Wade nodded. "I know what you mean. This is quite the expedition. I see Colonel Williams hasn't arrived yet. Hopefully he'll be along soon."

Just then the door to the office opened, and the subject of their discussion strolled in dressed in heavy winter Army gear.

"Good morning everyone." He nodded. "I don't know about you, but I'm psyched for this. My first dog sled ride. I'm ready. Let's go."

Troy chuckled. "Alright then. Give me about fifteen minutes to get the dogs hooked up and finish packing our gear onto the sled. It's going to take us two days of steady travel to get out to Peter's Glacier. We'll camp one night on the way out, one night at the plane then one night on the way back with two days of travel back."

"Understood." Colonel Williams nodded.

"Sir," Troy turned to his boss, "if you'll check the good colonel's gear to make sure it's all appropriate, I'll go get the sled taken care of."

"Certainly." Wade turned to Colonel Williams and started to check out his cold weather clothing.

"Now wait a minute," the colonel pulled his arm away. "This is the best cold weather gear the US Army has to offer."

"Be that as it may, I won't be responsible for frostbite or any other cold weather injuries, Colonel." Troy stopped and turned around on his way to the door. "Let the superintendent take a look. If there's something that needs to be switched out, we have extra gear here."

Troy disappeared out the door.

"Is he always so bossy?" Colonel Williams turned to the superintendent.

"Only when he takes his job seriously." Superintendent Wade glanced at him over the rim of his glasses. "If I were you, I'd listen to him while out in the wilderness. That man knows this park like the back of his hand. You don't."

~

Maggie followed Troy out to the kennels and helped as he packed the sled with supplies. She watched as he harnessed the dogs into their respective positions. Venture went into the lead position as usual. Followed by S'more, Party, Vista and Topo in the swing positions, then Summit, Disco, Cupcake and Polly in the wheel positions. The kennel yard came alive with the barking of nearly every dog in the kennels. The dogs hooked up to the sled were so excited, they jumped up on their hind legs and led the barking uproar. Maggie laughed and placed her gloved hands over her parka-covered ears.

"What can I say?" Troy spread his arms wide and attempted to yell over the loud den of barking. "They love their job."

The superintendent and Colonel Williams came out of the office and joined them by the sled.

"Is it always this loud?" Colonel Williams shouted.

"Always." Troy nodded and stepped over to the sled. He pulled back the covers from the seat where Colonel Williams would be riding. "Your chariot awaits, Colonel. If you'll climb aboard, we'll get this expedition started."

Colonel Williams turned to Wade and held out a gloved hand. "We'll see you in a few days, sir."

"May God be with you, Colonel." The superintendent shook his hand. "And remember what I said. That man will keep you alive."

Maggie watched a smirk appear on Colonel Williams' face. "I don't believe in God, Superintendent, so I'll just trust Mr. Donovan."

The superintendent smiled. "May God be with you anyway, Colonel. Just because you don't believe doesn't mean He isn't there."

He released the man's hand and stepped beside Maggie, his chin held high, a slight smile lifting the corners of his face. The smirk had disappeared from Colonel Williams as he turned to climb onto the sled. Maggie had the sudden urge to hug the superintendent but she wasn't sure how he'd take it, so she crossed her arms over her chest instead.

Troy tucked the colonel in, wrapping him securely with blankets to ensure he'd remain as warm as possible out in the wilderness. From her own experience the day they took the senator out, there would be little foliage and tree cover to block any wind they may encounter. It was wide open wilderness for the most part. Cold, snowy and windy. The forecast wasn't calling for snow today, but tomorrow could be a different story.

When the colonel was tucked in, Troy stepped over to the superintendent and shook his hand.

"We'll see you in a few days, sir."

"Stay in touch, Troy. Keep us posted as to where you are along the way. That's why we have that satellite phone. To stay in touch in the wilderness. Consider that an order."

Troy grinned. "Yes, sir."

His gaze trailed over to Maggie and his grin grew into a smile.

Wade coughed. "Um, I think I left something in the office. I'll be right back."

"Sure, he did." Troy winked at Maggie then grew serious. "I'll be back in a few days. Take care of Mom and Jeremy for me, will you?"

Maggie nodded. "Of course, I will. You be careful. Don't fall into any icy rivers or get eaten by any grizzlies or anything, okay?"

Troy scrunched up one eye and his mouth. "The rivers could be an issue. The grizzlies should still be sleeping yet so I don't think they'll be a problem. Wolverine on the other hand...."

Maggie slapped his arm. "You know what I mean. Just be careful."

Troy chuckled, then pulled Maggie into his arms and kissed her. It was a solid, short, sweet kiss that left her breathless. If he'd intended to leave her with something to think about while he was gone, mission accomplished.

Releasing her, he stepped back, winked and hurried to the front of the pack of sled dogs. He grabbed the tether and released Venture who became all business. The rest of the team followed his lead. Barking and play time were over. It was time to go, and they were ready to hit the trail.

Troy jumped on the sled's runners and he yelled, "Mush! Mush!"

Summit, Disco, Cupcake and Polly, the power dogs in the wheel positions, jumped forward giving the whole team the initial jolt they needed to get going, then the others leapt forward led by Venture. The team was off. Troy and Colonel Williams waved as they slid smoothly away over the snow.

Maggie thought she stood alone but was surprised when Wade spoke from beside her.

"Maggie, would you join me in a moment of prayer for our team as they head into the wilderness to perform their mission?"

Maggie turned her gaze to the man who was in charge of six million acres of this park. She was sure since he was a praying man, he prayed about every inch of it.

"I would love to."

He bowed his head and Maggie followed suit. "Father, we ask you to guide and protect our two men who are headed into the wilderness to perform a mission that is quite out of the ordinary. I can't say more, since Maggie isn't cleared for the information, but You know their mission. Guide their path and lead them to the plane. Help them find what they're looking for and protect them from all enemies. Bring them home safely. Protect the dogs and help them to perform as they're needed to. Help this mission to go smoothly if it would be Thy will. Help us to remember to give You all the glory. Amen."

Maggie lifted her head. "I liked your answer to Colonel Williams, sir. It was spot on."

He nodded and shrugged. "It was the truth."

~

Dafna sat in her cell looking at a fashion magazine. It was a little harder to see out of one eye, but she was managing. At least she had something to look at. Earlier, the inmate librarian had brought the library cart around with books, magazines and newspapers for certain inmates. She wasn't sure how she'd rated, but she wasn't going to complain. Her head was throbbing, and her left eye was mostly swollen shut, but she wasn't going to say anything to anyone.

No matter how she tried to not ever be alone, it didn't matter. There was always someone from the gang present to do a number on her. The guards didn't seem to care, or they didn't know who was doing it. And she wasn't about to tell them. The gang would kill her if she told.

She took a deep breath and gasped from pain. She suspected she had at least one fractured rib. Dafna dropped the magazine on the bunk beside her and slowly lowered herself onto the mattress. No matter what she did, it hurt. A lot.

As Dafna lay there for a few minutes trying to take in some good deep breaths, a female guard came to her cell and unlocked the door. She held a parka in one hand and a set of shackles in the other.

"Come on, Orlov. Get up. You have an appointment to go to. Let's go. Now."

The redheaded guard stood sternly by the cell door, but she didn't scream at Dafna as some of them did.

With great difficulty, Dafna stood up and grimaced as she got to her feet. 'What kind of appointment?"

"With your lawyer."

The guard looked Dafna in the face. "Hold up. What happened to you?"

"I had a run-in with someone's fists." Dafna avoided the woman's gaze.

"Who was it?"

Dafna's gaze in her one eye remained down. "It was dark. I didn't see their faces."

"You didn't see or you won't say?" The guard's voice grew soft and low.

Dafna remained quiet for a moment then asked, "Am I going to be late for my appointment?"

The guard helped Dafna into the parka then put the shackles on her and locked them. "Come on then. Let's go."

Dafna shuffled alongside the guard as the woman held Dafna's arm and led her outside to a running van where she was shackled to a bar and seat belted in.

"Good luck." The female guard half smiled then slammed the van door shut.

Another guard was already in the driver's seat and, when Dafna was settled, drove them away. When they reached the courthouse in downtown Fairbanks, Dafna was led inside to a small conference room and placed in a chair at a table. Her parka was removed and she was allowed to sit with her shackles and handcuffs not attached to anything. A guard stood behind her against the wall.

A few minutes later a thirtyish man in a suit carrying a briefcase came in, laid the briefcase on the table and took a chair across from Dafna.

"Hello, Dafna. My name's Grant Cooper. I'm your new lawyer." He extended his hand across the table toward her, a warm smile on his face.

Dafna stared at him with one lifted eyebrow. "My what? M...my new lawyer?"

"Yes, that's right."

She shook her head and eyed his hand. "I'm sorry, Mr. Cooper, but I can't afford a real lawyer. Who sent you? Did my mama send you? Because I know for a fact, she can't afford a real lawyer either."

His smile broadened. "No, your mom didn't send me. You don't have to worry about any fees, Ms. Orlov. Everything's been taken care of. All you need to be concerned about is lessening your sentence. And that's what I'm here to do."

When she failed to shake his hand, he folded his hands on the table in front of him and looked toward the guard. "You can step outside now. We'll be fine."

The guard eyed him then Dafna hesitantly before nodding. "I'll be right outside."

"Thank you." Cooper smiled and waited for the door to close behind the guard. He leaned slightly forward, his eyes taking in Dafna's disfigured face. "I can see that things aren't going well for you in jail. Am I right, Ms. Orlov?"

Dafna shifted in her chair. "Maybe. I get a little tired of being somebody else's punching bag, if that's what you mean."

"Yeah, that's what I mean." He opened his briefcase and pulled out a manila folder. "Ms. Orlov, you're about to be sentenced for attempted murder of a federal official. That could carry a minimum of forty years. Do you understand what that means?"

Dafna dropped her head until her chin nearly rested on her chest. She nodded as her body slumped in her chair.

"If you'll work with us, we'll seek to have your sentence reduced." Mr. Cooper paused before continuing. "Not only that, but I'm going to attempt to have you moved to a different federal prison."

Dafna's head snapped up, an expression of pain marking her features. She clasped her shackled hands on the tabletop. "Oh no. No. You can't move me."

"I'm sorry. Why not?" Mr. Cooper's face was blank.

"My mother comes to see me every week. She lives here in Fairbanks. She couldn't afford to travel anywhere to come see me."

"I see." Mr. Cooper nodded, a smile lifting the corners of his lips. He scrubbed a hand along his chin in thought. "Well, we'll have to do something. We can't have you getting beat up all the time and leaving you where you are isn't working."

Dafna shook her head and eyed him with her good eye. "No, it isn't."

"Does your mother own her home or rent?"

"She rents."

"Does she work?"

"Yes. She works in a local restaurant."

Mr. Cooper wrote down the information on a notepad. "Good. Now, for your plea bargain. Certain information is needed from you. If you'll give us this information, we'll talk about cutting your sentence."

Dafna eyed him again, this time her good eye narrowed. "What information do you want?"

"Who is Pavel Dubrovsky? What is his alias? Where does he come from and why were you and your brother working with him to kill Senator Scott?"

Dafna started to push away from the table but Cooper's voice halted her.

"Think before you act, Ms. Orlov. Forty years is a long time to be someone's punching bag. You're what? In your early twenties? You'll be in your early sixties when you get out unless you make parole. Attempted murder of a federal official? Good luck with that.

"Who are you protecting? Why won't you give him up? What is he to you? Your boyfriend?"

Dafna rolled her eyes. "*Nyet*. He is not my boyfriend, as you say. I am not protecting him nor were we working with him to kill the illustrious senator."

Dafna's voice was riff with disgust and sarcasm. She looked away, then after a few minutes, her gaze trailed back to the man across the table from her.

"Fine. I will help whoever this information is for, and you get me the absolute best deal you can. I don't want to be in prison any longer than I have to be. I'm done with this. The good senator is safe. I have no intentions of ever stepping near him again. And one other thing. You must keep my mother near wherever I am sent so I can see her often without her having to pay so much money to travel to see me."

Mr. Cooper smiled. "I'll do everything I can to get you that deal, Miss Orlov."

Dafna slumped in her chair and waited for the questioning to begin.

Chapter Nineteen

Troy and Colonel Williams were making good time across the snow-covered wilderness tundra. The sun had even peaked out a few times from behind a mostly overcast sky. Now that the early April days were growing longer it made it easier to make progress. The dogs were in their element and each one happy as a lark to be out in the snow-packed backcountry. Venture always did his job well by leading the team around obstacles and away from the snow-covered river. With spring coming on, the temperatures were starting to hover just above the 0 mark and the river ice would soon begin to thaw. Even with snow covering it, the river water would flow beneath, and if a dog or person stepped on it, it would be too late to know the ice wasn't thick enough to support their weight.

"How are you doing, Colonel?" Troy leaned forward to make sure his mission mate could hear him.

"Oh, I'm fine. Stiff but fine." Colonel Williams called over his shoulder from his seat on the sled.

"Ready for a break? You can get up and stretch your legs."

"Yeah. Sounds good."

"Whoa!" Troy's loud command to the dogs was obeyed immediately and they came to a smooth stop. Several instantly plopped to the ground panting while some sat. A few rolled in the snow then lay down with snow coating their thick fur.

Troy secured Venture and the sled so the dogs wouldn't drag it off if a snow hare or a ptarmigan wandered into view and the dogs decided to take chase. He'd learned early that chasing down an empty sled after a team of dogs on the hunt for a rabbit was not something he wanted to repeat.

He pulled a thermos of coffee from the sled supplies along with a couple of plastic cups. Pouring coffee into the cups, he handed one to the colonel who had extricated himself from the sled.

"Here you go, Colonel. This should help. It's still nice and hot. It will be for a while so help yourself."

"Thanks." The colonel accepted the cup and drank eagerly. "Mmmm. Yep. That's good. Spring might be on the way, but it's still super cold out here."

"Well, it's only 4° out. It's going to get down to - 6° tonight, but don't worry, I have a tent." Troy chuckled and walked away to give water to the dogs.

Just then his satphone rang. Reaching into his parka pocket, he pulled it out and answered it.

"Hello, sir. Miss me already?"

"Well, actually, I wish you were here now." The superintendent's voice raised the hackles on the back of Troy's neck.

"What's the matter, sir? What's happened?"

"We got the information we wanted out of Dafna Orlov."

"Sir? How in the world did you do that? Did you get the lawyer like you were hoping?"

Wade chuckled. "You bet we did. And he's good. He's not my lawyer but the lawyer who knows a lawyer who…well, you know what I mean. Anyway, the guy convinced Dafna to talk and in the end, he got her sentence cut in half with parole in ten years."

"Wow, he is good. I'm sure Ludmila will be happy. What did Dafna share?"

"You're not going to believe this, Troy. I had to sit down when I found out."

"Sir, the suspense is killing me. Can you just tell me?"

"Oh yeah. Of course. She told Mr. Cooper that Pavel Dubrovsky is…are you ready?"

Troy heaved a heavy sigh and shook his head. "Yes, sir. I'm ready when you are."

"Pavel Dubrovsky is none other than Jud Svenson."

Troy wasn't sure he'd heard his boss right. "Jud Svenson, sir? Are you sure that's what she said?"

"Believe me, Troy, I had the same reaction. She went on to explain that Jud is a Russian agent that was implanted several years ago. He was put here to wait for orders by the Russian government."

"What orders?" Troy couldn't understand how a man that he'd known for several years could be a Russian agent.

"Dafna wasn't sure about that, but I've already talked with General Harding. He wasn't in the least surprised. I have a feeling Svenson is an agent who has worked on a lot of missions, Troy. I doubt this is his first. This is likely his most current one."

"Was he out to kill the senator, sir? Was he involved in the murder attempts by the Orlov siblings?"

"Not according to Dafna Orlov. She said he had nothing to do with those, that they were planned and carried out solely by her and her brother. Dafna and Ivan hated the senator because he didn't rescue their father back in 1987. He was sent out by the US government to do so and failed. At least in their eyes he failed. When asked if she understood that her father was most likely dead when the plane hit the ground, she broke into tears and nodded. She still blamed the senator for not recovering the body."

"She just wasn't going to let him off the hook in any way, was she?" Troy toed a clump of snow with his boot.

"Not likely," Wade agreed. "No matter the outcome, he was her scapegoat. I'm sure her brother Ivan fed her frenzy as did Jud Svenson."

Troy paced back and forth along the line of his team of dogs, a thought forming in his mind. "Sir, there's something I'm concerned about in light of this new information."

"What is that, Troy?"

"Sir, Maggie dated Svenson once. I'm concerned for her safety. She has no idea about Pavel Dubrovsky or that he and Jud are one and the same."

"I'll give her a call and brief her on it if you think it would be a good idea." Wade paused. "Oh, and before you ask, Dafna was asked about Maggie's break-ins. She said she didn't know anything about them or the laptop. Seeing as how the second break-in where the laptop was stolen happened after she was taken into custody, I can believe that."

"Yeah, I suppose so. And yes, I think Maggie needs to know about Svenson, sir. For her own protection."

"Will do. I'll keep you posted. How goes the journey?"

"We've just stopped for a break. We'll get back on the trail soon and make more tracks. The dogs are doing great and Colonel Williams is a trooper. I'll phone you when we camp tonight."

"Godspeed, son."

"Thank you, sir."

Troy hung up and relayed the information the superintendent had given him to Colonel Williams.

"Well, it's good we know who the Russian agent is at any rate." The colonel climbed back into his seat on the sled.

"Yeah, but the question is, does he have the same information we have?" Troy tucked the colonel in. "We know he got the photograph of the plane at the glacier. Did he figure out the location? And is he on his way or has he already been there?"

~

"Thanks for letting me know, Superintendent. It's hard to believe. Just when you think you're getting to know a person, something like this comes back to bite you." Maggie paced the floor of her bedroom. "And to think Jud was behind the theft of my laptop. He got me out of the cabin so one of his cohorts could break in and steal it."

"I'm so sorry, Maggie." The superintendent's words were filled with genuine regret. "He has a lot to answer for and will as soon as the authorities track him down."

"Yes, sir, and I hope they will soon."

"Just be careful, Maggie. He thinks you don't know about his Russian name or the fact he's a Russian agent. My suggestion is to stay as far away from him as you can."

"I'll do that. The Scott's invited me over for dinner this evening. It should be a nice and relaxing time."

"Sounds good. They have plenty of security there so you should be fine. Have a great time, Maggie."

"Thank you, sir. I will."

Maggie ended the call and tossed her cell phone on the bed before dropping down to sit on the edge of it. Leaning forward she planted her elbows on her knees and her chin in her hands. She'd never been attracted to Jud, not with Troy Donovan around, but she was disappointed he'd turned out to be a Russian agent. She shook her head in disbelief. First the Chicago mafia at Cape Hatteras, now a Russian spy in Alaska. How did she manage to get tangled up in these situations?

Lord, I don't know what Your plan is, but please keep me safe. Please keep Troy and Colonel Williams safe on their expedition to the plane. I don't know what they're looking for, but whatever it is, Jud, a.k.a. Pavel Dubrovsky, wants it too. No telling what his plan is. I know it's important to our country so please don't let him get it. Please, Father.

~

Maggie parked her car in front of the Denali Wilderness Lodge and made her way inside. She climbed the wide staircase up to the Scott's suite where the security guards were awaiting her arrival.

"Good evening, Miss Lawrence. I hope you're doing well this evening. The Scotts are expecting you." One of them stepped over to the door of the suite and knocked on the rustic wood. He folded his hands in front of him as he waited for the door to be answered.

"Yes, thank you. I'm just fine." Maggie nodded and waited, her gaze wandering around the hallway. The housekeeper seemed to be taking longer than on Maggie's last visit.

After a while, the door finally opened and Hortense, the housekeeper, waved Maggie in. "Please, come this way."

Before the door closed, Maggie spotted the guard returning to his post. She felt better knowing they were there. Had the senator been told about Jud? Well, it wasn't her place to say anything so she wouldn't mention it.

She followed Hortense into the sitting room where the Scotts were watching a documentary on Africa. Talk about a far cry from Alaska.

They looked up as she entered the room.

"Maggie, dear. Please do come in." Miriam held out her hand as the senator stood to his feet. "Brad, let Maggie sit here beside me once Hortense takes her parka."

"Of course, dear. Calvin…." The senator looked toward the hallway just as another knock sounded. "I'll get it, Hortense. We're expecting Calvin Jacobs as well. That's probably him. Have a seat and make yourself comfortable, Maggie. I'll be right back."

Miriam patted the sofa beside her. "Please, dear Maggie. Have a seat."

Maggie walked around the coffee table and sat beside the senator's wife. "You look much better since the last time I saw you, Mrs. Scott. Are you feeling better?"

"Actually, I am, dear. I've been getting a lot of rest, and I do believe it's helped. But please, call me Miriam. This Mrs. Scott stuff is for the birds. Especially since we're here in a small group of friends."

"Alright, Miriam." Maggie smiled.

They turned as the senator and Calvin Jacobs walked into the sitting room. The senator took an armchair near the gas fireplace while Calvin took the other one across from him.

"Hello, Mr. Jacobs. How are you doing this evening?" Maggie pointed at the brace on his arm, injecting as much sympathy into her voice as she could. "How are the bones healing? And the gunshot wound? You've had more than your fair share of injuries recently."

"Don't I know it." The thin, middle aged and balding man crossed one ankle over the other and settled his braced arm in his lap. He settled the other arm along the cushioned arm of the chair and gazed at her over his wire-framed rims. "Eating is the most difficult, but I manage. I have to have help with dressing. It's all just too much for me by myself."

Maggie smiled at Calvin. "It's a good thing you're staying in the same building so you don't have to drive."

"Oh no." Calvin shook his head with vehemence. "I couldn't do that in my condition."

"I hired my assistant an assistant." The senator tried to keep a straight face, but he started chuckling. Then he slapped his knee and laughed out loud.

Calvin heaved a heavy sigh and rolled his eyes as Miriam turned to her husband and pinched her lips, pinning him with a look of tolerance.

"Brad, it's not that funny."

Maggie dropped her gaze to her lap and clamped her lips shut to prevent a giggle from escaping. No, it wasn't very funny, but the fact he thought it was and his laughter made her want to laugh.

Hortense came into the sitting room and called them to dinner. It was a small dining space and the food had been delivered and served from the hotel kitchen. It smelled amazing, and Maggie was ready to eat when they sat down. They shared a delightful time of discussion over the meal, and Maggie found she enjoyed herself immensely. When dessert was finished, they decided to take coffee in the sitting room around the fireplace and enjoy the more comfortable seating.

The discussion they all avoided was finally brought up by the senator.

"Have you heard anything from the men on their way to the glacier, Maggie?"

She shook her head. "No, and I don't really expect to. They don't have a reason to talk to me about anything. Since I'm not a part of the mission…."

"Ahh, you may not be a part of the mission, but I think you're a part of someone's heart on that mission." The senator stretched his feet toward the fire and smiled a knowing smile.

Miriam's eyes ping-ponged between her husband and Maggie. "What's this? Tell me. Tell me all."

Bump.

The slight sound came from the hallway outside the suite.

Bump. Bump.

"Did you hear that?" Maggie lifted a finger, pointing toward the front door.

"I didn't hear anything." Miriam shook her head. "What were you talking about, Brad?"

"Yes, I heard a noise in the outside hallway." Calvin's eyes were round as saucers. "Is it always that noisy here?"

"No," the senator said. "Most likely a new tenant arriving to another suite."

"Where is your assistant while you're up here, Mr. Jacobs?" Maggie turned to ask the man but his attention was still aimed in the direction of the front door. "Mr. Jacobs?"

He turned his gaze to Maggie just as a crash sounded in the hallway by the front door. They all leapt from their chairs, but before they could move any further, three men were in the entrance to the room, guns in their hands.

Maggie gasped as she recognized Jud Svenson, a.k.a. Pavel Dubrovsky. His gaze instantly met hers, a sneer on his face.

"Hello, Maggie." There was a slight trace of a Russian accent in his words. She wouldn't give him the pleasure of asking about it.

"Jud, what are you doing here and why have you broken in?" Maggie's gaze slipped to the guns in the men's hands. She would play the innocent, uninformed as long as she could. "Why do you have those and why are you aiming them at us?"

"Ahh. The sweet innocent woman. We could've had such a wonderful time, Maggie. But there are some things far more important than our... relationship." He pointed his gun at the senator. "You, sir, get your parka and boots and anything else to keep you warm. You're coming with me."

His gaze roamed the tiny group. He eyed Calvin and wrote him off immediately. His gaze moved on to Miriam. "Ahh, yes. Mrs. Scott. Perhaps you will do."

"No." Maggie took a firm stance between Miriam and Jud. She was thankful Hortense had taken the dinner dishes on a cart back down to the hotel kitchen. There was one less person to defend. "Mrs. Scott has just been released from ICU at the hospital. Whatever you have planned, she *won't* do well."

Jud stared at Maggie then around her at Miriam. "Fine, Maggie. Get your parka and boots. *You're* coming with me."

~

Troy called "whoa" and the dog sled team came to a smooth halt beneath the edge of a rocky ledge. It had grown steadily colder and windier throughout the afternoon. Now that nighttime was fast approaching, it was time to set up camp, and the ledge would provide some blockage from the wind at least.

"There's a stand of trees over there." Troy pointed at a stretch of black spruce, aspen and balsam poplars about fifty feet away. "There's bound to be some downed branches and possibly even a couple of small downed trees. There's an ax and a saw in the equipment on the sled. If you'll head over and start looking, I'll be over to help you as soon as I tether the sled and take care of the dogs."

"Roger that." Colonel Williams found the tools quickly and headed to the trees to get started.

Troy tethered the sled then fed and watered the dogs before heading over to give the colonel a hand. Before long they had enough wood to build a fire and keep it going through the night. Both men carried their bounty beneath the ledge, then Troy built a nice fire while Colonel Williams pulled out the cooking gear and food to prepare a simple meal.

Venture and the rest of the dog team moved closer to the fire and curled up, tucking their noses beneath their tails. Within minutes their eyes were closed, and they were fast asleep. They'd worked hard all day and were deserving of a good night's rest.

Troy and Colonel Williams made themselves comfortable around the fire as they devoured their supper of beef stroganoff and hot chocolate.

"It's amazing what a day out in the cold can do to an appetite." Colonel Williams leaned over to place a second helping from the tiny propane stove onto his plate. Once he'd served himself, he held up the pot of stroganoff for Troy. "More?"

Troy finished the last bite of his own food and waved a hand. "No thanks. I've had plenty."

The colonel sat back down and resumed eating. Between bites he asked, "So what's your gut feeling? Think we'll run into any trouble out here?"

Troy stared into the dancing flames of the fire and shook his head. "I have no clue. There's no telling what Svenson's up to. It's been a couple of weeks since he stole Maggie's laptop. I'm sure he has access to Russian intel, and if Maggie could figure out the picture, I'm pretty sure they can. It would only be a matter of time before they figure out the plane's location."

"Yeah, well they don't have you on their team." Colonel Williams set down his empty plate and put his gloves on. "Do you think Svenson knows the park like you do?"

Troy shook his head. "Doubtful. Yeah, he's had his share of flight-seeing tours over it, but that's not the same as knowing your way around on the ground. If he is depending on Russian intelligence to figure it out, they've got access to satellite imagery, and that'll go a long way to help find the plane."

"That I'm sure of." Colonel Williams shifted on the bedroll he was sitting on. "What concerns me is the timing. Has he already been there? Or will we beat him to the punch?"

"Yep. That's the question." Troy gathered the few dishes and washed them with the hot water he had boiled on a second tiny propane stove. Packing them away on the sled, he fed the fire then dropped back to his bedroll.

"We'd better get some sleep, Colonel. We need an early start in the morning." Troy tugged his toboggan down over his ears then adjusted his parka hood securely over it. He slipped down inside his bedroll next to the fire and pulled it up over his head. His next words were muffled. "Good night."

The colonel grinned and followed suit. Before long, the only sound was the wind beyond the rocky ledge and the crackling of the fire.

Chapter Twenty

Once the senator and Maggie were dressed in their parkas and boots, Jud and one of his underlings led them out the front door of the suite and into the hallway. Jud left the third man behind with Miriam and Calvin. Maggie noticed the two bodyguards that had been standing by the doorway when she'd arrived were nowhere to be seen. She hoped upon hope Jud and his guys hadn't killed them, but merely knocked them out and moved them somewhere else.

"Turn right, Senator." Jud pressed his handgun into the senator's back. "There's a stairwell back there. Take it."

Maggie was given a slight push by Jud's henchman. She followed the senator as the group made their way to the stairs and headed to the main floor. Once there, they exited the building by a side entrance, and Jud told them to walk toward a black SUV. He put the senator in the front passenger seat and Maggie in the back seat. Jud sat in the back with Maggie while Jud's underling drove.

Dusk had set in and it grew darker as they turned right out of the lodge parking lot. Jud hadn't said where they were going, but Maggie was pretty sure they were headed into the park. There really wasn't anything else past the park entrance until the tiny village of Cantwell. Surely, they weren't headed there. She was disappointed, however, when they drove past the park entrance and kept heading south on Parks Highway.

What in the world?

"Where are you taking us?" Maggie didn't want to look at Jud. Instead she kept her face forward and asked in a strong voice.

"Wouldn't you like to know." Jud chuckled. "Oh fine. I'll tell you. We're going to Cantwell."

Maggie watched the senator to see if there was a reaction, but nothing. He must not have any idea why they were going to Cantwell either.

"What's in Cantwell other than a zip code?" Maggie turned to stare out the window into the gathering darkness.

"Ahhh, yes. Cantwell is small but there's more there than a post office and a gas station. You see there's an…airport." He dragged out the last word to see what response he got.

Maggie turned her head and stared at Jud but said nothing.

"Hmmm. Got your attention that time, didn't I?" He waved the gun in his hand. "Bet you didn't see that coming, Miss high-and-mighty photographer."

Maggie turned her face back to the front.

"Well, don't you want to know why we're going to the airport in Cantwell?" Sarcasm dripped from his voice.

Maggie remained silent. She wouldn't give him the satisfaction of answering again.

"No? You seem to have a genuine lack of curiosity considering the situation you're in, Maggie. Well, that's okay. I don't mind telling you. We're flying from Cantwell to Kantishna. Tonight."

Maggie saw the senator shift his gaze slightly over his shoulder in her direction, but not enough to meet hers.

"That's right, Senator. Ever flown to Kantishna?"

The senator's gaze moved back to the front, but he remained silent.

"Wow. You're a tough crowd, you two." Jud leaned forward and poked the senator's shoulder. Senator Scott jumped and turned slightly but didn't say anything.

"It's okay, because that's all I'm going to tell you. You'll find out the rest in the morning."

Maggie wished Jud would just shut up and remain quiet. Whatever he was trying to do with all this chatter was mainly giving her a headache. In the end, she suspected his goal was the same as Troy and Colonel Williams'. Why else would he steal her laptop? Somehow the day she'd taken the picture of the plane he'd found out about it or somehow realized it yet couldn't remember its location. Once they reached Kantishna airport, would they be heading into the park interior as well?

Father, this morning I prayed You would keep me safe. I had no idea this situation was coming, but You did. I'm still asking for Your protection and safe care, only this time I'm pulling the senator under the umbrella of Your protective care. Wherever they are, please protect and care for Troy and Colonel Williams. Help them to reach the plane and get what they need and get out before we get there.

~

Miriam sat on the sofa and Calvin on the armchair near the gas fire. Jud's cohort paced around the room looking at the pictures on the walls and picking up the statuettes to look at them. Where in the world was Hortense? Miriam was terrified the housekeeper would come walking back in while this man was here and possibly get hurt. Would she see the guards outside had disappeared and know something had gone wrong? She had to disarm this man and get the upper hand. And now.

"Uh, sir? Excuse me. Sir?" Miriam leaned forward and lifted a hand, one finger in the air.

The brutish-looking man turned and stared at her. "What?"

"You know I've only recently been discharged from the hospital. I was in a terrible accident, and I was in ICU for several days before they transferred me to a regular hospital room. I'm still on medication and it's time to take it."

The man's features remained the same. Not even a shift of his eyes except to blink at her.

"So?"

"Surely you're a compassionate enough man that you would fetch my medication for me." Miriam turned on the charm and leaned toward him, placing a hand to her head. "If I don't take it now, my symptoms will only worsen, and it takes longer for the medication to help once I do take it. Won't you please fetch it for me with a glass of water?"

He pointed at Calvin. "Let him get it."

"I don't know what she's taking." Calvin gave him an expression that said the guy was off his rocker. "I don't do well with things like that. Leave me out of it."

The man's brows furrowed as he looked back at Miriam. She clasped her forehead. "Please, you must hurry. I don't feel well. Not at all."

Worry rimmed the man's features as he bit his lip. "Fine, but you both gotta promise to stay here."

"Oh, we promise, don't we, Calvin." Miriam looked from beneath her hand on her forehead to her husband's assistant. She winked her far eye, the one away from the bad guy.

Calvin stared at her for a few seconds, then said, "Oh, oh yes, of course we do. We promise."

"Alright. Where are they?" The man tucked his gun into his jean's waistband.

"The medicine cabinet in the master bedroom. And don't forget the water."

"Right, right," the man mumbled as he hurried through the door to the bedroom.

"Hurry, Calvin. Get the statuette from the table there and stand behind the wall." Miriam whispered as she pointed her directions. "When he returns, whack him over the head with it."

Calvin stared at her wide-eyed and whispered back. "That's your plan? Are you insane?"

"Well, I can't do it. He'll obviously see I'm gone from the sofa as soon as he nears the doorway. You on the other hand, aren't in the line of sight."

Calvin thought for a few seconds and realized she had a point. "Fine, but I'm not sure I have the strength in my left hand with my healing gunshot wound. With my right hand out of commission, that's all I've got."

"Give it your all, Calvin. My husband and Maggie are depending on you. Troy and Colonel Williams may be as well for all we know."

Calvin rolled his eyes then climbed to his feet and grabbed the statuette, taking up his position beside the doorway. He hefted the heavy metal statuette in his left hand to get a feel for it then lifted it over his head. Miriam saw his face grimace with pain, but he held it there.

He didn't have to wait long. The henchman came through the bedroom and passed through the doorway. Calvin met Miriam's eyes and she nodded, a small, supportive smile on her face.

"I guess these are the ones..."

Whack!

The man fell to the floor dropping the glass of water and the bottle of pills. He didn't move as Miriam hurried to his side. She checked his neck for a pulse as a gash on his head dripped blood.

She smiled at Calvin and held up a hand. Calvin dropped the statuette to the floor and high-fived with his left.

"Good job, Calvin. He's got a pulse. Now to call the police on this guy then I'll call Superintendent Wade. I'm pretty sure he's going to want to know Jud Svenson, a.k.a. Pavel Dubrovsky, has kidnapped my husband and Maggie."

The door opened and Hortense strode through the hallway and into the room pushing her cart. On the top shelf was a coffee carafe steaming with fresh coffee, clean coffee cups and napkins.

The sweet smile on her face turned to horror as she gasped at the sight of the man on the floor, blood dripping from the wound on his head. She swooned as she took in Mrs. Scott and Calvin Jacobs kneeling beside his body. Her eyes rolled back into her head as she crumpled to the floor.

Miriam rolled back on her heels as she sighed. "I suppose when we call the police we should ask for the EMTs to come take care of these two as well, huh?"

~

Glen Wade and his wife were watching a movie when his cell phone rang. Normally he would be tempted to allow it to roll to voicemail, but he recognized it as the senator's number.

"Excuse me, dear. I'd better take this. It's the senator."

"Don't be too long. You're supposed to be relaxing, you know." She blew him a kiss then turned her attention back to the TV as he left the room.

"Hello, Senator. What can I do for you this evening?" The superintendent stepped into his home office and sat in his office chair.

"Well, Glen, sorry to disappoint you," Miriam Scott's feminine voice met his greeting. "Brad's been kidnapped but he left his phone. I had a feeling you'd recognize the number. You didn't disappoint me."

"Mrs. Scott? What do you mean, the senator's been kidnapped?" Wade sat up straight in his chair.

"I'm afraid so. We invited Maggie Lawrence and Calvin Jacobs over for dinner this evening. We had just settled into the sitting room for coffee around the fireplace when that Jud guy and two of his men broke in. Apparently, they overtook our guards. I have no idea how, but the guards are gone. Maggie and Calvin both heard a noise shortly before they broke in so that's probably what they heard. They took Brad and Maggie and left one of their men to guard Calvin and me. We tricked him and Calvin whacked him over the head with a statuette. The police are here now. They're getting ready to transport the guy to the hospital. Calvin did a number on him, but he's still breathing and has a heartbeat."

"Did Jud say where he was taking the senator and Maggie?"

"No, not at all. He started to take me, but dear Maggie told him I had been hospitalized and wouldn't do well with whatever he had planned. He took her instead. Glen, Maggie sacrificed herself for me. We have to find them."

"Don't worry, Mrs. Scott. We'll find them."

~

Maggie and Senator Scott sat in the rear seats of the Cessna 185 as Jud and his henchman sat in the front, Jud flying the plane. Maggie remembered the day she'd arrived in Alaska and Jud had taken her on a flight-seeing tour. She'd found Denali to be amazing and gorgeous. That day she had no idea the trouble she'd land in. With a slight shake of her head, she glanced out the window and down into the darkness. Then glancing skyward, she saw there was no moon to see anything by, but the northern lights lit the sky, the stars twinkling through the transparent curtain of color. Somehow it warmed her heart knowing her Creator had fashioned that phenomena for his children to enjoy. She would hold it close to remember when she was back in New York. If she ever made it back to New York. A heavy sigh escaped her. She shook her head again to try and toss those thoughts out.

Maggie glanced back down into the darkness below. They were over the park, and somewhere down there Troy and Colonel Williams were camping for the night. They would have no idea that she and the senator were on their way to Kantishna airport and most likely tomorrow on their way into the wilderness as well. Why else would they be headed to a remote airport deep within the park? Troy had told her about it once. Kantishna airport was located at the end of a ninety-two-mile dirt road. That road was closed in winter, and the only access was by air.

Before long, the Cessna 185 began to descend and Jud clicked a button triggering runway lights on the remote runway. In spite of the wind that had begun to blow throughout the evening flight, Jud brought the plane in for a fairly smooth landing. Maggie was thankful the runway was cleared of snow. A snow-covered runway wouldn't have been fun at all.

Jud taxied the plane to the parking pad that ran parallel to the runway and tied the plane down with the help of his cohort. They placed an engine warmer over the engine, then shoved the senator and Maggie toward a cargo plane that sat on the parking pad, its engine running.

Neither the senator or Maggie spoke. They simply watched as Jud approached a man who climbed from the doorway of the plane. Jud shook his hand and they spoke briefly, but Maggie couldn't hear their words over the noise of the engine.

Jud and the man walked over to the cargo door as it was lowered. Two dog sled teams were led out of the hold and onto the tarmac of the parking pad. Maggie's stomach dropped. She hated being right.

Considering she'd been dressed for dinner with friends, she certainly wasn't dressed for an expedition into the Alaskan wilderness in near subzero temperatures. It was fortunate she'd worn her boots and brought shoes for her visit. The upper part of her would be fine beneath her parka. It was the lower half that would freeze in the evening slacks she'd worn. She hoped Jud had thought of that and would provide heavier winter clothing. Same for the senator who wore slacks and a sweater beneath his parka.

Once all the supplies were unloaded, they watched as the cargo plane taxied to the runway and lifted into the sky, disappearing into the darkness.

With Troy and Colonel Williams already in the wilderness and no one else knowing where they were, Maggie's hope of rescue disappeared with that plane.

A still small voice echoed through her mind.

I know.

She'd prayed, hadn't she? Maggie just needed to trust. Maybe no one else knew where they were, but her heavenly Father knew.

Trust Me.

Help me to trust You, Lord. We're out here in the middle of nowhere. With bad guys. Help me to trust You.

~

Troy woke in the night and realized the fire had died down to mere coals. No wonder he'd grown chilly. He climbed out of his semi-warm sleeping bag and grabbed his parka. He'd stretched it on top of himself inside the sleeping bag to keep it warm rather than leave it outside and have it frozen solid when he got up.

He grabbed logs from the pile they'd stacked by the fire pit and built the fire back up. Soon it was blazing again. He glanced at Colonel Williams' sleeping form bundled inside his sleeping bag. Steam rose from the small hole near his face. Troy heard a soft snore emanating from it, and he chuckled to himself. His gaze moved to the dogs. Most were sleeping with their noses tucked beneath their tails. A couple eyed him through contented gazes, yawning then tucking back in for more sleep.

Troy watched the flames lick at the logs as Maggie's face danced before his vision as it did more times than not these days. She was becoming the center of his world right along with Jeremy and his mom. Was she as important as family? His heart told him she was. He couldn't deny he was in love with her, no matter how hard he tried. When this mission was accomplished, it would be time to have a talk with her. Could he let her return to New York without sharing what was in his heart? *Lord, I need Your wisdom in this. You know my heart better than I do. It belongs in Alaska as much as it belongs to Maggie. You know I could never make it in the big city. Could Maggie give all that up for me?*

Troy scrubbed his gloved hand down his face and gazed up at the amazing greens and purples of the aurora borealis that danced in varying ribbons across the sky. Whoa! Where had that question come from? He was getting way ahead of himself and probably ahead of God. He needed to find out where Maggie's heart lay before he could determine if she'd give up New York for Alaska. It wasn't something he needed to worry about now.

Releasing a heavy sigh, he pulled back the top of the sleeping bag and slid in to snatch another couple hours of sleep. Only sleep deprivation could bring on such irrational thinking. As he zipped himself in and peeked through the tiny breathing hole, he spotted the colorful night sky and the zillions of stars that showed through.

He'd never been to New York City, but he doubted they ever saw this spectacle down there. Surely it was a check in the pro column as a reason for Maggie to stay in Alaska. Could she see this tonight? Was she as amazed by its beauty as he was? No matter the fact he'd seen the northern lights all his life, it never ceased to fill him with awe.

Lord, wherever Maggie is, please keep her safe. Help her to fall in love with Alaska and the beauty of this amazing state. And if it's Your will, allow her to love me too.

~

Maggie's gaze took in the gorgeous aurora borealis as it danced in bright ribbons of green and purple across the midnight sky. She sat on the lead dog sled wrapped in warm blankets as Jud mushed the dog team. She dropped her gaze and glanced back to the senator who sat on the other sled as Jud's cohort mushed the other team. Maggie was concerned they would be traveling through the night. Although Jud hadn't said where they were headed, she had no doubt it was to the downed plane, the same as Troy and Colonel Williams.

Before long Maggie's concerns were put to rest when Jud called the small expedition to a halt and he and his cohort began to set up camp. Jud put the senator to work gathering wood from a stand of trees nearby. Maggie strode over to help him.

"Are you alright, sir?" she whispered as she bent to pick up smaller branches.

He nodded. "Yes, I'm fine. You?"

"I'm fine. I just hope we get there after Troy and Colonel Williams have come, retrieved whatever it is they're looking for and gone."

"That would be nice, but I know their schedule. It's not likely." The senator glanced over his shoulder. "Shhh."

"What are you two doing?" Jud's cohort waved a gun in their direction. "Shut up and get on with picking up wood. It don't take talkin' to pick up some sticks. Hurry up."

"I hope you're wrong." Maggie filled her arms and stood straight.

"You and me both." Senator Scott loaded his arms and followed Maggie as she headed back to the makeshift campsite.

They dropped their wood beside the area Jud had cleared to make the fire. Within minutes he had one going and Maggie and the senator were warming themselves beside it.

"Don't get too comfortable." Jud tossed his small hatchet into the ground, the head sticking into the permafrost, handle upward. "After a few hours of sleep, we'll be back on the trail. Maggie, in that rucksack are trail meals. Scrounge and find something for us to eat. There are pots to cook them in there as well."

Maggie didn't particularly care to be bossed around like kitchen help, but she didn't have much choice. Cohort stood nearby with pistol in hand. Was she leverage to get the senator to do whatever it was they wanted him to do? She knew it had something to do with the plane. The plane that Troy and Colonel Williams were heading to the same as they were. Or were they both leverage? Time would tell.

Maggie scrounged in the rucksack and found several meals that just needed water added then cooked them over the fire to make a meal. In a short time, she was serving warm pasta and reconstituted warm cinnamon apples to her fellow travelers. They drank coffee and with the warm food eaten, everyone was soon ready to crawl into their sleeping bags.

Maggie doubted she would be able to sleep considering she was sleeping in -6° in addition to attempting to sleep near two bad guys. This was NOT her idea of a fun time.

In the not so far distance, she heard the mournful howl of coyotes. There was something in that cry that sent a chill down her spine. She sure wished Troy were here. He'd know if they were a threat to people or not.

Father God, please keep the senator and me safe. Protect us from whatever's out there that may harm us. Please deliver us from these men. Only You know how this will end. From my viewpoint it's not looking good at all, but You see the whole picture. Look after Troy and Colonel Williams and bring us all home safely. We need Your protection. Help Troy to find what he and the colonel are looking for. And please don't let Jud get his hands on it.

Chapter Twenty-One

Troy and Colonel Williams packed the last of the camping gear into the sled, then Troy led the dogs to their respective positions along the harness line and clipped them in place. Colonel Williams chugged the last of his cup of coffee and stuffed his cup beneath the sled cover before taking a seat on the sled.

"Are you ready?" Troy stood at the front of the team and watched the colonel settle in.

Colonel Williams gave him a thumbs up. "Ready when you are."

Troy petted Venture and released the tether. He jogged to the back of the sled and jumped onto the runners. He called "mush" and the team lurched forward. The team dogs at the rear of the pack gave the others the push they needed to get started and Venture took off leading the rest.

"Here we go, Colonel. Last leg of the journey." Troy leaned forward and spoke over the colonel's shoulder. "We should be there by this afternoon if all goes well."

"Let's hope it does."

Troy's satphone rang and he dug in his parka pocket for it. He retrieved it, and answering it, held it to his ear.

"Hello, Ranger Donovan speaking." He held onto the sled handles with one hand and the phone with the other as Venture led the team across a wide-open expanse of snow-covered land.

"Troy? It's Superintendent Wade. Got a minute?"

"Yes, sir. We're traveling west but go ahead. If I have to use both hands, I'll let you know."

"Sure, no problem." Wade cleared his throat. "I have some pretty bad news for you."

"Sir?"

"Yeah, Troy. The senator and Maggie Lawrence were kidnapped last night." Wade remained quiet as he let that news sink in.

"What?" Troy's heart dropped into his stomach as one of his feet nearly slipped from the sled runner. He steadied himself and stared with unseeing eyes at the scenery before him. Maggie's beautiful face was before him instead.

"Jud Svenson?" His voice came out like gritty sandpaper on stone.

"Yep. They overtook the guards in the hallway outside the senator's suite then broke in and took Maggie and the senator. They left a guy with Miriam Scott and Calvin Jacobs, but I have to give it to Miriam and Calvin. They outsmarted the guy and overpowered him. Calvin bonked him on the ol' noodle when he wasn't looking. They called the police and then me. I would've called you last night, but there wasn't anything you could've done except worry. You needed your sleep."

He was right, but Troy would've liked to have known last night. What could he have done? Nothing. He would've felt just like he did now. Helpless. He had to complete this mission.

"Sir, do you know where they're going?"

"I spoke with General Harding, he believes they're heading to the same place you are. We suspected as much since he stole Maggie's laptop and the picture of the plane."

"Yeah, but we never dreamed he'd take her and the senator with him."

~

"Get up. Now." Maggie was too warm and didn't appreciate being shoved in her side. Why would Clarissa do that? No, wait. The voice wasn't Clarissa's. It was male. Troy? Definitely not. She opened her eyes to find it dark inside…what was she inside? There was a small hole…Cold air came through the hole, and it looked like sky above the hole. Early morning sky. Where was she? It all came rushing back. No, it wasn't a bad dream. She really was out in the middle of nowhere Alaska in subzero temperatures trying to stay warm. Oh yes. She was with unsavory types. Two men heading further into nowhere Alaska looking for who knew what.

"Get up. Get up now." It was Jud's cohort.

"Stop kicking me." Maggie railed on him as she unzipped the sleeping bag. She was thankful she'd slept in her parka and toboggan hat. She stared the man down as she stood up. "I may be your captive, but you could try some common decency. How would you like it if the shoe were on the other foot? Would you like to get kicked? I don't think so."

Jud laughed from a few feet away as he fed the fire. "She's got a point, Harry. And a temper to match that auburn hair, I see."

Maggie glared at Jud before she turned to look for the senator. He was nowhere to be seen.

"What did you do with the senator?" Maggie turned her glare back on Jud.

"Calm down, spitfire." Jud chuckled. "We did nothing with him. He's using the little boy's room. He'll be back in a moment. Coffee?"

Jud held up a cup toward Maggie. Her first instinct was to knock it out of his hand, but it was far too cold to waste a good cup of coffee. She might not get another one.

She accepted it and glanced around to see if there was any sweetener.

"There." He pointed to a small container. "Help yourself."

Maggie doctored her coffee then took a swig, cradling the cup between her gloved hands. She cozied up to the fire and warmed the rest of her.

"Where are you taking us?"

"Now that's what I like about you, Maggie. You're direct and to the point." Jud stood and walked over to stand beside her. "I suppose it won't hurt to tell you. You'll find out soon anyway."

"You stole my laptop, didn't you?" Maggie took another swig of coffee, savoring its warmth and taste.

Jud smirked. "Of course not. I was with you that night, remember?"

"Perhaps not, but you arranged to have it stolen so that you could get the picture from it."

Jud's smirk faded to contemplation. "So, you know about the picture. What else do you know?"

"That's all I know. I have no idea what's so special about that plane, but you're taking us there, aren't you?"

Jud smirked and clapped his hands a couple of times. "Very good, Maggie. Why else would we be heading deep into Denali National Park? There's nothing else worth looking for in this forsaken place. Believe me, I've tried for years. It wasn't until your photograph that we were successful in pinpointing it. I didn't know what I was looking for. Of course, nature helped us out. A certain glacier retreated and has revealed its secrets. Not since the day that plane crashed has that glacier retreated so far back. It's as if the glacier decided to cover it over and protect it from prying eyes. Until now."

"What if you get there, and it's nothing like what you expect?" Maggie finished her coffee.

"Oh, my dear Maggie. That just goes to show you know nothing of what we're looking for. Take my word for it. It will be there."

"But if it's not?"

Jud's face twisted into an evil mask that made him almost unrecognizable. He lowered his chin and glared. "Then that would mean your boyfriend has gotten there first. That's why I have you and the senator with me. Try and keep up, Maggie. You're not here for a joy ride."

~

As the afternoon sun lowered on the northwestern sky, Troy spotted Peter's Glacier. He tapped Colonel Williams on the shoulder.

"There's the glacier we're looking for. Peter's Glacier. I judge we'll be there in half an hour. Hang tight."

The colonel nodded and Troy kept the team moving toward their destination. They had taken a break a couple of hours earlier so the team was happy to keep going. They would spend the night at the plane's location as planned.

Half an hour later, the plane came into view as they crossed a snowy hillock. The afternoon sun reflected on some of the glass that hadn't broken out of the frames when the plane had crashed. Troy guessed the plane must have crashed into the glacier further up the mountain and slid to the bottom where it came to rest on its belly, tail against the rocky side of the glacier. Ice had covered it years ago. As the glacier retreated, the plane stayed on the ground at the glacier's foot, leaving the front half exposed.

Troy halted the dog team several feet from the plane and stepped off the sled's runners. He tethered the team then watered and fed them as Colonel Williams climbed out of the sled and stood looking up at the red-colored plane that had once been an aerial ambulance.

"And to think that plane's mission was to rescue people." Colonel Williams folded his arms over his chest.

Troy finished feeding the dogs and came to stand by the colonel. "Yeah. One of the two men inside tried to save the other one. I'd say he was a hero in every way. I guess we'll never really know what happened to bring them down."

Colonel Williams turned his gaze on Troy. "Perhaps not, but we can give it a whirl. There might be an explanation inside or in the mechanics somewhere. Too bad we didn't bring an airplane mechanic along."

They stared at the wreckage for several minutes, each taking in what they'd only heard about before. The nose cone had been ripped off when it came to a halt in its resting place, taking the engine and various pieces and parts with it. The fire wall was exposed, trailing wires and various parts to the engine. All were rusted and oxidized from exposure to the weather. The glass in the cockpit window frames was either broken out or broken and still partially in the frames. The wing to their left was ripped off and was nowhere to be seen. It was most likely somewhere beneath the glacier between the summit of the mountain and where the plane rested. The other wing on their right was still attached but was partially hidden by glacier ice. Bits and parts of the plane lay around on the ground. A landing gear assembly with a wheel still attached lay to their left. Who knew where the other one was? Certainly not under the fuselage.

Troy tried to see inside the cockpit but with the reflection of the afternoon sun on the partial glass and the darkness behind the frames of missing glass, it was hard to see.

"Ready to head inside?" Colonel Williams turned to him, a wry expression twisting his features.

"After you." Troy held out his hand toward the plane. He held up a flashlight he'd grabbed from the sled in the other. "I'm prepared."

Colonel Williams tugged a small flashlight from a cargo pocket in his parka and led the way toward the plane.

They walked around the wreckage and moved back toward the left side of the fuselage.

"From the 1987 radio call from the plane's pilot," Colonel Williams moved his gloved hands along the crumpled and rusted red metal, "he identified the plane as Flight 1054 out of Nome. It was recorded by the Ft. Wainwright radio operator that particular flight was a Cessna Skycourier. General Harding and I looked up the specs on that plane and there should be a cargo door right above the wing on this side."

"Yeah, well, that's going to be a problem." Troy waved a hand in front of him. "This whole wing is covered in glacier ice at least twenty feet thick. There's no going in that way."

Colonel Williams released a heavy breath and scrubbed a gloved hand down his face.

Troy pursed his lips and thought for a few seconds. He walked back around to the front of the plane then around to the other side where the wing was missing.

"Hey, Colonel. Over here." He yelled.

Colonel Williams came around to join him. "What did you find?"

"Generally, they put emergency exits over the wings of most planes. This one's no exception. Look. It's not covered by the ice." Troy pointed at the exit just above where the wing used to be attached. "The glacier ice lays just behind it. I'd say God's smiling on us today."

Colonel Williams ignored that and stared at the side of the fuselage. "Got a crowbar on that sled of yours?"

~

Maggie grew colder and more tired the deeper they went into the park. The only things that kept her going were the beautiful view of Mt. Denali that played peek-a-boo through the clouds throughout the day, the knowledge that God was with her no matter how this situation would turn out, and the hope that Troy would get there and be gone before they got there.

Oh Lord, I need Your strength. Please keep us safe and please keep Troy and Colonel Williams safe. Would You allow them to get whatever they're after and be gone before we get there? I would so love for them to steal Jud's thunder and be long gone.

The words rang through her heart over and over as they traveled across the frozen tundra of the Alaskan backcountry. Maggie had never seen so much wilderness in her life. As many places as she had traveled in her career, she'd always been able to get back to civilization fairly quickly. Not this time. She was well and truly out here.

She spotted caribou, moose, wolverine and even a couple of mountain goats in the distance. It was just her luck. Jud had her camera. Oh, the photographs she could've taken if she had it.

The afternoon waned on until the sun lowered in the northwest and began to drop behind the mountains. It would be getting dark soon and the temperatures dropped with the daylight.

Maggie glanced over at the senator in his sled. He returned her gaze from behind sun goggles that Jud had given him and gave a weak smile. Jud had provided sun goggles for both of them against snow blindness. As bitter as she felt toward Jud at the moment, she was appreciative of the goggles. Staring at the white wilderness all day would have been horrible.

As the sun dipped ever lower and darkness began to grow, Maggie removed her goggles so she could see better.

A few minutes later, Jud and Harry halted the sleds at the top of a hillock, and she noticed there were sled tracks a few feet away from where they'd stopped. Following the tracks with her gaze, she realized they led to…the plane.

Maggie's heart flipped. Then sank. Was that what she thought it was? A dog sled team tethered in front of the plane? Oh no. That was not good.

~

Troy retrieved the crowbar from the sled then, after using a bungee cord to strap it to his waist, he began to climb up the front of the plane where the nose cone used to be. With care he made his way up to the cockpit then over that to the top of the plane.

"Hey, be careful." Colonel Williams followed his every move. "The top's going to be slippery, I imagine."

"Actually, it's pretty dinged up." Troy crawled on his hands and knees across the top of the plane. "Lots of places to grab hold of."

When he was even with where the top of the emergency exit door was, he lay down on his stomach and removed the crowbar from the bungee cord. Lowering his arms over the side of the plane, he jammed the end of the crowbar into the top edge of the emergency exit door and hauled back on the crowbar with all his strength. He did this several times, each time moving the crowbar deeper into the opening crevice that he was creating in the top edge of the door.

"That's looking good, Troy. It looks like you're making progress." Colonel Williams stomped his feet from the cold and shoved his hands into his parka pockets.

Troy's hands hurt, and he took a few seconds to flex the fingers on each hand before resuming his work. The edge of the door was bent out allowing him to shove the crowbar deeper. He wiggled it until it felt like it rested against another edge, then he leaned into it again with all his strength. It felt like something moved inside. Wiggling it in as deep as he could, he put his weight and strength into it and all of a sudden it popped open, but remained in place. Stretching, he shoved the crowbar into the sides of the door until he felt the mechanism that held the door in place from the inside, and he went to work prying it loose. Within minutes the door fell to the ground, forcing Colonel Williams to jump back.

He laughed and pumped a fist in the air. "That's great, Troy. You did awesome, man. Come on down. I'll wait for you before I go in."

Troy rolled onto his back and lay there for a few moments. "Thanks. I'll be right down."

After he caught his breath and flexed his cold and aching fingers again, Troy tossed the crowbar to the ground then jumped down and walked over to Colonel Williams' side. He pulled his flashlight from his pocket and climbed into the plane, Colonel Williams right behind him.

They had no idea from the outside just how much damage the crash had done to the plane. The glacier ice disguised much of the damage, but from the inside, they saw from the fuselage just behind the wings was completely missing. Glacier ice mixed with solid rock sat at the back of the plane.

Troy moved forward to the cockpit and found the bodies of the two pilots. One, who had been sitting in the pilot's seat, or rather half of him still was, had been thrown behind the co-pilot's seat when the upper half of his seat had been torn away from the lower half. His remains were mostly mummified now, his skin stretched thin over his skeleton.

"This was the ambulance pilot." Colonel Williams pointed at the upper part of the seat.

"So was this." Troy pointed at the lower half of the body that remained in the pilot's seat still in front of the console.

"And this was Evgene Orlov." Troy moved between the two seats as best he could and stared at the remains of the Russian defector who sat propped against the window of the tiny cockpit. He shone his flashlight on the erstwhile pilot then began searching through his pockets. "Pardon me, sir, but I'm here to complete your mission."

Troy found a variety of items in the man's flight jacket including a sterling silver cigarette lighter, but it wasn't until he checked the man's flight suit that he found what he was looking for.

He pulled out a small yellow manila envelope not much bigger than Troy's hand. He opened it and pulled out some papers. They were yellowed sheets of paper written in Russian. Just like General Harding had told them. He slipped the papers back into the envelope and with care moved away from the bodies.

"These are the papers." He waved the packet in the air. "General Harding will be happy when we get them back to him."

Colonel Williams grinned. "Good. Let's get out of here. It's depressing."

Troy slipped them into his parka pocket. "Yeah. It's been a long two days, but I think we'd better get back on the trail tonight. Knowing Jud's on his way here, we should beat feet and head back. We need to get these papers to General Harding ASAP."

As much as he hated to leave Maggie in Jud's hands, he doubted he would leave her and the senator out here. Once he didn't find the papers in the plane, he'd bring them back and use them as leverage to get the papers.

Colonel Williams swung his body out of the emergency exit doorway and Troy followed right behind him.

"What do you say? Ready to head back?"

Chapter Twenty-Two

As Troy's feet hit the ground, he glanced up to find he and the colonel had company. Jud Svenson and another man were aiming guns at them. Standing with them were Maggie and Senator Scott, both with expressions of fear and uncertainty stamped on their features. Anger coursed through Troy. At Svenson for dragging Maggie and the senator out here in the wilderness but more than that, at himself, for not hustling to get the packet and get out of here before he arrived.

"Oh, I don't know." Jud shoved his parka hood back from his face. "I think maybe you should stay with us tonight. I'm looking for something in that plane, and I suspect you might have already found it."

Jud glanced at Colonel Williams. "Has he, Colonel?"

The colonel unzipped his parka far enough to reach inside and pull a Sig Sauer P226 9mm handgun from an inside pocket. Troy thought he was going to aim it at Jud but was shocked when he turned and pointed it at Troy.

Colonel Williams nodded then spouted something in Russian. Then he spoke in his normal English. "He has. Found it right where we thought it would be. It's too bad Orlov didn't make it. I would have hauled him back to Russia and thrown him into a *gulag.*"

Shock swirled through Troy as he attempted to take in the last few seconds. He'd been traveling and working with a Russian spy all along. The thought threatened to overwhelm him. He had to hold it together and get a grip for Maggie and the senator's sakes as well as his own.

"You're a traitor." Troy spat on the ground at Colonel Williams' feet.

The colonel backhanded Troy across the face, eliciting a soft cry from Maggie.

"You can't be a traitor if you're not American." The twisted smile on Williams' face sent Troy's heart into a nosedive.

"I don't know how you ended up working for General Harding," the senator spoke in contemptuous tones, "but you'll be dealt with."

"Shut up." Harry turned a gun on the senator.

Williams stared at the senator for several moments through dead eyes. "You needn't worry about that, Senator. The good general will never know. When we all disappear, there will be no one to tell him, least of all the three of you."

Jud chuckled. "Why don't we all just sit down and have a nice warm meal and get some sleep. Everyone's tired and tomorrow's a new day. You just never know what a new day will bring."

He laughed. "Oh and, Williams, get the papers from Donovan, will you."

Colonel Williams glared at Jud. "You forget who I am, Dubrovsky. I'm the one who gives the orders here. This mission comes straight from Moscow. You'll do as you're told just as you've done up until now. Get the papers yourself and bring them to me."

Jud's light banter and smile disappeared. His gaze slid away from Williams. "*Da.*"

He strode over to Troy and began searching his pockets.

Troy knocked his hands away. "Don't touch me."

Jud sneered at him just before he lifted a fist and punched Troy in the face. Troy fell to the ground, blood spurting from his nose.

Jud leaned over him, the sneer spreading across his face. "You have no idea how long I've wanted to do that."

Maggie ran to Troy's side and knelt beside him. "Troy? Troy, are you okay?"

With gentle fingers, she swiped his hair from his forehead and stroked his cheek. Boy did that feel nice. His eyes opened and he attempted to sit up.

Jud shoved him back down as he pulled the yellowed manila envelope from Troy's parka pocket. "Thank you very much. It's been a pleasure. Punching you, that is."

He patted along Troy's parka until he felt something else, then he grinned and reached into his pocket and pulled out Troy's satellite phone.

"I'll just hang onto this as well, thank you."

Jud stood, slipping the envelope into one parka pocket and the phone into another. He turned and walked away.

Troy sat up and, leaning to the side, spat out a wad of blood.

"Hold on a sec." Climbing to her feet, Maggie marched over to the sled she'd traveled on, pulled back the cover and began rummaging through the gear.

Jud came over and grabbed her arm. "What do you think you're doing?"

Maggie yanked her arm away and shoved a finger in Jud's chest. "Back off, Jud. Or Pavel. Or whoever you are. You punched Troy, now I'm trying to find something to staunch the blood. Back off."

Without a word Jud took a few steps back and watched as Maggie rummaged. She grabbed some clean rags and a first aid kit and marched back to where Troy sat.

He leaned over the snow, blood dripping into the pristine white.

Maggie knelt beside him. Troy glanced around and saw Williams directing camp be set up. He even put the senator to work. No surprise there.

Troy turned his attention back to Maggie as she handed him a clean rag to hold against his nose.

"There you go. That was completely uncalled for. Jud is such a jerk. In more ways than one." She searched through the first aid kit for anything that might be of use. She found an ice pack and chuckled. "I doubt this will help any more than just sitting out here in -20°. What do you think?"

The rag held to his nose with one hand, Troy reached over and took Maggie's hand in his. "What do I think? I think you're one gutsy lady. Standing up to Jud like that on my behalf? You made him back down. That's something."

Troy's heart bumped erratically when Maggie lifted her gaze to his for several seconds. She gave him a faint smile and squeezed his hand then glanced down at their twined fingers.

"You need to put pressure on the bridge of your nose if you can." Maggie brought her gaze back to him. "I'm concerned he broke your nose, Troy. That's a lot of blood."

Troy pulled the rag away and checked it. "It seems like it's slowing down. I'll put pressure on the bridge for a bit and see if I can't get it to stop."

He watched Maggie's eyes grow wide as she stared at the ground right behind him.

"What's wrong, Maggie?" She had her back to the camp, and he didn't dare turn in case it brought the attention of the others to whatever she was staring at.

"Troy, there's a crowbar on the ground right behind you. Can you use it as a weapon?" Maggie's voice was little more than a whisper.

The crowbar. He'd thrown it to the ground after prying the emergency exit door off the plane. "Sure, if it hasn't already frozen to the ground *and* if we can find a way to hide it until we need to use it."

Maggie glanced casually around and saw the bent and rusted nose cone from the plane. It looked plenty long enough to hide the crowbar in. It would just be a matter of getting it in there without being noticed.

"What about the nose cone?" She took the rags and held them to his nose even as he pinched the bridge. Whether or not the bleeding had stopped it would give them some time to talk and no one would know if the bleeding had stopped or not unless they lowered the rag. "Keep this up over your nose."

Troy held the rag up and glanced at the nose cone. "Yeah, it would be a great place to hide it. Not easily seen unless you know it's there. Only problem is getting it there. I could distract them while you hide it."

"Oh, no you don't. What if Jud decides to use you for a punching bag again? He could rearrange your face the next time. I kind of like it the way it is."

Troy lowered the rag, his gaze seeking hers. "You do?"

A pained expression settled on Maggie's face. "Well, not at the moment. Your nose is swollen, and you're starting to bruise. Tomorrow you'll be a sight for sure."

He lifted the rag back to his face. "Great."

"Oooh, I could just…"

"You could just what?" Jud's snarky voice sounded as he approached them. He waved his handgun in Troy's direction. "You've had plenty of time to play with your nursemaid. It's time for you to pull your weight. Let's go. You can help the senator gather more firewood. There's more people to keep warm tonight so we'll need a big fire."

Troy climbed to his feet, and after a bit of initial dizziness, he was able to make his way toward a stand of scrub brush and small trees. The senator did the bending over and piled the smaller pieces of wood on Troy's arms then together they pulled the longer downed pieces back to camp.

The whole while Troy remembered how Maggie stood up to Jud for him. She was a strong woman, and he loved the thought of her standing by his side for the rest of his life. Before they could do that, however, they had to get out of this situation. *Lord, we need Your help….*

~

As soon as Jud and Troy walked away, Maggie stood, picking up the first aid kit along with all the bloody rags, and holding them in her hand, she backstepped three feet until she felt the crowbar beneath her boot. Casually glancing around the camp to make sure where everyone was and what they were doing, she knelt down and grabbed the crowbar. It was icy cold on her bare fingers that were already nearly numb from working over Troy. She wished she'd slipped her gloves back on, but it was too late now. They were in her parka pocket, and she was committed.

Maggie picked up the crowbar and wrapped the end of it in one of the rags then held it just behind her as she slipped quickly over to the nose cone. She kept an eye on where everyone was and what they were doing. No one paid any attention to her. *Thank you, Lord.*

Careful not to allow the metal crowbar to bang against the metal nose cone, she slipped it inside. It made a slight metallic scraping noise but at least it hadn't banged. Maggie turned to stand up.

"What are you doing?" Harry stood there, his brows furrowed, his gun pointed at her.

Maggie stood up, zipping the first aid kit closed and draping the shoulder strap over her neck. With a steady hand she pushed the barrel of the gun away from her.

"I would appreciate it if you would stop pointing that at me. Do I look like I can go far without you or your fellow criminals seeing me? Did it look like I was trying to escape? No and no." Maggie turned to observe the nose cone and shrugged her shoulders. "Actually, I've never seen a nose cone from an airplane before. Just thought I'd take a gander."

With heart racing, Maggie marched off to return the first aid kit to the sled. She snuck a surreptitious glance back at Harry. With his back to the nose cone, he'd turned to stare at her. His brows were still furrowed as if he didn't get her. After a few seconds he walked away. Maggie took a deep breath and released it slowly. *Again, Thank You, Lord. We'll do this step by step if that's how You want to do it.*

Maggie slipped her warm gloves on hoping her frozen fingertips would warm up soon. Troy and the senator had a good fire going and she stepped over to warm herself. With the sun gone now, the wind had picked up and the temperature had dropped.

"Get us something to eat." Jud dropped the rucksack of food fixings at Maggie's feet and walked away. Troy started after him, but she grabbed his arm and shook her head.

"Don't," she whispered. "It's okay. We all need something warm and this way, I know it's safe to eat."

He glanced down at her, his head tilted, a grin lifting one corner of his mouth. "I'll get you home, Maggie. Don't worry."

"Do I look worried?" Maggie grinned back, her voice a mere whisper. She winked the eye furthest from Jud, Williams or Harry. "Mission accomplished."

Troy's brows furrowed in confusion then rose when he realized what she was talking about. "You managed…?"

"I did. Right where I told you." She bent and rummaged through the rucksack. Maggie raised her voice so everyone could hear her. "Hmmm. Beef stroganoff with noodles, chili mac with beef, or chicken teriyaki. Looks like I'll have to make a couple of them to feed this crowd."

"I vote for chicken teriyaki." Harry raised his hand.

"You're a minion. You don't get a vote." Jud cast him a disdainful expression.

"Beef stroganoff." Williams spoke from his throne near the other side of the fire. He sat in a folding camp chair with one leg crossed over the other knee. "Make coffee. I want coffee."

Maggie deemed to glare at him then turned away. All of a sudden, a gunshot rang out. A painful yelp filled the air followed by deathly silence. Everyone scrambled to see what had happened. All the dogs from the dog teams began barking and howling.

Maggie screamed, "No." and ran to Troy's team of dogs. There at the back of the team lay Cupcake. Maggie dropped to her knees beside the still warm body as his blood seeped into the frozen snowy tundra beneath him. He was gone. Shot needlessly by a maniac. Maggie's tears froze on her face as she ran her hands through the thick black, gray and white fur.

Troy dropped beside her and wrapped her in his arms, just holding her as she sobbed. All she'd done is glare at the man, and he'd taken it out on Cupcake. Maggie shook her head and wiped her tears, as hopelessness settled over her like a heavy blanket. *Lord, only You can get us out of this alive.*

~

Anger twisted Troy's gut as Maggie filled his arms. Cupcake had been an amazing team dog and hadn't deserved to die like this. How could they have been so fooled by such an evil man as Williams? There was no way that was his real name. As a Russian spy working as Pavel Dubrovsky's handler, he had to have been in Alaska for a while and set himself up in the Army somehow. Was there a real Colonel Williams that he'd changed places with? Had he killed him? Who knew? Right now, he'd give anything to get hold of that crowbar and ….

"Get up. Both of you." Jud waved his gun at them. "Williams is hungry and wants to eat. Now."

Maggie lifted tear-drenched angry eyes at Jud. "You can tell him…"

"Now now, Maggie, that kind of talk will only get you killed. Just cooperate and feed the man. Keep him happy and you just might make it back home alive." Jud chuckled. "I wouldn't count on it, but who knows? Now get up."

Troy released her and helped her to her feet, his gaze returning to his dog. He doubted if he'd be afforded the opportunity to bury him. If he got out of this situation alive, he'd come back and take care not only of Cupcake, but the ambulance pilot and Evgene Orlov. These criminals might not respect anyone or anything but themselves, but he would see it done.

~

It was nearly impossible to clean the tin plates in the subzero temperatures, and Maggie was tempted to use them for frisbees rather than clean them. She attempted to hide her sadness and frustration as she poured boiling water from the fire and scrubbed them with a rag, only to see the water freeze on them within seconds. Whether true or not, she was determined Jud, Harry and Williams had left extra food on the plates on purpose just to make it more difficult for her. It seemed the more hot water she poured on, the thicker the ice formed on the plates on top of the food.

"Here, let me help you." Troy knelt beside her and set a small pan on the ground by the fire, filling it with boiling water. "It'll work better if you wash them in a pan like you do at home."

"Of course, it will." Maggie sighed as her shoulders slumped. "Thanks. Where did you find that?"

Troy added soap to the hot water and swished it around, creating bubbles. "On one of the sleds. I saw you struggling and went to see what I could find. Voilà. You have a dishpan. I'll wash. You dry."

He dumped all the plates, forks and cutlery into the pan and began washing. "let's do this quickly. The water won't stay hot for long."

"Senator Scott, it's my opinion that you and your search team did a poor job of searching for this plane." Williams allowed his Russian accent to slip into his voice as he sat in his camp chair staring into the fire, his Sig Sauer in his lap. "In 1987 it had not yet been covered over by the glacier. What excuse do you have for not finding it?"

Maggie held her breath as she lifted her gaze to the senator. She hoped he wouldn't glare at the man or speak with contempt. After what he'd done to poor Cupcake when she'd merely glared at him, no telling what he'd do now.

"We searched for over a month." The senator spoke with no emotion. "We ran into a lot of bad weather during the search, often having to call it off until another, better day."

"Well, it's just too bad, isn't it?" Jud leaned forward in his camp chair. "You had your chance years ago to find the packet that Evgene Orlov stole from the Soviet Union. Now, you've lost it. Those papers will be returned to Russia. The United States will never know what Orlov was about to hand over to them."

"Shut up, Pavel." Williams turned a glare on him and growled. "It is not their business."

Jud flinched as he clamped his mouth shut and grimaced, his eyes darting about with unease.

"Well, we know your name's not Colonel Williams, so why don't you tell us what it really is?" Troy wiped his hands on a rag and turned on his knee to gaze at Williams.

The man sneered at him. "Certainly, why not? You won't be returning with us in the morning to tell anyone anyway."

He uncrossed his legs and re-crossed them, making himself even more comfortable. He slipped his gun into the cupholder on the arm of the chair and linked his fingers together behind his head. The sneer remained on his face.

"My name is General Yuri Kozlov of the Russian army. I infiltrated into the US Army five years ago. I took the place of the real Colonel Jack Williams when he was supposed to transfer to Ft. Wainwright Army base in Fairbanks."

Maggie's heart dropped. The real Colonel Williams? Oh no. Did that mean...?

"You killed him, didn't you?" Troy's voice was gruff with anger.

Kozlov shrugged, his hands still behind his head. His features twisted into a careless expression. "I had the same bone structure, you see, and once they gave me a tuck here and another tuck there then changed my features to look like his, there was no way we could have two Colonel Williams walking around. It had to be done, you understand. It helped that the real Colonel Williams had no family. He was a bachelor and the only child of deceased parents. Did that not work out well for us?"

"It did." Troy dropped the rag beside the pan of hot water and before Maggie knew what he was doing, he grabbed the pan, stood and threw it in Kozlov's face.

Not expecting it, the man screamed. Maggie doubted it was from pain because the water wasn't that hot anymore. It was more likely from the suddenness of the action and from anger. She didn't wait to see what Troy did next, but reached for the pan of hot water next to the fire and threw it in Jud's direction. He howled in pain. Of this she was sure. Maggie followed up by hitting him over the head with the hot pan then grabbed his gun when he hit the ground. She turned in time to see Senator Scott whack Harry over the head with his camp chair. Then he hit him again and again until the man dropped to the ground. Troy stood over Kozlov with the gun he'd taken from his chair.

"And here I thought you were going to use the crowbar." Maggie smiled at Troy.

He winked then winced as the movement tugged against his bruised and swollen nose. He gave her a slight grin. "When the opportunity arises, use what's at hand."

Chapter Twenty-Three

Troy was torn between making Kozlov, Jud and Harry dig a hole in the frozen permafrost in order to bury Cupcake or taking him home to bury him near the kennels. In the end he decided on the latter. He'd rather his faithful team dog would be laid to rest nearer his teammates than out here in the wilderness. It just felt…right. He bundled Cupcake's furry body in a piece of tarp he took from one of the sleds and laid him tenderly near the landing area. Troy would send him back on the helicopter and bury his ranger dog properly when he returned.

After a long night of swapping watches with Maggie and the senator, the three of them had gotten little sleep, but it was the only way to keep watch over Kozlov, Jud and Harry. Troy reclaimed the satphone from Kozlov last night after capturing the three. This morning he'd called General Harding and explained the situation, telling him they'd need a helicopter to retrieve the captured men. They would also need two trained rangers to help Troy bring the dog sled teams out of the wilderness.

"Yes, sir." Troy nodded as he held the satellite phone to his cold ear. Having lowered his parka hood, he wore only his toboggan, the wind chilling his neck and ear. "I'll give you a full report on my return, sir."

"Excellent." General Harding sounded as if he stood right beside Troy. "I expect it'll be a good one."

"You bet it will be, sir. I'll let you go so we can prepare for the chopper."

"It's on its way. See you when you return." The phone clicked indicating the general had hung up.

Troy stepped closer to the senator and lowered his voice. "He's sending a helicopter to pick up these guys. I want you to take Maggie and go with them. He's sending a couple of rangers to help me take the dog sled teams back."

Troy reached into his parka pocket and tugged out the small, yellow manila folder, holding it out to the senator. "Here you go, sir. I'm passing this on to you. You can see the general gets it."

Senator Scott reached out a gloved hand and took it, slipping it into his own parka pocket. "Thanks, Troy. For everything you've done to secure this."

Troy smiled. "No problem, sir. I just hope after all this trouble it's not Orlov's mother's homemade recipe for borsch."

The senator laughed long and loud. As his laughter faded away, he pulled a handkerchief from his slacks pocket to wipe his eyes. "You and me both, my friend. You and me both."

Maggie stepped over to them, a gun in her hand, still pointed at the three forlorn-looking foreign operatives. "Did I miss a good joke?"

Senator Scott waved a hand. "Yep. You missed it."

He walked away, chuckling to himself.

Maggie watched him go, her brows drawn together. "Will he be okay?"

Troy followed her gaze and nodded. "He will be now."

He tossed a pack onto one of the sleds and turned to Maggie. He tilted his head toward the three men sitting near the fire, their hands tied behind their backs. "A chopper's coming. It'll arrive in about forty-five minutes to take them to Ft. Wainwright. General Harding's expecting them."

"Oh, good. I'm sure he's preparing a couple of cells for them at jail central, then?"

"In the stockade, actually." Troy nodded and grabbed a small pack to add to the sled. He slid it beneath the cover and turned back to Maggie. "One more thing. I want you to escort the senator back to his wife. I'd feel better knowing you're with him."

Uncertainty flared in Maggie's gorgeous green eyes as her brow furrowed. Troy had a feeling she wanted to argue the point and possibly stay with him, but he was going to win this battle.

"Besides, there are two rangers coming on that chopper to help me bring the teams back home. If I have the weight of someone on my sled, it'll slow me down. If all three sleds are passenger free, we can go faster and make better time. We'll get home sooner."

Maggie continued to gaze at Troy, a battle warring on her features. "And what about Cupcake?"

In spite of the bitter cold, Troy tugged off his glove and slid his hand behind Maggie's hair inside her parka hood. He leaned his forehead against hers. "I'm sending him home with you, sweetheart. If all goes well, we don't hit any foul weather, or anything happens to slow us down, I'll be home by tomorrow night. Superintendent Wade can arrange to have him stored until I make it back. Then we'll bury him."

Maggie nodded. They stood like that for several moments then Troy dropped a kiss on her forehead. "You'd better get back to watching the men."

"Yeah. You distracted me." Maggie grinned as she walked away.

It felt good to laugh out loud, and Troy allowed himself a good one as he strolled to the nose cone to retrieve his crowbar.

~

The UH-60 Black Hawk helicopter arrived forty-five minutes later as promised. Maggie watched as it approached from the north-northeast and landed on a flat area of snow-covered ground about two hundred feet from their camp. As the grasshopper-like machine set down on its steel paddle skids, the chopper blades sent the snow into a mini swirling blizzard. The pilot cut the engines to reduce the stinging effects of the snow.

The side door of the helicopter opened, and six men climbed out. Four army personnel dressed in cold weather clothing followed by rangers Bryce West and Jason O'Rourke, dressed just as warmly.

They all jogged over to the camp, the army personnel carrying M4 carbines.

"They're all yours, gentlemen." Troy waved in the direction of Kozlov, Jud and Harry. "Please, take them back to General Harding. I'm sure he's looking forward to some interrogation time with these fellows."

"You can count on that, sir." One of the army guys stopped by Troy as the other three headed toward the men in the chairs. They grabbed them none too gently and dragged them to their feet, leading them back toward the helicopter.

"I'm Staff Sergeant Edwards, Ranger Donovan." He pulled a slip of paper from his pocket and handed it to Troy. "General Harding would like for you to meet with him Monday, April 22."

Troy accepted the paper with the date and request on it. He glanced back at the staff sergeant. "What's this for?"

"I don't know, sir. All he said was for me to give it to you. I'm just obeying orders." A slight grin tipped up one corner of his mouth. "When the general says jump, I just ask how high."

He turned to the senator. "Are you ready to go, sir?"

"Yes, I certainly am. And I don't think I want to come back into the Alaskan wilderness again anytime soon." He turned to Maggie. "Ready?"

"Well, no, not yet." She glanced at Troy then over at the bundled body of Cupcake. She returned her gaze to Troy and smiled. "I'm escorting the fallen body of Ranger Cupcake."

Staff Sergeant Edwards lifted an inquisitive eyebrow in Troy's direction, his lips clamped in a straight line.

Troy nodded. "Yep that's right. Kozlov shot one of my dog team. Every one of those team dogs is employed by the park service just the same as the Army employs K9s for service. They are rangers. This ranger dog just happens to be named Cupcake."

Staff Sergeant Edwards eyebrow dropped as he nodded. "Understood. Ranger Cupcake will be flown to Denali in the company of Miss Lawrence once the foreign intelligence operatives have been taken to Ft. Wainwright."

He gave Troy a salute then did an about face and walked back to the helicopter.

Troy and Bryce carried Cupcake's body to the helicopter while the senator and Maggie followed close behind. Once the ranger dog was stowed safely onboard, the senator shook Troy's hand.

"I'll see you when you return, Troy. I'm not leaving for Washington until I know you and your dog teams have returned safely. We've come too far in this adventure for me to leave just yet."

Troy chuckled and returned the senator's hearty handshake. "Thank you, sir. It has been an adventure, hasn't it. We'll be back soon. Go kiss your wife and get warm again. Put your feet up by the fire and be safe."

"I'll do that." The senator clapped Troy on the shoulder and, with the help of two of the soldier's, climbed onboard.

Troy turned to Maggie who stood to the side. His gaze pierced hers as she stepped closer then stopped. Oh no, he wasn't going to let that happen. His arms reached out and tugged her close, wrapping them around her. He heard her gasp just before he claimed her lips. Pain radiated through his face from his nose injury, but it faded from his mind as Maggie filled his being.

He had a feeling the US Army wouldn't be happy with a long farewell, but he kissed her with everything he had in him. She would remember it until he returned, that was for doggone sure.

Several whistles sounded from just inside the open doorway to the helicopter, but it didn't stop Troy from sending Maggie a message he hoped she'd hold in her heart until they could have a talk. And they would be talking. Soon.

Troy's heart was racing and he could barely breathe when he released her. Maggie's eyes remained shut and he had to hold on to her until she finally opened them. She took a deep breath and her eyes focused on his face.

The helicopter engine revved and the blades began to spin.

"I think they're trying to tell us something." Troy grinned as he raised his voice to be heard over the engine.

"Miss Lawrence, you'd better get onboard." One of the soldiers leaned out and called over the whirring blades. "This bird's leavin'."

Troy wrapped his hands around Maggie's waist and helped her climb into the chopper. She scrambled into a jump seat and buckled her seat straps. The soldier handed her a set of headphones and plugged her in.

Troy grinned and waved as he stepped back. Maggie waved and smiled, sending his heart trip-hammering. He could still feel her lips against his. He drew in a cold breath as the soldier closed the door. Troy stepped back. Within seconds, the chopper blades were flinging snow into another mini blizzard, sending stinging particles of snow whizzing through the air.

Troy turned and jogged far enough back to be out of reach of the painful icy particles. He watched as the bird lifted into the air carrying away the woman he loved. He had mixed feelings about her being on that bird. She was riding with the three bad guys, but it helped knowing there were four armed soldiers there to protect her as well as the senator. At least she would be back home shortly where she would be safe and warm.

As he watched the metal bird fade and grow smaller in the distance, he realized it took his heart with it. Maggie Lawrence would forever and always be the love of his life. The only thing he was uncertain of was did she feel the same about him?

~

Maggie barely paid attention as the soldier helped her buckle in and plug in her headset. Her heart was racing to beat the band and her lungs were pumping like she'd just run a race. Her gaze met Troy's and she waved just before the soldier slid the door shut. Through the large rectangular windows in the door, she saw him retreat as the pilot revved the engines and the whirring blades sent swirling snow in a torrential blizzard surrounding the helicopter. It lifted from the ground and took off toward home.

Maggie dropped her head back against the headrest of her jump seat. She still felt Troy's kiss, and was tempted to reach up and touch her lips. Glancing at the audience of eight men, not counting the pilot and co-pilot, she nixed that action. Most of them were staring at her as it was. She glanced out the window at the passing scenery, wishing she had her camera. That and her laptop would be on the sled that Jud had brought out to the plane crash site, but Troy would bring it home. At least she would get them back.

The voices of the pilot and co-pilot in her ears weren't loud and she ignored them, closing her eyes and allowing her body to relax for the first time in a few days. It wasn't particularly warm in the cargo area of the helicopter, but it was warmer than the plane crash site. Maggie thought of Troy and the other rangers still in the wilderness, out in the cold and chill wind. They still had at least today and tomorrow to get through before they could truly get warm again.

Father God, please bring them home safely. Look after them and their teams. Protect them and help the dogs to be swift and sure footed. And, Father, I love Troy. Thank you for bringing him into my life. I don't know what Your plans are for us, but I can't see a life ahead without him. If You want him in my life, then please work it out somehow.

Maggie felt herself drifting as the helicopter sped through the azure morning sky. There may be bad guys onboard, but she was resting. Resting in her Father's care.

~

Troy turned from the disappearing dot of the helicopter in the distant sky and returned to camp. He bent to douse the campfire then joined the other rangers as they finished packing up the sleds.

"So that's how it is, eh?" Bryce walked over and elbowed Troy as he tightened the sled cover. "I turn my back for more than a day and you make your move on Maggie, you sly dog. Then get yourself caught up in an international spy ring. What the heck, Troy?"

"What can I say? I like to keep life interesting." Troy stood and grinned, then winced.

"And get the beautiful girl in end," added Jason as he tightened the cover on the sled he was working on.

"Yeah, well. We aren't there yet."

"What do you mean, you aren't there yet?" Bryce began harnessing his dog team. "I saw the way you kissed her. Looked pretty 'there' to me."

"Well, we need to talk first. I haven't told her about Liz." Troy straightened, a grimace etching his features.

Bryce gave a slow nod, his eyebrow lifting in understanding as he nodded. "Right."

"Well, let's get these puppies harnessed and this show on the road." Troy reached for a harness and he and Jason helped Bryce harness the dog teams and prepare to head home.

A short time later they were ready as the dog teams filled the wilderness air with their barking in their eagerness to get on the trail. With one final glance at the crashed ambulance plane, Troy sent a silent promise to the deceased occupants that he would return for them and remove them from the wilderness back to their loved ones.

Troy returned his gaze to his lead dog, Venture and called in a loud voice, "Mush. Mush."

Venture leapt just as the team dogs in front of the sled did, giving the whole team the initial jolt they needed to move the sled forward.

Troy grabbed the handles of the sled and jumped onto the runners as it gained momentum. Bryce and Jason did the same with their teams.

The dogs charged across the snowy tundra in the frigid morning air, steamy clouds puffing from their mouths as they eagerly did the job they lived for. Their mushers rode the runners of the sleds occasionally calling encouraging words to the teams, urging them on. This would be a long day for all three teams. A few short breaks to eat, water and rest, then back on the trail. Troy wanted to get home by late tomorrow night if at all possible. One night on the trail was pushing it. Only time and hard work by the teams and mushers would tell if they could do what they hadn't done on the way out.

Lord, I just want to get home. Am I being unreasonable? Bryce and Jason haven't said a word and they're willing to do the impossible. Help these teams to hold out and to be strong. Please keep the weather good for us. Protect us. And please protect Maggie. In Christ's name I pray.

Chapter Twenty-Four

Clarissa and Jeremy were tickled pink to have Maggie back. They would've been happier still had Troy come home, but they were used to his occasional odd hours and days.

"You needn't worry." Clarissa handed Maggie a bowl of popcorn as the three settled in front of the TV to watch a cartoon movie. "I'm used to Troy sometimes being gone for days on end. It was only yesterday morning since you left him out there, sweetie. He and the other rangers are trained to travel long distances with the dog teams for days at a time. I know he said he wanted to be home tonight, but if the weather out there turns bad, they may have to hunker down and wait it out. You have to be prepared for anything."

Maggie took the bowl of popcorn and held it out to Jeremy who was dressed in his dinosaur pjs. He scooped up a handful and crammed it in his mouth.

"I know, Clarissa. It was just so cold out there, and…."

"And you're in love with him." Clarissa dropped to the couch on the other side of Jeremy, her words matter-of-fact.

"Clarissa." Maggie's whisper scolded as her eyes dropped to Jeremy. "Someone may be listening."

Clarissa cast her glance over the rim of her glasses that begged "really?" then waved a hand in front of Jeremy's eyes. He didn't even blink. "Pshaw. He's watching the movie previews and isn't even listening."

Maggie heaved a heavy sigh and popped a piece of popcorn in her mouth. She wasn't going to have this conversation with Troy's mom. Not until she'd had a conversation with Troy, and he would have to start it.

"So-o-o-o?" Clarissa reached for the popcorn bowl.

"Shhh. The movie's starting." Maggie dropped more popcorn into her mouth and snuggled next to Jeremy.

By the end of the movie, Jeremy was fast asleep against Maggie's arm.

Clarissa used the remote control to turn off the TV and glanced at her grandson. "I'll take him upstairs."

Maggie shook her head. "No, please let me take him."

At Clarissa's smiling nod, Maggie gently drew him into her arms and cradled his head on her shoulder. Getting to her feet, she walked into the hallway to the stairs and climbed to the second floor. In Jeremy's room, Maggie carefully laid him on his bed and tucked him in. A gentle sigh escaped Jeremy as he rolled onto his side and cuddled against his pillow. Maggie stood watching him for a moment then turned to find Troy leaning against the doorframe, his arms crossed over his chest, a tender smile on his face.

Maggie started, placing a hand over her heart. She smiled as warmth flowed upward from her sweater neckline, a bit embarrassed she'd been caught watching over his son.

Troy stood away from the doorframe, crooked a finger, and tilted his head, nodding over his shoulder, indicating she should come with him.

Maggie's steps were silent as she left Jeremy's room and stepped into the hall. Troy pulled the door to, leaving a wide crack. A smile lifted the corners of this lips as he twined his fingers with hers and led her downstairs to the kitchen.

Clarissa was making herself a cup of tea. "I'm glad you're home, sweetheart. Maggie was pretty worried about you. She's not used to your trips like this, you know."

Clarissa glanced over her glasses at Maggie as she stirred honey into her tea. "You'll learn to trust him, sweetie."

Maggie's face grew warm. "It's not that I don't trust Troy, Clarissa, it's just…."

"Save it." Clarissa waved a hand. "I already know the truth. You two will have to figure things out on your own."

She headed for the doorway. "I'll take my tea upstairs so you can get started on that right now. Goodnight."

The warmth surging through Maggie grew as Troy's fingers tightened ever so gently on hers. He chuckled as he tugged her toward the living room. Was he taking his mother's advice? They were doing this now?

Troy led Maggie to the couch and even after they were seated, he didn't let go of her hand.

He turned to face her better. "Thanks for seeing the senator safely home. I'm sure Mrs. Scott was frantic to see him."

Maggie released a happy laugh. "Well, she certainly was, but she's one brave woman, Troy. It seems that after the senator and I were kidnapped, she and Calvin Jacobs managed to take down the guy who was left to guard them. Between the two of them they quickly concocted a plan to trick him into leaving the room, then Calvin bopped him on the head with a statue when he walked back in."

"Yeah, Superintendent Wade mentioned that to me when he called to tell me you and the senator had been kidnapped." Troy's brow furrowed as his gaze filled with doubt. "I just don't know where Calvin got the wherewithal to lift a statue in his condition."

Maggie lifted her shoulders in a shrug. "I have no idea. Adrenaline perhaps? He did pull some stitches and had to be re-stitched, but they got their man and called 911. That's when the superintendent called, and you were warned the senator and I were kidnapped as well as the fact Jud and Harry were on the way to the plane crash site. The only problem was no one knew when they'd arrive."

"Yeah, and no one knew Colonel Williams was a Russian spy. Much less the Russian spy General Kozlov."

Maggie nodded. "That did nearly turn things sour, didn't it? I'm so glad you took control and got the upper hand. If you hadn't, you, the senator and I would have been permanent company for Evgene Orlov and the ambulance pilot."

Troy reached over and stroked Maggie's cheek. "The Lord was looking out for us, sweetheart. He had a plan."

"Yes, He did." She whispered, his touch doing things to her heart rate. "Speaking of Orlov and the ambulance pilot, do you have plans to bring their bodies back? It just seems fair to do so. They've been lost out there long enough, and now that we know where they are, they should be brought home."

Troy nodded. "Later in the spring when it's warmer, I'll take Bryce and Jason back out to retrieve their bodies. I'm sure Ludmila

Orlov and her daughter, Dafna, would want their husband and father brought home. We'll have to research to find out who the ambulance pilot is, but I'm sure the Army can help us with that. Then we'll locate his family and return his body to them."

"And what of Dafna and Ludmila? What will happen with them?"

Troy smiled. "Dafna's got a great lawyer now. He got her sentence cut in half with parole in ten years. Wherever she's sent to prison, Ludmilla will be helped to set up a home and a job nearby so she can be close to support Dafna. Natalya and I visited Ludmila. She's a sweet lady who loves her daughter and prays for her to come to know the Lord. I'm sure in time with her support and prayers, Dafna's heart will soften and one day she may come around. Who knows?"

Maggie tipped her head until it rested against Troy's shoulder.

"I'm glad you made it home safely. Did all the dogs fare well?"

"Sure, they did. They're rangers." Troy chuckled.

Silence filled the room except for the snapping of the low-burning logs in the fireplace. One shifted all of a sudden, hissing as it sent glowing red sparks up the chimney. Maggie watched as the sparks flew then settled into low-burning flames over the charred logs.

"Maggie, I need to tell you something." Was that dread in Troy's voice? Maggie lifted her head and turned to look him in the face. Whatever it was, he wasn't eager to share it.

"Troy, I can tell it's something unpleasant, and if you'd rather not...."

"It's not something I like to talk about, but not only do I need to tell you, I want to tell you."

"Okay. I'm all ears." Maggie sat up straighter and clasped her other hand over their twined fingers.

Troy breathed in a deep cleansing breath and released it slowly. "As I've told you before, I met my wife, Liz, at UNC Chapel Hill. She was a North Carolina girl through and through. In some ways she was a lot like you, Maggie, and in other ways, well, she was nothing like you. When we met, I thought she was amazing. She was so full of life and so eager to travel and see the world."

Troy released Maggie's hand and stood from the couch. Maggie's hand felt cold and empty, while at the same time she felt bereft of his presence. She wanted to ask him to come back and sit with her, but when he started pacing, she understood he needed space and separation to tell her what he needed to say.

"When we married and I brought her to Alaska, Liz withdrew within herself and certainly from me. She got pregnant, and at first, I thought that was a good thing. She seemed happy for a while, then when Jeremy was born, she went into severe postpartum depression. She left us and headed up into Fairbanks. She met Jud Svenson and took up with him. The next thing I heard was she'd been killed by a bear up near the Arctic Circle. Jud had taken her on a hunting trip up where the grizzlies are. An investigation was done by the Alaskan State Police but it was determined to be a normal bear attack. I never agreed with those findings, but couldn't prove anything."

Maggie gasped and stood to her feet. Without thinking what she was doing, she went straight to Troy and wrapped her arms around him, her head resting on his shoulder.

"Oh, Troy. I'm so, so sorry. How horrible for you and for little Jeremy. He never knew his mother."

~

Wrapping his arms around Maggie, Troy allowed himself to soak in her warmth and her comfort. He released a heavy sigh and closed his eyes, just holding her. She fit so well within his arms. Could she hear his heartbeat as she rested her ear against his chest? Could she hear what it was asking of her?

"I love you, Maggie." His voice was little more than a whisper. "I can't go on any longer without telling you that. I've told you what happened to Liz. You're both North Carolina girls. She hated it up here in Alaska."

Troy pulled back and took Maggie's hands within his own. "My life is here, Maggie. It always has been and always will be. Alaska is my job, it's my family, and it's my heritage. I don't... know if... I could...."

When Maggie pulled her hand from his, she laid a gentle finger over his lips, sending his heart rate into overdrive. "Shhh. For one thing, I may be from North Carolina, but I'm not Liz. The cold isn't so bad, and since I've been here, I've certainly had my fair share of it."

Maggie chuckled and teased Troy's lips with her finger. "I could always work from Alaska and fly out for the occasional photo op, at least until our family starts to grow. Then there's Alaska that's chock full of photo opportunities. Oh, did I forget to say that I love you too?"

Troy covered Maggie's mouth with his own in a kiss he hoped she wouldn't soon forget. Tease him, would she? His own heart rate continued to climb as he let her go and his gaze met hers.

"So, you'll be staying then?"

Maggie released a happy sigh and dropped her head to his shoulder. "Uh huh, but I think you owe me some animal photo shoots. My boss will have my head if I don't get him some photos soon."

"We'll get going on that right away." Troy grinned and dropped to his knee there in front of the fireplace. "First things first, my love. I've been a little busy lately, so I haven't had a chance to shop for a ring yet, but will you marry me, Maggie Lawrence?"

Maggie smiled then dropped to her knees in front of Troy. "With my whole heart I love you, Troy Donovan. Yes, I'll marry you."

Troy gathered her in his arms and kissed her again, then pulled back ever so slightly. "We'll shop together when we can get up to Fairbanks and get whatever ring you like."

Placing her hands on either side of his face, Maggie pulled his head down for another kiss. "Whatever you want is fine as long as we do it together."

Troy kissed her long and deep, holding her close to his heart.

"So, she said yes?" Clarissa asked from the doorway, her cup of tea in her hand.

Troy and Maggie pulled apart and turned, surprised.

"Mom, how long have you been there?" Troy's brows furrowed in annoyance.

Clarissa raised one brow and grinned. "Long enough. Congratulations and welcome to the family, Maggie. Now call Skye, Troy. She's going to be tickled pink to have a sister."

~

General Harding's office
April 22

A sense of déjà vu washed over Troy as he was escorted to General Harding's office. Only this time it was Major Galloway who escorted him. He hoped the general would tell him the outcome of the investigation into Williams'—or rather General Kozlov's—espionage. Somehow, he doubted it. Considering it was a matter of national security, he didn't have a need to know.

Troy had been back for two days, and he hadn't heard anything from Senator Scott, which was a little surprising. He'd told him he wouldn't leave until he'd made sure Troy was back safe and sound. Surely the senator was busy with state matters. Checking up on Troy was the least of his worries.

Major Galloway stopped outside the general's outer door and opened it, motioning Troy inside. The same sergeant sat working on a computer at a desk near the door to the general's office.

"Good morning, Sergeant Phillips."

The sergeant stood to attention and saluted the major. "Good morning, sir."

Sergeant Phillips held the salute until the major returned her salute then she retook her seat. "How can I help you, sir?"

"I believe the general is expecting us. This is Ranger Troy Donovan."

"Yes, Major Galloway. I'll let him know you're here." The sergeant picked up the phone and called the general. Within a couple of minutes, they were walking inside the door.

"Come in, come in, gentlemen."

The major walked to the general's desk and saluted the general who returned his salute, much as the sergeant had done for the major.

"Have a seat, Troy." The general indicated a chair in front of his desk. Major Galloway took a chair at the rear of the office. No sooner did he take a seat than the phone rang, and the general answered it.

"Yes, please send him in." General Harding returned the receiver to its cradle and looked up as the door opened.

"Senator Scott. Please come in and have a seat. Thank you for joining us."

Both Troy and Major Galloway stood and shook the senator's hand then retook their seats as he sat down.

"Gentlemen, I've asked you all here today to inform you that the four of us will be making a trip to Washington, D.C., in three weeks. On Monday, May 13, we will be joining the president at the White House for a ceremony in which Ranger Donovan will receive an award for his part in the capture of the foreign intelligence operatives. Not only did he capture the three men who attempted to retrieve information that was brought by a defector to the US for our government, he also prevented the murder of Senator Scott, not on one occasion, but on two occasions. I put Ranger Donovan in for the Presidential Medal of Freedom and he will be awarded this medal on May 13."

Troy wasn't sure if his extremities had gone numb or if he was about to faint. He'd never fainted in his life. Somehow, he didn't think that's what was happening. He moved his fingers to see if they would move. And they did. He shifted his foot. Good. It moved too. He swallowed. Hard. If he understood right, he thought the general just said the president of the United States was going to award him, Troy Donovan, the Presidential Medal of Freedom. That was the highest award that could be given to a civilian.

He took a deep breath and swallowed again.

"Ranger Donovan." General Harding clasped his hands on his desk, leaned forward and addressed Troy in a low voice. "Are you alright? Did you hear what I said?"

Troy nodded. "Yes, sir. At least I think I did. Let me make sure I understand. You said the president of the United States will be awarding...me...the Presidential Medal of Freedom. Am I right?"

General Harding's bulldog face twisted into a grin. "Yes, Ranger Donovan. That is correct. Don't worry. Just spruce up your park service uniform and polish up your boots. We'll get you there. And bring Miss Lawrence along with you."

Epilogue

Maggie walked beside Troy, her hand in his, as they followed Senator Scott, Mrs. Miriam Scott, General Harding and Major Galloway through a corridor of the west wing of the White House. Surely her eyes must be as big as proverbial saucers and her head must be on a swivel. It was her first visit to the White House and most likely the last. Feeling a bit overwhelmed, Maggie couldn't grasp it all. A squeeze of her hand drew her gaze up to Troy's. His familiar grin and wink did what he surely intended. The butterflies in her stomach settled a bit as she returned his squeeze and smile. She was proud to be at this man's side. Dashing didn't do justice to describe his appearance in his dress park uniform.

Too bad Superintendent Wade had been unable to attend. His eyes had grown misty when he'd gotten the news about the ceremony to honor Troy's actions in capturing the foreign intelligence operatives. He couldn't have been prouder had Troy been his own son.

A White House aide met them and led them to the oval office where the ceremony would take place. He gave each of them directions as to what would happen, where they would stand and what to do and when.

As they stopped just outside the oval office door, the aide turned to Maggie. "Ma'am, you'll need to wait out here until the ceremony is over. Ranger Donovan will be back out shortly."

Before Maggie could even think to say anything, Troy shook his head. "No, that's unacceptable. She's coming in with me."

The aide shook his head and spoke in a low voice. "I'm afraid that's not possible. She's not been cleared to enter the oval office, Ranger Donovan. She's not on the list."

"And why isn't she? It was planned all along that Maggie Lawrence, my fiancé, would be attending the ceremony with me." Troy turned to General Harding. "General?"

The bulldog face of General Harding stared down the aide as he clasped his hands behind his back. "Ranger Donovan is right. A request for Miss Lawrence to attend the ceremony was sent along with all the others three weeks ago. I don't know who dropped the ball, but Miss Lawrence *will* be attending the ceremony. Do I make myself clear? I'll have a word with the president myself if I have to."

All color faded from the aide's face as he nodded. "Uhh…yes, sir, General. That's…clear as a bell. You'll have to give me a few minutes, but I'll see what I can do."

Senator Scott stepped forward. "Hand me that paper, son. I'll sign off on it. I think I've come to know this young lady pretty well over the last few months. If a senator can't take care of this, then other than the president, I don't know who can."

With only a moment of hesitation, the aide handed his clipboard of papers to the senator, who signed his name with a flourish.

"There. That's taken care of." The senator handed the aide back his clipboard and pen just as the door to the oval office opened.

"Please come in." Maggie assumed this was another aide who stepped back and waved them into the president's inner sanctum.

As she stepped onto the thick plush carpet, her hand still clasped within Troy's, Maggie noticed there were cameras and reporters everywhere. Great. As much as she would prefer to be behind one of those cameras, she was beyond proud of Troy and happy to be at his side.

Click click click click. The cameras in the room began clicking as their small group followed the aide across the room. There was the president *and* the first lady. Somehow, Maggie hadn't expected her to attend. Her smile was gracious and welcoming. The president stood with his hands folded in front of him, rocking back and forth on his heels, a kind smile on his face. He and his wife walked forward and shook hands with General Harding, then the senator and his wife, then Senator Scott introduced Troy and

Maggie. The president and first lady shook their hands and welcomed them to the White House.

As the president shook Troy's hand his face turned serious. "Ranger Donovan, thank you for your service to our county. You stopped men who have been working subversively for some time and prevented them from doing further damage to our country. Sadly, one of our own US Army officers was killed and impersonated by one of them. Colonel Williams will be given an honorary memorial service in which he will be remembered."

Troy returned the president's handshake. "I'm glad to hear that, sir. It's a tragedy that it happened, and I'm sure he was a good officer simply serving his country as he wanted to."

"Certainly." The president turned to Maggie. "And who is this young lady?"

"This is my fiancé, sir. Maggie Lawrence." Troy smiled as his gaze met Maggie's.

The president shook Maggie's hand. "Miss Lawrence, I understand you were there when Ranger Donovan captured the foreign intelligence operatives."

Maggie smiled at the leader of the free world. "Yes, sir, I was. He did a magnificent job of it too. I'm super proud of him." Maggie's gaze wandered back to Troy.

"From what I hear, you had a hand in capturing the foreign intelligence operatives as well. Did you not?"

His words snagged Maggie's attention and her gaze flew back to the president.

"Yes, sir, she did." Troy wrapped an arm around Maggie's shoulder, drawing her close to his side.

"They both did, sir." Senator Scott piped in as he leaned close to the president.

The president smiled and stepped back. "Well, let's get this ceremony started. I have another appointment this afternoon. An obligation with congress. Believe me, I'd much rather visit with you fine folks."

The aides hustled to direct everyone where to stand then the ceremony began. Maggie watched proudly as the president of the United States placed the Presidential Medal of Freedom around Troy's neck. *Click click click click.* Cameras clicking again. Oh, but Troy was handsome in his dress uniform. Hmmm. What was she thinking? He was handsome all the time.

Maggie thought she heard the door to the oval office open and close quietly, but she didn't turn to see who had come in or left. It wasn't important. Troy, standing there in his uniform with the white-edged blue ribbon draped around his neck, was all that mattered. Hanging from the ribbon was a white enameled star with a field of blue and tiny gold stars in the middle, all surrounded by golden eagles in a circle, their wings touching. Pride welled up within her.

"Miss Maggie Lawrence, would you please come forward?" Maggie wasn't sure she heard right, but the president was looking directly at her and holding out his hand. Her gaze moved to Troy's and he nodded, tilting his head in a movement as if to say, "Come on."

The president grinned and waved her forward. "Miss Lawrence, please."

Maggie felt a slight shove from her right. She glanced at the senator who stood beside her. He leaned toward her and whispered, "It's your turn. Go."

Maggie's heart jumped into her throat and her feet felt like lead as she stepped toward the president and first lady. Warmth rushed upward and over her as she tried to remember what Troy did.

"Miss Lawrence had no idea that she was receiving this medal today, so understand her bewilderment. General Harding put in for Miss Lawrence to receive this medal and when I heard why he recommended it, I agreed. This young lady assisted Ranger Donovan in capturing the three foreign intelligence operatives, and she took one of them out single handedly. Thank you, Miss Lawrence, for your assistance in protecting the interests of our country."

He reached over to the silver tray the first lady held and picked up the Presidential Medal of Freedom, placing it around Maggie's neck. Her heart was full as her gaze swept the small crowd that filled the oval office. Then it halted on a familiar face and she released a soft gasp. There, at the back of the room, stood her dad, Owen Lawrence. His endearing salt and pepper hair and tortoise shell rimmed glasses nearly brought tears to her eyes. He was smiling the proudest smile she'd ever seen on his face.

The president wanted to shake her hand but all she wanted to do was get to her dad. Maggie turned to the president and shook his hand and the hand of the first lady. She spent the necessary time greeting all the right people and posing for all the right pictures. Her jaws were starting to ache from smiling. Thank goodness Troy stood beside her.

A couple of reporters wanted to ask questions but she finally said, "Can you hold on just a minute please? My dad is back there, and I haven't seen him in several months. I'd just like to say hi and give him a hug."

Before they could respond, Maggie grabbed Troy's hand and tugged him in the direction of Owen.

She wrapped her arms around him. "Oh, my goodness, Dad. What are you doing here? It's so good to see you. I've missed you so much."

Owen chuckled and returned Maggie's hug. "I've missed you, too, kiddo. Oh, my. Where do I begin? I got a phone call from a certain young ranger, then I got another call from a senator and another one from a general. Next thing I know I got a call from the White House. Boom. Here I am. Who knew it was that easy to get an invitation to the White House?"

Maggie held him away and stared at him then at Troy. "You two knew? And didn't tell me?"

Troy grinned. "Maybe."

"So have you two met?" Maggie's gaze ping-ponged between them.

"No, just talked on the phone." Owen shook his head. "Perhaps you should do the honors."

Maggie held the hands of the two men she loved the most in the world and introduced them. "If we're making introductions, I'd like you to meet Senator Scott and his wife, Miriam. They're wonderful people, Dad."

Before he knew it, Owen had been introduced not only to the Scotts but also to the president and the first lady. For a short time, Owen chatted with the senator and the president about his latest fishing trip to Florida and they were swapping fishing stories. Troy took the opportunity to snag Maggie's hand and pull her just outside the oval office and the business that was happening there.

Wrapping her in his arms, he leaned his forehead against hers. "What a day. Happy?"

"Yeah. I'm always happy when I'm with you." Maggie grinned and snuggled within his arms. "Thanks for arranging for my dad to come. Not only was I surprised to receive the medal, I was thrilled to look up and see him standing in the back. I think I heard him enter when you were getting your award."

Troy lifted his head. "Yep. It was him. I was afraid he was going to be late."

"I love you, Troy," Maggie whispered, reaching her arms up and slipping her fingers into the hair at the nape of his neck, "and I can't wait to begin my life with you."

Troy slipped his arms around Maggie's waist, tugging her close. He lowered his head, his gaze on her lips. "Then let's not wait too long. Think your dad will come to Alaska for a wedding?"

Maggie chuckled. "You haven't seen his RV. I'm sure he will."

As Troy's arms tightened around Maggie, he kissed her with a promise for the future. She had no doubt that he loved her with his whole heart, and he'd spend the rest of their lives demonstrating that fact.

Maggie barely heard the sound of the oval office door opening. Then she heard the president say as he closed the door again, "Tell my secretary I'll be a few minutes late to my next appointment. Love's *far* more important."

The End

Keep reading for a sample of The Peaceful Valley Wounded Soldier's Anthology

Author's Notes

In the middle of the night on August 13, 1961, trucks filled with construction workers and soldiers drove through East Berlin to the border of West Berlin. These men began building the well-known Berlin Wall. It was rebuilt four times over the years, each time fortifying it to prevent escapes from the east to the west. There were many escapes in the early years, but as the years passed and the wall was fortified, escapes grew fewer until they were nearly impossible. Hundreds of east Berliners died attempting to escape the socialist regime of the Soviet-held German Democratic Republic. When the wall was first built, it separated families and friends. When they went to bed that night and woke the next morning, there the wall was. If they were from the west but were visiting in the east, they were stuck there. And vice versa. They were stuck for nearly three decades under communist rule. There were over 5,000 escapes and at least 171 East Berliners died attempting to escape.

In the fall of 1984 while serving in the US Army, I was given the opportunity to take the Berlin Orientation Tour. This was a tour not available to just any US soldier. I was chosen, along with two other soldiers from my base in Italy, to attend with other soldiers from around Europe. We took a night train from Frankfort, Germany, to West Berlin, Germany. This was before the Berlin Wall came down. Our train traveled through the night and stopped once somewhere in communist East Germany. I risked a peek out a pulled shade to see where we were and was shocked to see our train was surrounded by armed Soviet Soldiers. I admit it gave my heart a jolt, but I remembered Who was looking out for us, whether I was the only Christian on that train or not, I'll never know. Peace settled over me. It was the only stop in the night, and I was able to get some sleep. Over several days we toured Western Berlin held by the US, Britain and France, but what I remember most is our trip into East Berlin. Our tour bus had US ARMY emblazoned across both sides as we drove through the famous Checkpoint Charlie. A Soviet officer came aboard and took a head count. We were dressed in our Army dress greens but we weren't allowed to wear our name plates or our unit citations to identify us. We only had a few hours that we were allowed in East Berlin, and we had to be back at Checkpoint Charlie at a certain time. We needed to have the right head count or there would have been a major problem. I still remember the buildings facing the west and how they were painted to look prosperous but on the backs to the east they were dilapidated and in need of paint. There was poverty everywhere. We passed stores where there was little food on the shelves. If a loaf of bread was in the window, it didn't mean it was on the shelf in the store. The cars there were old and broken-down looking. We were openly followed everywhere we went by agents speaking into their collars (no kidding) and into their wristwatches. We saw the grotesque and modern statues that communist countries erect to their leaders such as Marx and Lenin. Then came the famous Brandenburg Gate which was stuck in no man's land between the walls. Of course, we made it back to Checkpoint Charlie for our appointed headcount. I left East Berlin with mixed feelings. I was an American who was even more proud to serve my country, more grateful for the blessings God had given me, and determined I would share my experience whenever I saw the opportunity. I wished that day that every American in the US could've been on that bus and witnessed the things I had seen. If they had, would we be where we are today? Would they have raised their children to appreciate the free country we've been blessed with up till now? I don't know. It's a moot point because they didn't see it. All I can do is pray for our country that it will never fall into the hands of socialism.

On June 12, 1987, Pres. Ronald Reagan stood before the Brandenburg Gate and the Berlin Wall in Berlin, Germany and challenged Gen. Sec. Mikhail Gorbachev to tear down the wall. It's believed this was the beginning of the end to the cold war.

As the cold war thawed throughout Eastern Europe, on November 9, 1989, the spokesman for East Berlin's Communist Party announced there would be a change in the city's relationship with the West. He said that, beginning at midnight on the 9th, the citizens of the German Democratic Republic, or GDR, would be free to cross the eastern border into the west. Both West and East Berliners converged on the wall. Chants of "To auf!" ("Open the gate!") filled the air. When midnight came, they flooded through the checkpoints. Families and friends were reunited after nearly three decades. People began hammering and chiseling the wall away. Bulldozers and cranes soon appeared and the wall was torn down. The symbol of socialism that had separated free and oppressed people was no longer a barrier.

I was proud to serve under President Ronald Reagan and to call him my Commander-in-Chief. The challenge he gave Mr. Gorbachev that day in Berlin, may not have dropped that wall immediately, but it set in motion what would bring about the end of the cold war and the freeing of socialist countries all over eastern Europe.

"There is one sign the Soviets can make that would be unmistakable, that would advance dramatically the cause of freedom and peace. General Secretary Gorbachev, if you seek peace, if you seek prosperity for the Soviet Union and Eastern Europe, if you seek liberalization, come here to this gate! Mr. Gorbachev, open this gate! Mr. Gorbachev, tear down this wall."

~ President Ronald Reagan

Dear Reader,

If you enjoyed reading this book and want to help me to continue writing and publishing more books for your enjoyment, please take a moment to leave a review. They are very important to authors. We depend on them to let other readers know what they think about our books so they in turn will know whether or not to purchase and read them. Should you not care for it, I would appreciate an email to me rather than a negative review. And remember, the author has no control over prices, so please keep that in mind if you're not happy with the cost.

You can find me at Amazon, Goodreads and BookBub should you choose to leave a review.

Thank you again for reading my story. I hope you enjoyed it.

For His glory,

J. Carol Nemeth

Author Bio

A native North Carolinian, J. Carol Nemeth has always loved reading and enjoyed making up stories since junior high school, most based in the places she's lived or traveled to. She worked in the National Park Service as a Park Aid and served in the US Army where she was stationed in Italy, traveling to over thirteen countries while there. She met the love of her life, Mark Nemeth, also an Army veteran, while stationed in Italy. After they married, they lived in various locations, including North Yorkshire, England. They now live in West Virginia, where, in their spare time, Carol and Mark enjoy RVing, sightseeing and are active in their church. They have a son, Matt, who serves US Army active duty, and a daughter, Jennifer, her husband Flint, who serves Air Force active duty, and three grandchildren, Martin, Ava and Gage. Their four-footed kid, Holly, is pretty special too. She loves traveling in their RV, and when they pack up to go, Holly is waiting inside for them to head out. Carol, a multi-published author, is a member of ACFW, and she loves traveling to research for her books. She and Mark enjoy taking the RV and heading out on research trips.

Social Media Links

Yorkshire Lass- Buy Link https://amzn.to/2Ivddxd

Dedication to Love - Buy Link https://amzn.to/2IJMnBF

Mountain of Peril - Buy Link https://amzn.to/2MBoIIF

Canyon of Death – Buy Link https://amzn.to/2MC06Q3

A Beacon of Love – Buy Link https://amzn.to/2K8KzoU

Ocean of Fear – Buy Link https://amzn.to/2F2LpPF

The Peaceful Valley Wounded Soldiers Anthology – Buy Link https://amzn.to/2Kb6QRa

Sign up for my newsletter at www.jcarolnemeth.com/ and receive a free short story.

www.facebook.com/J.CarolNemeth

https://twitter.com/nemeth_jcarol

https://www.amazon.com/J.-Carol-Nemeth/e/B01F45LWY8/ref=sr_ntt_srch_lnk_1?qid=1485890302&sr=8-1

https://www.goodreads.com/author/dashboard

https://www.bookbub.com/profile/j-carol-nemeth

The Soldier's Heart

"Have you heard who's back in town, Myra?"

Beth Hayes couldn't miss Myrtle Brown's voice from the next isle over as she searched Hoover's Pharmacy shelf for the supplies she needed.

"Nope," Myra Washington replied. "Can't keep up with who comes and goes in this dadblamed town. Seems the young'uns are always leaving and coming back. Never satisfied. Want to leave because the town's too small. They leave and they don't like what they find in the big world so they come back."

"Myra, would you just hush up and listen to me?" Myrtle said.

Beth grinned. The two women had been best of friends for at least fifty years but were always going at it. They were pretty much inseparable, but to hear them talk, you'd think they couldn't get along.

"What are you going on about, Myrtle? Which young'un has returned this time?"

Beth reached for a bottle of peroxide.

"Why it's that Alex Hunter, don't you know. He's back from the Army. And he's a looker too," Myrtle added, "Mmmhmmm. He sure is. They say he's a major."

The plastic bottle of peroxide slipped from Beth's fingers and hit the floor, rolling under the edge of the display unnoticed.

Alex Hunter? Her Alex Hunter? No. *Not* her Alex Hunter. Her Alex Hunter left for the Army twenty years ago never looking back. Why would he return? He wouldn't. And he wasn't her Alex Hunter. Not anymore.

Beth glanced into the shopping basket hanging from her arm. What was she doing? Her brain had gone numb. Myrtle's words had thrown her for a loop and she needed to focus. Even if Alex Hunter had returned to Grace Ridge, there wasn't anything she could do about it, and she needed to keep moving on as if he hadn't.

With a determined nod she peered around. Hadn't she been looking at a bottle of peroxide? Oh yes, there it is. She grabbed it from beneath the edge of the display, dropped it into her basket, finished her shopping and headed to the cash register. She'd get on with her day as if she hadn't heard this...extraordinary news. Grandpa was waiting for her.

"Have a good afternoon, Beth," Mrs. Compton said from behind the register.

"You too, Mrs. Compton," Beth said, "and stay cool. It promises to get really warm today."

"Don't I know it?" The lady fanned herself in spite of the air conditioned pharmacy. "The heat just shoots in that door when someone comes in or out. Well, have a good day."

Waving her fingers, Beth grabbed her bag of supplies and rushed out the pharmacy door. Turning toward Grandpa Hayes' office, she ran smack into a hard chest and bounced backward losing her balance.

Hands reached out and grabbed her before she could fall backward and hit the pavement. Stunned and with the air knocked out of her, it took several moments for her to realize what had happened.

"Take slow deep breaths, Beth." A deep voice said as she was half led, half carried to the bench that sat between Hoover's

Pharmacy and Valley Hardware next door. "Take it easy."

Beth did as she was told because she needed to breathe again. What was that wall she'd hit? Or rather who had she run into? Then as reason began to return and her breathing settled back to normal, she looked at the man beside her, and her face warmed. She knew it wasn't the end of the June warm day that caused it. Of all the people in the world she had to physically run into, why did it have to be Alex Hunter?

The last time she'd seen him he was eighteen years old. He was good looking at eighteen, but he was devastating at thirty-eight. Apparently, the Army had been good for him. It had been twenty years and he'd never returned. He'd left a skinny kid right out of high school. He was anything but that now. He was taller and muscular, his dark brown hair cut in the high and tight favored by the military guys. But his face…his face looked as if he'd seen things. Hard things. His jaw had become more square and stronger.

Beth's gaze was drawn to Alex's and there she saw strength. The same gorgeous gray gaze looked back but there was a maturity that hadn't been in the young Alex. What could he have seen and done in his years in the military to build this man from that untried and untested teenager?

Right now compassion and concern filled his gaze. "Are you alright, Beth? You ran into me pretty hard. Where were you going in such an all-fired hurry, anyway? You could've been seriously hurt."

Beth's breathing had returned to normal and her ire rekindled. Standing, she grabbed the bag of pharmacy supplies he'd thoughtfully placed on the bench beside her. "You've been gone a long time, Alex. You can't just come back and pretend twenty years away."

Without a second glance she hurried toward Grandpa Hayes doctor's office. She could feel the anger coursing through her veins. Who did he think he was? After leaving her high and dry twenty years ago to show up now out of the blue and act like nothing had changed. They had been inseparable since sixth grade. They did everything together. Then in high school they'd planned to go to the same college, and then the future? Who knew? But it probably would've been together. Right?

Then Alex decided he wanted to serve his country. There

wasn't anything wrong with that. Beth's father was an officer in the US Army and had died serving his country when she was sixteen. She was very proud of him and his service. But Alex had just up and joined without talking to her. They'd made plans and he'd ruined them.

Beth flung open the back door of the doctor's office and stomped up the hallway, by this time in a fine dander.

She hurried into the supply room where Jeannie Mason stood surveying the shelves with her clipboard.

"Oh good. You're back. The supply company said they could get the shipment out by early next week so we'll just have to plug along with pharmacy supplies until then." She turned as Beth dumped her bag of supplies on the work table. "What goodies were you able to find?"

It was only then she noticed the steam pouring from Beth's ears. "Uh oh. What happened?"

"He's back."

Jeannie was not only Beth's co-worker but her best friend. "Ok. I'll bite. Who's back?"

"Alex Hunter. That's who's back." Beth paced the small floor of the supply room then stopped in front of Jeannie. "What am I going to do?"

Jeannie chuckled and put her hand over her mouth to cover it up. "Why should you do anything? It's been twenty years. The man has served his time. He can do whatever he wants. Yes, even come back to his hometown if he wants to. Hello! He did grow up here."

Beth felt as if a bubble popped inside her. Jeannie was right. This was his hometown. He'd been born and raised here the same as her.

"You know, Beth, just because he went off and joined the Army and decided to have a different life than you doesn't mean it was the wrong thing for him to do. Maybe it's time for you to get over it."

"Beth, I need you to prep the rooms ASAP." Grandpa stuck his gray head into the supply room. He peered at her over his wire-framed glasses. "Everything okay? You don't look so good. We're running behind this morning, and the first patients are already in the waiting room."

Beth nodded numbly. Jeannie's words had stung but she didn't have time to think about them right now. Getting the supplies at the pharmacy and running into Alex had made her late. She'd have to hurry to get things back on schedule

~

A grin lifted the corners of Alex's mouth as Beth marched away. Yep. She still had that same spitfire spunk she had as a kid. Her auburn ponytail swishing back and forth as she walked was just as cute as it had been then too.

Had she changed in twenty years? Oh yeah. A lot. She was always a cute kid but she'd matured into a gorgeous woman. Now to have her come flying out of Hoover's Pharmacy like a tornado and smash right into him had been a pleasant surprise but it had been nearly disastrous for her. She'd had the wind knocked right out of her.

It was pretty obvious she was none too happy to see him. Her hazel eyes had always changed colors when she was angry and their darker hue now indicated ire. Twenty years ago he'd tried to explain his reasons for wanting to join the Army but she'd refused to listen. It had been important to him to serve his country, but every time he'd tried to tell her, she'd slammed the door in his face. For six weeks before he was due to leave for boot camp, he'd tried to talk to her, but Beth would leave when he came into a room. She'd lock the door when he came over to talk to her. She'd hang up when he called. She wouldn't let him explain.

Glancing at his watch Alex remembered his appointment with the bank manager, Mr. Edwards, and walked over.

"Alex, please come in and have a seat." Mr. Edwards waved him to a chair in front of his desk. "I have all your paperwork ready for you to sign. I know you're excited to get to work on your grandparents' property. It's an amazing thing you're doing out there."

"Thank you, sir. I'm excited to get going on it. It's a much-needed ministry," Alex said.

"And you're just the man to fulfill that ministry, Alex. Here you go. Just sign here, here and here, and we can get this project going."

Alex leaned forward, signed the papers and stood to shake hands with the bank manager. "Thank you, sir. Have a good day."

"You, too, son. I look forward to seeing great things from this ministry."

"Yes, sir."